THE SEVENTEENTH YEAR

IAN W. SAINSBURY

For Olive

Previously in The World Walker
Series (contains spoilers for
books one and two)

Join my (very occasional) mailing list, and I'll send you the unpublished prologue for The World Walker: http://eepurl.com/bQ_zJ9

What you need to know about Manna:

Manna is nanotechnology accessible by a minority of people born with a certain genetic disposition. The Earth was seeded with stores of Manna at the dawn of multicellular life. These stores are known as Thin Places, regularly visited by Users when they need to refill their personal stock of Manna. Different Users manipulate Manna in different ways; some to attack by manipulating their physical environment, some to sense the proximity of enemies, some to heal the sick. All can use it to produce food and water in seconds from their surroundings.

Seb Varden has almost god-like powers given to him by Billy Joe, an alien who had been kept in a secret government facility since 1947. Unfortunately, these powers— essentially a massively upgraded version of Manna—come with no instruction manual, and, while Seb tries to work out how to use them, he is pursued by various interested parties. The most tenacious of these is a Manna user called Mason, who uses ruthless mercenaries to try to gain access to Seb.

Despite killing Seb's friend Bob and kidnapping Seb's on/off girlfriend, Meera (Mee) Patel, Mason is eventually thwarted. In The Unmaking Engine, he redoubles his efforts, and, in a confrontation with Seb, is finally defeated. A brain tumor, keep at bay since childhood by Manna, is healed and the real person trapped inside Mason is revealed. Mason is actually John, Seb's older brother.

As well as defeating Mason, and gaining a brother, Seb has to take on the Rozzers - the alien race who created humanity and provided the Thin Places billions of years in our past. They are en route to Earth to wipe out a failed experiment and start over. The Unmaking Engine will be dropped into the ocean to achieve this end. Unfortunately, their failed experiment is the human race, and the only person standing in their way is Seb. Seb is now further into the process that began when he was first given his powers - he is evolving into a World Walker, an incredibly rare being. The Rozzers try to manipulate or neutralize him. Even their ship—which is, in fact, a sentient being itself, part of a hive mind that evolved from nanotechnology into a new species of artificial intelligence—attempts to dissuade Seb from interfering.

Seb takes on the Rozzers and prevents them from wiping out humanity. To do this, he must make two huge sacrifices. The first is his removal of humanity's Manna ability, achieved by adapting the Unmaking Engine. From this point on, no child will ever be born with the genetic makeup necessary to manipulate Manna. Seb's second sacrifice is to finally allow his entire body to be replaced by nanotechnology.

On a personal level, this may be a tragedy rather than a triumph. Seb has finally found happiness with Mee, and their relationship has deepened. But, by saving humanity, has Seb lost his own? He becomes distant, struggles to relate to those around him and, finally, vanishes from the island of Innisfarne where he and Mee were hoping to build a new life together.

Mee is left behind, wondering where the man she loves has gone.

And she's pregnant…

Chapter 1

Innisfarne

Joni died on her ninth birthday, but she didn't let it spoil her party.

There were only two other children on Innisfarne that spring. Evan and Hattie were eight-year-old twins. Evan was quiet, solemn and watchful. Hattie was loud, spontaneous, unreliable. They looked so alike that the gulf between their personalities seemed even more pronounced. And they didn't think dressing up as magical characters was silly, which some of the visiting children did. When Joni announced her fancy-dress theme, Evan consulted his books for ideas. Hattie, who had little patience for the written word, drew her inspiration from movies and tv.

"I'll be Tinkerbell," she said, dancing under one of the giant oak trees that marked the center of the small island. "Or…Peter Pan. No! They're not creatures, are they? I'll be the ticking crocodile, a unicorn, a dragon. No, Rumpelstiltskin, um, a phoenix, no—I know—I'll be a robot." She danced out of the shade and skipped across the small clearing before breaking into a run as she headed back to the Keep.

Evan picked up his book and gave Joni a rueful grin. "She'll come back dressed as a mermaid," he said. "She's always a mermaid. Meet you back here in half an hour."

Joni smiled and waved as he walked out of sight. Half an hour was enough time to climb a tree, or take a quick swim in the bay. A grownup, keeping the sea in sight on their right side, could walk the perimeter of the entire island in under three hours. But, as far as Joni was concerned, Innisfarne had everything she could possibly want. Well, nearly everything. It had the sea for swimming in, the forest to explore, trees to climb. She had friends who came back year after year with their parents to be part of the community for a few months. And she had Mum. And Uncle John. And Kate.

She chewed her lower lip and wondered if Mum would let her dye her hair green as part of a costume. It was a long shot. Mum always said she looked perfect as she was. Joni wasn't too sure. Her hair never did what she wanted, sticking out at funny angles, although Mum had fixed it into a plait today. And her eyes weren't deep brown like Mum's, they were gray, which she thought looked a bit weird in her light brown face. But she couldn't talk about her eyes to Mum. Mum said she had her dad's eyes.

She'd have to fetch an adult if she wanted to swim. Mum always looked sad when they went down to the best beach for swimming. She didn't like to go there. Uncle John might come. Joni already had her outfit in the backpack at her feet: a long dress made of green and brown rags sewn together, complete with a matching headband.

She was going to be a dryad, a tree-spirit. Joni wondered if she was cheating, as dryads weren't imaginary. After a few seconds thought, she concluded that since everyone else thought they were imaginary, it would probably be ok. It was her birthday, after all.

She decided to climb the oak tree.

As soon as the decision was made, the tingling started. It was a bit like pins and needles, only this was in her head. It had happened before, every now and then, for as long as Joni could remember. It always went away after a few seconds. She was about to start climbing when she hesitated, one foot already in the first knothole.

The tingling sensation was so *insistent* this time. And she could *hear* something, too. If Joni had known what tinnitus was, she might have blamed that for the cause of the constant sound. But the hum she heard didn't have the high-pitched tone familiar to tinnitus sufferers - it was, instead, a low whispering rumble deep in the bass end of the frequency range.

There was also something happening to Joni's vision. She blinked a few times, but the strange sensation remained. It was as if the area directly in front of her was normal, but everywhere else was darkening. Slowly, Joni turned her head. A bright area stayed in focus around the tree. Everywhere else, colors were muted and faded, becoming a twilight monochrome. She looked back at the oak and up into its branches, following the path she would climb. It, at least, was still perfectly lit by the early-afternoon sun.

Although the day had suddenly—*magically*, thought Joni, as excited as she was nervous—become twilight, some areas were far easier to see than others. There were two slightly brighter paths leading away from the clearing and a patch of clear daylight. One path led toward the bay, the other back to the Keep. The clearest path was where Joni had been sitting while talking to the twins. What she saw there made Joni let go of the tree and gasp.

"Oh, frogspawn," she said. Although Mum cursed more than anyone else on Innisfarne, she wouldn't let Joni do it, which was totally unfair. So Joni had developed her own swearing lexicon.

She chewed her lip again as she tried to make sense of what she was seeing. There was someone else sitting exactly where she had been sitting less than a minute ago. There was no way anyone could have crept up that quietly and quickly. Joni was the only one on the island who could move around without a sound. She'd had her whole life —*nine years,* she reminded herself proudly—to learn every rock, every bush, and every tree.

The figure she was staring at was strange and maddeningly familiar. Joni squinted. The reason it seemed so strange was easy enough to pinpoint. Joni could see right through the figure to the rough grass beneath where it was sitting. It wasn't exactly *transparent,* though. It was more like it was *there* and *not-there* at the same time. Joni knew this didn't make sense, but she also knew it was true, the same way she knew this was happening in her head; *real* and *not-real.*

Maybe it was a fairy. It was her birthday, after all. And Joni suspected she was half-fairy. *Faerie*, Joni corrected herself. In the grownup book she'd found in the library, it had been spelled that way, so that was probably how real faeries spelled it. Joni didn't know much about her dad, but it was certainly possible he was a faerie. *King of the faeries*, Joni corrected herself. Joni knew her dad wasn't dead, that he loved her very much, that he would come back if he could, that Mum would tell her more when she was older. Old enough to understand why he wasn't here now. Joni didn't think Mum really understood why her dad wasn't here, but she didn't dare say so, especially because Mum might admit it was true.

If Dad was the king of the faeries, who only left his magical kingdom for one night every hundred years, he might have visited Innisfarne and fallen in love with a human woman. Which would make Joni half-faerie. It would certainly explain a lot. Including, perhaps the presence of this magical creature sitting a few feet away from her. Joni looked more closely, trying to take in every detail in case it suddenly disappeared.

It was definitely female. Although the figure had its back to her, the part of her face that was visible looked like a girl's features. Her hair was styled in a plait like Joni's. Joni was thinking of asking Mum if she could have a pixie-cut. *Would a faerie call it a pixie-cut? Did that mean pixies might have a faerie-cut?* Joni wondered what that might look like.

The figure even had a T-shirt like Joni's. White, with sunflowers. *Wait.* Joni took a long look at the weird, indistinct shape. It wasn't a faerie. It was something even stranger. It was her double. Then she realized she knew better than that. It wasn't her double, it was—somehow —*her.*

The other Joni was frozen in exactly the position Joni had been sitting when she had decided to climb the tree. When she had thought about swimming instead. Or going home. Joni realized those two possibilities were the two paths that were still lit in the semi-darkness.

Whatever was going on, it was probably important, almost certainly magical (*faerie magic*, Joni reminded herself). She should probably go and tell Mum, or Uncle John. But…the oak was such a great tree to climb. And Joni was such a great climber. And the view from halfway up was amazing. One day, she'd make it all the way to the top, but Mum would have a complete fit if she saw her and it was a bit scary when you got that high, so maybe not today. Maybe when she was ten.

She turned away from the other Joni and started to climb.

Chapter 2

The lower part of the trunk was massive, but it wasn't smooth. It looked like hundreds of arms were stretching around the trunk, trying to grasp something on the other side. Joni stood on these arms and quickly clambered up to the first branches. Progress after that was easy, and the ancient oak was so huge that it was possible to climb near the center and remain totally invisible from outside. Of course, anyone close enough would have heard what sounded like a giant squirrel making its way up the tree. Joni could climb quickly *or* quietly. Just not both at the same time. Joni was in the mood for speed today. She reached her marker within three minutes. She knew she was now halfway up the tree because of the piece of yellow rag a few feet out on the branch. The rag marked the furthest point she'd ever climbed. She looked at the scrap of yellow cloth. She hadn't been able to see it from the ground today. Probably because she'd tied it there in Fall, and now new leaves had unfurled in their thousands, obscuring her marker.

Joni decided to move it further out so she could see it from the ground again.

She started her journey along the branch, crawling carefully, and soon came level with the rag. Quickly untying it, she looped it around her wrist before setting off again. As she inched away from the trunk, her weight caused the branch to dip. Her stomach lurched and she hissed out a surprised breath. She stopped for a few seconds, her heart beating rapidly. She looked down. It was a very long way. Much higher than the main building, which was two stories high. Twice as high as that. Joni looked at her fingers - white and shaking slightly due to the grip she had taken on the swaying branch. This was no way for the daughter of a faerie king to behave. Joni pushed herself upward and bounced on the branch experimentally. It bounced with her, flexible but strong. She realized it would take a lot more than her slight weight to break a branch this big and strong. She decided to go on.

The branch was now getting too narrow to crawl on, so Joni latched her fingers together, crossed her ankles and let herself slide off the branch and dangle beneath it like the baby orangutan had done on the TV program Mum had let her watch. She hung there briefly, almost losing her nerve, before resuming her progress along the branch, now upside-down. Hand over hand, foot over foot. It was easier than she had expected, and Joni looked up as more and more of the sky appeared through the branches above. The sky was a pale blue, and wispy clouds were moving at different speeds across it. The effect was almost hypnotic, and Joni began to feel as if none of this was really happening. Her thoughts slipped and slowed into a daydream.

"Hey, Joni, where are you? I'm a mermaid." It was Hattie's voice from below. Joni let her head hang down so that she could look directly beneath her. A bizarre figure was hopping across the clearing. Hattie had used sticky tape to cover her body and hair with shells and had fashioned a rudimentary tail out of a blanket, a shopping bag, and a great deal of industrial-sized aluminum foil. As her legs were stuck together (more tape), Hattie couldn't walk properly, so her progress toward the oak was awkward and —frequently—painful, as her costume made it hard to remain upright for long. When she crashed to the ground for a fourth time, she called more loudly.

"Ow! Joni!? Where are you? Come and see my costume."

Joni realized her earlier thought had been correct - Hattie couldn't see the strange darkness, or the second Joni. Only she could see it. She knew this was a secret she would be keeping to herself. One day, she would be able to tell the fairy king, he would smile and explain and it would all make sense.

She took her right hand from the branch to wave at Hattie, and that's when it happened. The piece of bark under her left hand suddenly sloughed off from the wood underneath, and her upper body fell away from the tree. For a quarter of a second, she still had the hope that her crossed feet might bear her weight, but that hope disappeared as her feet were wrenched apart and away from the branch, one sneaker sent spinning away.

She fell.

And that's when the first impossible thing happened.

She wasn't there any more. She was somewhere hot. Really hot. But the flames weren't burning her. She looked around and didn't understand what she was seeing. It was night-time. There were three moons in the sky. Two really scary looking people—goblins, maybe, they were ugly, ugly, ugly—were having a fight. There was a lot of blood, which was really yucky. Then lots of things happened quickly and it was like her brain couldn't make sense of it. The goblin on the floor looked right at her and smiled and it wasn't a goblin at all it was her dad but how could it be her dad? he was a fairy king not a goblin. She felt a big rush of love and happiness all the same and wanted to go to him even though she didn't have a body and he was a goblin then suddenly -

- she was back on Innisfarne looking at the branch she had just fallen out of.

She didn't scream, she didn't breathe, she didn't think.

Her body relaxed all on its own. Joni was passive. The fall was something that was happening *to* her. She had no say in what was coming next, no control over it. The fall was going to continue whatever she did. As would, of course, the end of the fall. Which was the next thing that was going to happen.

It happened. Her body had twisted slightly as she fell, but she was still traveling headfirst, as her hands had slipped half a second before her feet. So Joni's head hit the ground first, about seven feet away from an open-mouthed Hattie, who didn't have time to shut her eyes before her friend's neck snapped loudly on impact. More than a dozen other bones were shattered in the fraction of a second that followed, many of them piercing various internal organs including her spleen, liver, and one of her lungs. Any of which may have led to her death. None of which did, however, as the fragment of skull which had been driven through Joni's brain like a badly designed but extremely effective bullet, was already doing the job.

Joni held on to a tiny shred of consciousness and—before it winked out of existence—saw, clearer than any hologram, an image of herself. It was her as she was just before she had decided to climb the tree. Joni desperately tried to reach out to it. There was a humming sound and she felt pins and needles all over.

Hattie saw the life fade from the eyes of her friend,

whose head was now stuck onto her body at completely the wrong angle. She opened her mouth to scream.

That was when the second impossible thing happened.

Joni was sitting at the base of the big oak tree. She looked up to see Evan smiling at her.

"She'll come back dressed as a mermaid," he said. "She's always a mermaid. Meet you back here in half an hour."

Chapter 3

The party was fun. There was jello, hot dogs, ice cream, chips, cookies, soda, milkshakes, sandwiches, party games, hide-and-go-seek, apple bobbing, pass the parcel, dead lions, L-O-N-D-O-N London (which was the same as What's The Time, Mr Wolf) and gifts. The gifts were all books, of course. Joni was a reader. One day, she was going to be a writer.

Mum had half-hoped Joni might turn out to be a musician, like her. She'd even named Joni after some ancient singer. The birthday gift last year had been a half-sized acoustic guitar. It was in her room now. It was useful for keeping the door open in summer when it was hot.

"Everything ok, Jones?"

Only Mum called Joni *Jones*. It didn't sound right when anyone else said it.

Joni had been thinking about her fall. Trying to puzzle it out. She rubbed her neck, remembering the sensation when it had snapped. She smiled at her mother.

"Yes, Mummy. Just thinking about a book."

Joni couldn't have articulated clearly to anyone, even

herself, why she lied at that moment, but she did it without hesitating. Something inside her suspected that telling Mum what had happened would make her go into the Sad again. Mum hardly ever went into the Sad these days, and when she did, she was usually back the same day. Since Joni's last birthday, Mum hadn't been to the Sad properly. Not like that time when she couldn't get out of bed, and Kate and Uncle John looked after her for two days.

"You and your books, Jones. Never thought I'd produce a bookworm."

A fit, lean man in his fifties appeared at Mum's shoulder, holding a wrapped gift which was obviously a book.

"Uncle John!"

John shrugged mock-apologetically as he handed the book over.

"Happy birthday, honey," he said. "Here's another one for the collection."

He winked at Joni.

"It's a good thing, Mee," he said. "Some kids don't read at all. If I hadn't had books when I was growing up…" His voice tailed off. His childhood had ended with him killing his father and becoming a violent criminal mastermind. Possibly not the best advertisement for encouraging kids to read.

Mee smiled at him. "Well, you turned out ok. Eventually." She turned to Joni. "He's ok, isn't he?"

"Best. Uncle. Ever." Joni finally managed to squeeze a finger under the paper and free the book from its wrapping.

"A Wizard Of Earthsea," she said, looking at the cover, her eyes wide. "Wow! Thank you, Uncle John."

She jumped up from the table and hugged John hard, squeezing him tight until he pretended he was struggling to breathe and had to cling onto a chair to stop himself falling over. Joni giggled, then released him and skipped away to the corner of the communal dining room, flinging herself onto a well-worn beanbag and beginning to read. Within seconds she was lost to the world around her.

Mee and John cleared up dishes and started to wash them as the other children and the few members of the community who had come to the party began to drift away.

"A book about a wizard?" said Mee, quietly, handing John a plate to dry.

"It's a beautiful book," said John. "Joni loves fantasy - well, she loves every genre of book as far as I can tell. But give her a choice and she wants fairies, goblins, giants, dragons…and magic."

"I know, I know," said Mee. "But I've decided I'm going to start telling her a little bit about Manna, and I'm just worried she's going to get confused. Reading about wizards, dragons, all that Middle-Earth crap."

John flinched a little to hear Tolkien's opus dismissed so casually, but decided this probably wasn't the time to defend the Lord Of The Rings. Instead, he put the plate away and held out his hand for another.

"She's a very bright kid," he said. "And A Wizard Of Earthsea will teach her more about responsibility than magic. Don't underestimate her. I'm glad you're going to talk to her, though. She won't be on this island forever."

Mee sighed. "I wouldn't want her to be," she said. "Ten years ago, I'd have been horrified at the idea of living in some weird hippy community on a three-mile by two-mile island. Now, I can't imagine living anywhere else. But Joni has her whole life ahead of her. She's going to want to get out there, explore, see the world."

John was silent for a while, wondering how best to phrase his question. In the event, Mee beat him to it.

"Yes, I'm going to tell her about Seb," she said. "Just in simple terms, at first. It's not as if anyone really understood him, anyway. *Understands* him."

John nodded at Mee's change of tense.

"He'll be back, Mee."

"Yes, I know. I know it, John. I just don't know when. And once that first year had passed, when he had missed seeing his daughter born——," she stopped talking and attacked a frying pan with a scouring pad using more vigor than was strictly necessary. John lifted it gently out of her hands when she showed no sign of stopping.

"He loves you. He'll love Joni. And he'll be back."

Just before she fell asleep that night, Joni thought about her father, the Fairy King. He had given her some of her magic. She smiled. She knew he would come back for her.

Chapter 4

Rome

The covert photographs showed a married couple drinking cocktails on a hotel balcony. They seemed happy enough. Not young, not old. No children yet. Both successful in their chosen careers. Successful in their marriage, too. Neither had taken lovers. Adam's employers would be pleased by that last detail. Not because of any moral stance. Abandoned lovers sometimes asked questions, and —in Adam's line of work—the fewer questions, the better.

Adam had lived with a girl for a few months, once. It hadn't ended well. Not for her, leastways. He struggled to remember how it had felt, having someone to come home to. Someone waiting when you opened the door. Someone who wanted to know how you were feeling. Someone who cared enough to be there, even in the bad times. Then he remembered: he'd *hated* it. Even her corpse had annoyed him.

Spreading the photographs out on the hotel room desk, Adam took a small roller out of his backpack, removing the protective cover. As he rolled it briskly and firmly across all four images the top layer of the photographs disintegrated into tiny shreds of paper. When he had finished, a rough, pockmarked surface remained, leaving no recognizable trace of its original subject. He collected the particles into a pile, tapping the roller to release any stray pieces, then swept them into his cupped hand and flushed them down the toilet.

He'd invented the roller device himself, using a lint remover as a prototype, then having a more robust model tooled - each piece at separate shops. The roller's blades tore the outermost layer of a sheet of paper or photograph away, producing a tiny pile of dust to dispose of. It also— Adam had discovered—made a surprisingly effective instrument of torture.

It was typical of his approach to his work: a low-tech, elegant solution to a problem.

Adam ripped up the unrecognizable photographs and put them in his suit pocket. He sat down and checked his reflection, angling the desk lamp onto his face to make sure every detail was right. His skin tone was olive today, the wig black and neatly trimmed. The stubble shading his face was another product of his inventive mind. Adam's entire body was hairless, so he drew upon his expertise with makeup to match his skin tone to the local Italian businessmen he had observed in the nearby cafes and bars. The fake stubble was actually the real thing, collected from barbers' garbage bags and applied to his makeup before it dried. His eyes, behind lightweight designer glasses, were rendered dark brown by contact lenses.

He closed his makeup bag and replaced it in the backpack, pushing it right to the bottom, so that he could quickly reach the weapons tucked into pouches nearer the top. The backpack was black and anonymous-looking. He replaced it every few weeks, or after every job, whichever came sooner. It was part of his routine. Adam had spent years perfecting the art of being unseen, unremarkable, unnoticed.

Before leaving the hotel room, he threw a couple of towels onto the bathroom floor. He squeezed a little toothpaste onto his finger, smearing it across the side of the sink. He messed up the sheets on the bed. He opened the minibar, tipped a few tiny bottles of vodka into a glass, swirled the contents briefly, then poured it down the toilet. He carefully placed the glass on its side on the table, next to a copy of yesterday's Figaro.

Pausing at the door, he looked at the room dispassionately. Untidy enough. Overly tidy rooms stood out as much as trashed rooms to hotel cleaners. Adam didn't want to stand out.

The chambermaid was young, her features regular and her blouse slightly too small. She smiled as she moved her trolley to one side to let Adam past. He was about to walk on when a slight stiffening of her posture reminded him of his role. He slowed after passing her and turned back, whistling softly. She looked over her shoulder and caught him admiring her ass. She made a disapproving noise to mask her obvious pleasure and Adam shrugged, mock-apologetically, giving her a little smile as his gaze moved up to her face, down a little to her breasts, then back up to her face again. She decided to return the smile, but he was already walking away toward the elevators. Reassured that the young man in room 1104 was a healthy, good-looking, arrogant pig after all, the chambermaid returned to her duties.

⸻

HE FOUND them in the second café he tried. With only two more days of their vacation remaining, they had become predictable in their habits, taking lunch at pavement cafes within walking distance of the hotel, to which they would return for sex and sleep before setting out once more in the early evening.

They were sharing a dessert - gelato, four scoops of amaretto ice-cream in the long glass accessible only after disposing of the whipped cream and flaked almonds on top. They fed one another with long-handled spoons and laughed at each other's jokes. Adam supposed they were happy. Happiness was a fairly easy trick to pull, so long as you were prepared to ignore the facts.

They ordered cappuccino. They almost could have passed for Italians, with their designer clothes and manicures, but no Italian would be caught dead ordering a cappuccino after 11am. Adam detected a tiny sneer in the smile of the waiter as he placed the cups on their table. Adam ordered a second espresso and paid the check, strolling over to the fountain in the middle of the square.

Sitting on a bench that gave him a good view of the cafe, he pulled out a cellphone and started to talk into it, his tone low and urgent. The phone was a brick - he'd carefully taken a soldering iron to the SIM card and fused it to the surrounding circuitry. It was a simple precaution. He supposed he could carry a phone with no SIM at all, but if it was ever mislaid, stolen, or—worse, still—if he ever ended up in custody, it would draw attention. This way, it looked like a malfunction had recently occurred. And the phone served its purpose very well. Adam had discovered that those few people who managed to overcome the unease they felt around him enough to approach him, were quickly put off by the serious expression he adopted while jabbering nonsense into a silver rectangle.

When the couple finally left the café, he followed at first, then, as they approached the hotel, walked briskly ahead of them and pushed the button for the elevator. Adam's timing was perfect. As the doors slid open and he stepped inside, he heard them pick up their pace slightly. As the doors slid back into place, he prevented them closing fully by sticking his foot in the rapidly decreasing gap. The couple thanked him. They were both smiling, flushed, anticipating getting back to their room. Oblivious to Adam, whose talent for invisibility was hardly necessary when each only had eyes for the other.

The man went to push the button for floor nine, but stopped when he saw Adam had already done it. The woman's face was flushed, her eyes shining. The man had placed his body between Adam and his wife - not out of any defensive instinct, but because he wanted to hide the fact that he was touching her through her skirt. Adam was relieved when the elevator doors opened and they spilled out, the amorous couple stifling their giggles. The sexual urge was very powerful, but it clouded judgement. Adam had mastered it through years of mental and physical training. He was able to feel sexual desire, even take plea-sure in it if the circumstances were correctly arranged, but he could summon or dismiss the urge at will.

Adam pulled the envelope out of his jacket pocket and placed his other hand on the gun in his right-hand pants pocket. The gun had a long silencer screwed to the barrel. The first thing Adam did when he bought a suit was to slit away the right hand pants pocket. A simple holster on his thigh kept the weapon easily accessible.

No one else was in the corridor, which made the process a little simpler. As the man opened his hotel door and watched his wife go in, Adam called after him, jogging slightly and waving the hand-written envelope. The envelope had never failed. Adam had experimented with waving a wallet, a phone, money, a book - anything to get the attention of the target for a moment. The envelope worked best because the target had to take a look at the name on the front before he knew if he were the intended recipient. And, in this day of email and instant messages, who could resist the allure of a crisp, white envelope?

The man waited for Adam, who kept the envelope in motion so that the writing stayed blurred. When he reached the man, he handed it to him with a smile. The second the target's eyes fell to the meaningless scrawl on the envelope, Adam shot him in the skull and pushed the body into the room, lowering the corpse silently to the floor and shoving the door closed with his foot. Stepping over the man, he took three quick steps into the room, which was laid out exactly the same as the one he'd booked for himself. As he walked, he looked to his right, where the mirror gave him a view into the space. The woman had hitched up her skirt and was bending over the bed, her silk panties stretched tightly over her buttocks. He placed a hand on her rear, and she sighed with desire. He shot her in the back of the head and she collapsed forwards without a sound.

Adam scanned the scene. Two kills, no witnesses, no complications. The gun he was using was not powerful, and the silencer slowed the progress of the bullet slightly. Those two factors, combined with the flat-tipped ammunition he used meant the bullet would enter the skull, but would not retain enough kinetic energy to punch out an exit wound on the far side of the brain. Also, the bullets expanded on impact, doing enough damage to ensure one shot was enough. Very efficient, very little mess.

Adam closed the door quietly behind him, hanging the Do Not Disturb sign on it. He took the stairs down to the lobby and ducked into the bathroom, heading straight for a stall. Once inside, he took a canvas bag from the backpack. Peeling off the suit, he balled it up and placed it at the bottom of the bag. He put on shorts, a T-shirt, and sneakers and carefully removed the black wig. He pulled out a baseball cap which had strands of blonde hair glued into the front and back. Sunglasses completed the change. He put the backpack in the canvas bag and grabbed it, hoisting it over his shoulder.

No one looked twice as he exited the hotel and headed for the train station.

Twenty-nine kills. He doubted many in his profession could boast as many. Most were eventually terminated by their employers to prevent any trail leading back to them. Adam had been very careful to make sure he wouldn't meet the same fate. Firstly, his work was impeccable. It would be a bad business decision to get rid of him. Secondly, no one had ever actually met him, either to give him instructions for the next job or to pay him for the last kill. Adam was very, very careful. But he knew his unblemished record of hits was finally becoming a liability. It was nearly time to retire and disappear.

Adam bought a ticket to Berlin and boarded the train to Milan. It was busier than he liked, but he'd learned to screen out the noise and smells of the cattle, and they—in their turn—seemed to instinctively know to keep their distance. They were so easy to fool, but when he had finished a job and was able to let the mask slip a little, Adam knew his presence made others uncomfortable. He was glad of it.

His training was progressing well. His physical strength and stamina were still growing, and his temperament was improving as he worked with the darkness at his core. With each job, he had become more level, calm, and weathered by experience. He knew he must not rush anything. What were a few years when you were going to make history? When he was ready, he would pay the Broker a visit. By that time, he would have the knowledge and the ability to make the kill that would change the world. The kill he had been born to make. The kill his father's successor had messed up so comprehensively.

Chapter 5

Innisfarne

The summer after she fell/didn't fall from the tree, Joni got sick with glandular fever. At first, it was just a sore throat, which was initially treated with a little skepticism due to her fondness for the chocolate ice cream which seemed to provide the only relief.

After a week, her throat was obviously swollen, and she couldn't get out of bed at all. Her arms and legs felt like they were being held down by invisible goblins and she couldn't even lift her head off the pillow when Mum came to bring her some breakfast.

"Yoghurt?" said Joni, her voice a croak like crumpling paper.

"Yoghurt," said Mee. "I'm not sure three meals consisting solely of ice-cream is providing you with a nutritionally balanced diet."

"Ok," said Joni, and closed her eyes.

"What do you mean, 'ok'? No argument, just 'ok'?" Mee leaned over her daughter and smoothed back a lick of dark black hair that had stuck to her forehead. Joni was sweating, and her forehead was hot. Too hot.

"Jones?" said Mee. There was no answer. She was asleep.

"Shit," said Mee as she backed out of the door. "Shit and buggery."

She leaned out of the door.

"Kate? Kate?" There was an answering shout from the kitchen downstairs. Mee walked to the top of the stairs and leaned out over the bannister.

"Joni's running a fever. Her throat is worse. Anyone on yesterday's boat still carrying Manna?"

Although Innisfarne had no Thin Places where Users could absorb Manna, visitors to the community sometimes showed up with their reserves brimming, reluctant to let go of the safety net provided by its power.

Mee heard footsteps, then Kate's face appeared below.

"You sure, Mee? It's fine with me, but…"

"Well I'm not overjoyed about it, but she's really sick."

"Ok, Paula always shows up with a full tank. I'll go find her."

Mee took a wet flannel in to Joni and held it against her forehead. She was burning up. Mee frowned at the thought of letting Manna near her little girl, but what choice did she have? She knew her distrust of nanotechnology was based solely on the fact that it had led to her losing the only man she had ever loved. Sometimes it was convenient to forget he wouldn't even be alive without it.

Seb had been gone more than a decade now. Mee had been eleven weeks pregnant with Joni when it had happened. He had saved the world, but lost himself. Over the course of a few short weeks, he had become distant, disconnected. She could still see the old Seb in him, but it was as if he was being pulled in a different direction by an irresistible force. He had told her that he didn't have a single organic cell left in his body. He had allowed the alien nanotechnology, which had saved his life more than once, to replace his human cells completely. As a result, he had certainly averted the deaths of more than seven and a half billion of his fellow humans.

"If, that is, you think I can call myself human any more," Seb had joked, feebly, in one of the rare moments when they were talking properly, just days before he had gone.

"You're the most human man I've ever known, Sebby." He hadn't flinched when she called him Sebby. Not a good sign.

"I don't know what I am, Mee," he had said. "Maybe it will get clearer, but…" He had stopped talking, looking up at the stars.

Mee had looked at his profile in the moonlight. His ready smile was absent, his jokes, his spontaneity. She couldn't begin to imagine what he had gone through, or how it must feel to begin to doubt your connection to your own species. She had stroked his face.

"Maybe you're overthinking this," she had said, choosing her words carefully. "Maybe you get to decide now. Choose who you want to be. What do you want, Seb?"

The silence that followed had gone on far, far too long. Finally, he'd turned and looked at her, but it was as if he couldn't see her at all.

"Mee?" he had said, not seeing her face half-illuminated by the fire they'd lit, not hearing the crackle of the flames, not feeling the soft breeze or the touch of her hand on his skin.

"Mum? Mum?"

Mee thought of how Seb had changed physically, during the fifteen days he had stood unmoving on the beach. The memory of pushing a hand right *through* his shoulder, as if his body had been semi-solid, still woke her up some nights.

"Mum? I don't feel so good."

With a start, Mee looked down at Joni, who was sweating. Her eyes were dark, her skin pale. For a second she looked like a very old woman rather than a ten-year-old tomboy.

"I'm sorry, honey, I know. Someone's coming to help you."

Mee held a cup up to Joni's lips and winced at the obvious pain her daughter experienced when trying to swallow.

━━

PAULA BUSTLED around Joni's bedroom like an anxious tie-dyed nightmare, muttering about Feng Shui, reflexology, and crystals. When she started moving her hands around Joni's body, trying to 'sense her aura,' Mee finally snapped.

"Look, Paula, do me a favor, would you?"

Paula stopped chanting. She had been trying to produce overtones with her voice, something she'd read about in a magazine. She felt sure her technique was showing improvement, but an unfortunate side-effect was the dribble of mucus sliding out of her right nostril. She wiped it on one purple sleeve.

"Yes?"

"Cut the mumbo-jumbo crap and help her. Or piss off out of it."

Paula elected to respond to Mee's rudeness and cynicism with a display of quiet, unruffled dignity. She shook her head sorrowfully while pursing her lips and raising her eyebrows, which was intended to register as a mixture of pity and selflessness. Unfortunately, it made her look like a bulldog that had just been given an unexpectedly large suppository, sideways.

Kate stepped in as mediator.

"Please, Paula," she said. "Mee's stressed. We'd be very grateful if you could help Joni."

Paula lit a joss stick and reminded herself to reject the negative and replace it with a positive. Her interpretation of that particular psychological technique meant that she allowed herself cake whenever anyone was mean, narrow-minded, or sneered at her spiritual beliefs and practices. Which had resulted in a slight weight problem.

"Thank you, Kate," she said, ignoring Mee. She bent over the bed and laid her right hand on the child's head and her left on her solar plexus. These, as she had been taught in module four of *Chakra Consciousness: Awakening The Shaman Within* (internet-based course, £699), were the seats of self-healing within the body. She closed her eyes, taking a deep breath through the nose, releasing it through the mouth with a long, "OM…"

"Oh, for fuck's sake," said Mee. Paula promised herself a Bakewell tart. She took another breath, then let the Manna flow out of her as she released it. She always pictured Manna as a healing stream of tiny blue crystals, entering the body and stimulating the chakras with their life-giving energy. She could feel the flow leaving her fingertips. She looked up at the other two women, unable to stop a slightly triumphant smile appearing on her face.

Mee nodded curtly.

"Thank you," said Kate. Paula took a step backward

from the bed. As she did so, Joni groaned in her sleep. Paula looked at the little girl's face. Manna did its work pretty quickly. She expected to see signs of recovery within a minute or so. Back to full health in a couple of hours, no more.

Suddenly, Paula leaped about three feet into the air - a surprising maneuver for a woman of her age and size. Mee stared at her in consternation.

"What is it? What's wrong?"

Paula looked at Mee but felt unable to speak for a few seconds. She had never experienced anything like it. The Manna she had released had been restored to her. Not gently, either. It was as if it had been fired out of a cannon back through her fingertips into her body. Which explained the gymnastics. It was unprecedented. Manna was never rejected; it adapted itself to every task, it was unstoppable once released. Paula shook her head firmly. First there was Year Zero. Now this. The world was surely ending. She made a mental note to send off for the prayer wheel she'd seen on discount.

"It's no good," she said. "The Manna - it came back again. Her body won't take it."

Kate stepped forward and looked at Joni, who had opened her eyes and was staring at them. She took the child's hand and looked up at Paula.

"That's impossible," she said, flatly.

"I know that," said Paula. Kate held up the hand she'd burned on the stove that morning.

"Try this," she said.

Paula, still shaking a little, touched the burn with one finger. Mee noted—with a snort—that she didn't bother with the runny-nosed chanting this time.

The burn shrank as they watched, disappearing as the shiny skin was replaced by fresh new cells.

"Humph," said Paula, feeling vindicated. She could still channel the healing power of the universe. The problem obviously resided with the rude woman's daughter. Probably some kind of karmic judgement regarding her mother. She picked up her joss stick and swept out of the room in a cloud of purple and yellow garments.

"More ice-cream, honey?" said Kate. Joni nodded feebly. She tried to push herself up on the pillows, but couldn't do it. Mee and Kate propped her up.

"Back in a sec, Jones," said Mee.

In the kitchen, Kate put a hand on Mee's arm.

"If she can't be helped with Manna…" she said.

"I know," said Mee. "What choice do I have? I'll call Stuart, see if he can come right away."

While Kate took a bowl of ice cream up to Joni, Mee used the island's only phone—an ancient landline device—to call Stuart, the retired fisherman who ran the daily ferry service between Logos Bay and Innisfarne on his old trawler.

Her hands were only shaking slightly as she replaced the receiver. She hadn't left Innisfarne for ten years.

Chapter 6

Berwick-Upon-Tweed

The hospital on the mainland was on the outskirts of a city. A city! Joni had read about cities, seen some TV shows that showed them, but the reality was markedly different to a moving picture on a twenty-inch screen.

For one thing, there was the noise. Joni and Mee had arrived in the back of Stuart's car, and—as it was rush hour when they reached the city—the roads were packed with vehicles: vans, trucks, motorcycles and buses, most of them electric, but some still pumping clouds of smoke into the sky. At one memorable point, they drove under a bridge at the same time as the silver-blue streak of a train passed overhead.

Joni would have had her face pressed against the window, drinking in every last detail, if it hadn't been for the fact that her head was lolling against Mee's shoulder and she couldn't summon enough energy to move it.

Before they reached the hospital, she had fallen asleep again. Asleep! In a city!

━━━

WHEN JONI FINALLY WOKE UP, it was night-time. There were soft pillows under her head and an unfamiliar smell in the room. She moved a little. Her back hurt. She managed to reach behind her and found a dressing covering the skin just above her butt. She flinched when she touched it. Her throat felt much better, and she was thirsty. The room she was in wasn't completely dark, She could see Mum sleeping in a big chair next to her. Joni really needed a drink, but didn't want to wake her. Mee was twitching and mumbling in her sleep. She looked exhausted, her skin gray, her dark black hair lank and uncared-for, a few streaks of white coming through in places.

Joni could see a glass of water on a table next to her. She reached out her hand for it. Her arm still felt heavy, but it wasn't as bad as it had been back on Innisfarne. She closed her fingers on the glass. It was still cold. Joni guessed Mum must have been refilling it with fresh cold water every so often ready for when Joni woke up. She was about to pick up the glass when she saw the tube on her arm. Pieces of tape attached the tube to her skin. There was a clear liquid inside the tube and, when she looked closely, there was a needle at the end of it going right into her flesh. Joni jumped in shock, and the glass slipped out of her hands, smashing on the hard floor.

Mee's eyes opened, and she was on her feet instantly, ignoring the glass and taking Joni's hand. She saw the expression on Joni's face as she looked at the tube going from her arm to the transparent bag hanging at her bedside.

"It's ok, Jones, it's there to make you better. You were dehydrated—you needed fluids—and this is how they do it in hospital. It means your body can have a drink, even when you're asleep."

Mee perched on the bed and stroked Joni's cheek.

"You're going to be fine. The doctors and nurses have taken good care of you."

"What's wrong with me?"

"It's called glandular fever. It gave you a sore throat and made you very tired, but you're on the mend now. We'll be able to go home in the morning."

Joni smiled and pushed herself up a little on the pillows.

"Can't we stay a bit longer?" she said. "In the city, I mean. Just to see what it's like. Just for a little while."

She looked up at Mee's face. She was frowning.

"There's nothing for us here, Jones. We have everything we need on Innisfarne."

"But, Mum-"

"But nothing, lovely girl. I have medicine for you, and the doctor said you're going to need plenty of rest for the next week or so. Home is where you need to be."

Mee smiled at her daughter, but the smile didn't look right.

"I'll get you some more water."

As Mee poured the water, a nurse came in and started picking up the pieces of broken glass. Mee's thoughts were whirling. She hated being away from the island, and a decade of self-imposed exile had made her feel like a stranger on the mainland. Even the small town of Berwick-Upon-Tweed (which Joni had insisted on calling a city) where the hospital was located seemed overwhelming, despite the fact that Mee had grown up in north London.

She had already called Stuart to arrange transport back to Innisfarne in a few hours.

She couldn't tell Joni the truth. Not yet. How do you tell a ten-year-old child that her father was some kind of super-being? That most of the Order thought he was the Messiah? That plenty of other Users wanted him dead? And that if anyone found out that Meera Patel—Seb's girl-friend—was alive and well, there would be plenty of inter-ested parties who might track her down, not all of which who would have harmless intentions. And what happened when they found out about Joni? The Messiah's daughter? The biological offspring of the most powerful being on the planet?

And how could she ever leave Innisfarne? That was where Seb had spent the last few weeks before he disap-peared. That's where he would come back to. She would need to be there if he returned. *When*. When he returned.

———

JONI WAS GIVEN a wheelchair for her trip back to the car the next morning. That was kind of fun, but it also meant she couldn't explore some of the places they passed which looked interesting. She was curious about the rest of the children's ward. There were sixteen children in there—Joni counted—and, as she'd never been in a room with more than four other children before, that in itself was pretty amazing. Some of the kids were in bed, some were wandering around in their pajamas, three small boys were taking turns pushing a wooden train around a track. Two of the children—one of them a girl a little older than Joni —were bald, which was a little strange. Joni didn't know if this was because some girls just didn't grow hair or if it was the fashion in the city. She self-consciously gave her own curls a little tug just to reassure herself her hair was all still there.

The lobby of the hospital was a big, open room, with balconies on two levels above them, lots of glass letting in the sunlight, and an amazing machine which gave people drinks whenever they held a plastic circle up to it. Joni watched this process with fascination, while Mum spoke to a doctor.

"I'm glad I caught you, Ms Patel," the doctor said. He was young, bright-eyed and remarkably presentable considering the two hours sleep he'd managed to snatch while on duty the previous night.

Mee was glad her name was not an uncommon one in the UK. As far as hospital records were concerned, they had treated Joni Patel. Mee knew her caution bordered on paranoia at times, but she also knew how easy it was to track someone in a hyper-connected world. She wanted to leave as little of a trail as possible, should anyone made a real effort to look for her. She left Joni looking at the vending machine, and stepped out of earshot.

"What can I do for you?" The doctor flicked through some notes until he found what looked like a computer-generated image of a human skull, with a solid black blob representing the brain.

"Your daughter—," his eyes flicked down to the chart, "er, Joni, presented fairly serious symptoms when she was admitted. We needed to rule out meningitis."

He noticed the look on Mee's face. "We *did* rule out meningitis."

"The lumbar puncture," said Mee. That was an experience she never wanted to go through again. Even though she knew Joni was anesthetized and could feel nothing, the sight of that needle going into her back was something Mee was going to live with for a long time.

"Yes." The doctor held his chart up a little higher. "We also took a CT scan of Joni's brain."

"But she's ok?"

"Yes, yes, she'll be fine. Make sure she completes the course of tablets, and she'll be up and about in days. It's just…well, we weren't able to complete a proper scan."

"What do you mean?" Mee gestured toward the image he was holding. "What's that, then?"

"I think it's some kind of malfunction." The doctor tilted the image, as if it might impart its secrets more clearly if held at an angle. "Instead of a clear image of Joni's brain, we got this. It's weird. Like her brain is covered, or shielded."

"You just said it was a malfunction." Mee turned her body, signaling clearly that she wasn't going to be staying long.

"Well yes, yes, of course, what else could it be? So, naturally, we reset the machine and tried again."

"And?" Mee tried, and failed, to restrain her curiosity.

"And this time, the CT scanner shut down. Completely. All the computers turned themselves off. At first, we thought there had been a power cut. But it was just that room - and all the lights stayed on anyway. The machine was dead. We sent out for specialist maintenance, but they weren't needed. The scanner turned itself back on before they arrived. They checked it and could find nothing wrong. To be honest, they thought I was wasting their time."

"And why should I be interested in your computer trouble?"

"It's just the timing, Ms Patel. That's what was strange. I came in to see Joni yesterday evening and told you my diagnosis. When I left the room, I had a call. The scanner had just come back online. That very moment."

Mee lifted an eyebrow and gave the man her best withering look. As withering looks go, hers was world-class. The doctor blushed and stammered under its glare.

"So, what are you suggesting? That my daughter broke your machine, then magically restored it to life? While she was unconscious?"

"Well, well, no, but, well, with this Manna stuff out there I just wondered…"

Mee sighed. She had forgotten how the world had changed beyond the island since Year Zero. Manna users weren't in the shadows any longer, and those who had emerged were feared, mostly with good reason. She shook her head.

"She's just a sick little girl, doctor, that's all. And I need to get her home."

"But, Ms Patel, if we could just try the scan again, we might rule out any possible—,"

"No," said Mee. The doctor saw the look on her face and backed away. It probably was just a malfunction, anyway.

"Time to go, Jones," said Mee as she helped Joni out of the wheelchair.

"Mum, can I ask a question?"

Mee braced herself. How much had Joni overheard?

"Sure, Jones, what is it?"

Joni twitched her thumb toward the vending machine.

"Can I have a hot chocolate?"

Chapter 7

Six Years Later
Innisfarne

A few months after her sixteenth birthday, Joni met a boy, fell in love and had her heart broken. Then she unmet the boy, thinking that would mean she could unfall in love and unbreak her heart. She was disappointed, but not entirely surprised, to discover love didn't work that way.

━━

THE BOY'S name was Odd, and Joni met him on a creative writing course. The course had been advertised in one of the free local newspapers that occasionally reached Innisfarne on Stuart's boat. It wasn't cheap, it was nearly a hundred miles away, and it was residential - nine nights in a remote hotel just outside Haltwhistle on the southern edge of Northumberland National Park.

When she'd finally found the right moment to ask her mum, Joni had discovered a universal truth which came as a complete shock to her, just as it had to countless other teenage daughters since the beginning of time. She had discovered her mother was capable of doing something utterly surprising, something that completely confounded her expectations. Joni had gone to Mee expecting a huge argument, involving Joni having to point out that she was nearly an adult, that—although she appreciated that Mum was just trying to protect her—she couldn't be expected to live out the rest of her life on a tiny island, that she had ambitions of her own, she wanted to be a writer, dammit, this was her dream, it had always been her dream, couldn't anyone understand that, and if Mum stood in the way of her dreams, what did she think would happen, that -

"Yes," had been Mee's initial response, while folding laundry. When Joni, uncertain she'd heard correctly, had asked for clarification, Mum had handed her a basket of bedclothes and smiled. "It sounds great, Jones. I think you should go. I'll call the bank tomorrow. Who do I need to transfer the money to?"

Joni was happy—*very* happy—but for about thirty seconds, she couldn't feel it. She had been so ready to be disappointed, angry or wretched that these emotions still hovered around her like ominous storm clouds. Finally, she saw them as the illusions they were, they evaporated, and she hugged her mother.

"Thank you, Mum," she said, "thank you, thank you."

"Of course, Jones," said Mee, stroking her daughter's hair, inhaling her scent and marveling that the smell of her daughter was still as uniquely hers as it had been when she was a baby.

Mee knew daughters rebelled. She had done it herself, spectacularly, when she was only a few months older than

Joni was now. She had discovered boys, alcohol, and marijuana during the course of a single ill-advised party lasting most of a weekend. Following that, she had bunked off school for half a year, failing every exam when her mother had finally forced her to return. It had taken years to bridge the distance between the two of them. She wasn't going to let that happen with Joni, however much she wanted to protect her, however scared she was.

Joni kissed Mee and ran back to her room to get the newspaper ad. So far, her education had been taken care of by the steady flow of teachers who regularly spent periods of weeks, or months on Innisfarne. Now she was going to sit in a room full of people her own age. People who wanted to write! People like her! She danced around the room, then headed for the door.

When her hand closed on the door handle, she was aware of a strange tingling sensation, like mild pins and needles in her head. The sensation was accompanied by a subtle, low humming noise that seemed to be coming from everywhere. It all seemed slightly familiar. Joni knew she had felt this many times before, but normally it was brief and obvious. It was one of those things she assumed everyone must get every now and then. Like hiccups.

As she left the room, she glanced over her shoulder. The door was swinging toward her, but, just before it closed, she caught a glimpse of someone on the other side, holding the handle. She gasped and stood still, looking at the door. She knew she hadn't imagined it. But she couldn't have seen what she'd thought she'd seen. It was impossible.

Come on. You're sixteen, not six.

She put her hand on the handle and pushed slowly downward. There was no resistance from the other side. As soon as she heard the *click* of the mechanism, she pushed the door hard and leaped into the room, shouting, "Ha!" as she landed, fists raised, in a fighting posture.

The room was empty.

Not sure what the ninja pose was supposed to achieve, Jones.

Joni smiled at how ridiculous she must look. Then she went to find her mum, but not before checking over her shoulder twice before the door shut behind her.

Chapter 8

Haltwhistle

First love is supposed to be special. It's supposed to be an emotional rollercoaster. And, almost without exception, it's supposed to hurt. It's a rite of passage very few avoid and, like most rites of passage, the participant, ideally, emerges wiser, more realistic, and better prepared for the rest of life's journey. Joni, although she was in some respects—unlike every other teenager who believed the same—unique, was dismayed to find herself on the same emotionally volatile path countless others had followed before her.

Odd was a beautiful boy. There was no other word for him. Fourteen teenagers attended the writing course, of which only five were boys. Of the five, only Odd had broken with tradition. He upended the idea of the spotty, bespectacled, introverted teenage boy who wants to write. He was tall, his blonde hair unfashionably long, falling onto his broad shoulders in heavy, Byronesque curls. His blue eyes were very blue. Amazingly blue. The blue of an unexpectedly bright Spring day. A glacial blue. Joni was in trouble the moment she saw him.

Then there was his accent and his slightly halting way of speaking. Odd's parents were Norwegian and had only moved to Britain the previous year. Odd had quickly discovered that his name attracted attention and some amusement in his new country. He might have even been bullied, especially combined with his lilting accent. But, either by instinct or design, Odd made it impossible for his name to be used as a weapon against him, by bringing it up himself and disarming everyone around him.

As excruciating as it was unavoidable, the first evening at the hotel hosting the course had opened with the group tutors introducing themselves, then making everyone else do the same.

Joni, blushing to her roots, had managed to stammer out something about wanting to write fiction. Others had fared little better, some almost inaudible as they stumbled over their own names. Mell, perhaps half a year older than Joni, was an exception, cool and poised as she announced her intention to write a bestselling novel before she was twenty. It was hard to doubt someone with that much confidence.

Then Odd stood up. Joni saw an older female student unconsciously part her lips slightly, her eyes widening. He certainly had a palpable effect on those around him.

"I'm Odd, hello," he began, and waited for the inevitable giggles to die away. He laughed himself, and everyone relaxed. "You might interpret what I am saying in two ways. Both the ways are right, so well done to you. My name is Odd, it is a common name in Norway, but in the UK you hear me say it and think, 'hmm, is he saying he is odd?'"

More giggles.

"So, let me tell you now, yes, you are right, it is also that I am a little odd. The way I speak is odd, my face is a little odd. If you get to know me, you will find other odd things, but I am thinking you might find fun things, too." He smiled and everyone, *everyone* smiled back. Joni was acutely aware that she wasn't the only one who wanted to get to know him and find out what the other things, the *fun* things, were.

"Don't feel sorry for me, though, if you please," said Odd. "Feel sorry for my sister - she is Randy."

He sat down amidst gales of laughter.

⸻

JONI HAD ALWAYS FELT an inner confidence, always been comfortable in her own skin, and being brought up in an ever-changing community on a small island meant she was used to being around people she didn't know. But suddenly being thrust into the company of a group of strangers her own age propelled her into an uncharacteristic introversion. She became more of an observer than a participant. She was fascinated by everyone, but couldn't seem to find a way of initiating conversations. She spoke when spoken to, then clammed up again.

Jones, what are you doing? These guys are just like you. Talk to them.

There were two sessions every morning. The first ninety minutes were set aside to discuss the exercise they had worked on the previous afternoon, with students randomly selected to have their work read aloud and critiqued. This was a painful process for most of them, but as Rae (the lead tutor, and a published author of a series of best-selling thrillers, plus three impenetrable literary novels) pointed out on the second morning, they'd better get used to it.

"You want to write without any criticism? Fine, never show anyone your work. But you're here, you've all expressed an interest in writing for a living, so I'm telling you to prepare yourself for some pain. You put a piece of writing into the public domain with a price tag on it, and someone will hate it. Guaranteed. The more copies you sell, the more people you'll unearth who'll tell you it's a pile of crap. You'll find readers who love it, too, but if you spend your time worrying about the ones who don't, you'll never write anything worth shit."

She picked up the pile of paper next to her - everyone's attempts to write a horror story in one hundred words. She flicked through, pausing occasionally and making uninterpretable noise at the back of her throat.

"There are some pieces here that show real promise. Others are bad but contain one or two lines that display a spark of life. Then there are a few that are dead in the water. I'm not going to tell you which are which, but I'll make you a promise. On your last morning, if you come and see me, I will give you my honest opinion about your future as a writer. If you have the potential to sell books, I'll tell you. If I think you should consider an alternative career, I'll let you know. I won't sugar-coat it. I don't want you to waste your time if you have no talent, but—more importantly—I don't want you to waste the time of your readers."

Before sitting down again, she raised an eyebrow and half-smiled.

"I've run this course every summer for seven years now. That's around one hundred students. Guess how many students have taken me up on my offer during that time?"

There was silence, everyone assuming, correctly, that her question was rhetorical.

"Six. I wonder how many of you will knock on my door that last morning? And, if you don't, you might want to ask yourself why not. Writing's a tough game. Don't misunderstand me. Anyone can write, but very few ever write something worth reading."

Joni went for a walk before lunch. She told herself she needed some fresh air after being stuck inside all morning, but she knew that wasn't the truth. She just wanted to be able to sit alone, not make conversation. She had ended up at a table full of shrieking girls the previous evening, all of whom quickly bonded over a common currency of music, movies, and online entertainment. There was one television on Innisfarne. It was over twenty years old and could only pick up four channels - five, if the weather was particularly clear. There was no internet. Joni knew what the internet was, but there was no way of getting it on Innisfarne. Even visitors quickly abandoned their cell phones once they realized there was no signal. Joni listened to the girls talking for ten minutes. She dropped out of the conversation and slipped away from the table as soon as she could.

Once back from her walk, she grabbed a sandwich and a soda and sat down in the corner, fishing in her bag for her copy of Gormenghast. She was quickly lost in the world of Titus Groan and his nemesis, Steerpike.

"Ooh, Mervyn Peake, how very gothic."

Joni jumped, nearly dropping her half-eaten sandwich. She looked up. It was Mell. Tall, popular, confident, auburn-haired, unfairly attractive, and unfeasibly large-breasted Mell.

"I *love* Peake, isn't his prose just scrummy?" She sat down without asking and plucked the dog-eared novel from Joni's hands. "Wow. You've read this a few times, haven't you? Now be honest with me. Even though Steerpike is the bad guy, don't you just want to have a good rummage inside his pants?"

Joni just stared at Mell for a second, then both girls started laughing.

Underneath the bluster, the make-up tips and the encyclopedic knowledge of the current crop of male movie stars, Mell turned out to be well-read and a genuine lover of literature. The two girls soon discovered a shared love of Catcher In The Rye and Lord Of The Flies, as well as a passion for the slyly mocking novels of Jane Austen. Joni convinced Mell to read Graham Greene and, at Mell's insistence, agreed to try Lord Of The Rings one more time.

"We can never be friends if you don't. And I think we should be friends. Because you're a reader. No one I know reads. Come on. Friends for life!"

Mell extended a crooked pinky. Joni stared at it before realizing she was supposed to do the same. They linked pinkies and shook them up and down solemnly.

"That's it," said Mell. "Friends for life. You have to be my chief bridesmaid, or turn off my life support machine if I'm hideously injured in a car crash. Right, we're supposed to write something like a Shakespearian sonnet this afternoon. I always thought iambic pentameter was a close-harmony singing group. Come on, I've found a window seat with cushions. There's room for two. And I have wine for later."

Finding herself swept into Mell's confidence was the first surprise. The second happened a few days later. Joni had taken to walking in the middle of every afternoon for an hour, partly to clear her head and think about her writing without Mell's regular 'helpful' interruptions, partly to fulfill her longing for solitude. She had never thought about how important her 'alone time' was until it had gone.

She walked up the hillside at the back of the hotel. Once over the crest, a long, low, sunlit valley stretched to the west for about five miles. At the top of the ridge on the right, Joni could see the regular line of stone denoting the path of Hadrian's Wall, the ancient border dating back to Roman-occupied Britain. She felt a little shiver at being so close to a real piece of history. The biggest, most successful, most famous empire in human history - and this was as far north as it got. Climb over that wall—an easy task now, as time and weather had reduced much of it to an uneven line barely three feet high—and she would step into a country the Romans never succeeded in claiming for Caesar, or anyone else.

As she stared up at it, the sight was abruptly blocked by a pair of hands placed over her eyes. She sighed theatrically. Couldn't Mell have stayed behind for a smoke?

"Mell," she said, "I'm supposed to be clearing my head. I told you, having a 'nip of vodka' doesn't have the same effect for me. I need to be outside. On my own. Just for a little while."

"Oh. Shall I go, then?"

Joni's body stiffened. It was a male voice, and the lilting tones could only belong to one of the group. She put her hands up to her face and took hold of Odd's hands, turning to face him as she gently pulled his fingers away from her eyes.

He was smiling.

"Shall I?" he said again. "Do you want that I should leave?"

Joni was aware, *intensely* aware, that Odd was still holding one of her hands. On one level it seemed like the most natural thing in the world but on another, she found it was all she could think about. The beauty of the landscape seemed insignificant, Hadrian's wall no more than a boring pile of stone. Gosh, Odd's eyes really were incredibly blue. This close, she could see he wasn't wearing contact lenses.

"Can I walk with you, Yoni?" Joni loved the way he said her name. No one else said it like that.

"If you like," she said, trying very hard to sound casual. As they walked across the edge of the ridge, he finally let go of her hand. *Shit*.

Odd was disarmingly honest about himself and his literary prospects. He admitted he was no great writer and had no real hope of becoming one, although he enjoyed reading. He just wanted to be able to document the times he was living through. He had three brothers, and the house they had moved into in London was smaller than the house they had lived in just outside Bergen. His mother was an anesthetist, his father a radiologist, and the UK had offered them a very generous package to bring their skills to the National Health Service.

"London?" said Joni. "Aren't you scared of Manna gangs?"

"No, not really. It's not as bad as the people are thinking. They control certain areas. No one would want to go to Putney, for example. But they are not coming into the city much. The police are many and if Users get caught, they know of the tags."

Joni knew most of this, the various ways government had cracked down on Manna users—now they were out in the open—was old news, even on Innisfarne, but she liked Odd telling her about it. She liked hearing his voice, the way he constructed his sentences. She liked looking up at him while he explained, the way he tucked stray blonde curls behind one ear when he was thinking. The curl of his lips when he smiled. Those eyes.

Joni had read about romantic love and had formed the considered opinion that it was, well, a bit overrated, if not downright silly. Despite Jane Austen's acerbic subtext, her heroines still swooned. Still dreamed of romance, still longed for a good marriage. Characters in other books—thrillers, horror, science fiction, fantasy—fell in love and allowed their feelings to cloud their judgement. Even in the fairytales she read as a child, humans were forever falling in love with a fairy, leading inevitably to disaster.

Joni was a daydreamer, a romantic in the true sense of the word. Her heart was moved by a beautiful old tree, the sun setting over a stormy sea, the smell of the forest after rain, the music of Bach, Mahler and The Beatles. She rhapsodized over a well-turned sentence in a novel, an inner thought of a fictional character expressed in such a way that she suddenly felt linked to that character—and the writer—in some profound way that transcended time and space. But going all gooey-eyed over a boy? Hardly. She had decided that *falling hopelessly in love* was a literary cliché bandied about by hacks who wrote cheap trashy nonsense. She was certainly not going to *fall hopelessly in love*. She would never *fall hopelessly in love*.

Joni fell hopelessly in love.

Chapter 9

The last few days of the course passed in a blur. Mornings critiquing, usually in smaller groups with Rae coming around to offer her pithy insights. Lunches with Mell, followed by writing sessions on the window seat. These sessions were broken up by frequent interruptions whenever Mell was stuck on a particular word, or couldn't quite think of a metaphor, or was bored, or wanted to start on the vodka *for inspiration.* The afternoon walk belonged to Joni and Odd.

By unspoken agreement, they hadn't mentioned anything to anyone else, and barely did more than exchange pleasantries at any other time. But, walking the ridge, or heading into the forest for an hour and a half that always passed too quickly, they talked to each other as if no one else existed. Their walks seemed to take place in a bubble, a separate space which would admit no other.

Odd told her a little more about his family and the move to Britain, but Joni always felt he wasn't telling her the whole story. Norway had escaped most of the problems associated with Year Zero. Its Manna population was small and confined to just one area of Oslo. Why leave such relative security for the uncertainty of London?

"I think they just want to help people," said Odd. "We are coming from a long history of people who love freedom. We do not like it when people try to take this from us. Manna users deserve freedom, too. I think we do not like how the government is so quick to lock them up, you know?"

He looked sidelong at Joni. They were holding hands again. Neither mentioned it, but Joni felt as if her hand was a new kind of limb which had an existence all of its own, sending messages of happiness back to her brain. She could feel the pressure of his long fingers. Sometimes he squeezed when he was empathizing a point. She wasn't going to let go of that hand, even if she got cramp.

"My family has used Manna," she said. "I don't see a problem."

Odd looked startled at her bold admission. His eyes darted left and right as if scared they might be overheard.

"You have to be careful what you say, you know," he said. "I am happy you have told me this. I know Manna is ok, it depends on the User, but not everyone is agreeing with this. Some people would have you tagged if they heard you."

Joni looked at him doubtfully.

"It's got that bad?"

"Yes. In the cities, yes. People have to be very, very careful. A boy at my school, his father was tagged. One day, coming home from work, there was a Manna gang looting some shops. He tried to get away when the police came, but he was rounded up with the rest. The police found the tag, so the boy never saw his father again."

"But that's terrible! Surely, if he was caught up in it by chance, if he has no criminal record, they can't just—,"

"But no, they can. And they do. There is much, oh, what is the word I need? Much…panorama?"

"Paranoia."

"Yes, that is him. Paranoia. The government tells us we are in danger, it tells us the Manna users hate us, they want to take over the world, and everyone must stop them. And, of course, we know some Manna users do want power, they are violent, they do not care who they hurt while they are taking what they want. But that is just a tiny number, tiny, compared to all Manna users. Good Manna users have to hide, pretend they are normal, not help someone who is bleeding on the street in case someone sees and they get tagged. It is a bad time, Yoni. A bad, bad time."

"But it doesn't have to be this way. If people stand up for what's right…" Joni thought about the incomplete picture she had of her father. Mum had warned her to be on her guard with strangers, to avoid speaking about Dad as far as possible. She knew he was a Manna user, but something more than that. Mum had promised to tell her the whole story, but when? Joni knew how hard it was for Mum to talk about Dad, but she had to know. She had to know why Uncle John and Kate (or Martha, as members of the community sometimes called her) looked at her *that way* sometimes. Sadly, pityingly, lovingly, but also curiously. As if they were waiting for her to do something. Maybe something that would scare them. Or perhaps she was just being ridiculous. She looked at Odd. He was still speaking.

"But how often do people stand up for what is right, Yoni? It is so much easier to look the other way, tell yourself it is important to protect your family. How can you be worrying about other people's families? Who can be so brave? I do not know. It is easier in books."

Joni decided to take a risk.

"I don't know much about my father," she said. "I

never met him." Joni was used to speaking about Dad this way. People assumed he must be dead and didn't ask many questions. But Odd just waited for her to go on. So, she did.

"He wasn't like other people. He had something people wanted, he was powerful. But he never asked for it."

Joni paused. This was already more than she'd spoken about her father to anyone other than Mum, Uncle John or Kate for the whole of her life.

"He and Mum, they had to hide. Change their names. Everyone wanted something from him. Some wanted him dead. But he wanted to help people. I think he would still be helping people now if he could."

"What was his name, this Mr Patel?"

Joni shrugged. She wanted to say her father's name to someone. Make him feel more real.

"Patel is my mother's name. His name was Varden. Seb Varden."

He looked at her, his expression hard to read. She looked back. Neither said anything. Then they were kissing, and Manna users, tagging, riots, even the woods and the rain that had begun to patter onto the branches above them, faded into the background until there was just her, a boy, and a kiss.

THE LAST MORNING of the course was the best and worst day of Joni's life so far.

The best bit came in the morning. Joni had packed her clothes back into her suitcase, said her goodbyes. The group were exchanging addresses, emails, social media nicknames. Joni hung back a little. She had Mell's number in one pocket. In the other was Odd's London address and cell phone number. He had laughed when she said she had no email address - in fact, no internet presence at all. Then, when he'd realized she was being serious, he'd written his email down anyway.

"One day you will be joining civilization, you know. Can't hide away on your island for the rest of your life."

He'd kissed her again. He'd kissed her a lot during the last two days, even risking being seen on a couple of occasions in the hotel itself. But nothing had felt like the first kiss. Joni imagined that was how it must always be with first kisses in relationships. It was always good, but it could never compare to the first time. Not that she would ever have another relationship, of course. Because this was true love.

Joni didn't know then that she'd got relationships backward. They didn't start at the peak, then plateau. They were supposed to get better. She didn't realize until much, much later why that first kiss had felt quite so intense. It was because Odd had known then that there would be no relationship.

He had been kissing her goodbye.

As Joni made her way to the downstairs room that Rae had used all week as an office, she was surprised to see Mell coming out, her expression grim, her eyes slightly puffy and red-rimmed.

"Mell? Are you ok? What happened?"

Mell shrugged off her attempt at a hug and looked at Joni, sniffing loudly.

"It's all right for you, it all just comes pouring out, doesn't it? Some of us have to work hard, you know, we sweat blood to come up with one sentence that doesn't sound like tired crap. Well, Miss shit-for-brains in there thinks I might be better off as a trolley-dolly for British Airways. Apparently," raising her voice now, "I have the *tits* for it. Well, FUCK YOU." This last was delivered as she half-ran down the corridor.

Joni stood alone for nearly a minute, wondering if she wanted to go in or not. Did she really want to find out that Rae thought she'd make a great flower arranger, or perhaps an accountant? Could she bear someone stomping on her dreams? The problem was, she respected Rae's opinion. She's read some of her work and the prose was tight, spare and powerful. Joni *cared* what she thought.

She took a deep breath and knocked on the door.

"Miss shit-for-brains is now in session," came the reply. Joni went in.

As she headed back to the hotel lobby to pick up her bag, say her goodbyes and wait for the taxi that would take her back to the station, she felt as if she were floating. Rae had been direct and unflattering, as she had promised. She had started with Joni's weaknesses: an occasional tendency towards flowery prose, which needed to be reined in, a preponderance of dark metaphors, the occasional unnecessary adverb, a slightly simplistic black/white, good/evil world view which could only be partly excused by her age. But…but. A strong voice, a cohesive style, an inexhaustible curiosity and a willingness to learn.

"You're a writer, Joni. Whatever else you may be, you will always be a writer. It's obvious. As plain as the nose on my face. Don't look quite so happy. You'll need to feel the lows as well as the highs if you ever hope to move anyone with your words. Good luck."

Fifteen minutes later, as Joni reached the lobby, found her bag and started scanning the faces for Odd, she didn't realize how quickly she would be feeling the lows to which Rae had referred.

She couldn't see him in the lobby, so Joni left her case and went outside. There was a gravel turning circle directly outside the hotel's old-fashioned brass-framed doors, and it was full of parents' cars, picking up their offspring before returning them home for Christmas.

As she walked along the line of nose-to-tail cars, Joni smiled at all the hugging going on, the shouts of greeting. She was still smiling when she saw the back of Mell's head. She was standing by a tree. There was a hand stroking her hair while its owner was enthusiastically delivering what looked more like mouth-to-mouth resuscitation than a kiss. Funny, Mell had never mentioned a boyfriend. Then the kissing couple disengaged for a moment, before finding a new position, the hand moving from her hair to one of her breasts.

Joni stopped smiling as the familiar blonde curls came into view. Then those blue eyes locked with hers and she turned and ran, stumbling as she made for the hotel. Blinded with tears, she headed upstairs and flung herself into the nearest restroom, finding the furthest stall and locking the door behind her.

She waited there for an hour before drying her eyes, going back to the lobby and calling another taxi to replace the one that must have given up and gone.

There were no cars at all left on the drive. As she watched, a coach crunched across the gravel and came to a halt. The door opened, and about forty children emerged, whooping, laughing, screaming and running around the lobby, pursued by tired -looking adults. Joni saw the taxi. She picked up her bag, walked out of the hotel and climbed into the back of the car. The driver set off. They passed the tree where Mell and Odd had been kissing. Joni didn't look.

Chapter 10

It wasn't until she had flung her luggage into the overhead rack, slumped in a seat, spent half an hour crying and almost as long sleeping that Joni calmed down enough to become aware of the tingling sensation. Even then it took a long time for her to recognize what was happening, what it meant.

The ticket collector had taken one look at her red face and tear-streaked cheeks and said, not unkindly, "Eh, well, pet, if it's over a bloke, don't waste your tears. Most of us are complete bastards."

To her relief, the train was quiet and her carriage was almost empty. She knew it was likely to take on more passengers at the various stops between Haltwhistle and Newcastle, where she would have to wait nearly two hours for the bus north.

She watched the countryside go by in a blur. The blur wasn't due to the speed of the train, rather the state of the windows, which looked like they hadn't been cleaned since Year Zero. The monotonous green-brown view of the landscape, the gentle swaying of the carriage and the metallic clatter of the wheels had a soporific effect on the exhausted Joni, and she slipped into a dream.

In the dream, she was falling from a tree. She knew the tree, it was one of the tallest oaks on the island and had once been her favorite for climbing. She had stopped, abruptly, years ago, and although she continued climbing elsewhere, she had an almost superstitious fear of that particular tree. She couldn't remember the last time she'd climbed it.

Her dream-self had no fear of the oak and had climbed a good distance into its branches before the dream properly began. When Joni became lucidly, consciously aware, she was upside-down, pulling herself along a branch, as confident and nonchalant as a spider monkey.

When she fell, the initial fear and disorientation were almost immediately replaced by a sense of curiosity and wonder. Her fall slowed, her stomach unclenched after the initial lurch when she had lost her grip. She opened her eyes. Her body was turning as she fell in slow motion. She looked up at the sky first, noticing—with a jolt of recognition—a piece of yellow rag tied around the branch from which she'd fallen. Then she twisted and looked down at the clearing below. She could see a small girl walking towards the main cluster of buildings on the island. She was wearing a white T-shirt. White with sunflowers. Another jolt of recognition, a fizz of memory. Joni twisted in the air. She saw another, identical figure, the sunflowers clearly visible on the T-shirt, frozen in mid-skip, heading toward the beach. Dream-Joni looked at her own T-shirt then as it rippled slowly in the wind, seeing the same sunflowers. She twisted again and looked directly below. A third girl, a fourth if you counted the falling Joni, was sitting at the base of the tree.

I remember this. I remember falling.

Suddenly the speed of the dream decided to align with real-world forces, and without warning, Joni's lazy, sycamore seed descent turned into a plummet. She heard her neck break on impact. For a moment, although her body was facing away from the tree, her broken neck meant she was looking straight at the seated girl. She was looking at the seated girl at the same time as she was looking at her broken body through the eyes of the seated girl.

An announcement was made over the train's tannoy and Joni was pulled into the hinterland between sleep and full wakefulness. She was only there for a couple of seconds, but it was long enough for her to remember why this dream seemed important. Why it seemed more than a dream. With the strange, slow clarity that can arise before the conscious mind is fully engaged, Joni remembered the other girl she'd seen in her room that day. The day she asked Mum if she could go on the writing course. And her unconscious mind cajoled her conscious brain to make the connections - and realize the dream hadn't come out of nowhere: it was a memory.

She was fully awake, and—now that she was paying more attention to the tingling sensation—she became aware of a deep, rumbling tone underscoring the rhythmic metal dance of wheels on tracks. The sound wasn't external, it had an intimacy which was both familiar and unnerving.

Joni had grown up with a child's fantasy of being different, special, chosen. Because of the mystery surrounding her father, she'd never quite grown out of it. If Dad had wielded some strange power, how was it possible that she could be so…normal? She'd done the math. She had been conceived before Year Zero. Two months before. There was no reason why she wouldn't be able to use Manna. But she remembered what had happened when a User had tried to cure her glandular fever. Her body had rejected the Manna completely. She remembered the sensation. So, not only couldn't she Use, but she couldn't even be helped by other Manna users. Great. Sub-normal.

She felt a frisson of fear. If this wasn't Manna, what was it? She could *feel* a build-up of power inside her, like a massive subterranean generator coming online. And as she turned her attention fully toward it, she felt the significance of the moment like a physical pressure. She only half-believed something was about to happen. But she knew, if it did, that nothing would ever be the same again.

For a moment, she hesitated. But only for a moment.

━━━

JONI CLOSED her eyes and focused on the tingling. At first, it was hard to do. Other thoughts started jostling for attention, insistent and distracting. Initially, she fought against the distractions, before remembering her daily Innisfarne meditations. She tried to shift her mindset, allowing the distracting thoughts to exist without feeding them.

It was like a soccer player Joni had seen once. Half the community had gathered around Innisfarne's only TV set to watch a match which was considered significant in the world outside the quiet island. A man called George had explained some of the rules as the game had progressed, and, with less than a minute left before the end, Joni felt she had a fair understanding of what was going on. No one had scored a goal, despite numerous attempts, and, as the seconds ticked away, one of the teams had focused completely on defense, bringing all their players back into their own half and fending off every attack by sheer weight of numbers. George had explained this was a sound strategy, if a little frustrating to watch, as the defending team would win some sort of league if they didn't lose this match. The attacking team had to score a goal if they wanted to win.

The player Joni remembered had lined up a free kick. He was a long way out from the goal. Too far, Joni had thought, but George had assured her it was possible for a great striker to score from that distance. Every other player had been forced to back away from him until the referee blew his whistle. When he did, the player had begun his run-up, but, as he did so, every player in the opposing team had sprinted toward him, shouting, looking for all the world like an advancing army intent on pulling him apart. But the player had taken his shot as if they didn't exist and the ball had sailed over their heads, curling in the air before burying itself in the top left corner of the goal, thereby winning the match.

The slow-motion replay had fascinated Joni. She looked at the man's face as he ran toward the chaotic scene: the snarling faces of the opposing team, the huge spotlights pinning their dark shadows to the artificial turf, the roar of tens of thousands of fans on their feet as the fate of their favorite team came down to one single moment. One single kick. And yet the player's face was utterly calm, completely focused, clearly completely unmoved by everything that was conspiring to distract him. In those few seconds, he was just a man kicking a football to the best of his ability. He might have been doing it in his backyard, he was so relaxed.

Joni thought about the football player as she turned her focus inward and concentrated. But it was no good. Her brain seemed unable to screen out what wasn't necessary. She kept seeing Odd's face. And every time it appeared, she saw him kissing Mell. Over and over, her mind adding details she couldn't have seen: his tongue sliding between Mell's lips, his hands pulling her closer, their bodies pushed hard together, his fingers unbuttoning her shirt. Then she started imagining what might have come next. Did the pair of them sneak away? Find a quiet spot in the forest? Tear each other's clothes off, frantic in their desperation to feel naked skin against naked skin?

Joni opened her eyes again.

"For God's sake, Jones, get it together," she said, her voice suddenly loud in the quiet carriage. An old man she hadn't noticed lowered his newspaper and gave her a look full of despair at the prospects of the younger generation.

"Sorry," she said, and shuffled further along her seat until she couldn't see him.

She remembered the football player again. *Concentrate. Nothing else exists*. She needed to narrow her focus to one event. She just needed to kick the ball.

She forced her mind away from Odd and Mell by focussing instead on that moment in her room when she had the newspaper lying on her bed, folded to show the advertisement for the writing course. She had read it over and over, getting increasingly excited. She had known she *had* to go. She had been preparing her arguments, as she was convinced Mum would be against it. Decision made, she had been about to get up, go and find Mum, ask her if she could go. She'd been sitting on the bed at the moment she'd made the decision.

As she remembered this, the low hum became more

prominent. It wasn't that it got louder, more that its constant presence became suddenly obvious as other thoughts were pushed aside. The tingling became more pronounced, too—almost painful— as her bedroom on Innisfarne appeared in front of her closed eyes, the details filling in on their own. She could see herself sitting on the bed. Then the hum became a roar, swelling within the space of one second, to a cacophony that overwhelmed everything, bringing darkness as it reached an unbearable peak of sound which shook her entire body.

Abruptly, everything stopped. The roar, the tingling. And, Joni realized, the sound of the train had stopped too. She could hear a blackbird's song, the murmur of distant voices. Hesitantly, she took her hands from her lap and placed them next to her. She felt the distinctive padded patchwork quilt she'd had on her bed for as long as she could remember.

Joni opened her eyes. The train was gone. She was sitting in her bedroom on Innisfarne. It was morning, not early afternoon - she could tell by the light which had only just begun to creep up the far wall toward her bookshelves.

On the quilt, carefully folded, was a newspaper. An advertisement had been ringed with green pen.

Creative writing course for under 18s. Led by novelist Rae McCall, students will discover the tools needed in the craft of writing, improving their technique through a series of exercises followed by group and individual critiques. All within the stunning setting of the Winterbourne Hotel, Haltwhistle, on the edge of Northumberland National Park.

Joni stood and drew a few shaky breaths. She looked out of the window, registering the unbelievably ordinary sight of the yard. Then she looked back at her room. She had done it. She had actually done it. What was she, a time traveler? She snorted in disbelief. Time travel was too riddled with problems to ever be feasible - Mum was fairly hot on science, and she'd ripped apart that concept one night when they'd been discussing HG Wells.

Joni picked up the newspaper with trembling fingers and dropped it into the trash.

Chapter 11

France

The Broker lived in a chateau in northern France. He lived alone, protected by a handsomely paid security team, a hand-picked mixture of Manna and non-Manna users. A helipad on the croquet lawn meant he could receive visitors from anywhere in the world. The Broker himself had not left the grounds of the chateau for almost fifteen years. Technology had offered him a painless way of growing his business from anywhere in the world, and he had delicately slid his virtual fingers into the lives of hundreds of influential individuals from his satellite-linked lair.

He had chosen his contacts carefully over decades, amassing information and storing it in his purpose-built databases. Then a series of creatively programmed algorithms connected the dots between the individuals, their associates, and their business interests. Criminal activities carefully concealed from view were dragged into the light of the Broker's scrutiny.

To his clients, the Broker described his business using a simple metaphor: he ran a currency exchange. His exchange wasn't the largest in the world, but it was certainly one of the most useful, and powerful. And the only currency it accepted was information. Ten years ago, with the sudden disappearance of Mason, who—up to that point— had been his only real rival in the information business, he had unexpectedly found himself the market leader.

The Broker had no price list for his services, but his Swiss account—the details of which he was always happy to supply to new clients—was regularly topped up with amounts he would have been embarrassed to ask for. It was almost as if his clients were competing with each other to prove their gratitude for his unique service.

The Broker treated the occasional assassination attempt as a backhanded compliment, as well as an occupational hazard. Those behind the attempts were given a lesson in how assassinations should be carried out. For these specialist assignments, the Broker used the only person who made him truly nervous - the only person about whom he had been able to discover *nothing*, despite his best efforts. But the risk of using this invisible individual, a man who didn't appear to have left a single trace of himself anywhere on or offline, had been more than compensated for by his remarkable skills in getting the impossible done. Killing the un-killable. The Broker suspected that one day, Adam—his first name was all he had—would want to erase all trace of their dealings. He just hoped that day would come far into his opulent future. His prediction about Adam was correct. Unfortunately, his hopes regarding the timescale were as inaccurate as they were optimistic.

———

ADAM WAITED PATIENTLY, the night scope pressed to his eye. If patience was truly a virtue, it was the only one Adam possessed. It had been six years since the hit in Rome. Since then, he had only made himself available for one or two jobs a year. During that time, he had become indispensable to the Broker.

Gaining access to the Broker was a four-part operation taking forty-one days in all. Staking out the chateau had been first. The location was known in certain circles - it was impregnable, so the Broker felt little need to conceal his whereabouts. Adam had watched the comings and goings from a tree on a neighboring hillside. He set a camera to record while he slept or fetched supplies. After sixteen days, he found what he needed. A small Citroen approached the gates, where the first security team checked the vehicle and its occupant. The security operatives were first-rate, one keeping a safe distance, his weapon cocked and ready while his partner asked the questions. The car drove inside at 11:17pm and did not re-emerge until 5:14am. Adam was ready, his belongings packed and the immediate area cleared of evidence. He dropped out of the tree and made for the car he had concealed nearby. Part two of the operation began.

He picked up the Citroen on the main Paris road and followed it to a small, exclusive housing estate in the suburbs. Adam watched as the driver locked the car and limped into his house. A couple of nights later, he broke in and questioned the driver, whom Adam's research had revealed to be a high class escort commanding eye-watering prices for his services. There was no need to threaten the man - he was glad to give up the information Adam required. The bruises, cuts, and burns he showed Adam had been carefully placed in order to be hidden when he was clothed.

Adam thought it unlikely the Broker would use the same prostitute twice, and bugging the offices of every high-end escort agency would be inefficient. Instead, the third part of his operation involved bringing in a little help. He hired a local petty criminal to watch the Paris road at the junction with the smaller lane leading to the chateau. Visitors other than shift changes for the security detail were rare, so any car containing a single occupant prompted an empty text being sent to Adam's burner phone. It happened twice in eleven nights. The first time, on the ninth night, was a false alarm - a laborer working in a neighboring vineyard had taken a wrong turn after a night of heavy drinking. A very brief conversation with security led to him weaving his way back to the main road.

The car that turned in on the eleventh night was an anonymous Peugeot, new, slightly sporty. Adam picked it up in his night scope from his perch in a tree three-quarters of a mile further up the hill. Silently dropping to the floor, he jogged down the hillside, his night-vision goggles making the otherwise treacherous descent easy.

When he reached the road, Adam looked for the tree he had marked. Finding it, he took off the goggles and reached behind a nearby bush. He dropped the goggles beside the bag containing his next outfit and picked up a large metal sign and a cap.

He placed the sign on the road. It read: Halte, Gendarmerie. Adam ripped away velcro patches on his jacket and pants, revealing hi-vis 'police' badges. He turned on his flashlight and waved it slowly as the Peugeot appeared and slowed to a stop a few feet away. The window slid down as Adam approached.

"Is everything ok?" said the driver. Adam shone the flashlight on the man's face. Mid-twenties, quite heavily made up, dark red wig, a smart three-quarter length emerald dress and a silk shawl.

"Get out of the car." Adam could speak four languages fluently besides his native German, and he cultivated a neutral accent, trying to sound as bland and anonymous as possible.

"Was I speeding?" The driver did his best to appear unconcerned as he swung his legs round and slid from the seat. He was already opening his purse. A small bribe was occasionally necessary to placate over-zealous members of the local gendarmerie.

━━

ADAM DIDN'T GO to great lengths to conceal the escort's body. He just dragged it into the bushes along with the police uniform and the sign, making sure they weren't visible from the road. By the time they were discovered, he would be long gone. He took the clothes from the concealed bag and dressed quickly. Part Four of the operation was reliant on his own abilities, and he was at the height of his powers.

The guards were expecting 'Chantelle'. The pair on the gate let Adam through without a problem. They searched the Peugeot quickly and thoroughly, then did the same to Adam. They asked his name, the name of the agency plus a four-digit code that had been texted to the real escort's cellphone while he drove. Adam had the phone now, as well as the silk shawl, which added a classy touch to his own black cocktail dress. The escort had given up all the information he needed immediately - it had only taken the police uniform to persuade him. Adam had been prepared to get more physically persuasive but was glad when it proved unnecessary. It meant he didn't arrive later than expected.

There were two more guards on the front door. That only left the Broker's personal bodyguard, Katrina. Adam had done his research. She was a truly exceptional hand-to-hand fighter, trained to a high level in knife work and a skilled Manna user. She met Adam in the huge marble-floored lobby. The other two guards were sent to patrol the exterior of the chateau, with instructions to report back in two hours. Now it was just the three of them in the building.

Adam knew he would only have one chance to get this right. He felt a small surge of adrenaline - not so much because of what he was about to *do*, more what he was about to *learn*.

Katrina led Adam into a bathroom as big as most living rooms. She turned to face him.

"Strip," she said. "Naked. Now." She waited until Adam had wriggled free of the dress and the panties beneath. He folded them and placed them behind him by the door. Katrina examined his body thoroughly, starting with his feet and slowly working up. Then she pulled out a latex glove and lubricated one finger, Adam feigned shock and reluctance before allowing her to check every orifice.

Katrina raised an eyebrow at the hairless scalp beneath the wig but said nothing. She was a little taller than Adam's five feet eight inches, but their physique was remarkably similar . Both were lean and wiry, muscled more like dancers than fighters. Professional killers had no room for vanity in their fitness and training regimes. They trained for speed, strength, and stamina. Of the three, stamina was the least important. Ideally, there would be no prolonged fighting. One blow, properly placed, should be enough. Sometimes two, if your opponent was experienced, lucky, or both. Speed meant you stood the best chance of winning. Surprise increased your chances significantly. Katrina, by the time she had finished examining Adam's teeth and looking under his tongue, was finally satisfied. She relaxed a fraction, concluding there would be no surprises from the hairless, naked man in front of her. Her confidence was misplaced.

Adam winced. "There was no need to be so rough," he said. "I think you broke my filling. It hurts." He put a finger into his mouth, exploring the area gingerly.

"Poor baby," said Katrina, flatly. "Now get dressed. He is waiting for you. Upstairs, first door on the right. Knock and wait until he calls you in. When you are finished, ring the bell on the table in the lobby."

Five years ago, Adam had helped a skilled dental surgeon avoid losing a kneecap to a local mobster collecting gambling debts. The mobster had gone home with three fewer fingers, and the dentist had agreed to do anything Adam wanted. Particularly when Adam explained that his debt, far from being paid, would now be personally handled by Adam himself. He paid the first installment by performing some specialist dental work.

Adam slid his fingers back to the first upper molar, twisted it forty-five degrees clockwise and pulled it down, tilting it as he did so. The blade attached to it, concealed in a narrow hollowed-out chamber in the two teeth behind, was razor-sharp. Adam groaned a little to cover any sound, then pivoted on his toes and swung his right arm in a scything arc, catching Katrina's throat and opening her jugular in one blur of motion. Her eyes widened, but her reflexes were incredible. Adam could see why the Broker had singled her out. Even as the fatal wound opened and sprayed crimson jets through the fingers she had instinctively jammed onto her neck, her right leg snapped up to deliver a kick that would have stopped Adam in his tracks, had it landed. It didn't. Another advantage of surprise was the fact that you were one move ahead of your opponent during the crucial first few seconds of an engagement. Adam had dropped into a squat just as Katrina moved. He used his right leg to sweep her off her feet, just as her kick passed harmlessly over his head. As she fell, he pushed her backward, hard, and there was a satisfying crack as the back of her head made contact with the substantial freestanding bathtub.

While Katrina bled out, Adam checked himself in the mirror. Only a few flecks of blood. He dabbed at them with some wadded tissue, careful not to smear his makeup. He replaced the tooth and retrieved his clothes from near the door. As planned, they were free of stains. He put the wig back on and smiled at himself in the mirror.

"Showtime," he said.

Chapter 12

The Broker woke up slowly, in some discomfort. The last thing he remembered was the thrill of anticipation as the lithe, trembling escort had approached him. Now he was disoriented and confused. His shoulders hurt. He opened his eyes. Then he shut them quickly, before trying again, hoping he had just imagined what he had seen. He hadn't.

His wrists were tied to large iron hooks screwed into the wall, stretching his arms uncomfortably. He was sitting on a high stool, facing the wall. He could only see straight in front of him - something was obscuring his vision on both sides. There was light in the room, but it was flickering. Candles. He couldn't stop himself groaning when he realized where he was. He was in the Games Room. Next door to the master bedroom. He couldn't see left or right because he was wearing blinkers, handmade to his specifications to fit a human head. He was naked. Naked, tied up, unable to see his enemy. In a soundproof room. This wasn't good.

He heard a noise behind him and tried to twist to see better. As he did so, the stool was jerked away from under his naked buttocks, and he fell. The sudden shock of pain in his shoulder sockets as the ropes abruptly stopped his fall made him hiss through his clenched teeth. His feet found the floor. He was only able to stand on tiptoe. Just as he had specified when he had commissioned the construction of the Games Room almost two decades previously.

"Let the fun begin," said a soft voice behind him. "That's what you say to them, isn't it?"

For a few seconds, the Broker allowed himself the comfort of believing this was a simple act of revenge. Maybe he had injured one of the escorts more permanently than he had intended. Maybe this was a jealous boyfriend, or——. He stopped his own delusional train of thought. Just to get into the chateau, through his security team, was supposed to be impossible for anyone wishing him harm. Each pair of guards comprised one soldier and one trained Manna user. The Manna users could not be fooled, they could sniff out violent intentions a mile away. They had proved invaluable on a number of occasions. How had this one slipped through? Was it possible his team had been compromised? How? Besides paying them every year what most people earned in ten, the Broker had the power of life or death over their families. They could not be turned against him. What did that leave? There was no chance at all of betrayal from Katrina. She had been trained since the age of three to serve, unquestioningly, the master or mistress to which she was assigned. For life. He had been forced to sell a small Caribbean island to pay for her. She was worth it.

He cleared his throat. "Katrina..." he said.

"Was a Majji fighter," said the soft voice behind him. No real accent, hard to place. No tension, either. A pro. Shit. Wait. Did he say *was*?

"You know about..."

75

"The Majji? Yes, of course. I make it my business to keep abreast of my peers. And the Majji feature heavily among them. Bred to kill. Impressive. She's dead."

"I don't think so," said the Broker. Even now, hanging from the wall in this impossible situation, he didn't believe Katrina could have been overcome.

"I wish I could tell you that she put up a good fight, but I'd be lying. And I do think we need to be totally honest with each other in the short time we have together. I think it will expedite things a little if I explain who I am and why I'm here. Although, surely you have guessed the answer to both of those questions by now."

The Broker could feel his mental processes coming back online as every second passed. The side of his neck hurt. That must have been from the blow that incapacitated him. He didn't see it coming, and it must have been extraordinarily accurate to render him immediately unconscious. But who? And what did he want? The fact that his captor wanted something gave the Broker a sliver of hope.

"I described the Majii as my peers, but that's not quite true. I have no peers. I'm the best at what I do. You should know. I've allowed you exclusive access to my talents for the last six years."

Oh. Fuck. Adam.

Adam chuckled. The Broker heard a tiny whining sound. Now he knew who was standing behind him, he started to picture some mechanical instrument of torture being prepared to inflict unimaginable pain on him. Then he heard the tapping of keys and realized the first sound had been Adam turning on the laptop.

"You have a printer in your bedroom. I want to print some information, then delete all trace of the files. Username, password."

The Broker told him. After Adam had first contacted

him, he'd sent him on a few impossible hits, suicide missions. Adam had succeeded where no one else had got close. As soon as he realized the value of the asset he had acquired, the Broker used Adam to consolidate his position, take out competitors, cement his reputation as the only serious source of illicit corporate and national information globally. Adam had enabled him to build his empire. He was unstoppable, a ghost, a nightmare. Once unleashed on a job, he didn't get back in touch until blood had been spilled. And tonight, if he didn't play this very, very carefully, the blood would be his own.

The fact that Adam had trussed him up facing the wall was surely a good thing. He was still protecting his identity. Why do that if he intended killing him?

"I am here to collect my payment. You promised you would pay me in full when I wanted it—,"

"Of course, of course—,"

"—but I'm afraid I don't trust you. Granting you exclusive access to my services has made you rather dependent on me. I don't think you would be prepared to give up all the information I require and risk losing me in the process."

The Broker started to say something, then thought better of it. Adam was no fool. Better, perhaps, to play along. For now. An opportunity to talk his way out of this may yet arise.

"Where is the information I asked you to gather?"

The Broker named the file.

"And everything is contained here? All the information I need?"

"Yes. That's everything."

The Broker had answered quickly. Adam was an excellent liar. He had grown up among people who spent much of their existence lying. He himself only answered to the

Father of Lies. The *real* Father of Lies. So he knew a false-hood when he heard it. He opened the file and pressed print. He walked up to the Broker, stuffed a balled-up pair of socks into his mouth and opened the soundproofed door to the master bedroom. The printer was spitting out paper on the desk in the corner.

Back in the Games Room, Adam shut the door behind him. He was carrying two heavy hardback books. He dropped them onto the floor next to the dangling man. The Broker was sweating profusely now. Heavy and out of shape, his tendons, joints, and muscles were silently screaming at him as he struggled to find a position that didn't cause constant agony.

"I'm going to ask you a question," said Adam, "Then I'm going to do something a little unpleasant. After that, I will ask the question again. Does that make sense?"

"Yes," said the Broker. He wondered how a creature like Adam defined "something a little unpleasant" and immediately wished he hadn't.

"Good. Please listen carefully. The file I just printed is supposed to contain all the information you have gathered for me over the last six years. Now, despite your vulnerable position, and your prior knowledge of my capabilities, you may be tempted to hold something back, so that you still have some chance of regaining my loyalty."

"No," said the Broker, "no, of course not. I—,"

"Shh," said Adam and waited until the Broker had fallen silent. "You are an intelligent and successful business-man. I would expect you to lie to me - even in this extreme situation. But I would advise strongly against it. My question is the same one I asked a minute ago. Think carefully this time before answering. Does this file contain every piece of information you have gathered on the subject?"

The Broker hesitated this time. He couldn't show weakness, couldn't give him a different answer. There was no way Adam could know, either way. He took a deep breath.

"That's everything," he said.

There was silence for a moment, then Adam walked up behind him. He forced the Broker's legs apart. The agony in his ankles and toes increased. He screamed.

"Don't move," said Adam. "You wouldn't want my hand to slip."

A shiny white object floated into view between the Broker's legs. For a surreal moment, he thought it was a balloon. He blinked sweat and tears out of his eyes. The balloon tilted, revealing eyes, a nose, and a mouth. It was a bald man. No eyebrows. Adam was completely hairless. He had something in his hand. The Broker wondered if the pain was making him hallucinate. It looked like a tooth. A tooth with a tiny blade sticking out of it. The hand came upwards. Without warning, Adam sliced open the wrinkled skin of his testicles, following this with another quick incision inside his scrotal sac. The bald head disappeared again.

There was a half-second delay before the pain kicked in. Then there was thirty seconds of frenzied thrashing. The Broker lost control of his bladder and covered the wall with rancid urine.

When he finally stopped moving, he realized the stream of urine had ceased, replaced by a thin patter of blood seeping from between his legs. On the floor below him was a dark, round piece of gristle. One of his testicles. He moaned, just as Adam's hand appeared, holding one of the hardback books. The hand slapped the book onto the floor, flattening the piece of flesh below it. The Broker sobbed.

After a few minutes, Adam spoke again.

"I'm going to ask the question one more time, after

which I will do the same thing to your other testicle, with one slight difference. This time, I will flatten it *in situ*. It's why I brought two books. They used to use bricks to do the same when castrating cattle, you know. Books seem more appropriate for a man as well read as you."

Adam stopped talking. He was making a strange sound. It took the Broker a few seconds to realize it was laughter.

"How appropriate," said Adam, tilting the spine of the second book as he brought it over. "It's Dickens."

"There's a second file," screamed the Broker, "THERE'S A SECOND FILE."

Chapter 13

Adam assumed, correctly, that the Broker's guards would have an armory near the roof and that sniper rifles would be available. The chateau was surrounded by open space so any intruder could be picked off by a shooter at the building's highest point.

While the printer continued producing pages of information, Adam—now wearing a black pair of sweatpants and a T-shirt he'd found in the bedroom—used the combination the Broker had given him to open a heavy cabinet on the third floor. He took out an AWSM, a British-made sniper rifle. He made sure the five-round chamber had its full complement of .338 bullets. He didn't anticipate having to reload. The AWSM held the record for the longest confirmed sniper kill at a distance of nearly two and a half kilometers. Adam had kept an eye on the odometer of the Peugeot as he drove in. The gate was just over a kilometer from the house. It was a virtually windless summer night, and the cloud cover had lifted since he arrived, revealing a three-quarter moon. Adam attached the scope and took position on the roof.

He dropped to the surface of the chateau roof and crawled on his belly until he could use the scope to check out the gate. He knew the guards' routine - he had watched them for many nights. Every ten minutes, one of them would leave the small guard hut and move to the gate, listening and watching for a few minutes before returning to the hut. Adam settled down to wait.

Four minutes passed before there was movement. Adam waited until the first guard was as far away from the hut as he was going to get. The window of the hut was open, as it was a humid night, and Adam had a clear line of sight to the man within. Adam's breathing was very slow and steady. He inhaled, held his breath for a count of three, feeling the stillness and silence as he relaxed. As always, he felt the darkness inside him swell in approval, his mind clearing and the world shrinking until it contained only his finger on the trigger and the sandy-haired man eleven hundred meters away in the guard hut.

Adam squeezed the trigger and immediately moved his shoulder a fraction of an inch to bring the second guard into view. Adam saw the man react to the sound of a bullet hitting his colleague in the back of the skull, but he had barely moved before the second bullet caught him in the face, punching a coin-sized hole in his eye socket, emerging at the back of his head just below his military-style hair-line. His knees crumpled under him as his brain stopped sending the messages necessary to keep him upright.

Adam waited. The two guards in the house checked in with the gate eight minutes later. He heard the voice of a man below him growing increasingly tense as he failed to get an answer. Soon, Adam heard another voice. The two remaining guards must have been standing almost directly below his position. Adam's guess was that the guards would think a communication problem was the likeliest explanation for the sudden radio silence. No one had breached the gates, and they wouldn't even consider the possibility of an attack from the chateau itself as Katrina was in charge. Such misplaced confidence in the legendary skills of the Majji.

Sure enough, after a brief conversation one of the guards set off toward the gates. Adam immediately got to his feet and ran silently back to the stairs, the AWSM in his hands, making his way quickly through the house to the main door. He could have waited and shot the guard out in the open, but that would leave the final guard expecting an attack. Messy.

Instead, Adam placed the rifle near the heavy front door and peered out through the spy hole. Sure enough, the guard was standing with his back to him, watching his colleague jog down the drive. It would only be a few more seconds before he spotted the body by the gates.

Adam turned off the lobby lights, pulled the door open and was outside before the guard had even half turned. He jabbed him in the windpipe to prevent noise, then followed that blow with another under his ear. This combination— one of Adam's favorites—completely disoriented the guard, who staggered as if drunk, suddenly onset by severe vertigo and nausea. Adam had plenty of time to take the knife from the sheath on the guard's belt and bury it in his throat. As the dead man fell, Adam gave him a push that sent the body spinning out of sight behind an ornamental bush. He then ducked back into the chateau, leaving the main door open. Lying on the cool marble floor, he picked up the rifle, slowed his breathing again and looked through the scope toward the gate.

The last guard had just spotted the body. He stopped jogging and turned back to the chateau. When he regis-tered that his colleague had gone, he had to choose quickly: run on to the gate, or go back to the house. He hesitated for approximately quarter of a second, which was long enough for Adam to release a shot that made either choice obsolete.

Upstairs, the printer had fallen silent. Adam found a finely balanced Japanese meat knife in the kitchen and a briefcase in the ground floor office. He took them upstairs and placed the few hundred sheets of paper inside the briefcase. He stood in the doorway of the Games Room for a few moments. The Broker was whimpering, the full weight of his body now on his wrists, arms, and shoulders as his toes and feet had finally cramped and given way. Adam stepped forward and, using the knife, sliced open the femoral artery in the groin. Blood started pouring down his leg. The Broker then understood the long, slow, painful death Adam was planning for him. His voice was a shaky whimper.

"You can't leave me like this. Just kill me, make it quick. Please."

Adam shook his head, even though he knew the Broker couldn't see him. He despised the dying man's weakness. It came from a lack of understanding about life. About the order of things in the natural universe. Amazing how otherwise intelligent people couldn't see the truth that was right in front of them.

"Embrace the pain," said Adam. "Learn from it. In life, you were a merciless, powerful, self-serving man. Be the same in death and claim your reward."

In the few seconds that followed the only sounds were the labored, ragged breathing of the naked man hanging on the wall, and the regular drips of blood still falling from his groin.

"You're insane," said the Broker.

"By almost every measure known to science and medicine," said Adam. "Yes, I am. But the measures by which I will be judged are far greater." He turned and walked away.

"No!" shouted the Broker. "I lied! There's more information, there's more!"

"You didn't lie. Goodbye. You could always try shouting for help."

With that, Adam closed and locked the heavy door of the soundproof room on the second floor of the isolated chateau. He placed the key in his pocket and went back to the Peugeot, retrieving the AWSM from the lobby. It was a very fine rifle.

The next shift change for the guards was due at dawn, still nearly four hours away. If they realized the whereabouts of their employer and could lay their hands quickly on some industrial cutting equipment, they might get through the soundproof room's heavy door in another hour. But the man inside would have bled out long before that.

Adam had meant what he had said; the Broker had shown great potential in life. He might yet be rewarded by the Master. Although, Adam considered, as he remembered the whimpering sound the Broker had made as he walked away, his legs covered with blood and shit after finally losing control of his bowels, probably not. Probably not.

He rested one hand on the briefcase as he drove. He was going to spend the next few days carefully perusing its contents. The information the Broker had tracked down for him was beyond price. He knew people must have suffered and died to assemble the reports he now had in his possession. And there would be many more who would kill to know what was contained in the few hundred printed pages. The Broker's computer security would be unbreakable - his reputation had depended on it. After his death, all the information would be erased. If the Broker did not log in at least once during any twenty-four hour period, using a password which changed each time according to an algorithm only he knew, a virus would be automatically released which would turn all the data into incomprehensible garbage.

Sometimes, the offline, old school approach could have its advantages. Once Adam had memorized the most pertinent information, he could simply burn the documents, and their contents would be lost for ever. He had glanced at the titles. The first one had caused a surge of excitement as he realized he was finally within sight of his quarry. The second one meant nothing to him. Yet.

The first file was titled, *Sebastian Varden*. The second, *Innisfarne*.

Chapter 14

Innisfarne

Joni couldn't have said why she didn't tell Mum what had happened. She knew she had said nothing when she'd fallen out of the tree as a child. It wasn't that Mee wouldn't believe her - she had seen too much crazy stuff not to. But the few times she'd spoken at length about Seb - her dad - she'd made it clear that his power had caused as much heartache as it had joy, if not more. And it had changed him. The man Mum loved would never have left her, but that's exactly what Dad did. Mee never spoke in detail about the time when he left, but it was clear that she blamed the power, for changing him and taking him away from her. And she was only kept from despair by her certainty that he would be back. Well, that and the fact that she had a daughter to bring up.

The first few days after Joni returned, she tried to spend as little time around Mum as possible. Mee wasn't stupid. She could see something had happened, that Joni was quieter, unhappy, dealing with some kind of internal struggle, but she could also see it wasn't a conversation Joni was ready to have. Like all mothers of teenage daughters, Mee knew there was a time when you had to back off. It didn't come easily to her. She was especially puzzled by how sudden the change in Joni had been.

Joni started taking a long walk around the northeast tip of the island every afternoon to help her process what had happened, as well as to avoid Mum's questioning glances.

In reality, the long walks were as much about getting over Odd as mulling over the physics-bending trip she'd initiated on the train home. It was her feelings for the Norwegian boy that convinced her, more than anything else, that she hadn't had some kind of mental breakdown and imagined the whole thing.

She knew she'd been in love with Odd. She was sixteen years old, well-read, very imaginative, and had grown up on an island where she hadn't mixed with many people her own age on a regular basis. She knew an objective observer would think it highly likely she would have fallen head over heels with the first boy who'd paid her attention. But Joni wasn't stupid. She wasn't ignorant. She was naive—certainly—but she was aware of her naivety and took it into consideration when examining her feelings. The connection between her and Odd had been intense, considering it had been formed over the course of a few afternoons. But that didn't mean it could be trivialized. It was real, and it was deep. They had begun to open up to each other in a way that she had never felt before, never been able to truly imagine. As they got closer, she had begun to see herself as Odd saw her, and that had begun a process of transformation which was still continuing. She was growing up - and the person she was going to grow up to be would be partly determined by the way an eighteen-year-old blonde boy had looked at her. And spoken to her. And kissed her.

And kissed Mell, she reminded herself. It was doubly bitter because she'd lost Mell, too. Although she could understand Mell more easily. She'd just been told she wasn't going to make it as a writer, she would have been glad of the attention - and the distraction. Joni had kept her burgeoning relationship a secret. And Odd was irresistible. Joni only had to glance at the other girls on the course to see that. But she still couldn't understand why he had behaved as he did.

A week after her magical return—Joni thought of it as a *reset*—she managed to face the worst of it. The sea was pounding against the rocks as she picked her way along the shingle in bare feet, her sneakers knotted together and slung around her neck. She watched the waves for a long time. It was something she loved to do, but it freaked Mum out for some reason, so she only indulged herself when alone. Joni loved the enormity of the sea. The curve of the Earth visible at the horizon where tiny-looking ships were silhouetted against the sky. The cry of seabirds searching for scraps. And, most of all, the constant growl, roar and *shuuuush* of the waves as they clawed at the beach then withdrew.

Joni faced the thought head on, at last. *It's not that I will never see him again. The writing course won't start for weeks yet. He doesn't know me. He never will.*

She allowed the truth of it to settle over her like a clammy fog, before taking a deep breath and howling her anguish, as loudly as she could, at the uncaring waves.

It took an hour. Afterward, she walked slowly back to the Keep. The keep was the center of the community on Innisfarne. A collection of stone buildings, plus a few wooden dwellings added at times when visitor numbers were greater. The biggest building held a dining room, kitchen and meeting/meditation room, plus bedrooms upstairs for the longer-term residents. Which meant Kate, Mee, Uncle John and Joni, usually. It had only been known as the Keep since Joni had read a book on castles and started imagining she might be called upon to repel invaders from their tower. She had been about seven at the time, and no one had pointed out that a long, low, two-story building was hardly a tower. Instead, the name stuck.

As she rounded the corner of the Keep, Uncle John emerged from one of the wooden buildings. Disused for a long time, he'd taken it over and converted it into a workshop, building tables, chairs, stools, and desks. They were utilitarian items, but beautiful in their way. Simple, strong, functional. The community sold them on the mainland to help pay their few, regular bills.

"Hey, Joni, what's up?" Uncle John was Dad's brother, although they hadn't even known about each other until they were adults. Stranger still, John said he was sick before he met Seb, that his brother cured him. He didn't talk about his life before then at all.

"Hi, Uncle John. You got a minute?"

"For you, honey? Of course. Coffee?" Joni had recently discovered the joy of coffee, mostly because of John's passion for it and his almost ritualistic approach to making it. Coffee beans arrived weekly on the boat, he ground them by hand and used a personally modified heater to drip water onto the grounds in a steel cafetière. Even this wasn't as good as a pressurized system, he'd told Joni. It was on his to-do list.

"Yes, please." She followed John into the workshop, and he grabbed a handful of beans, weighing them on an old-fashioned set of scales before tipping them into the grinder. Joni leaned over and grabbed another handful.

"This is going to be a two-pot conversation," she said.

———

THE TELLING TOOK some time because Uncle John wanted as much detail as possible. He wanted to know everything she remembered from her ninth birthday. Then he wanted to hear how it felt when she was on the train, what was the same, what was different. Exactly what steps she took to make it happen, the *reset*.

"So, you're buying all this, then?" she said, draining her third mug of black coffee. One more than her usual limit. She could feel the buzz.

John spread his hands and shrugged.

"Why would you lie? And this kinda runs in the family. Well, not *this*, exactly, but, well." He fell silent for a moment, thinking.

"You don't remember us taking you to the Thin Place, do you?"

Joni looked at him, blankly.

"You were three years old. We had Stuart take us out on the boat. Just me, you and your mother. Mee didn't want anyone to know what we were doing. She told everyone we were going fishing."

Joni laughed at the thought of her mum fishing. She was a vegetarian for a start.

"Great cover story," she said.

"You think? Well, she was nervous. We went out to sea. Funny, people forget this planet is mostly ocean. No one ever looks for Thin Places anywhere but on land."

"They're at sea, too?"

"You bet. Probably many more than on land. I guess

91

most are difficult to get to. You have to be real close to be able to draw on the Manna. It's not gonna work if you're floating a few hundred feet above it in a boat. So we headed for the shallows, kept close to the coastline. After about twenty minutes, Mee had Stuart slow the boat. She could feel it, close. She always was sensitive that way. We got a little further in, then Stuart cut the engine. I guess we were sitting in about ten to twelve feet of water. She leaned out, put her hands in, and the Manna just rocketed up from the seabed into her body. She was fairly crackling with energy. Then she picked you up and dangled you over the water."

"What did I do?"

"First of all, you laughed. You thought it was some new game. Then your mum told you there was something special under the water. You wanted to know if it was a water-baby. Don't know where you picked that idea up from, but when Mee said, 'maybe', you tried real hard to get to it. Mee said if you concentrated, it might come."

John took a sip of coffee and pulled a face when he realized it had gone cold. He put the mug on an old table covered in coffee rings.

"We waited about a half hour. It was getting cold, you were tired. When we turned around for home, you started to cry a little because you hadn't seen the water-baby. Then when your mum said we wouldn't be fishing, you fair howled all the way back."

Joni smiled.

"I don't remember it," she said. "So, I'm not a User. Mum said so when I asked, but I didn't realize she had tested it."

"Yup," said John. He fell silent again, waiting. Eventually, Joni spoke.

"So what am I, exactly?"

"That's the sixty-four-million-dollar question, honey. I guess we might have to ask your father when he comes back."

Joni looked him in the eye. She had known Uncle John all her life. He was a quiet man, kind, gentle and patient. She had never heard him raise his voice and he had always made time for her, never told her to run along or come back later. And he had never, ever lied to her, answering every question she posed carefully, but honestly.

"Do you really believe that?" she said. "Do you really think he's coming back?"

John nodded slowly, his eyes never leaving hers.

"I know it."

Joni stood up and stretched. It was late afternoon now and she could hear the sounds of food preparation coming from the kitchen.

"Ok. Ok." She walked to the door, but John said her name, quietly, and she turned. He looked older in the lengthening shadows. He was in his sixties but had always seemed like a man decades younger. Now he looked his age. A trick of the light.

"Two things. First, what are you going to do with this power?"

"I'm going to try to figure it out a little, explore it. See if I can make it happen, rather than wait for these moments. If I practice, maybe I'll be able to get some control over it. I'm going to try."

John sighed and shook his head.

"Of course. Of course. I guess you have to find out what's going on. When your mother had that little chat with you about changes going on in your body she had no idea, right? But that's the second thing. You gonna tell your mom?"

Joni shook her head. John nodded slowly back.

"I guess it's wise. Unless you have to."

Joni knew they both wanted to protect Mum. Finding out Joni wasn't a User must have been a relief - and she knew Uncle John's refusal to talk about his past had something to do with Manna, Mum had said so when pressed. If Mum thought Joni had some kind of power inherited from her father, she would, inevitably, consider the possibility that she might lose her daughter the same way she had lost her soul mate. Joni remembered Mum's last episode - what Joni used to call 'going into the Sad.' She had laid in bed ten days, getting up only to go to the bathroom, eating almost nothing. Silent, unreachable. Looking at her daughter as if she didn't know her. It had been almost unbearable. That had been three years ago. Joni wasn't about to be the cause of it happening again.

"And Joni?"

"Yes?"

"Be careful. This ability may have saved your life once, but I can tell you that true power always comes with a price. I guess this time, you had a taste of that."

Joni said nothing, the ache of Odd like a physical knot in her side.

"I'll be careful. I promise."

She would start practicing tomorrow.

Chapter 15

Joni decided to be disciplined about her attempts to *reset*. She put aside two hours each morning and asked for privacy, telling Mum she was going to work on her writing. She kept a journal and noted the time before each attempt. In the afternoons, she kept up her solitary walks. She had a lot of thinking to do.

The first few days were frustrating. It was hard to know how to start. She looked for a link between the fall from the tree and the moment on the train. The only common element she could find—other than the humming and the tingling—was the fact that she had seen a version of herself. A shadow-self. There had been a shadow-self sitting near the tree on her ninth birthday. On the train, she had brought to mind a shadow-self, sitting on the bed, weeks before. Now, though, she couldn't seem to consciously make it happen. She tried concentrating hard, listening for the low hum, flexing her fingers as she waited for the tingling to begin. It never did.

Dozens of times, Joni got up from her bed and made

for the door, turning at the last moment, hoping to see her shadow-self still sitting on the bed. Nothing.

She joined the community regularly for morning meditation at 6am, much to Kate's pleasure and Mum's surprise, taking seriously for the first time the attempt to be fully awake to the moment. To her disappointment, this seemed to be virtually impossible. Her legs hurt as she sat on the cushion, she developed itches in places she didn't even know *could* itch and she spent the whole hour thinking about not thinking about scratching them. Or she would think about Odd, and spend sixty minutes indulging in miserable self-pity. She persevered mainly because she knew it was this daily—well, twice-daily for most of them —activity which had kept Mum functioning. Without it, the depression she sank into so rarely would have swallowed her whole.

Kate put a hand on Joni's shoulder after one of the early sessions.

"This is why it's called *practice*, Joni. We are not trying to achieve anything. There is no goal here. Stop trying."

That just annoyed her for a few more days, until sheer boredom made her stop trying one morning and she suddenly—only for a fraction of a moment—understood what Kate had meant. It was as if something inside her had cracked open to reveal the real person. She carried the knowledge of that into her two-hour *reset* sessions, logging her failures day after day in her journal.

The breakthrough, when it came, was laughably ordinary. She was sitting on her bed—her journal documented this as attempt number seventy-three—when there was a quiet knock at the door.

"Can I come in?" It was Mum's voice.

"Sure," said Joni, remembering at the last moment as the door swung open, to grab her pen in an attempt to look as if she was in mid-sentence. "Hmm?" she said, distractedly, as Mee's face appeared.

"Sorry to disturb you, Jones," said Mum, "but McG is on the roof again." McG was one of Innisfarne's five goats and the most adventurous. His full name was Goaty McGoatface, although no-one could remember who had christened him. His occasional forays onto the roofs of the Keep's various single-story buildings occurred at least once a month, and Joni was the only one who could reliably talk him down.

Joni hesitated. McG could wait, it wouldn't hurt him to spend another forty-five minutes on the roof. He might even find his own way down. And she was determined to remain disciplined in her pursuit of the secret behind the *reset*. She was about to refuse when she remembered it had rained the night before, and McG might slip and hurt himself. She was too soft-hearted when it came to that stupid animal.

"Ok, I'm on my way," she said, uncurling her legs from under her and sliding off the bed.

"You're a star," said Mee, then looked at her, frowning. "You all right?"

Joni was standing stock still. The tingling was there, so subtle she would have missed it if she hadn't spent the last few weeks trying desperately to make it happen. She closed her eyes briefly. She could feel, as well as hear, the faint hum; such a deep note, it seemed to be heard with the whole body, not just her ears.

"You ok?" said Mee again. "Jones? You with us?"

"Yeah, yeah, sorry. Just lost in my writing, I guess." She headed for the door and turned as she got there, holding her breath.

Sitting on the bed was a faint shadowy outline of a figure, its legs tucked under itself, holding a journal.

"That's good," said Mee as they walked out to find the recalcitrant goat, who was bleating furiously from the roof of Uncle John's workshop. "You're finally getting somewhere with it, then?"

"Yes," said Joni, "I think I am."

She successfully rescued McG and moved the trellis leaning against the workshop wall which had enabled him to get up there in the first place.

"Sorry," said Uncle John, as he moved the trellis to a safer location. "I clean forgot he thinks he's a mountain goat."

He looked at Joni quizzically as she turned to go back to her room.

"Any luck yet?"

"Ask me tomorrow," she said, walked a few paces, then stopped. "Actually, can I come in for a second?"

They sat in the workshop together. Joni refused the coffee this time.

"It just happened," she said. "I think I can *reset*. I'm going to try."

"Now? Here?"

"Why not?"

John poured himself some coffee and looked at her, intently.

"You need to stretch first? Warm up? Seriously, though, Joni, if this works, come straight back and tell me about it. I guess I won't remember this conversation, right? It won't have happened?"

"Yes. No. I don't think so. Ok, here we go."

The tingling sensation had continued ever since Joni had left the room. It had faded a little, but it was easy to relax and let it come back, along with the low hum. This time, it happened fast. The moment she looked inward and focused all her attention on what was going on inside her, the tingling increased, the sound roared and—

—she was back on her bed.

There was a quiet knock on the door.

"Can I come in?" It was Mum's voice.

"Sure," said Joni. When Mee's face appeared this time, Joni kept her eyes on her journal and chewed her pencil as if she was lost in concentration.

"Sorry to disturb you, Jones," said Mum, "but McG is on the roof again."

Joni glanced up then. Her mouth dropped open, and the pencil fell out. She was about to make a decision. *That's it, that's how this works. I'm at a fork in the road.*

"You ok, Jones? Did you hear what I said?"

Joni took a couple of deep breaths, excited at her discovery and eager to test it. She realized she was flushed and breathing rapidly.

"Um. Yeah, I heard you, Mum, but I just had a great idea for a story. Let me just get some thoughts down, then I'll come and take care of McG. Twenty minutes. Thirty, tops."

"Ok. Let's hope he doesn't eat his way through John's roof in the meantime."

When the door closed, Joni stood up and looked at the bed. The shadow figure was still sitting there. She picked up her journal and made some notes.

Key element: a decision.

1. The fall from the tree. I decided to climb the tree, instead of going to the beach or heading back to the Keep.

2. I decided to ask Mum if I could go on the writing course, rather than stay on Innisfarne.

3. I decided to help rescue McG, rather than stay in my room.

Consequences of decisions:

1. I fell out of the tree and died .(Did I?)

2. I met the Norwegian shithead, and he stomped all over my heart.

3. A goat climbed down from a roof.

Number three seemed a little out of place. No one got hurt. Even as she considered this, there was a bang from outside, shouts, and some very loud bleating. Joni ran.

McG had found his own way down from the roof. He had chosen the most direct route—straight down, backward, letting gravity do all the work—and had broken a hind leg as a result. The poor creature was screaming in pain. Joni took one look, stopped running and looked inward.

The *reset* was practically instant this time. She was back in her room. There was a knock on the door.

"Can I come—oh!" Mee stepped back in surprise as Joni flung open the door and came out. Mee hurried to keep up with her as she headed for the stairs.

"It's—,"

"McG?" Joni finished her mother's sentence for her. Mee stopped in confusion, halfway down the stairs.

"Yes. How did you—,"

"Intuition," said Joni as the front door shut behind her.

Five minutes later, McG was safely back in the yard, and Joni was heading back up to her room to try again.

Chapter 16

The rest of the morning passed extremely quickly, and very slowly. Quickly because now that she had found the trigger, Joni discovered she could bring on the conditions for a *reset* at will, so she continued experimenting. Slowly, because each time she *reset*, she had to live through the same time period again.

This year is already 375 days long.

She had been on the writing course for ten days, then lived through the same period on Innisfarne after the *reset*. She thought about the implications for a while, then shook her head in a futile attempt to clear it.

She reviewed her notes. The first time she had *reset*, it had saved her life. The second time had been an attempt to avoid severe emotional pain. In that regard, it had failed. She remembered everything, including the pain, despite the fact that—now—it had never happened.

"Arse biscuits," she said aloud. It was one of Mum's tamer expressions. It felt strangely appropriate.

The third *reset* had prevented a goat suffering a broken leg. Not life or death like the first time, not emotional distress like the second (she wasn't sure if McG was capable of existential angst brought on by a disastrous love affair, but she rather doubted it). The third attempt differed in another key regard: she had not been personally involved. The events she had changed had benefitted the goat, not her.

The rest of the morning was a series of increasingly successful attempts to trigger a *reset* moment without a significant event occurring. By the time she went for her walk that afternoon, Joni could make it happen at will, just by making a trivial choice between two inconsequential outcomes. She tested it one last time that night, just before bed.

The blue pajamas or the cotton T-shirt?

The blue pajamas won out, and she climbed into bed. As she closed her eyes, she *reset* and was standing in front of her closet again. This time, she pulled out the old white T-shirt and put it on before getting into bed.

As Joni drifted into sleep, she could almost imagine Dad's smell was still on his T-shirt. It couldn't be, of course. He hadn't worn it for seventeen years, and it had been washed countless times since then. But it was a comfort to imagine some part of his presence might still be clinging to the tattered cotton garment.

That night she saw him. It was a dream, of course—Joni knew it must be—but it was more than that, too. For a start, it interrupted a different dream, which had never happened before. And Dad *saw* her.

Joni was walking up a hill. She recognized the location. It was behind the Winterbourne hotel, where she had never attended a writing course and certainly hadn't met any Norwegians. She looked over her shoulder. Odd was about two hundred yards behind her, looking up, calling to her, waving and gesturing her to slow down. She increased her pace and headed toward the top of the hill. Odd was also waiting there, his blonde hair blowing across his face. He was smiling. She wanted to go to him, but she also wanted to get away from him. She hated herself for wanting both, or either. Or neither. She felt completely confused and frustrated.

She heard bleating above her and looked up. McG had sprouted a glorious pair of white wings and was flapping his way to the summit, gliding and darting like a fat, hairy bird of prey. He was chewing her journal. Joni jumped to try to snatch it from him, but the flying goat was too fast and beat his powerful wings, gaining height quickly. Within seconds he was just a speck in the clouds.

Joni carried on climbing. Although she had picked up her pace, she noticed she wasn't getting any closer to the Odd at the summit. Looking behind her, the Odd trying to reach her wasn't making any headway either. The distant bleating above her sounded a lot like laughter.

That was when she woke up within the dream. She knew she was still asleep, but she felt fully awake, conscious, totally aware of the ridiculous nature of what was happening. The confused, circular nature of the dream seemed suddenly to be under her control. She looked ahead and blinked. Odd vanished. She looked behind her to confirm the other Odd had also disappeared. McG remained - she could hear him bleating excitedly. As she looked up, she saw him experimenting with loop-the-loops. Since she now felt in control, she decided to join him. She wouldn't need wings. If she could imagine it, she could do it. She grinned, squatted then threw herself upward toward the sky, aiming squarely at the winner of the World's Ugliest Bird competition.

It didn't work. Instead, she was somewhere else. Somewhere hot. Very hot. There were flames all around her. She could feel the intensity of the heat, but it didn't burn. She knew that if this was real, it would scorch the eyebrows from her face. Her skin would be reddening, wrinkling, crackling, splitting, and popping. Her eyeballs would melt, her tongue would turn black. Somehow none of these things were happening. And there was no pain.

At first, she could see nothing at all. Orange, red, yellow, blue-black, green, purple, the flames danced across her vision. After a moment, she found she could move. She looked down toward her feet and was unsurprised to find she didn't have any. No arms, either. She didn't have a body at all. She was a wraith, a spirit, a movement within the flames themselves. She thought herself forward, and it happened, her awareness dancing through the heat-haze to a place where darkness began to interrupt the constant colors. There were specks of light within the dark patches. Then the darkness grew greater, a vastness opening up above her. The specks were stars. The night sky stretched above her, every constellation clear. Joni was no cosmologist, but she knew what The Plough looked like. And The Bear. Orion's Belt, that was an easy one. They weren't there.

Joni forced her eyes away from the sky. At ground level, the flames threw light out to a distance of about fifteen meters before becoming lost in the shadows.

I'm in a fire. I am a fire.

At that moment, she realized how familiar all of this seemed, and she remembered why. This wasn't a dream - it was a *memory.* A memory of the vision she had had while falling from the tree on her ninth birthday.

At the edge of the clearing, she could make out trees, comfortingly familiar yet disconcertingly unusual. Some kind of fruit was hanging from one, dark, swollen, longer and thinner than a banana. As she watched, there was a flash of movement and some kind of furry creature a little like a squirrel, but with far longer arms, dropped onto one of the fruits and was gone, climbing up through the branches in a blur of movement.

She heard shouting somewhere, then silence. She tried to move. The result was disconcerting. She didn't move, but the entire scene seemed to pivot around her. It was as if she was at the center of a slow-motion spinning top, or at the hub where the spokes of a bicycle meet.

Then she was able to see what the shouting had been about and—if her flame-body had been equipped with a beating heart—she was sure it would have stopped during the following thirty seconds.

Around the edge of the clearing, men and women were sitting or kneeling. Except they weren't men or women. They were humanlike in appearance, but there was something *off*, something wrong about them. They were small, for a start - although it was difficult to get a true sense of scale when she didn't know how big the trees were. Their faces were flatter than humans, their eyes set too far apart.

She would have studied them more closely if it hadn't been for the events taking place in the foreground.

Between the fire and the watching crowd, two half-naked figures made up a tableau that looked like a movie poster. One figure was standing, his arm raised in an obvious gesture of victory. Blood ran down one side of his face, and there was a shallow cut down his side. He was breathing heavily and shouting something incomprehensible.

On the ground another figure lay still, his face turned away from the fire. He was breathing in short, shallow gasps and his hands were pressed over a wound in his stomach. He groaned and rolled over, his face now visible. It had the same flattened features, the strange eyes, but as he groaned in pain, the face morphed, flickering and sliding into something else. The face Joni saw then was one she knew intimately, even though she had only ever seen it in photographs.

It was her father. It was Seb.

She tried to move forward, go to him, but she was unable to get any further than the outermost limit of the fire which, somehow, contained her consciousness.

Joni didn't know where she was, *what* she was, or how she could possibly be where she seemed to be, but she knew *why* she was there. Dad needed her.

She thrashed around impotently, trying to get to him as she watched thick, dark blood seeping through his fingers. His *three* fingers, she noticed. Three fingers and a thumb. Long, powerful-looking fingers, dark, with tapered, sharp nails at their tips. That must explain the injuries on both combatants, who were otherwise unarmed.

As Joni frantically tried to do something, anything, to help, she found herself screaming soundlessly and wordlessly.

It's not working. He's going to die. This is real, and he's going to die in front of me.

Seb's eyes flicked open. He looked right at her. He *saw* her. There was a long moment, outside any familiar measurement of time, when they connected. Somehow, Joni felt his confusion - he recognized her but didn't know her, he loved her but didn't know who she was.

The moment passed, and he smiled.

It was as if she was seeing him as he really was, simultaneously with this other creature, knowing they were one and the same. His eyes never left hers, but they slid apart and narrowed, becoming more deep-set as his nose simultaneously flattened itself into the hard, bony face that was re-appearing. He moved his hands away from the wound and Joni watched in awe as the blood stopped flowing and the gash closed up. It was as if it had never been there.

Seb stood up. His attacker still had his back to the fire and was pacing back and forth, pumping his fist, shouting something at the watchers, their alien features unreadable as they watched him. Then, as their eyes swiveled back to Seb, the fist-pumper stopped and spun around. Even on a face as physically unfamiliar as his, the expression on it was instantly recognizable as shock. He recovered quickly, though, raised his lethal-looking fingers and threw himself toward his opponent, snarling with fury.

Joni woke up. She was in bed in her room in the Keep on Innisfarne. She sat up and listened to the birdsong. It was dawn. One of Mee's occasional expressions, reserved for special occasions, came spontaneously to her lips.

"Fuck-a-doodle-do."

She pulled on a pair of jeans, before running down the hallway to the furthest door. She knocked and waited. After a few seconds, Uncle John's unshaven face appeared, his thin hair sticking up in tufts. He had a book in his hand.

"It's 5:30," he said. "What's wrong?"

"Sorry to wake you," she said "but—,"

"I'm always awake before dawn," he said. "I don't sleep so good." He looked at her face. "What the hell happened? You still working on your magic powers?"

"I had a dream."

"A dream?"

"Yes. Well, no, maybe not. But I need to tell you about it. And I think we should tell Mum. And I want you to tell me everything about Dad."

"Everything?"

Joni nodded. John sighed, shook his head, then held up a hand.

"You know what I'm going to say, right?"

"That it's better that I don't know everything? That it's Mum's decision? That she's only trying to protect me? That's bullshit, John. Things are happening, and I need to understand why. Or at least get a sense of where I come from, what's going on and—,"

She stopped. John was now holding up both hands.

"You wanna wake up the whole entire house, hon?" He smiled, resignedly. "Anyways, that's not what I was going to say."

"Ok. Then…"

"I was going to say we need coffee. Lots of coffee. My workshop in five minutes."

He shut the door.

Chapter 17

Joni told John that the dream had been a memory of a vision she had had when she was nine.

"I had totally forgotten it, had no memory of it at all. But all this practicing with *resetting* somehow triggered something, brought it back."

John asked some questions about the dream, got her to describe Seb as he was when she saw him as human, not as some alien creature. He sat in silence for a long time as a half-finished cup of coffee went cold beside him. Then he reached over and took Joni's hand.

"Honey," he said, "I want you to consider the possibility that this was a dream after all."

Joni started to speak, but he stopped her with a gesture and squeezed her hand.

"I'm just asking you to think about it. I know it was incredibly vivid, that it seemed utterly real. Just a couple things make me question it a little. First, you had a long day yesterday, right? I mean, if you were practicing your *resetting* in the morning, I'm guessing your morning was a lot longer than mine, right?"

"Yes," said Joni. "But when I *reset,* I'm back where I was - my body is no more tired than it would have been anyway."

"Ok, maybe, but mentally, you live through these different time lines, different futures. There must be some kind of impact from that."

Joni considered this. In one sense, he was right. She had been thinking along similar lines the previous afternoon on her walk. The main by-product of multiple *resets* was a feeling of confusion, a sense of reality as being something slightly slippery, not reliably solid. It wasn't a pleasant sensation, and she'd already decided to keep her experiments down to one or two every morning. Otherwise, she might run the risk of losing her sense of what was truly real, or important.

"Yeah, ok, I have thought about that."

"Another thing. You described how Seb looked. Just think about that for a second. He's been away a long time, Joni. You were nine years old when you had this vision of him. By then, he'd been away nearly ten years. Ten years. But you described him looking exactly the same as he did the day he left. The same as he looks in all those photographs you've seen."

His voice was gentle. He smiled sadly at her. "He wouldn't look that way, honey. I know you thought it was real, but just consider the possibility you were seeing what you wanted to see."

"But you said he'd be back. You think he's out there, somewhere."

"I do believe he'll be back. And I want to believe that, somehow, you connected with him wherever he is, that you truly saw him and he knew you were there."

"He did," said Joni. "I know he did. He didn't know it was *me,* exactly, but he knew someone was there, someone close to him. I could feel it. And if this whole thing was just my brain-fucked fantasy, he would have known who I was, would have known I was his daughter, but he didn't. He didn't know."

She was standing up now, her eyes full of tears. John reached over for his coffee, took a sip and spat the cold liquid straight out again.

"Brain-fucked?" he said. After a moment, they both laughed.

"Joni," he said, "don't get me wrong. On balance, maybe you're right. Maybe this was—in some weird way— real. But Seb's been gone so long that I'm doubting my own motives. I want to believe it, but I'm scared to. And I'm scared about how Mee's going to react."

"You think I should tell her?"

"Yes," said John, and stood up. He checked his watch. It was just after seven. Meditation was over, and breakfast would be served in a half hour. "I'm on washing up duty this morning. I'll meet you after, and we'll go talk to her. And you're right. It's time we told you everything."

THAT WAS the day Joni finally found out the truth about her father.

Breakfast had finished, the washing up and cleaning done. Members of the community had gone to weed the vegetable patch, muck out the goats, or repair a wall. The island was always busier during the summer and—since no one paid to stay on Innisfarne—guests were expected to help out, picking jobs from the list Kate pinned on the noticeboard.

"Oh god," said Mee, looking at the expressions on Joni's and John's faces. "This looks a lot like an intervention. I should remind you both, I'm down to about two spliffs a day now." Neither John nor Joni smiled at this, and Mee sighed heavily, put her hand in her purse and brought out rolling papers.

"Don't worry," she said, "I'm not going to smoke it. Yet. I'm going to listen. This will help me concentrate. Once I've heard what you have to say, *then* I'll probably smoke it."

While Mee started the ritualistic rolling of a giant spliff, Joni took a deep breath and looked at John for encouragement. He smiled at her.

"Mum, I'm going to tell you about something that happened to me this summer. Then I'm going to tell you about a dream I had last night. I think the two are connected in some way. Both things might freak you out. And the thing that happened this summer that started all of this didn't actually happen. That's part of what I need to explain."

Mee had stopped what she was doing and was now holding the joint halfway to her lips, ready to lick and seal it. She tilted the spliff first one way, then the other, peering at it as if confused.

"Nope," she said, "haven't smoked it yet. Thought for a second I already had." She put it back on the table and smiled at her daughter.

"Jones," she said, "you're everything to me. I've tried hard not to smother you, I've tried to let you know that you're loved and that you can tell me anything. Right?"

Joni could already feel her eyes brimming with tears. Mee kept talking.

"These last few weeks, I can see you've been struggling with something. I could see you considered talking to me about it, but felt you couldn't. Here's what I kept thinking - tell me if it sounds crazy. There's no one on this island your own age or even close to it this summer. And I pretty much know how you spend your days. It's not as if anyone gets much privacy here. So why do I think you've fallen in love and been dumped?"

Joni threw herself into her mother's arms, and the two of them cried together, while Mee stroked her daughter's hair and spoke the same soothing, meaningless words that everyone needs to hear.

John went back to the workshop to brew a decent jug of coffee. He took his time. When he came back, the two women were dry-eyed. Joni was just coming back into the dining room with a box of tissues. She had already explained the details of her ability to *reset*.

"Shame you can't demonstrate, really," said Mee. "It's kind of scary, but kind of abstract, too."

"I can demonstrate it," said Joni.

"How?"

"When you were almost exactly my age, you stole a ring from Granny."

Mee froze, saying nothing.

"It was her grandmother's ring, a family heirloom. You pawned it to buy dope but didn't get back to the pawn shop for months. When you did go back, it had gone. You were in a terrible state. You always intended to get the ring back. Then one night, you saw the ring on Granny's finger. She must have seen it in the window of the pawn shop, bought it back, and said nothing about it. You realized she knew you had stolen it. You kept meaning to apologize, thank her, hug her, but you didn't know where to start. You finally told her when she was in hospital, just before she died. She smiled, said there was nothing to forgive."

Now it was Joni's turn to console her mother as she wept. When she could speak again, she only had one question.

"How?"

"When I went to get tissues, I created a *reset* point."

"A what?"

"I'm getting in the habit of doing it whenever I make a decision. Even one as small as 'do I get a box of tissues, or wipe my eyes on my sleeve?' I make sure I feel the tingling, hear the hum. It takes half a second. I didn't go for the tissues the first time. I stayed. You said it was a shame I couldn't demonstrate, so I thought of a way. I asked you to tell me something you'd never told anyone. Something no one else in the world could possibly know. You told me about Granny's ring. Then I *reset* and went to get the tissues."

Mee had a strangely unfocused look in her eye. Joni knew she was about to curse in her unique and infamous way. It showed the depth and profundity of her shock that all she managed to come out with was a whispered, "Shit."

Next, Joni told her about the dream. Her reaction to this was nothing like Joni had feared. There was no lapse into depression. If anything, it was the opposite. The sadness that underscored even Mee's happiest moments seemed to lift temporarily as she digested what she had been told.

"He's out there," she said. "Wherever *there* is. And he's helping someone. It's what he does. And he saw you."

"Well, yeah. Kinda. I don't think he knew who I was."

"But seeing you did something, changed things. He was losing the fight before you showed up."

"Yes," said Joni, remembering the dark blood between Seb's fingers as he lay on the ground.

"Did he go on to win? Was he ok?"

"I don't know," said Joni. "I woke up."

"But he healed himself?"

"Yes."

Mee stood up and paced. Then she smiled.

"Well, ok. And this was a memory. You saw all this when you were nine years old. The first time you *reset.*"

"Right."

"Well, whatever you inherited from your father, maybe that first use of it triggered that dream, vision, whatever it was. In a way, who cares? He's alive, he's out there in some shithole with three moons and people with faces that look like they ran into a wall. But he's out there. And—as soon as he can—he'll be back. The selfish bastard."

Joni smiled at her. John got up.

"I'm gonna make up some sandwiches, some fruit, fill up the water bottles. I don't know about you, but I need some air. It's lunchtime already. Let's eat in the forest, then walk along the north beach. That's your usual spot, right?"

"Yes," said Joni. "And you two can tell me everything about Dad."

"One more coffee before we go?"

"Are you trying to avoid the subject?"

"Not at all, nope. I agree. It's time to tell you." He exchanged a meaningful look with Mee. They'd agreed many years ago that—when this day came—Joni didn't need to know that John had once been Mason, the man who had tortured Mee and killed Seb's friend.

Mee took Joni's arm as they headed for the door.

"I was going to tell you when you turned eighteen," she said. "It's a lot to take in. First of all, your dad isn't just some powerful Manna user. In fact, what he uses isn't really Manna at all. And it's not separate the way Manna is. It's something far more powerful. He's a World Walker. And he's entirely responsible for Year Zero. That's how he saved the world."

Chapter 18

The world Joni knew was very different to the one in which her mother had grown up. Mee, along with the vast majority of people, hadn't even known Manna existed. Joni had grown up surrounded by people who had Used all their lives and came to Innisfarne knowing their era was passing and the next generation would have to live without the power they had taken for granted. The island had no Thin Places, yet Manna users had been drawn there for decades. Most of them were members of the Order who had found that daily meditation sessions, rather than the power to create food from dirt, was what they truly needed. No one ever managed to adequately articulate what it was about the place that kept them coming back, but certain words were heard again and again in people's halting attempts to describe their experience: honesty, reality, solidity. *Ordinariness*. Joni hadn't realized how much more grounded than the average sixteen-year-old she was until she had gone to the writing course and, among her peers, felt alone. Not lonely, *never* lonely, but alone.

Accepting the truth about her father was straightforward in a way, because—despite the scale of what had happened to him, and the extent of his power—Mee made it clear how his humanity had always come through. Until those last few weeks. He was no saint, but a complex man who had always tried to do the right thing. In the end, doing the right thing had come at a cost they had yet to understand. It was why she'd given Joni Seb's surname, rather than her own. She'd wanted Joni to know she had two parents who loved her, wanted her father to be a real presence for her. However long it took him to get home.

Joni wondered why she was so different. Although she had been conceived before Year Zero, she couldn't use Manna; yet she had a powerful ability, possibly unique. It was certainly an ability Dad had never demonstrated, although genetically she assumed it had come from him.

"He never really understood what Billy Joe had given him, Jones," said Mee, "so try not to stress about understanding why you can do what you do. That alien freak saved his life. Then Seb went to Roswell and, after that, he saved *my* life." She sighed heavily and shook her head. "I had kind of hoped to spare you all this superpower shite. It's not as much fun as it looks in the movies."

Uncle John had been even quieter than usual during their picnic in the small copse of trees they all generously, if inaccurately, referred to as 'the forest.' He spoke up now.

"He saved my life, too, in a situation when pretty much anyone else wouldn't have."

Joni looked at him, suspecting there was a lot more to that particular story. She also knew Uncle John would have told her if he'd wanted her to know. There was hurt there, and regret. She knew she'd never deliberately upset him by dredging up a personal history he had long decided to leave behind. She nodded at him and smiled, saying nothing.

They finished up the sandwiches and walked out to the north tip of the island. The beach they were heading for wasn't the one from which Seb had disappeared. Joni knew Mum still found it hard to be there. Mee had been lost in thought as they walked and, just before they reached the beach, she put a hand on Joni's arm. All three of them stopped.

"The *reset*," she said. "I think I know what it is, what you're doing."

A couple of seagulls screamed high above them. They ascended in a spiral, seemingly without any effort, before heading out over the open water. Mee sat on the coarse grass that grew wild on the edges of the rocky shore and patted the ground for John and Joni to join her.

"Seb almost gave up Walking once," she said. "It was after he rescued a family from a fire. He came back home afterward, but I thought he had failed. I'd seen it all unfold on TV. The fire had spread, the building had been gutted, and the young mother and her family had all been killed."

"But you said he rescued them," said Joni.

"He did," said Mee. "Just not in this universe."

She explained the concept of the multiverse, and it all started to make sense...slowly. In his 'home' universe, Seb had been too late to rescue anyone, but in a parallel universe, the family was still trapped, still alive. It was only when he got back to Mee that he had discovered what had happened. And, for a while, he had been unable to deal with the consequences; the knowledge that for all the people he helped, countless others would always be unreachable. In the end, he had continued to help, to do good, because that was all he knew - and the people he saved were real people who might have suffered or died without his intervention.

"So the universe splits at certain moments?" Joni was

trying to piece a coherent picture together out of the information she had just been given.

"At certain moments, possibly, if there are a finite number of universes," said Mee. "But there are plenty of respected physicists who suggest the number is infinite. Every time a choice is made, any time a situation arises with different possible outcomes, all of the outcomes occur, and new universes form. You've heard of Schrödinger's cat?"

John started whistling Give Me The Simple Life, but as neither Mee nor Joni knew the song, his attempt at humor went unrecognized. He stopped whistling.

Joni was rubbing her forehead.

"Shrew-who's what?"

"Schrödinger's cat. It's a thought experiment. You put a cat in a box with some decaying uranium and a bottle of poison. The uranium may or may not leak radiation before you open the box. If it does, the poison is released, and the cat dies. If it doesn't, you open the box and the cat jumps out, perfectly healthy."

"Which means what, exactly, apart from never trust a physicist with your cat?"

"Schrödinger said that—and this occurs on a quantum level—the cat, at the moment before you open the box, is both alive and dead. Both possibilities exist alongside each other, with an equal probability of becoming a reality. What you need to think about is what triggers the event that cements one possibility into reality."

"Opening the box?" said Joni.

"Exactly. By opening the box, one of the possibilities becomes actual, the other collapses. The observer causes the reality."

"At the quantum level."

"Right. At a fundamental level, observation *shapes* reality."

It was a still, sunny afternoon and the sea was sparkling under the deep blue sky. A fishing boat bobbed about half a mile out. Joni had seen it before, but it had always been further out to sea.

"So. Let me make sure I have this right," said Joni. "It's possible that I could be consciously splitting the universe every time I set up a *reset*? The moment I make a decision and hear the humming, a new universe forms?"

"Either that, or a new universe forms whenever you, or I, or anyone, makes a choice. I have a question."

"Shoot."

"You can't go back any further than your last *reset*, can you?"

Joni considered the question. It had never occurred to her to try. She said as much.

"Ok," said Mee. "That fits my theory. Try it now. We'll wait."

"Now?"

Yeah, sure. Go for it. When was your last *reset*?"

Joni thought back, letting the tingling grow, hearing the low sound, following it to the moment she refused a last cup of coffee back in the dining room. The process was become fast now, almost automatic.

"The dining room," she said.

"And before that?"

"Er, it must have been when I went for the tissues - before you told me about the ring."

"Ok, fine. Go back there."

Joni reached for the moment, but she knew even as she tried that it had gone. There was no connection to it at all. She shook her head.

"Can't do it," she said.

Mee nodded. "I wondered. I'm glad. If you could do that, it would be like traveling in time. But you could get lost in the labyrinth of your own past. How could you resist the temptation to keep going back? What would that do to you in the end? You might have lived a thousand years of experience over one lifetime, constantly branching off, avoiding problems. You'd have nothing in common with anyone. It would be a nightmare."

Mee was gazing out to sea, her eyes fixed on the fishing boat, but not really seeing it. Joni wondered if she was still talking about her. From what Mum had said, Dad was immortal. What did that mean for their relationship?

John coughed, breaking the mood. He stood up.

"I don't know about anyone else, but I need to clear my head. Coming? Or do you want to go back?"

Joni smiled and, virtually unconsciously, created a *reset* point. As soon as she'd done it, she tried reaching back to the last point. It had gone. Interesting. Finding a definite limitation was strangely comforting.

"I'm game," she said.

Mee linked arms with her, and the three of them walked out onto the rocky beach. Joni smiled at the two of them as they walked. She felt unexpectedly buoyant. She hadn't realized the stress keeping something from Mum had put her under. And having Mee's sharp mind applying itself to the situation had already thrown up some really fascinating possibilities. The sun was shining, and anything seemed possible.

So she was totally unprepared when the shooting started.

━━

IT HAPPENED JUST after Joni waved at the boat. She had

121

seen it there a few times recently, and she had the sudden urge to acknowledge its presence. She raised her arm and gave a long slow wave. She could see the figure in the boat take something away from his face and wave back. Binoculars? Maybe the boat wasn't for fishing at all. Perhaps it was for birdwatching. Joni knew the island attracted arctic terns and some rarer little terns each year, but that was normally in the autumn. She wasn't sure if there was anything worth seeing in summer.

The figure squatted in the boat, then lay down on his— or her—front, picking something up from the bottom of the boat.

Joni turned away and was about to ask Mum more about how Dad navigated the multiverse, when a flash of light distracted her. She turned back to the boat, frowning. It came again - a flash of sunlight reflected on glass in the bottom of the boat.

There was a sound to her left. Joni had once knocked a melon off a table, and it had split as it hit the floor. The sound she had just heard was eerily similar. She turned just in time to see John spinning like an out of control ballerina. As he spun, she saw an arc of blood spiraling with him. He hit the ground face down, making no attempt to break his fall.

She turned to Mee in time to see part of the side of her head disappear, one eye blown backward through her skull so quickly that Joni saw daylight through her head before she crumpled.

Joni opened her mouth to scream, but something punched her in the back, and suddenly she was lying on her side. She could see the waves gently breaking over the rocks about fifteen yards away. There was a sound. It was getting louder. An engine?

"Mum?" She tasted blood in her mouth when she

spoke. She must have bitten her lip when she fell. Funny how that hurt so much, but there was no pain at all in her back.

She knew she had been shot, but it didn't seem important. Something had happened to Mum and Uncle John, but they had to be ok, really, right? She called out again, her voice a little stronger this time.

"Mum? John?"

There was no answer.

Joni tried to move. Her brain sent the usual automatic signals to her legs, commanding them to move. Nothing happened. It was such a bizarre feeling. All her life, she had only had to decide to move, and her legs had done the rest. Now they had rebelled. Nothing was moving at all down there. She tried her arms instead and found that some movement was possible. With a huge effort, feeling as if something heavy was squatting on her upper body, she managed to lift herself up onto her elbows.

She looked back up the beach toward Mum and John, then immediately wished she hadn't. John had fallen face first into a rock pool. Even if the sheer amount of blood-loss he had suffered—evidenced by the color of the sand and stone all around him—hadn't killed him, the fact that his mouth and nose were underwater would have finished the job.

Mee was worse. Her body looked like a child's discarded rag doll, limbs flung out at unnatural angles, unmoving. Her remaining eye stared lifelessly back at Joni.

Joni was sick then, her stomach spasming weakly as she spat hot, acidic bile from her mouth. She turned away from the horror behind her.

The engine noise had stopped. She could see the boat bobbing on the water just far enough out to avoid the hidden rocks closer to the shore. There was something else. She blinked away salty tears and tried to clear her vision.

At first, she thought it was a seal. They came in close on occasion, curious or friendly. Then the head rose out of the water, revealing a pair of shoulders. Not a seal. And not friendly. As the figure waded out of the water, she could see it was a man. Not tall, but wiry and lightly muscled. Bald. And naked.

Great. The first naked man I get a good look at is going to kill me. That's just brilliant.

Fear managed to introduce a little clarity into her mental state as she saw the curved knife in the man's hands. He stopped about three feet away from her and knelt on the stony beach. He glanced at her, then bowed his head as if at prayer.

"Ialdabaoth," he said, "I offer you this life, this final sacrifice. Joni Varden, the daughter of Sebastian Varden. Come back to your creation and rule over us."

Oh, super, a religious nut job.

Joni was dimly aware that there was something she had to do, something important. The urgency of this was obvious, but her brain was struggling to cooperate with the request for action. Everything was slowing, becoming treacly, her awareness shrinking as the bald man picked up his knife.

She realized she was staring at his penis.

Something I need to do. Something I should do right now. Something, something…

Chapter 19

Germany
Three months previously

Adam went to Father's cottage, south of Munich to read the files. He needed somewhere away from other people, somewhere he knew he wouldn't be disturbed.

The cottage stood in twenty-five acres of Bavarian forest, invisible from the road. Adam used the back entrance. The turning was unmarked and looked like a farmer's track. There was a gate, and a large sign warning of disease and pronouncing the area quarantined. A plastic box on the side of the gate revealed a keypad. Anyone breaking the perimeter without entering the correct eighteen digit code would trigger a silent alarm. A phone would ring in a nearby military facility, and two helicopters would be dispatched. There would be no attempt to engage with whoever was responsible for breaking the perimeter. The *Oberst*, who enjoyed a generous monthly retainer, would simply order the bombing and destruction of the building as part of a training exercise. Any accidental loss of life during the exercise would be considered a matter of regret, but would not warrant any further investigation.

Adam entered the code, swung open the heavy gate and drove the 4x4 through before closing the gate behind him.

Father had always valued privacy, and the cottage had proved to be the perfect place to do his real work, hold meetings and discuss strategy with his most trusted advisers. He had led a worldwide organization for decades until his sudden death. Adam, at one time a rejected child and embarrassment to his father, had—during his father's last years—become closer than anyone else to the old man. Most of the senior members, including Adam himself, had believed he would eventually succeed his father and bring about the event their organization had dreamed of for centuries.

His father had never entirely accepted Adam's view of Manna. The organization had been built by powerful Users, and to them it was an ancient Magick available to initiates. Adam told his father it was most likely Manna was alien nanotechnology. It seemed it was available to anyone with a particular genetic predisposition. A cursory study revealed it had nothing to do with what you believed, who you worshiped or what kind of arcane word you muttered before Using. If you were genetically predisposed and were exposed to it, you could use Manna.

Adam had found supporters in the organization, but Father had been blind to the truth. He had spent a lifetime collecting and studying ancient Satanic documents, obtained from archaeological digs or private collections around the world. He could not let go of his precious

Magick, so Adam finally gave up and practiced patience. His time would come.

Adam opened the cottage door with a key he took from under a stone in the garden. The perimeter security was such that it seemed pointless to waste money on securing the building itself.

Dust sheets still covered everything inside. Adam went back to the car and took out a backpack and a sleeping bag. He had enough food for three days, but he expected to have finished his planning before then. He threw the sleeping bag into what had once been the boardroom. He stopped for a moment, his eyes searching out the darker patch on the polished floorboards. It was still there - Adam had forbidden the staff to remove it. It was good to be reminded that there was no place for complacency. He would not suffer the same fate as Father. He stood in silence for a few moments, then went upstairs.

The study was the room Adam most closely associated with Father. He pulled back the dust sheets from the desk, chair and bookshelves. With a little effort, he could still see the old man sitting there, brow furrowed in concentration, his beloved books close at hand. Adam had only read one book since dropping out of Oxford a term before he was due to graduate. The recognition and opportunities academia offered were already of no interest to him, even then.

The crystal skull was still there. Father had paid hundreds of thousands of dollars to have it stolen from a museum in Peru. After discovering its fabled supernatural powers to be disappointingly absent, Father had demonstrated his sense of humor by using it as a paperweight. It was sitting on top of the last Acolytes of Satan newsletter.

Naming the organization The Acolytes of Satan had been Father's masterstroke. No one ever took them the slightest bit seriously and, in its latter years, the organization had even managed to obtain some European funding set aside for under-represented religious groups.

Adam pushed the skull and newsletter to the corner of the desk and sat down. He pulled the two reports out of his backpack. *Sebastian Varden. Innisfarne.* He settled down to scan the printed sheets. He would read slowly, and in detail, tomorrow. This afternoon was about getting the big picture.

Two hours later, he looked up to see the first tinges of red appearing in the sky outside. He put down the last page and steepled his fingers. He smiled, thinking how much this gesture reminded him of Father. He had respected the old man, despite his shortsightedness and naivety.

The files had contained two major surprises. He was impressed at how much information had been gathered during the last decade. The Broker had been an impressive figure and his network of informants and researchers were obviously talented, hardworking, flexible around legal constraints, and thorough. The man's death had been regrettable, but the endgame was approaching, and Adam couldn't afford to leave a trail.

The first surprise had been the fact that Sebastian Varden had been responsible for killing the woman who had murdered Father. Sonia Svetlana had underestimated Varden's strength and her own abilities. She had paid the ultimate price. She had been as blind as Father in her own way, also believing her power—which was considerable—was based on some kind of Satanic Magick. She had swatted Father aside like an insect as she took over the leadership of the Acolytes, reducing him to a shriveled pile of blackened bones in the boardroom downstairs. Then she had gone to America to kill Varden. She hadn't returned. The Acolytes of Satan had never recovered.

Most of the senior figures had disappeared, and the catastrophic failure of Svetlana had convinced the organization's less committed members to quietly abandon the project.

Father had failed to bring about the reign of Satan on Earth. Svetlana had convinced the Acolytes she could make it happen by wiping out the most powerful Manna users. She had failed. Now there was only Adam left. And he knew the Master. The darkness inside him was intimately connected to its Master, and he knew he would succeed where the Manna-loving fools had failed. Year Zero had proved beyond a doubt that his path was the right one. The generation of Manna users currently living would be the last. Adam was surely the forerunner of a new society. He had paid his dues. He had done his research. He had accepted the quest.

He knew Satan wasn't coming back anytime soon. He was as much a piece of fiction as God. A promise of eternal life, a threat of damnation. The carrot and the stick. But Adam had seen through the charade, had spent his years at Oxford perusing ancient texts that revealed a different possibility. As the truth had become clearer, Adam recognized the role he had to play. He, and he alone, had the loyalty, commitment and power to restore order to the mess that was humanity.

The project was still alive. Varden was dead, but—on a tiny island off the northeast coast of England—his daughter still lived. Adam would kill Joni Varden.

And no one would ever see him coming.

Chapter 20

Adam often dreamed, and his dreams were always variations on the same few key moments in his journey to the Master. The cottage was so full of memories that he wasn't surprised when they emerged from his unconscious mind during the night. Adam paid close attention to dreams, believing that the gray area where consciousness becomes malleable often provides signs to those who knew how to interpret them.

There were two dreams that night, both clear and memorable. It was very unusual to experience these dreams together in this way. Adam took it to be a clear sign that he was getting close to his goal.

In the first dream, Adam was twelve years old.

Father had taken him shooting on the estate. Their wet coats were hanging in the pantry, and the two of them were warming themselves in front of the fire. Adam felt empty inside, a coldness spreading within him even as the fire brought warmth to his physical extremities.

"Why, Father? I want to stay here. With you."

"I am not prepared to discuss this. I have work to do which you are not yet old enough to understand."

"But, Father, I——,"

"Be quiet, Adam. I have made my decision. You are aware that our beliefs are not shared by the rest of the world. You know how important secrecy is. You will be expected to play your part. The school in England you will be attending is not completely unsympathetic to our way of life. I will give you the names of certain books you should seek out in its library. I will also have certain tutors contact you from time to time, to broaden your education. You will respect them as you would me. Is that clear?"

Adam knew that to continue to object would be futile.

"Yes, Father."

"You will live with your mother in the school vacations."

Adam tried to interject. His relationship with his mother was an uncomfortable one. His parents had been estranged since he was five, when his mother moved abroad. She seemed to tolerate Adam for the most part, but it had always been clear she didn't like her only son.

"If you are to live amongst the cattle and walk among them unde-tected, you must learn their ways. This is absolutely crucial. Do you understand?"

Adam nodded, miserably. Then Father stood and delivered the worst blow of all.

"You have no Manna ability, Adam. I can no longer deny the truth of this."

Adam leaped to his feet.

"No, Father! I can learn, I know I can. You said so yourself! I am a late developer, but my power may be stronger when I come into it."

Father simply shook his head slowly from side to side.

"No, Adam, you have no ability to summon Magick. My wish for it to be so has done us both a disservice. I wish it were otherwise. Now sit down."

"But, Father, you said——,"

"Sit down, Adam!"

Adam never disobeyed Father, but he could feel the life for which he thought he was being prepared slipping away from him. He knew Father was the respected leader of a powerful organization. Lately, Adam had been allowed to take part in some of the rituals with the robes, the goat-skull masks, and the curved knife. He knew the sleepy young people who were brought to the cottage in the middle of the night never left. And he knew he was supposed to be by Father's side. He took a step toward Father.

"I will learn to Use. I will. This is my destiny, Father, you must not send me——,"

Father glared at him in anger, and a great invisible hand pushed Adam in his chest, almost lifting him off his feet as he was tossed into the chair behind him. He could hardly breathe, but the worst pain wasn't physical. Father had never used Manna against him before.

The old man turned his back on him.

"One day, Adam, you will return to me. You will be well-educated, both in the ways of this deluded world and in the ways of its true Master. There will be a place for you in the organization then, but it will be commensurate with your abilities. You leave first thing in the morning. You are dismissed."

Adam walked out of the room with a new desire burning in his core. He would either learn to use Manna, or he would find a way to overcome those who flaunted their abilities.

Adam unzipped the sleeping bag and stood up, stretching. He drank some water and thought about the years he had spent in England, first at a small boarding school, then at university.

His academic career had seen him go to Oxford two years earlier than was normal. Great things were expected of him. His early abandonment of his studies caused consternation and disappointment.

His mother had died during that last term. It may have been a stroke, but he was no doctor. He had found her lying on her side on the bedroom floor, one leg encased in pantyhose, the other bare. Her skin had displayed a purplish tinge where it met the carpet. Adam had delayed calling the authorities for five days. He had been intrigued by the corpse now that the spirit within had gone. It was the first time he had been given an opportunity to study death, and he hadn't wanted to waste it. He'd spent many hours watching her corpse. Her body had stiffened, changed color. There had been some astringent odors. But it hadn't been her anymore. It hadn't been his mother.

Adam left England liking his mother a little for the first time. She had contributed a valuable lesson. Her death had been an education in itself. Adam, although a bright student and well versed in the sciences would, nevertheless, not disregard the evidence of his own senses, his own observations. *Humans are more than their bodies. There is an animating agent, known as spirit, soul. It exists.*

During his time at Oxford, Adam had begun to explore the darkness he detected inside himself. This was not a metaphor, some ignorant abstract attempt to explain away depression, rage, the periods he had experienced since early childhood during which he had felt himself entirely separate, different, *superior* to everyone else. It was a real, palpable part of him. And it was growing. He had encouraged it, got to know it, developed a respect for it and, yes, even a little fear of it as it had become more and more of a presence within. And, as he had watched his mother's dead body, he had felt the darkness coil and shift, its power building. Some experiments involving local Manna users had finally proved to him that he could end their deluded sense of entitlement. Now it was time to show Father.

Adam got back into the sleeping bag. He closed his eyes.

The second dream followed the first so closely it was as if he had opened a door in one time period and walked straight into another. He was back in Germany, years later.

Adam remembered this moment well.

He was standing on the roadside, close to the cottage. Father's life had been threatened in recent weeks, and had surrounded himself with his most powerful Manna-using advisors. No one could get within half a mile without being sensed and—if they kept coming—the combined power of six senior Users would crush any enemy foolish enough to take them on. At least, that was the theory. Adam believed differently. He was about to risk his life finding out if he was right.

He was dressed in black. He carried no weapons other than an adapted taser - commonly known as a Manna-spanner.

Before moving, Adam looked within, found the darkness and let its coils reach out from his heart to fill his mind and body. He knew enough about psychiatry, a pseudo-science if ever there was one, to diagnose what the profession would make of him. Schizophrenia, with regular psychotic episodes. Schizophrenia because Adam heard voices, psychosis because the voices told Adam he was better than other people, and hurting—or killing—those who got in his way was perfectly acceptable behavior.

The voices spoke to him now. There were no words, but Adam could interpret the soundless void that opened up to him when he turned to it. He knew he was a psychopath. He embraced it. Why would anyone want to be anything else? He was the best of a new breed. The voices, the darkness, came from his Master. And it was abundantly clear that Adam was superior to other people. He was more intelligent than most, certainly more physically adept and incredibly focused. But the quality that made him truly stand out was his realism. He looked at the world—violent, selfish, unforgiving, cruel— as it was. He didn't flinch. He had come to understand the true nature of creatures by discovering the true identity of their creator. And now it was time to share his discovery with Father.

Shrouded in his personal darkness, Adam walked toward the cottage, keeping close to the tree-line. He hadn't expected any guards outside the cottage, and he was both relieved and disappointed to find this was, in fact, the case. Such confidence in their own power!

Adam climbed the ivy at the west end of the cottage, easily forcing the window of the storeroom on the second floor. Once inside, Adam unscrewed the lightbulb, then stood in the pitch-black room for a full three minutes, listening intently.

There were sounds coming from Father's office, a murmured conversation. It was 11:15pm. No self-respecting Acolyte would go to bed before the witching hour of midnight. Other voices came from downstairs.

He opened the door and waited. Just as he was about to move, someone started to come upstairs. Adam took a few paces back into the room and stood absolutely still in the darkness. The footsteps stopped at the top of the stairs. Adam hoped the open storeroom door would seem unusual enough to raise suspicion. It did.

He felt the Manna wash into the room and around his body. The User was probing the room, knowing any intruder would be sensed immediately. They hadn't reckoned on Adam. The Manna-sense parted around him and continued as if he were a pebble in a stream, then retreated.

Satisfied that no one was in the storeroom, the User walked in and flicked the light switch. During the second in which the User registered the missing lightbulb, Adam stepped silently forward and punched the figure in the throat. He caught the falling body and lowered it noiselessly to the floor. In the light from the hallway, Adam saw it was Petter, a much respected and feared senior Acolyte. He very nearly laughed at the ease with which he had neutralized him. He had even shown some restraint, pulling the punch slightly so as not to kill the man. The fact that he would almost certainly never be able to speak again would be an appropriate reminder of the dangers of complacency.

Adam closed the storeroom door as he left and walked to the study. Its door was slightly ajar. Adam took a small mirror from one pocket. A magnet attached the mirror to the end of a piece of thick wire. Adam crouched and slowly pushed this past the edge of the door, angling it slightly upward. After three seconds, he pulled it back. The *office had two occupants. Father and, to Adam's pleasure, David. David headed up the Acolyte's security operation. He was a sadistic killer and very good at his job, but Adam wasn't going to let his admiration for the man deter him. He stood up.*

Adam knocked on the study door. Petter had been heading this way, so knocking seemed an obvious approach.

"Enter," came the voice from within. Adam reached into his left pants pocket and took out the Manna-spanner. Then he stepped inside. Father had his head bent over some papers and didn't even look up. David was far more alert - he had got to his feet when Adam had knocked and only took a fraction of a second to react to the situation. But that fraction of a second was all Adam needed. The steel tip of his right shoe caught David under the chin and lifted him off his feet as the bone shattered. Adam stepped forward to catch him as he fell, simultaneously firing the spanner at Father.

Adam had spent some time adapting this particular weapon. Rather than hit the victim with enough voltage to cause uncontrollable spasms, this one released a high voltage burst for 0.8 seconds, then dropped the voltage to a level which was painful, but not agonizing. This meant Father's Manna had been disabled, but his mental processes were reasonably functional. Adam explained as much as he checked David's pulse.

"That's a pity," he said, "I always liked David." Father's eyes widened in horror, only to be replaced by a new, unfamiliar expression as he looked at his son. Then he chuckled, despite his body's painful twitching. Adam realized what the unfamiliar expression was. It was pride.

"Could you….?" Father tried to point at the spanner, but his hand jerked wildly out of his control.

"Of course," said Adam, flicking a switch on the device. The prongs detached themselves from Father's chest, and the wires retracted. Adam replaced it in his pocket.

"Impressive," said Father. Adam smiled, thinly.

"The prodigal returns," said Adam.

Adam opened his eyes. It was dawn.

ADAM SPENT NEARLY a week in the cottage. Longer than he had planned, but he knew preparation was more important than haste. He shot rabbits and cooked them over a spit the first couple of extra nights, then hunted and killed a wild boar, using no weapon other than a knife. His physical condition was still excellent, and as the blood of the conquered animal seeped into the loamy earth, Adam felt a savage joy. He was gloriously alive and so close to the end of his quest.

He had digested all the information in the two reports and burned them both. He had spent hours communing with the darkness, allowing it to fill him, no longer able to sense where he stopped and the darkness began. He was Chosen, and he felt unstoppable.

Before leaving, he finally collected what he had come for. Rolled in a dirty piece of cloth in the top drawer of Father's desk, exactly where it had been the night Father first showed him. A curved dagger at least eighteen hundred years old. Lethally sharp. Adam wondered how many lives had been taken by the dagger, how much blood spilled over the centuries. Father had certainly sacrificed dozens to Satan, unaware of his true Master. Adam handled the knife reverentially before rewrapping it in the cloth and stowing it in his backpack. He had researched its true provenance and was confident he would be the one to bring about the purpose for which it had always been destined. It was time to reward those who saw the world as it was, not as they had been taught it was. The worshipers of Ialdabaoth, the Demiurge.

Chapter 21

Northumbria, Northeast England

Adam bought a boat a hundred miles from Innisfarne and made his way up the coastline over the course of two days.

He needed accurate, up-to-date information about Joni Varden's movements. The information in the Broker's report had been obtained by operatives infiltrating the island. The authors had spent a week there and confirmed the earlier report's assertion that Sebastian Varden had gone. After an absence of over sixteen years, the presumption was that he was dead. Adam didn't like presumptions. It hadn't done anything for his father, who had faced Sonia Svetlana presuming his devotion to the Satanic cause would make him victorious. Or Svetlana herself, who had presumed her dominant abilities combined with the help of a hand-picked team of powerful Acolytes would be enough to defeat Varden. The safest course to follow was to presume nothing about a situation until you had all the information. Varden had been gone for seventeen years now. That was enough information to be reasonably confident about discounting him. It didn't mean he was definitely dead, it just meant it was safe to proceed as if he was.

When he reached the small island, Adam kept his distance, passing it from every conceivable angle before looking for a suitable spot to moor up on the mainland. The best mooring was taken by *Penelope*, an old fishing vessel, which acted as a ferry to and from Innisfarne. He passed it some thirty yards out. A white-haired man emerged from the boat's small cabin and watched him. Adam waved, a pair of binoculars and a long-lensed camera hanging round his neck. He had elected for a pasty pale complexion set off by curly ginger hair for this trip. He also sported round, gold-rimmed spectacles. The white-haired man watched impassively for a few seconds, then raised an arm and gave a short wave back. He watched until Adam was out of sight.

That night, Adam moored in a secluded cove about five miles further south. When night fell, he made his way overland back to *Penelope* and looked for a suitable spot to set up camp. He found it in a small copse halfway up a neighboring hill. It gave him a good view of the boat and enough cover to render him virtually invisible, especially in the camouflage he now wore.

According to the Broker's reports, *Penelope* made the crossing every morning at 5:30am. Adam arrived on Sunday night. Sure enough, the boat didn't move until Monday at 5:15am, when an old Landrover pulled up alongside it. The old, white-haired man got out and started the boat's engine, warming her up. No one else got on, and at 5:30am it departed. Two hours later it was back. The crossing took about twenty-three minutes, but the old man obviously hung around for his breakfast. There were four passengers on the return trip.

Tuesday saw three new arrivals. The reports had suggested the vast majority of visitors were muesli-eating, sandal-wearing tree-huggers who spent their time on Innisfarne meditating, doing menial work or walking around the island. It was just over six miles from north to south, so that wouldn't account for much of their time.

Adam had tried meditating on a few occasions. Mostly during the time Father thought he could develop some Manna ability. He was supposed to watch his thoughts without engaging with them, that much he remembered. But what he saw in his head didn't resemble what the meditation teachers spoke about. He was aware of darkness, fear, pain and horror. It had terrified him at the time, before he had begun to recognize that the darkness was there to teach him. If he embraced it.

Adam watched the new guests board the boat. One was male, old, feeble. The other two were more interesting. Both women, one of them tall, confident - she looked every inch a Manna user. The other subdued-looking. Beaten. The reports had mentioned that Innisfarne had become a refuge for women who had suffered violent domestic abuse. Many of them had been physically and psychologically traumatized. The island had quietly earned somewhat of a reputation among professionals in the field for undoing damage that no other treatment had been able to touch. Adam focused the binoculars on the shorter woman. Her head was bowed, she shuffled rather than walked, and when the older man asked her a question, she turned away quickly. Interesting.

Adam had considered going to Innisfarne himself, but

the risk was too great. He knew the island was Manna-free, and—even if a Sensitive with active reserves was there—the darkness within him would enable him to move among them without arousing suspicion, but…But. Joni Varden was too much of an unknown. Her father had possessed power beyond the comprehension of the Broker's team of informants. She might have inherited no power at all. Or she could be her father's equal. No one knew. It was pointless to risk getting to her only to find she knew exactly who Adam was immediately and could stop his heart by simply clicking her fingers.

He hadn't got this close only to mess up now. Once again, his disciplined, almost serene patience came into play.

He went back to his boat and started surveilling the island from a distance of about a mile, using image stabilized binoculars to counter the movement of the vessel. He covered the island coastline systematically, the engine always running so he could move along if anyone took an interest in him.

On the eighth day, he saw her. She emerged from the tree line at the northern tip of Innisfarne and walked along the shingled beach. She looked lost in her own thoughts. No photograph had been available, but she matched the physical description. Adam had to admit she was striking. She had her mother's unruly black hair, combined with unusually light gray eyes. She walked around the headland, then headed back toward the group of buildings just south of the center of the island.

She kept up the same routine the next day. On the third day, Adam laid the AWSM sniper rifle on the floor of the boat and sharpened and oiled the knife. He then stripped naked, removing the ginger wig and makeup.

With thirty minutes to go before she normally

appeared, Adam reached within himself to contact the darkness, letting it fill him with its cold, dread purpose.

With five minutes to go, he lifted the binoculars to his eyes and waited.

Chapter 22

Innisfarne
Present Day

The bald man knelt beside her and looked into her eyes. Joni looked back and saw nothing in his expression. Just blankness. If the eyes truly were the windows to the soul, this guy was either missing a soul, or he really needed to clean his windows.

Joni was suddenly aware of just how quiet everything was. She could hear the waves on the rocks, but no seabirds were shrieking. Close to, it seemed the bald man was able to breathe soundlessly. And Mum and Uncle John weren't breathing at all anymore.

He looked away then and raised the knife. It was curved and had some kind of intricate design carved into the handle. The sunlight caught the blade and dazzled her for a second.

He paused and whispered a word reverentially. Almost like a lover.

"Ialdabaoth."

Oh. Yeah. I remember.

As the knife came down toward her chest in a blur of speed, Joni *reset*.

———

JONI LOOKED AT UNCLE JOHN. He was smiling at her as if waiting for her to say something. On other occasions, when she had *reset*, she had been prepared, calm, ready to pick up from wherever she had left off. This time, she burst into tears, grabbed Mee and hugged her, then did the same to John, her body wracked with sobs.

She pulled them both back further into the trees and away from the beach, where she could see the boat bobbing in the water, the figure in it watching the shore. She shuddered.

"What is it, Jones, what's the matter?" Mee and John both looked completely confused by Joni's sudden outburst, but before she could start to explain, Mee looked at her shrewdly.

"Was that a *reset*?"

Joni nodded, still sobbing occasionally, holding her mother's hands tightly like a toddler who had just been lost and was scared of it happening again. She had a sudden thought and shot a look back at the boat, just visible through the trees. It hadn't moved. She created another *reset* point.

She told them. She didn't hold back any details. They all sat down. No one interrupted. When she had finished speaking, Mee looked at her for a long moment.

"Good job you got your heart broken this summer and not next, then."

Joni realized she must still be in shock. It took a while to process the logic - that without the writing course, without Odd and Mell, she might not yet have learned to use her ability to *reset* the multiverse. And they'd all be dead now. She was still thinking about it when Mee and John stood up. She realized she had missed much of what they had said. But one word had sunk in.

"Police?" she said. "No. We can't. What are you going to say? There's a bald guy on a boat who looks funny? Can you please search his boat, because we think he's got a gun and a really ornate knife on board. He's probably trying to kill us. Yeah, they'll totally arrest him. Or you, maybe."

Mee started to object, but she could see the logic. She turned to John.

"What the hell shall we do?" she said. John shook his head numbly, thinking.

Joni surprised herself by finding that, despite the lingering horror of the last hour, she was able to think logically. She wondered if that was a quality of her ability. She remembered what had just happened as clearly as any other memory. More clearly, since it was so horrific. And yet it hadn't, actually, happened at all. They hadn't walked onto the beach. Yet.

"I have an idea," she said.

She knew she couldn't explain what she really wanted to do. There was no way Mum or Uncle John would let her do it. But the bald man had been there to sacrifice *her*. It was Joni he wanted. If she was going to protect Mum and John, she was going to have to do this alone.

Mee was looking at her closely. And she was thinking. Joni could see her begin to work out what Joni was thinking of doing.

"No, Jones. Don't. We can work this out together. You're safer here, with us. We can protect you."

But Mum hadn't seen the emptiness in the bald man's eyes. She hadn't felt the certainty. The commitment. He had come for Joni, nobody else. No one would be able to protect her. And there was no need for them to get hurt trying.

She made her decision.

"Joni!" said Mee. "No!"

She *reset*.

She was back. Standing again, not sitting. They were still in amongst the trees, the sea just in sight. Mum and John knew nothing about what had happened on the beach. They were waiting for her to explain why she was suddenly so upset.

She lied to them. It wasn't easy, but she turned her thoughts away from the awful pictures still fresh in her brain - John spinning as the bullet caught him, Mum's head caving in. She desperately wanted to be comforted, but she knew it wouldn't be possible if she wanted to protect them. So she lied. Told them she was crying because it had only just hit her how much she wanted to know her father, how much she had missed out on because he wasn't there. There was enough truth in what she was saying to make her tears convincing.

Mee wrapped her arms around her daughter.

"You still want a walk? Or shall we just go home?"

Joni nodded dumbly and let herself be led away, back toward the Keep, her head on her mother's shoulder.

―

BEFORE DAWN THE NEXT DAY, Joni was up, packing.

She threw everything she thought she might need into a backpack.

She wrote a note for Mum, leaving it on her pillow. She couldn't allow herself to think too hard about how Mee would react. She'd already lost Dad. Joni's note reassured her that she would be back, that only she could take care of this problem and she was sorry she wasn't able to share it.

She made it to the small quay before *Penelope* arrived and hid the backpack in a clump of long grass around the base of a tree.

She went to breakfast as usual. Her quietness and tension would, she hoped, be put down to the emotional day she'd had, finding out about her father. No one seemed suspicious, even though she felt like she had a neon sign above her head, flashing, *WARNING. ABOUT TO RUN AWAY.*

She kissed both Uncle John and Mum before excusing herself. She didn't cry. She even managed to agree to meet Mum later to talk about a distance-learning writing course.

Stuart, *Penelope*'s owner, was a man of regular habits, and Joni had already spotted him going to the bathroom. She figured she had about a ten-minute start over him.

At the quay, she *reset* before retrieving her backpack, then got onto the boat, squeezing under a pile of tarp in one corner. There was still a faint smell of fish although *Penelope* hadn't been used as a fishing boat for many years.

The ten-minute wait seemed more like thirty, but finally Stuart's heavy boots could be heard and, a few seconds later, he was onboard, the boat tipping and rocking. She heard him whistling to himself as he started the engine and cast off, then the engine noise increased as they headed out to sea.

When they reached the mainland, she kept perfectly

still while the process was reversed. After she heard Stuart's Landrover roar away, she waited fifteen minutes before moving. Then she crawled out from under the tarp, pulling her backpack after her. She took out an envelope addressed to Stuart and left it tucked under the steering wheel, in a clear plastic bag in case of rain. It was August, but this was northeast Britain.

She pulled the backpack onto her shoulders and set off, heading inland.

Joni had stolen twenty £500 cash disqs from the Keep. Although she hadn't really had a choice, she couldn't stop herself feeling guilty, all the same. Most were in the backpack, but, as she walked, she took one out of her pocket to look at it. She needed to be able to handle it as if it was something she'd done all her life, otherwise, she'd draw attention to herself.

The disq was black, shiny, about the same size as a £5 coin. Disqs had replaced cash almost completely during Joni's lifetime, although, living somewhere where no one paid for anything, it wasn't as if she had noticed the difference. All she really knew was that the disq would gradually change color as she used it, first the tip, then the rest, red replacing black. When it was a solid red, it needed topping up. This was done online or at ATMs. Since Innisfarne was — quite possibly—the only place in the country with no internet and only one ancient computer, Kate replenished the store during her infrequent trips to the mainland.

Joni replaced the disq in her pocket and walked on. The main road was about three miles. She knew there was a bus stop there. She couldn't help but feel a little thrill of excitement as she walked. She was on the mainland. She could walk for hundreds of miles with the sea at her back before finding it again. And then it would be the Atlantic Ocean, not the North Sea. Not that she intended going

West. She was going to London. That much she knew. After that, her plans got a little hazy.

Then she remembered the bald man's eyes and shivered. If Stuart played his part, she had a forty-eight-hour head start. She just hoped it would be enough.

Chapter 23

London

Joni disembarked at Victoria coach station and immediately wished she hadn't. The coach station was vast, and it was teeming with people. She stood with her back against the bus for a couple of minutes, trying to gather her thoughts. In an attempt to distract her mind from the enormity of the situation, she counted the number of buses she could see. There were twenty-four of them in sight, and she could hear the electric engines whirring their warnings as more approached, parking in numbered bays.

She had finally succumbed to exhaustion and slept the last hour of the journey. She had missed the sight of London taking shape around her in the early evening, the sinking sun reflecting from glass skyscrapers that rubbed shoulder with medieval churches.

Joni had been last off the bus, grabbing her bag after the driver gently touched her shoulder to wake her. It was her second bus ride ever. Her first had been earlier that day - the short hop from the main road nearest Innisfarne south to Moilburgh. The second bus was bigger, the seats wider and there was so much more to see through the tinted windows. So many cars! And houses, and shops, and people, and animals: cows in the field chewing grass and looking bored, a pair of horses galloping around a field. Sheep moving in one amorphous mass as a dog herded them. Pigs, memorably, lying in a brown field; fat, pink and muddy, basking in the sun.

Now she pushed herself upright and walked away from the bus, trying to look like this was something she did all the time. She deliberately took longer breaths in an attempt to stop herself gasping at every new thing she saw. A sign twice the size of Uncle John's workshop wall flashed every few seconds, showing up-to-date information about the routes offered. Joni saw that she could, if she chose, get on another bus during the next fifteen minutes and head for Oxford, Bristol, Birmingham, Cork, Antwerp or Paris.

She realized how little she really knew about geography in the real world. It all looked much more straightforward on a map. All she really knew about London was that it was enormous and densely populated - ideal for someone who wanted to disappear. She would stay here, lose herself alongside the other nine million souls and work out how she could use her ability to draw out and stop the bald man. As plans go, it was pretty poor, she knew. But what choice did she have? Stay on Innisfarne, and she'd be putting everyone's lives in danger. At least here, it was only her own life she was risking.

Joni's mouth was dry, and she was beginning to feel lightheaded. She realized she was dehydrated and hungry. *Not forgetting scared shitless.* She shifted the backpack more comfortably onto her shoulders and walked purposefully under the departures board as if she knew exactly where she was heading.

She joined a line of people at a sign saying *Underground* and copied them as they held their disqs against some sort of device which beeped and opened a gate. There were moving stairs beyond, leading down and out of sight. She created a reset point. Taking a deep breath, she held up her disq, walked through the electronic gate and perched carefully on the top step of the moving staircase—*escalator*, she remembered—and slowly descended into an unknown chamber, full of echoes, snatches of music and the roar of distant trains. She half-wished she believed in some kind of traditional god, so she could pray for protection, but then decided that any personal god worthy of the term would hardly have allowed her to get into this situation in the first place.

There was a stall near the bottom of the long escalator, and Joni stocked up with bottled water, some fresh fruit and a chocolate bar called a Smudge, which tasted sweet and oily but made her feel slightly sick.

She decided that if she chose a destination randomly and found a hotel to stay wherever she ended up, there was no way the bald man would be able to find her. Not quickly, at any rate, and if she could keep moving, surely she'd always be a step or two ahead of him.

Between leaving the bus and boarding the underground train, Joni's image had been captured by seventeen security cameras.

Chapter 24

Near Innisfarne

From his boat, Adam watched the beach again, the sniper rifle at his feet.

He was prepared, mentally and physically for the task ahead. Yesterday, he'd had to watch impotently as the girl came tantalizingly close to the beach before suddenly walking away.

She hadn't been alone. The descriptions had matched those of Meera Patel, her mother, and John Varden. According to the reports, John Varden was a long-lost brother who'd shown up on Innisfarne a few weeks before Sebastian had died, or left, or taken a particularly long swim. John Varden was of no interest. Neither was Meera Patel. If they stepped onto the beach with the girl, he would simply take them out first, before bringing her down in preparation for the sacrifice.

He'd waited an hour after they had gone, but they

didn't return. Today was another no-show. It was already well past the time she would usually show up. He knew there was no way anyone could know he was there, let alone who he was or that he represented any kind of danger to them. It was a puzzle.

Adam could feel the frustration start to build. Even his patience had limits. Only the fact that he knew there was no way the girl could have been warned allowed him to keep his mood fairly level.

He still watched the old man's boat go back and forth from Innisfarne every morning. Sometimes, the only thing the old man carried was mail. There had been a single visitor this morning - a frail, stooped, gray-haired woman. No one had left the island.

So it was a surprise when, mid-way through the after-noon, *Penelope* hove into view, heading directly toward his boat.

Adam made sure the knife wasn't visible and rewrapped the AWSM in its sacking. He put down the binoculars as the other boat approached.

"Guess I picked the wrong time of year for it," he called as *Penelope* drew up alongside. "Nothing but the common gull so far."

The old man grunted in return. Not the talkative type. That was fine with Adam. "Got this for you," said the old man, pulling an envelope from his pocket. It was sealed and there was no name on the front.

Adam looked at it but didn't take it. "For me?" he said. "You sure?"

"I'm sure." The old man leaned forward and tossed it into Adam's boat. It landed at his feet, on top of the hidden rifle.

"Well. Thank you, I guess."

The old man nodded and pushed the throttle, guiding his craft away from Adam, heading back to the mainland.

He opened the letter.

Dear Bald Man, it began. Adam didn't react outwardly, but he felt suddenly cold. The handwriting was neat, the grammar precise. There were no misspellings. The report had said she was intelligent.

I don't know your name. I don't know who you are. No one here knows you even exist except me. I left a note for Stuart asking him to deliver this to you the day after he found it. If you're reading this on your boat, that means I left Innisfarne hours ago.

Adam looked around him, using the binoculars. If this was a set-up of some kind, he couldn't see how. And there was no sign of anyone apart from *Penelope*, which was shrinking rapidly as it headed back to land.

You're wondering how I know about you. And how I know you're bald. Well, perhaps you're not quite as clever as you think. I certainly found it pretty easy to get the better of you, didn't I?

He took a long breath in. No one had got the better of him since he'd been a child. He wasn't about to let that change because some kid thought she had the measure of him. And she'd shown her hand - he knew now that she must have some kind of enhanced sensing power. He'd been far enough from the island that no Manna user could have sniffed him out, but perhaps Varden's daughter had no such limitations. And he had felt no trace of it at all. An impressive ability, if it were true. In the absence of a better theory, he would proceed with that in mind. He would have to cloak himself with the darkness when he next came within a few miles of her.

I've left Innisfarne forever. No one has any way of getting in touch with me. The world's a big place. We won't meet again.

Goodbye.

It wasn't signed. Adam smiled. The letter was bad news

in one way, certainly. The girl—somehow—knew a little about him. But not enough. And she wasn't as smart as she thought.

Firstly, the world was not a big place at all, these days. Adam was an expert at leaving no trace as he passed, but Joni Varden had no such experience. He could track her.

Secondly, she'd made a mistake including that word: *again*. She hadn't said they'd never meet. She'd said they wouldn't meet *again*. He'd been mistaken about her ability. He remembered the report on her father. Reputedly, he'd been able to travel vast distances instantaneously. No Manna user could do that. What abilities might his daughter have? Something new, something unique. Whatever it was, it was some kind of defensive mechanism. She hadn't counter-attacked, she had run. Which showed weakness.

Adam was used to dealing with weakness.

Chapter 25

London

Joni got off the tube after three stops. There were two reasons why it seemed a good idea. Firstly, she was unable to prevent herself squealing every time the clattering, swaying, screeching train came to a halt, or set off. She guessed this wasn't a normal reaction, by the looks she was getting from the other passengers, who seemed to number in the hundreds just in her carriage. *There are more people in this tin box than live on the whole of Innisfarne!* Secondly, she knew Westminster was the seat of government. She just had to see the Houses of Parliament. She couldn't let the opportunity go by. Surely even a runaway girl with weird powers being pursued by a mad killer was allowed to be a tourist for an hour?

As she emerged from the almost unending maze of white-tiled corridors and sets of staircases, Joni had a sense of being outside herself, looking in. She could see a terrified teenager in a city for the first time, trying not to make a fool of herself. She could see the deeper fear, the dread that would underscore every conscious moment until the bald man was locked up. *Or, even better, dead.* She wondered at her lack of compassion. Surely she should think of him as unstable, ill, not evil. Yet she couldn't think of him as anything other than evil. The blank expression, the dead eyes, the sense of emptiness, of a brutal simplicity of purpose. She had felt no hint of common humanity - it was as if he were a different species entirely.

And yet, separate from the fear, and somehow managing to free itself from being dragged down by it, was an undeniable feeling of happiness. It seemed ridiculous under the circumstances. But, as she stood at the top of the steps and looked across the street at the iconic government buildings and the ancient clock tower that dominated them, her heart felt light. Happiness bubbled up unbidden. She had to fight a sudden urge to dance about like a toddler.

About twenty yards from the station exit, a large statue gazed across at the Houses of Parliament. Made out of some dark, solid material with which Joni was unfamiliar, it was roughly double the size of a normal human. Its subject was an old, powerful-looking man in an overcoat, hunched slightly, leaning on a walking stick. His expression was so real-looking, it held Joni spellbound for a few minutes. At first, he looked determined, defiant, proud and strong. The inscription identified him as Winston Churchill, the leader who led Britain through the war years, fighting—and defeating—the Nazis under Adolf Hitler. Joni enjoyed history and had been studying the Second World War, but seeing this statue made it all seem *plausible*, somehow. She knew it had happened, but looking at the dark carved figure, she felt the shock of a historical event freeing itself from the pages of books and taking on an undeniable reality.

I wonder what he would have made of Manna? And the Manna War?

It was what journalists had taken to calling the regular clashes between police and gangs of Manna users. Areas of London were now considered off-limits to all except battalions of police, properly tooled-up with EMPties, Manna-spanners, and tags. The suspicion voiced by some of the press was that these highly visible raids were staged more to allay public fears than actually make any difference. Everyone knew that the authorities were playing a waiting game. Manna users were dying out, their numbers shrinking all the time. Those Users who had gone public were circling the wagons and seeking strength through numbers. They were holed up in various London boroughs. The same ghettoization was mirrored in cities worldwide. But the majority of Users had hidden their abilities; scared, on the one hand, by the brutal behavior of the gangs and, on the other, by the failure of new anti-Manna legislation to differentiate between criminals and law-abiding citizens. These days, if you Used, you were an enemy of the state.

Joni carried on staring at Churchill's face. Over time, more subtle expressions emerged. She felt sure she could see regret now, a weight of sadness, a world-weariness.

Never mind Manna. What would he have done with my *ability? Would World War Two have been over faster? Would millions of lives have been spared?*

For the first time, Joni thought about what her power might mean for the future. She had inherited it from her father, which meant, according to what Mum and Uncle John had told her about him, that her body must contain alien nanotechnology at a level far beyond that offered by

Manna, which had been present on Earth before her most distant ancestor crawled out of the slime. Her power, the integrated technology woven into her molecular structure, felt entirely natural to her. Its use was becoming instinctive, almost effortless. Which wasn't Dad's experience when he became a World Walker. Whatever that meant.

She crossed the street and joined the rest of the tourists looking up at Big Ben, many of them taking pictures of the famous clock tower.

If she survived long enough to have children, what abilities might they inherit, if any? She had no sense at all of the tech inside her being in any way separate. It was *her*, all of it. She felt like she was just beginning to stretch herself, explore the possibilities of what she could do.

Dad couldn't die, apparently. Joni knew the same didn't hold true for her. Lying on the beach, she had felt her consciousness swirling away into nothingness. If she died, she died. And yet she had a strong feeling of continuity that was hard to explain; hard—even—to formulate in a way that made any sense. In some peculiar way, she felt far, far older than sixteen. Her afternoon walks on Innisfarne had supplied a metaphor that gave her a way to express how she felt about her mortality. She had watched the waves as they crested and broke, thinking about their relationship to the body of water that produced them. A wave seemed—no, *was*—individual, discrete. And yet it was also an illusion of individuality. Without the sea, there was no wave. Before it was a wave, what was it? Where was it? And when it rejoined the water, where did it go?

Joni wondered if she would only be able to think so deeply about life while she was a teenager. She felt as if no one else would ever understand. She imagined a future self, worn down by age, experience, and worries. Surely even that version of herself wouldn't remember, or understand, the profound connections Joni was making as a sixteen-year-old.

She giggled out loud, causing an Italian family posing for photos nearby to move their children away to a safe distance. Joni giggled again. She realized she was having a proper, clichéd, teenage moment.

Nobody understands me. Even the future me, apparently.

She walked to the street, clogged with a bewildering variety of vehicles. She pressed a button on a waist-level box, as she'd seen others do. It would make the lights change so that she could cross the road back to the underground station. As she waited, she looked across at Churchill's statue. At this angle, he looked completely bald. She stopped smiling as she remembered why she was here, and who would be trying to follow her.

As she descended once again into the sticky heat of the station, heading toward the roaring echo of the rattling trains, she found she could still hold on to a faint sense of happiness and peace.

I may only be a wave, but I'm also the ocean.

———

SHE TOOK the tube to Canary Wharf. There was no logical reason to pick that destination, but she liked the sound of it. *Wharf* meant it must be near water, which she would find comforting. And Joni liked birds.

As the train clattered her closer, she pictured an idyllic riverside row of cottages, the street lined with trees, the branches of which struggled to bear the weight of the hundreds of bright yellow exotic birds perching there.

The reality, when she finally emerged, was about as far removed from her mental picture as it was possible to be.

Canary Wharf had once been touted as a center to

rival that of the City, London's traditional financial heart-land. It had prospered for decades, its great glass and steel hymns to capitalism thrusting out of a coveted piece of real estate, proudly squatting inside a loop of the Thames.

During the past decade and a half, things had changed.

As Joni exited the station, she paused and created a reset point. She was doing it habitually now, whenever she could look around and feel she was—temporarily, at least —safe. A small man sweeping up looked at her, stopping what he was doing. His gaze was so intense that Joni stopped walking, her pretense that she knew what she was doing dropping momentarily. The man shuffled closer to her before speaking.

"Miss? You know where you going? Someone meeting you?"

Joni felt the unease of being in an utterly strange place. She was suddenly, uncomfortably, mistrustful of the man's motives in approaching her.

"Yes, actually, I am meeting a friend. She's expecting me, I'd better go."

She started to walk away, but the man moved more swiftly than she expected, grabbing her arm.

"Not safe here," he said. "Trouble every night now. The gangs, they have been moving in. Police can't stop it. You should get back on the train, Miss. Go back into town. Not good here, not good."

Joni shook free of his arm and forced a smile onto her face.

"I really am meeting someone. I have to go. I'll be late."

She walked quickly away, risking a look over her shoulder to make sure he wasn't following. The small man was leaning on his broom, watching her, shaking his head. His expression was unreadable.

"You take care please, Miss," he shouted after her. "I have daughters. Please. Take care. If you change your mind, the station will be clo—,"

She hurried away, feeling bad about her unwillingness to trust him. It was so hard to know how to behave here. She was deliberately trying to cultivate a more street-wise cynicism, hoping to avoid appearing as some guileless, clueless visitor. Which was exactly what she was.

She kept her head down as she hurried around the corner, not looking at her surroundings until she had put a few hundred yards between herself and the station.

The sun was beginning to set, and the tall buildings on either side cast long deep shadows onto the concrete walkways. There were trees here, but they weren't the old, established oaks, elms, and yews Joni had pictured. They were saplings, for the most part, planted in squares of earth, fenced off from the concrete. They hadn't been well looked after, most of them either wrenched half out of the ground, some missing entirely. Joni looked to the left and right and saw that many of the buildings had once contained stores or offices, with big signs advertising brands she'd never heard of. But the windows were smashed or boarded up.

Joni looked at the scale of the buildings around her. Tens of thousands of people must live and work in a place like this, she thought.

So where is everybody?

It was colder in the shadow of the buildings. She shrugged off the backpack, had a drink and put her jacket on before continuing. She felt suddenly stupid. It had seemed like a clever idea, picking a random name on the Underground map. Now, she wished she'd done some research first. It would be dark soon, and she was in a place she didn't know, which was eerily deserted.

She turned and made for the station, walking fast. As she walked, she felt increasingly vulnerable. Every building rose for many stories above her. Each window might contain someone who was watching her, right now. A young girl, on her own. She quickened her pace.

As she turned the final corner before the station, she stifled a sob. The gates were locked, the doors closed. The small man was nowhere to be seen. Joni ran across and stood in front of the glass doors which had slid apart automatically for her just twenty minutes ago. They stood motionless now. She tried to force her fingers into the tiny gap between them, but they were shut fast. She kicked them in frustration.

"Hello?" she called, as loudly as she dared through the quarter-inch gap where the doors didn't meet. "Hello?" Her voice echoed away into the empty station. The cleaner must have gone home for the night.

Ok, Jones, what now?

Oh.

She *reset.*

Chapter 26

She was back at the station gates. The small man was looking at her. She smiled, turned on her heel and went back into the station.

"Changed my mind," she said. He went back to his sweeping.

Joni didn't know how many different train lines converged on this station. Some of the ones she'd seen on the map at Westminster seemed to have four or five different colors heading in different directions to places she knew as little about as Canary Wharf.

She decided to head back to the platform where she'd disembarked. There had been trains heading in the opposite direction as hers had arrived. She would do it right this time. Get back to the heart of the city and ask for help at a tourist information center. She had no idea how the bald man intended to follow her, but she knew he would try. She could make things difficult for him by asking for details of lots of hotels, then picking one at random. That would throw him off the scent, surely. She would stay one night in a place, then move on. She had enough money to last her a few months if necessary. But she didn't want to run forever. She was going to need a plan - sooner, rather than later.

Joni realized she couldn't remember exactly which of the wide corridors she needed to take. She felt a slight flutter of panic.

Calm down, Jones.

She shrugged off her backpack and placed it at her feet. After taking another mouthful of water, she listened carefully. If she could hear the announcements they made, she could head toward the sound and find her train. She created another *reset* point.

As she listened, she heard the sound of approaching footsteps. They got closer quickly. Someone was running toward her.

Joni looked around for somewhere to hide. She was standing in the middle of an open concourse. There were small stores on either side, but they were locked.

While she was still standing frozen with indecision, the runner appeared. It was a girl who looked to be in her twenties. Her long red hair, pulled back into a ponytail, was swinging wildly as she pumped her arms, sprinting as fast as she could.

When she saw Joni, her eyes widened comically, and she skidded to a stop, unsure as to whether this newcomer represented a threat. It took her about half a second to decide that she didn't, then another half-second to make a decision.

"Hide!" she hissed. Joni looked at her blankly, then registered another sound in the empty station. Another runner heading toward her. No, this time there were multiple footsteps, heavier, approaching fast. The redhead grabbed Joni's arm and pulled her to the side of the concourse. Joni made a grab for her backpack as the surprisingly strong woman dragged her.

"My backpack!" she said, pulling against the woman.

"No time!" Joni continued to resist and was shocked and horrified when the strange woman slapped her across the face.

"Do you want to find out what they do to pretty girls?"

Joni followed her as she ran toward the door of a boarded-up store. The door had a heavy padlock on it. There was no way they would have time to open it before their pursuers reached them. As they approached, the redhead raised a hand and the door suddenly looked less substantial, more like heavy drapes than solid wood. The woman didn't even attempt to slow before jumping at the previously solid door, and Joni followed without thinking.

It felt like jumping through spray from the ocean, only warmer. The woman held up a hand, and the door was solid again.

Joni looked at her. "You're a—,"

"Yes," whispered the woman, putting a finger to her lips. "Now shush."

The two of them crouched behind the door and listened. The running footsteps got much louder, then slowed suddenly. Joni, her heart sinking, realized they must have spotted her backpack.

"You see her?" The voice was male, the accent East London, like Mum's. Joni wondered how Mum felt about life on a tiny island when she'd grown up in such a busy city. Then she marveled at her brain's ability to focus on trivialities when she was in imminent danger. She wasn't sure it was a particularly useful quality.

She glanced round to look for another way out if their hiding place were discovered. The store's interior was dark, but not pitch black. The light from the fire exit still emitted a sickly green glow. Enough for Joni to see the door was blocked by piles of boxes.

Knackers.

Another one of Mum's favorite words.

Joni nudged the stranger and pointed at the back door. Surely she could use Manna to get them through the barricade? The woman shook her head, whispering, almost inaudibly, "I'm all out."

With a sudden chill, Joni remembered when her last *reset* point had been set, less than a minute earlier, too late for her to choose anything other than run, or follow the redheaded woman, as she had done this time. She was in a corner - her ability couldn't help her now.

She jumped as the door was rattled a few feet away from where they were crouching. The woman took her hand and looked at her levelly, seemingly willing her to stay calm. Joni concentrated on keeping her breathing as slow and quiet as she could manage.

"They're all locked up." It was a different voice, another male. There was another voice, calling from a little distance away. Joni couldn't make out the words. At least three of them, then.

The first voice spoke again. It sounded like he hadn't moved. He had sent the others to search. The leader.

"Forget it. She's fast, I'll say that for her. Once we'd lost sight of her, she could have gone anywhere. Forget the stupid bitch. We've got summat far more interesting right here, lads."

Joni could hear the sound of her backpack been upended and shaken out onto the hard floor of the station. She started to get up, but the woman shook her head slowly and firmly.

"Well, well, some girly clothes, chocolate bars - 'ere you go, Tone, don't say I never give you nothin'. Couple of books."

Joni heard the zip of the inside pocket. It contained

eighteen of the twenty £500 disqs she'd taken. Nearly all of her money. It took all her strength not to groan aloud.

"Four, no five, disqs, chaps. All full. Might be a score on each. It's our lucky day." He must have pocketed the rest himself. No honor amongst thieves after all.

"Oh, hang on, hang on. This one fancies herself as a bit of a writer. Pages and pages of stuff. Looks like we'll be 'aving a bedtime story tonight."

There were appreciative laughs from his friends. Joni wasn't sure which was worse. Being robbed of everything she had, or having her private thoughts read by this idiot. No, she did know, actually. It was the latter.

"Get a load of this. Proper chick lit." The leader started reading aloud, adopting a proclamatory tone that heaped even more humiliation upon Joni.

"'Why did I let myself be taken in by him?'" The others laughed. "'It's not as if I'm unintelligent. I wouldn't just fall for a pretty face, blonde hair or blue eyes. I could only have felt as I did because there was some kind of genuine connection between us. I know he felt it too. How could he have treated me that way?' Blah blah blah, broad shoulders, full lips, blah blah blah, long talks, some snog-ging. No shagging at all, as far as I can see. Sorry, lads." There were murmurs of disapproval.

Joni felt the grip on her arm loosen as the voices finally moved away. Just before they became inaudible, one sentence floated back clearly: "What kind of name is Odd, anyway?"

The red-haired woman shot her a shocked glance, then shook her head, as if dismissing what she'd heard.

"We'll give them a few minutes to clear out, then we'll make a move," she said.

Joni didn't answer. After a few seconds, she sniffed.

"Oh, Jesus," said the woman. "Don't cry. Was it much money?"

"Enough," said Joni, wiping her face on her sleeve. "But they took everything. And my journal…I don't know why I brought it really. Stupid. It's just a habit, writing every day. I couldn't bear to leave it."

Joni realized she was rambling, and giving information away to someone she knew nothing about. Then she decided that if she was going to have to start trusting someone, she might as well begin with this woman who had saved her from the three men.

"I'm Joni," she said, sticking out her hand somewhat awkwardly.

"Charlie," said the redhead. "Nice to meet you."

She pulled Joni to her feet and led her to the boarded-up window. She listened for a few seconds, then started pulling at one of the boards.

"Give us a hand, will you?"

Joni grabbed the same corner Charlie was pulling and, with a sound of splintering wood, the nails tore free of the surround, and the board came away. There was just enough room for them to step through.

"It's getting late. You got anywhere to stay?" Joni shook her head.

"We've got the best squat on the Wharf. You'll be safe there tonight." Charlie looked Joni up and down. "I'm not going to pry, but you look seriously out of your depth. No one comes this far along the Jubilee line alone unless they're packing serious firepower of one sort or another."

She shot Joni a lopsided smile.

"You're not, are you? I don't need to worry, right?"

Joni shook her head again. Charlie led the way to a different set of automatic glass doors. Joni frowned.

"The station's shut now. The doors don't work anymore, do they?"

In answer, Charlie walked toward them, and they swung silently apart.

"They always open from the inside. So no one can get trapped. Health and safety, innit? First time in London, right?"

"Is it that obvious?"

"'Fraid so, kid. You're lucky you bumped into me first. I don't fancy your chances much otherwise. Run away from home?"

She looked up at Charlie now and nodded.

"Something like that. I don't want to talk about it, really."

"Wasn't going to ask, Joni. It's your business. But if I can peg you as a teenage runaway, so can others. And a lot of them won't have your best interests at heart, see?"

Joni nodded again. She had been creating *reset* points every minute or so, not wanting to repeat the experience of feeling like a trapped animal. As soon as she'd created the first new reset point, she'd realized she'd lost her only chance of retrieving her backpack, but she couldn't risk going back and finding she and Charlie didn't manage to escape in every scenario.

They walked on, away from the skyscrapers. The buildings were smaller, here. Not all of them were boarded up, although a few were just burnt-out shells. As they rounded the next corner, Joni finally saw the water. Not the sea, but water nonetheless. She felt happier immediately. The street they were walking down had red-brick buildings facing the water.

Charlie ducked into a gap between two buildings.

"Nearly there," she said. "Just got to fill up. Not too smart of me to let it get so low." At the end of the nondescript passageway, Charlie knelt on the floor and placed her palms on the ground. Her body shook and she grunted as energy poured into her. Joni wondered again at her own lack of Manna ability. She couldn't even sense the power when she was practically standing on top of a Thin Place.

Joni was beginning to formulate a theory. She remembered Uncle John telling her about closed systems. She had been trying to understand computers - a subject that was hard to study when the only example on Innisfarne was probably old enough to appeal to collectors of vintage technology. Luckily John was something of an expert. He told her that a closed system meant no third-party software could be installed. In an open system, anyone could write programs, or contribute improvements, but that openness meant the system was vulnerable to malware and viruses. Closed systems protected the software. That's how Joni felt about her ability. It was installed at birth.

Charlie stood up, bobbing on the balls of her feet.

"That's better," she said. "Come on, nearly there."

Joni followed her along the street. She looked at the water parallel to the buildings. It wasn't the Thames - it was too regular. More of an artificial lake, fed by the river that snaked through the center of the city. The setting sun turned the water red-orange. It wasn't a particularly large body of water. Less than half a mile away, Joni could see a couple of airplanes. One was missing its wings, and the other was a blackened hulk. The runway itself was covered in grass and weeds. It was obviously a long time since any plane had taken off or landed there.

Charlie had stopped outside one of the buildings.

"Those men who were chasing you," said Joni. "Were they a Manna gang?"

Charlie laughed then, a genuine cackle that made her

look quite different. Her face softened, and her eyes sparkled with humor.

"You've got it all arse-backwards, kid," she said. "They were vicious small-minded thugs. They're trying to wipe out Users."

She walked up the path and pushed the door open. She smiled at Joni's reaction.

"No need for security," she said. "We've got the twins. No one could get within half a mile of here without us knowing about it."

Joni hesitated on the path.

"You got it," said Charlie, smiling. "We're the Manna gang. We're not all bad, you know. We've had a lot of bad press, that's all. Come on in, I'm dying for a brew."

Joni *reset*, then followed her into the house and shut the door behind her.

―――

NORTHUMBRIA

ADAM SPENT an hour changing his appearance. The ginger birdwatcher disappeared and a goth, black-haired, with dark mascara and funereal clothing, took his place. Adam thought of this as hiding in plain sight. Sometimes, drawing attention to his appearance was the best way to conceal his identity. No one would ever link his last two personas.

He had unloaded the boat in a secluded bay, then tied the steering wheel in place, started the engine and sent it out to sea. It would be discovered drifting, eventually, and might even be traced back to the cash purchase by the quiet ginger man. After that, the trail would dry up. He'd wiped the boat clean, the knife was now strapped to his leg, and the rifle was at the bottom of the North Sea.

He walked to the road and caught a bus to the nearest town. From there, he took a train south. He disembarked after three stops, well short of the destination on his ticket. A trip to the bathroom and he came out looking like a student - mousy brown hair, heavy glasses and a T-shirt with an Oscar Wilde quote on it. He dumped the goth clothes in different trashcans, then shopped for his next outfit.

By early evening, he had checked into an anonymous hotel and was able to make a private call on a burner cellphone he'd picked up in town. He had memorized the number he needed to call, along with hundreds of similar numbers, during his years working for the Broker.

The call was picked up after the fourth ring.

"Martin, this is Adam," he said. There was a pause at the other end of the line. Very few people called this number asking for Martin. The voice, when it spoke, had a very slight cockney accent. Adam had dealt with him before. He was reliable. And fast.

"The Broker's not in business no more," the voice said.

"I know."

"Price has gone up."

"I'll pay you double the usual rate if you have this information to me within twelve hours. Within six, triple."

"What if it takes longer than twelve hours?"

"Then I won't pay you at all. Lost your touch?"

"Yeah, right. You're funny. Tell me what you need."

Adam gave him every detail he could think of that might make the search easier. He had confidence in Martin, but he couldn't help but wonder how the girl's ability—whatever it was—might affect things. As it turned out, he needn't have worried.

The phone rang after two hours and twenty-eight minutes. Adam picked it up and listened.

"I have a location for you. She got there tonight. Let's talk money."

Martin named an inflated figure. With the Broker out of the picture, he obviously saw no need to honor existing business arrangements. Still, Adam's purpose would soon be fulfilled. Afterward, maybe, he would gut Martin and wrap his intestines around his throat.

Adam agreed to the figure, giving the location and combination of a self-storage locker in Kings Cross station, which contained slightly more cash than the opportunistic Martin had demanded. Adam used similar lockers in major cities all over the world.

Adam removed the burner's sim card and swallowed it. He did some quick mental calculations.

He would need to stop at one of his lockers to replenish his wardrobe, makeup, and wigs.

He would need firepower, quickly.

He would need to steal a car.

He could afford four hours sleep before leaving. He lay down and closed his eyes, a small smile playing around his lips.

Joni Varden was in London.

Chapter 27

London

Joni took a while to get to sleep. It was night, but there were still lights outside, and distant sounds were audible over the occasional snore from others in the room. She doubted London was ever silent. How could people stand it? Not being able to find a refuge where the only sound was a gust of wind through the leaves of the trees, or the distant murmur of the ocean? She lay awake in the semi-darkness, wondering if another aspect of her abilities might be the knack of attracting trouble. She'd come to the capital to escape a killer and walked straight into the middle of the Manna War. She'd heard what was going on from visitors to the island and more had been filled in by a couple of books left behind. But this wasn't like the events in her history lessons. This was happening right now.

Her mind finally caught up with her body's insistence that she needed to sleep and she closed her eyes.

After Year Zero, it had taken Manna users a few years to confirm their worst suspicions. Year Zero marked the point after which no more Manna users were born. There were many theories as to why it had happened, but none offered sufficient evidence to be convincing. Manna was still there, and its Users could still fill up with the power they craved as easily as ever. But they would be the last.

One unexpected result of Year Zero, after Users spent a few years looking for answers which never came, was the end of secrecy. Manna users were a very small subset of humanity, able to focus their minds in such a way that they could draw power from Thin Places around the world. Some had used this power to help heal, or feed the hungry. Most had used it to wield power over their fellow humans. All had kept to the shadows, as those who had more openly revealed their abilities in the past had often been reviled as monsters and slaughtered. Vampires, werewolves, golems, witches, wizards, shape-shifters…these were myths and legends drawn from real encounters with Manna users. And, although less easy to kill than normal humans, the most powerful Manna users on the planet died just like anyone else if beheaded or consumed by fire. And they were outnumbered thousands to one. Secrecy had, over the centuries, became as important to them as their abilities.

But the last generation of Manna users wanted answers, wanted to give their children the chance to develop the same power. The children of Manna users were statistically around five times more likely to be Users than those born into regular families. Some Manna users went to the scientific community for answers. They did it carefully, paying for their own labs, scientists, and technicians. The majority of Users had accepted that Manna was some kind of advanced nanotechnology, buried in Thin Places. Some stubbornly clung on to a belief in magic, God, or Satan, attributing the gift of Manna to their preferred candidate. For the majority, two theories vied for supremacy as to the origin of Manna. One named aliens, the other an advanced human civilization, long since gone. The latter explanation had gained the most traction.

Science proved to be a dead end. Any attempt to discover what was happening at a cellular or molecular level inevitably failed. Manna users at the peak of their powers gave samples of blood. It was normal. Scans were taken—CT and PET—while a User was demonstrating their power. The moment the equipment was turned on, the Manna turned off. Any attempt to measure Manna was thwarted. It didn't want to be observed, and human ingenuity was nowhere near advanced enough to persuade it otherwise.

Those who wielded this ancient power reacted in different ways after the permanent effects of Year Zero had been confirmed. Some global players began the slow process of legitimizing their businesses. Others liquefied their assets and retired into obscurity. Smaller criminal groups fought among themselves or disappeared. But the most significant outcome was the rise of Manna gangs. Based in major cities, where certain districts soon became virtually no-go areas, the gangs used their power to fuel their private fantasies, no longer trying to hide. Their combined power was such, that—after early failed attempts by the police and military to reclaim the gangs' territories —they were, in general, allowed to live relatively unmolested.

An uneasy peace existed for a short while.

After the first, lawless years, the police and courts were given powers to keep Users in check. Germany was the first to come up with bespoke weapons, its lead followed quickly by the rest of Europe, then the world. Australia introduced tagging devices into its criminal justice system after a few false starts and—once again—the rest of the world was quick to copy a workable method designed to curb the Manna gangs.

The weapons were a combination of existing tech combined with some new ideas. Tasers, a way of immobilizing a potentially violent suspect, had been popular in some police forces for years. It soon became known that a taser, besides overriding the central nervous system and causing muscles to spasm, also knocked out any Manna currently active in the victim. Every police officer in Manna gang cities was issued with the devices, nicknamed 'Manna-spanners.'

The second weapon was the EMPty - an electromagnetic pulse grenade. A holy grail of the military for more than two decades, scientists, weapon designers and technicians in the field suddenly found their budgets increased. This was accompanied by huge political pressure. Within eighteen months, the first prototype was being tested and, a year later, the EMPties were in use. Thrown into a crowd of Users, the EMPty would explode three seconds after its pin was pulled. It wasn't designed to inflict physical damage, although some damage was inevitable in any explosive device. Its Unique Selling Proposition was the tightly targeted electromagnetic pulse it produced, knocking out any cellphone, computer or electronic device within a thirty meter radius. Also, of course, disabling any Manna. The shock to a person of a sudden, complete loss of Manna had the useful side-effect of producing unconsciousness.

The Manna-spanners and EMPties turned the tide.

Soon, Users stopped any open raids of areas outside the districts in which they had settled. The situation was pretty much a stalemate, but the Australian approach to justice made it possible to contain the Users and dissuade them from making any attempts at a major power grab. Again, it was based on existing technology.

It was a brutally effective, simple system. Any Manna user caught by the police was tagged. This, much to the horror of human rights advocates, included those who used their power to help their fellows. The rise to government of hard-line right-wing parties in the West had been another notable trend following Year Zero, so the same human rights advocates found themselves comprehensively ignored. The tags were simple in design - they sent a signal if tampered with or removed. The wearer's DNA was on record. If a tag wearer ever found him or herself in police custody again, the DNA on record removed the need for a trial. The prisoner automatically qualified for a life sentence in one of the purpose-built facilities far from any Thin Place. With no chance of parole. Tag removers qualified for the same treatment the moment the tag was tampered with.

So Joni knew what she was looking at when she woke up in the squat the next morning to the sound of—to her exhausted and slightly paranoid brain, at least—someone assembling various metal instruments of torture on a work surface. She opened one eye and cautiously tugged the sleeping bag away from her face. She was looking at an old, cracked, tiled floor. About eight feet away a pair of ankles came into view. Bare feet. She shivered inside the sleeping bag, fully clothed. One of the ankles sported a bright orange band. A Manna tag.

Joni quietly pushed herself into a sitting position, sliding her back up the wall behind her. She hadn't really got an impression of what kind of place she was in the previous night. She had been so exhausted, Charlie had taken pity on her and set her up on a thin mattress. Now, sitting in the early morning light, she could start to fill in some details about her location.

The ground floor was one, big, space. Judging from the abrupt changes in flooring materials over a few different areas, the house must have originally been more traditionally laid out, as a series of rooms. The conversion to an open-plan arrangement had obviously not involved any architects, interior designers, or anyone by the name of Quentin. Instead, it looked like someone had taken a sledgehammer to the interior walls and kept swinging until they were gone. Which was, in fact, exactly what had happened.

Diagonal stripes of mote-filled winter sunlight fell across the floor and up the side wall, illuminating the first four steps of an elegant staircase, its tattered and faded carpet hinting at a more salubrious past.

Around the walls were various piles of clothing, sleeping bags and personal belongings. All but one of the four sleeping bags were occupied. Joni could see a tuft of Charlie's unkempt red hair poking through a small gap in the sleeping bag nearest to her.

The unoccupied sleeping bag must belong to the tagged ankles. It was a man, his back to her, wearing long shorts and a camouflage jacket. He was tall, his blonde hair shaved close to his scalp. The noise that had woken her was him making his breakfast. Joni was amazed that everyone else seemed able to sleep through the racket. He had filled up a battered metal stove-top kettle and turned on the gas hob, lighting it with a flourish before flicking the match behind him. Now that Joni looked more carefully, she could see dozens of burnt match heads littering the floor.

While the water was heating up, Ankles grabbed a mug from a shelf and set it down on the counter, before tapping out a salsa-like rhythm on it with a teaspoon. There was an old, filthy looking toaster on the counter and he grabbed this next, pulling it toward him before dropping two slices of white bread into it. He pushed the lever. The bread slices disappeared inside, then immediately reappeared. He pushed it down again, with the same result. This was followed by about thirty seconds of what looked like a vicious attack on the defenseless appliance. Finally, it yielded, and the bread stayed down.

The kettle began to whistle as it came to the boil. Rather than removing it from the heat and stopping its rising shriek, Ankles started whistling too, trying to match the ascending tone. As he did so, his teaspoon salsa resumed, and he started dancing, singing something loudly in a language Joni didn't recognize.

Finally, he stopped singing and drumming. He used the teaspoon to flip the teabag against the window, where it began sliding down a well-worn brown trail toward a pyramid of teabags, suggesting an interval of many weeks between any cleaning attempts. He then used the same spoon to force a blackened piece of bread from the toaster and take a bite.

"Well, are you wanting a cup of tea and some jammy toast, or will you be staring at my tag the whole bloody morning?"

Joni jumped, startled. How could he…? Manna?

"I just know when someone is staring at me, that's all."

Was he reading her mind?

"And I'm not reading your mind, so no need to be

worrying about what you are thinking. It's a simple enough question, noob. Tea?"

He turned, while taking a long sip from the hot tea. When he lowered the mug, Joni jumped again, and only just managed to stop herself blurting out his name.

It was Odd.

Chapter 28

Northumbria

Mee stood at the Thin Place, shivering. It wasn't cold - in fact, a long-promised area of high pressure had finally done whatever it is that areas of high pressure did and brought on one of Britain's fabled heat waves. This meant very little to Mee, who was trembling for two reasons, neither of which were weather-related. The first was the fact that she'd only left the island on one other occasion since Seb vanished. The second was the fact that Joni had gone, and was almost certainly in danger. Joni. Her little girl.

She hadn't suspected a thing before Stuart had seen her that morning. Joni hadn't slept in her bed the previous night. The morning before, she'd been up before dawn. She'd left Mee a note.

I need a day or two alone to think about Dad - and this weird power of mine. I'll be in the crofter's cottage. I'll be back when my food runs out! Love, J xxx

The crofter's cottage was a one-room stone dwelling on the northeast tip of Innisfarne. It was weatherproof but basic, a simple camp bed in one corner and an ancient washtub in the other. A rudimentary toilet. Visitors sometimes used it for silent retreats.

Mee had given Joni the space she wanted. She understood the power of solitude. Stuart's news that morning had come as a huge shock.

He'd handed her an envelope at breakfast. It was addressed to her. Joni's handwriting.

Mum,

Don't give Stuart a hard time over this. I wrote him a separate note and told him if he didn't do exactly as I instructed, it could mean you, Uncle John, and maybe others might be killed. I'm sorry, but it's the truth. I had to lie to you the other day.

Please trust me. This is the only way I could think of that might keep us safe until I can work this out. I can't explain any more than that, but I want you to stay where you are. Don't come after me. I will get in touch soon.

I know this sounds crazy, but I think you could see I was more upset than I should have been the other day. Something happened. I reset, but I know it will happen again unless I find a way of stopping it.

I'm sorry. I love you. I will be back as soon as I can,

Jones xxx

Mee had read it twice, feeling numb. Then she looked at Stuart. He wouldn't meet her eye.

"She left me a note, Mee, said it was life and death. Now, she's not your average teenager, that one. I know she wouldn't say it unless it were true. She also asked me not to tell you anything else."

That was the longest speech Mee had ever heard Stuart make.

"What do you mean, *anything else?* What aren't you telling me?"

Stuart had simply shaken his head, looking down at the table. Mee had waited until he finally looked at her.

"Bugger," he had said. "All right, then." He told her about the letter he'd delivered to the ginger man in the boat. After he'd finished, he added that he had a 'bad feeling' about the man.

When Mee had said she was going after Joni, John and Kate had both wanted to come with her. It had taken a while for Mee to talk them out of it. For a start, someone Joni knew and trusted had to be on Innisfarne if she got back before Mee did. And Kate ran the place. They had both eventually seen the sense of this, but neither of them liked it. Kate had shown her the missing disqs, not upset at that loss, just relieved that Joni would have enough money. She'd also given Mee a cellphone and a wireless charger from a cupboard, taking note of the number.

"Call us, keep us informed."

Mee looked at her slightly cynically. The island's landline was notoriously unreliable. Kate had responded by punching a number into the cell's contact list and handing it back.

"Send texts to this number." She held up a second cellphone. I'll give this one to Stuart. He can pick up the signal on the mainland and pass on any messages." The thought of Stuart using any kind of technology invented after 1970 was comical, but Mee wasn't in a laughing mood.

She'd hugged Kate and John and left Innisfarne.

Now Mee had a bag full of clothes and no idea where she was heading. Stuart had delivered a letter to a man on a boat. It wasn't much to go on. He had promised to look for him today, but Mee had the sickening feeling he wouldn't find him. Because he was with Joni? Had they run away together? No. Joni wouldn't lie about the danger they were in. This man was a threat to her somehow. To all of them. He was the danger.

She looked at the remains of the stone circle in front of her. It was at the edge of a meadow, hidden from the road by the undulating landscape. There were five stones, gray, smoothed by centuries of exposure to wind, rain, hail and snow. The tallest stone appeared to be three feet high, but this was due to the fact that only the tips were visible. The bulk of each of the stones was buried underground, like landlocked icebergs.

Mee could feel the power. It had been a long time—many years—but she knew what to do. She allowed her mind to empty. She stepped forward, knelt and placed her hands on the warm earth. Almost immediately she felt her brain light up as tendrils of energy shot through her limbs, filling her with a power she hadn't felt for nearly two decades. God, it was a rush. Her whole body shook as the force of the energy took hold of her, the Manna responding to her need. Despite the situation, she grinned. *This must be how an alcoholic feels downing a scotch after years and years on the wagon.*

"Oh fuck!" she screamed. "Fuck, yeah!" A sheep in the neighboring field interrupted its chewing and gave her a long stare, before moving briskly away as if offended.

Twenty minutes later she was on the bus. The driver remembered Joni well and, when they reached Moilburgh, so did the lady at the ticket office.

"Oh, yes, lovely girl. Your daughter? I can see the resemblance."

If there was some kind of data protection regulation to

stop public transport companies revealing the private travel arrangements of their passengers, news of this had yet to filter through to the northeast fringes of the network.

"Oh, yes, dear," said the woman, beaming happily. "Of course I remember. She was off to London, dear."

Chapter 29

London

Adam arrived in the city driving a stolen Honda. He parked it in an area of North London most people were careful to avoid. He left the keys in the ignition and walked toward the nearest Tube station. It was dawn. He wore a hooded top. The hoodie was still the favored outfit of the petty criminal, so any security footage linking him to the vehicle would be unlikely to elicit any police action. A stolen car abandoned in a dodgy part of town by a hooded figure with a backpack wouldn't be worth the paperwork.

Adam almost made it to the Tube station without incident. Almost. For a while, he was worried he would have to explore the area a little more to find the kind of trouble he wanted. Then, luckily, it found him.

He was about two blocks from the station, and the street he was on was worse than most. The smell of dope seemed to cling to the very bricks of the old Victorian houses, most of which were boarded up and silent. A couple that weren't had a sentry on duty. Kids, no older than fourteen. They sat on the steps, sullen and blank-faced, eyeing Adam as he walked unhurriedly. The first kid he saw leaned backward as he passed and called something back into the house behind him. Adam assumed he was raising the alarm. He certainly hoped so. It had been a frustrating few days, and he could do with a workout.

He smiled when he saw them. About two-thirds of the way along the street, they strolled nonchalantly out of one of the houses. Only three of them. Adam didn't project an intimidating physical presence and he was used to being underestimated. He didn't slow down but turned as he walked, checking behind him. Two heavy-looking men had appeared at the end of the street. They were leaning against a wall, smoking. If they were armed, their weapons were concealed. So it was no more than handguns, and they stood little chance of hitting him from that distance. He was blocked in. Perfect.

Adam had already checked the cameras in the street. There were only two of them, and they were both wrecked. Judging by the extent of the damage, Adam guessed shotguns had been used. Messy. But also, a clear warning to anyone coming into their territory.

The three men in front moved slowly into the center of the street, blocking his way. None of them spoke. Adam took just a few moments to assess the situation. The man to his left was small, white and twitchy. He looked malnour-ished. Crack, probably, possibly heroin. He was bare-chested, his head shaved to a fine stubble. He looked impa-tient, shuffling from one foot to the other. Not much of a threat. If he was going to get involved, Adam guessed he'd use a blade.

The man on the right was huge. Another shaved head,

this one black and gleaming with sweat despite the fact that the sun had barely begun to give off any warmth. He was wearing a tracksuit, the top unzipped a little to show an impressive number of gold chains. He had a heavyweight boxer's build, but it looked like his time in the ring was a few years behind him. His stomach was big, and he moved slowly. Adam wasn't deceived. He'd wager good money that the ex-fighter still had some moves. He was standing with the right side of his body slightly forward. A south-paw, then.

In the center of the group stood the leader. He wore a cheap, dusty gray suit. The suit jacket had three buttons, all of which were fastened. He was older, a white goatee contrasting with the dark, scarred skin beneath. Goatee looked slightly more wary than his companions, weighing the situation. Not automatically assuming he had the upper hand, despite the numbers. That kind of caution made it obvious he was in charge. That, and the fact he had made it into his fifties in such an unforgiving environment. From the way his jacket hung, the right-hand pocket contained a reasonably heavy handgun. Possibly a Browning Hi-Power. Adam knew the British Army had phased out the Browning a generation ago, and many of them had found their way onto the streets.

Having assessed the threat in the immediate vicinity, Adam slowly turned a full three hundred and sixty degrees, checking windows and doorways. No one. Sloppy. They didn't think he was enough of a threat to warrant armed cover. That simplified things considerably.

Satisfied, Adam spoke.

"Excuse me, I'd like to get through."

Crackhead hawked and spat on the road.

"Well, no one's stopping you, pal," he said. He couldn't

keep still for a second, twitching and bobbing about like a kite in the wind.

"On the contrary," said Adam. "The three of you are deliberately blocking my way. I don't want any trouble. I don't have any money. Please let me pass."

The leader relaxed just a fraction. He nodded at Crackhead, who stepped forward and brought out a knife, which had been tucked into the back of his pants. He approached Adam with a big grin on his face, weaving from side to side and throwing the knife casually from one hand to the other. It was probably supposed to look intimidating. Adam tried not to laugh. He felt the first touch of the darkness. It felt good. He held up both hands as the man danced closer.

"All right, all right, I was lying, ok?"

Crackhead stopped a few feet away, still counting on his toes, still tossing the knife from hand to hand.

"Yeah, thought so. Hand over the fucking money."

Adam pretended to look confused. Then his face brightened, and he smiled at the wired, spittle-lipped drug addict.

"Oh, the money! No, I wasn't lying about that. I was lying about not wanting any trouble."

As he said the word 'trouble,' he took a quick step forward and plucked the knife out of the air in mid-flight. He turned it in his hand, pointed the tip upwards, and rammed it into the scrawny turkey skin under the man's chin with enough force for it to bury itself to the hilt. The blade was short, only about four inches, so it wouldn't quite reach the brain. Death would instead be due to blood loss, and might take up to a few minutes. Crackhead had obviously neglected his studies of anatomy and did the worst thing imaginable, under the circumstances - he pulled the knife out. The blade did some more damage on its return journey, leaving no major artery uncut. A gush of blood spurted out, he coughed wetly, voided his bowels and fell over.

During the three seconds it had taken Adam to take the knife and stab Crackhead, the heavyweight had done no more than begin to register what was happening, but Goatee was much quicker to react, as Adam had suspected. He put his hand into his jacket pocket and began to swing the gun inside upward.

Adam realized why the leader wore a cheap suit. He didn't take the gun out of the pocket before shooting someone. Why spend good money on a jacket you're going to ruin?

Adam moved fast, directly toward the man, punching him in his left shoulder, which sent him spinning off balance. Adam stepped to the left and, as the spinning man's back appeared, he grabbed the suit jacket and pulled it down over his shoulders, pinning his arms to his sides. Then he pushed him forward, hard. He fell on his face.

The heavyweight was heading toward him now, massive hands balled into fists, his footwork precise and solid. Adam stepped forward to meet him. As he did so, he trod on Goatee's right hand, now trapped in the suit pocket. The finger was hooked around the trigger, and with Adam's weight forcing the gun to turn outward at a forty-five-degree angle, there was a satisfying crack as the bones in the finger snapped in two places. Adam just had time to kick Goatee in the face, smashing his nose, before the heavyweight threw his first punch.

Adam was pleased to see that the punch was a jab, coming from the right hand. The heavyweight wasn't all brawn and no brain, and was upping his game. The boxer could see Adam was far more dangerous than they had suspected, and wasn't going to unload his most powerful punch until he had the smaller man where he wanted him. Unfortunately for him, that was never going to happen.

Adam ducked the first jab, then swayed backward to avoid the second. Boxers, if they were to successfully launch a post-professional career as a bodyguard, had to be prepared to unlearn much of what they had been taught. A boxing ring is a purpose-built mini-arena of around twenty square feet. Competitors have to observe certain rules. Unsporting punches lead to deductions on a fighter's scorecard. Low punches may be penalized by verbal warnings, a standing count, or even—in extreme cases—disqualification. Years and years of training involving scrupulous observation of these rules were hard to forget in a real fight with real opponents like Adam, who was only familiar with boxing rules insofar as it enabled him to exploit the weaknesses written into them.

He dropped to his knees and punched the heavyweight, hard. His beautifully placed uppercut hit the man's testicles with such velocity that one of them was sent back up into his body. Ten days later, once the swelling had subsided sufficiently, a surgeon would locate and remove the errant testicle, slitting the scrotum to replace it, all the time wondering how it had traveled such a distance.

The heavyweight looked for all the world as if he was about to sing an operatic solo. Instead, he expelled every last cubic inch of air from his lungs with a sound almost identical to that of air-brakes being applied by a forty-foot truck.

As the fighter fell, Adam looked back. The rearguard had woken up to what had happened over the course of the previous sixteen seconds and both men were running toward him, handguns raised. Adam smirked. Most petty criminals carried guns for reasons of intimidation and were usually less than competent in their use. If they fired now, they would be almost certain to miss. They were running, they were still fifty yards away, and the sound of shots would certainly attract police attention, even on a street like this one. But the two henchmen were keen to show their loyalty. They started firing. And shouting abuse. Adam wasn't sure exactly what result either action was intended to produce.

He calmly knelt next to Goatee and wrenched the gun from his pocket. The prone figure made a strangled sound but didn't move. The gun—a Browning, just as he'd guessed—looked to be well looked after. He checked the clip. Eight of the thirteen rounds were present.

Sliding the clip back in, cocking the gun and thumbing off the safety, Adam took a two-handed grip on the weapon and waited until the men were roughly forty yards away. Then he took his first shot - for calibration purposes. He aimed for the largest mass - the center of the man's chest. A puff of red from the man's shoulder as he jerked back gave Adam the information he needed, and the second shot stopped him dead. Literally, as his heart was shredded by the bullet and the splinters of rib that came with it.

The second man was skidding to a halt, adjusting to the changed situation, hoping to get an accurate shot at the hooded lunatic. When he tried to aim, his eyesight blurred as liquid obscured his vision. If he'd still had the capacity for rational thought, he might well have surmised that he'd just been shot in the forehead, and that the liquid was his own blood; but since much of his brain had just been punched through the back of his head, he died in ignorance of either fact.

Adam took the gun from the closest corpse. Always better to have a spare weapon. He jogged away, and was lost to sight before any backup from the street could attempt to avenge their stricken comrades. As soon as the underground station was in sight, he slowed to a walk and joined the crowds heading for their places of employment. His face was one amongst thousands. He boarded a tube packed with commuters and removed his hoodie. Underneath the hood, Adam wore a close-fitting cap and a pair of heavy-rimmed glasses. He put earbuds in and nodded rhythmically, despite the fact that they weren't plugged into anything.

As he pretended to listen to imaginary music, he briefly reviewed the encounter with the five combatants. He replayed every move carefully, examining his logic in deciding on each defensive or offensive measure. In the heat of battle, training, experience and instinct—in that order—were called upon to prevail. Adam found it hard to fault his actions. A little flamboyant with the knife, perhaps. Crackhead had been the weakest. A neck jab would have been faster and just as effective.

Well, there was always next time. Then he remembered who it was going to be next time. It wasn't as if a sixteen-year-old girl was going to put up much of a fight.

He would wait until dusk, but no longer.

Adam had time for one more visit before then. This was going to be a beautiful day.

Chapter 30

There were five of them around the big table in the squat. None of the chairs matched the table or each other and were in various states of disrepair. Much like their occupants—including herself—thought Joni, as she sipped at a hot liquid that Odd had claimed to be tea. It was brown, certainly, but that was where any similarities to tea ended as far as Joni was concerned.

She looked at the 'family,' as Charlie had referred to them, only semi-ironically. Charlie may have been the most senior, but her actions made it clear that everyone had a voice and no one was more important than anyone else. She said her husband described her as the most annoying kind of socialist - one who actually allowed her beliefs to affect her personal life. She mentioned Mark—her husband—a couple of times before Joni asked where he was.

"Fenland," said Charlie. Joni had heard the name somewhere but must have looked a little blank. "It's the biggest prison for Manna users in the country. First time they caught him, he was in a soup kitchen, using Manna to

197

feed people. Second time, he was on his way home the day of the Oxford Street riot. He tried to get out, but he was trapped inside the cordon when they started throwing in the EMPties. He got rounded up with everyone else, and when they saw his tag, that was it."

Joni remembered hearing about the Oxford Street riot - it had been nearly three years ago. It had started as a peaceful protest against the Manna Laws. As was often the case, no one had been able to prove whether the police had sent the marchers down a blocked street deliberately, or if it was just an administrative error. Either way, thousands of people—some of them Users, but the majority sympathizers—had found themselves with no way forward and more people being herded in behind. Panic had been quick to spread in the resulting crush, and Manna users had destroyed buildings to clear a path through the blockage, at which point the police had charged. Cellphone footage posted online had showed a number of vans containing tooled-up riot police arriving at the scene with suspicious speed.

Charlie looked at Joni, who was struggling for the right words. She laughed, humorlessly.

"Don't worry, Joni, there's nothing you *can* say, really. We've just found ourselves on the wrong side of history. I'd fight for him, do anything to get him back, but I know it won't do any good. It'll just get me locked up too, and then what would this lot do?"

She waved her arm at the other occupants of the squat. Odd was calmly sipping his 'tea,' his fourth of the morning. His shaved head made him look older, somehow, although that wasn't the whole story. He didn't smile as much as Joni remembered, and his blue eyes didn't sparkle with excitement and curiosity the way they had on the writing course.

If he even went to the writing course in this universe.

Theo and Cass were both letting their teas go cold. They had obviously endured Odd's tea-making skills before. They were twins, twelve years old. They had grown up with their Jamaican grandparents in London after their parents had been killed in a fire. The whole family had been strong natural Manna users. The children had been separated from their Grandparents shortly after the Manna gangs had moved into their neighborhood. The twins were both very powerful Sensitives, able to detect anyone within a mile of them who had hostile intentions. Joni knew her mum used to be able to pull the same trick.

The twins rarely spoke. Charlie had rescued them from a Manna gang who had used them as scouts while looting. Powerful Sensitives were rare enough that those gangs who boasted good ones were very keen to hold onto them.

"How did you get them out?" said Joni, looking across at Theo and Cass.

Charlie stirred her drink. She did more stirring than drinking. How was it possible Odd couldn't see that everyone hated his tea? Joni found she was beginning to get better at not looking at him every few seconds. This morning had already taught her that the word 'heartache,' far from being the exclusive province of bad romantic novels, could actually describe a physical symptom.

It's not him. You've never met this person.

It didn't help.

"It wasn't my finest hour." Joni realized she'd missed Charlie's last few sentences. She tried to review the few words that had broken through her daydream.

"You were in the gang?" she said. Charlie shot her a look that suggested she was reappraising Joni's level of intelligence.

"I'm not proud of it," she said. "The gang took what

199

they wanted, they preached a mixture of common sense and hatred. You know, 'we have to protect ourselves, we're an unfairly persecuted minority.' They mixed that with 'non-Manna users will never understand us, they hate all of us,' which led to 'let's drive these people out of their homes and take everything they have because they'd do the same to us.'"

Charlie sighed. "I was angry about Mark. So angry. I could barely think about anything else - every second of every day. Then, one night, I saw Theo and Cass for the first time. They were kept in the basement, treated like animals. They were powerless, and the gang leaders—for all their preaching about Manna users being better— showed their true colors when it came to looking after their own."

Cass and Theo looked at Charlie while she spoke. Neither showed much emotion, but they didn't take their eyes off her face.

"We were out one night. Foraging, Gregor called it. We knew it was looting. I doubled back to the house, unlocked the basement and got Theo. We picked up Cass on our way, crossed the river and looked for somewhere far enough away that they wouldn't find us. Ran into Odd just when we needed him and the rest is history."

"You make it sound easy," said Joni.

In answer, Charlie stood up and turned around. She pulled up her sweater, revealing three scarred marks on her back - two on her left shoulder and the other nearer the middle of her torso. She dropped the sweater back down and turned to Joni.

"I asked Odd to put the scars back so I could feel them and remember."

"Remember what?"

"That even those who claim to be on your side might shoot you in the back one day."

Joni could imagine the pain - she could clearly remember the sensation of being shot on the beach. But Charlie had been shot three times - and still escaped. How? Joni's face must have betrayed her confusion.

"Yeah, some people are born lucky, right?"

"Not really what I was thinking. You did get shot, after all. Not so lucky."

"Maybe. I'd got the twins into my car, but Gregor—the gang leader—had come after me. He didn't shout a warning, he just started shooting. I managed to get in and start driving. I could feel the blood running down my back. I was struggling to breathe. Made it across Putney Bridge and got to Parsons Green before I felt like I was going to fall asleep. Then I realized if I fell asleep, I probably wouldn't wake up again. But I was too far gone. I managed to pull the car to the side of the road. There were trees there. Dying didn't seem so bad if I could see trees. Silly, really."

She looked at Odd. "I was unconscious for the next bit. You tell her."

He smiled a strange, tight little smile aimed at no one in particular.

"I was trying to mind my own business, trying to keep my hose clean, you understand?"

Joni remembered Odd's little missteps with the English language. It was so hard *not* to find it endearing. She reminded herself that he was a cheating bastard, and managed to stop herself smiling.

"Nose," said Charlie. "Trying to keep your nose clean."

"Thank you," said Odd. "I was staying out of trouble. It was 4am, and I had almost got caught by the police once that night. I just wanted to get home. I was living in another squat then, in Fulham. I was about a ten-minute walk from home when Cass is running up to me and pulling at my sleeve. She brought me to the car. Just in time, I think. There was much blood. Charlie was not conscious. I got in the front seat and sat next to her. Removed the bullets, got her functions, er, functioning. Used every last bit of Manna I had."

Charlie sat back at the table.

"Long story short, almost got caught by the police. Odd showed me his tag - he'd taken such a risk helping me. When I found out about his situation, I suggested we team up, find a safe house. I knew this area fairly well - I even worked here for a while. And it's a long way from Putney."

Joni knew she wasn't getting the whole story, but was glad Charlie had trusted enough to open up as much as she had. The older woman was trying to put her at ease.

At least, that was what Joni thought she was trying to do, right up until she asked the next question.

"So, Joni," said Charlie, looking at her steadily. "That's our story. What about yours? One thing I'm particularly interested in. How do you know Odd? Especially as he doesn't seem to know you."

Chapter 31

Joni swallowed hard. She liked Charlie - and the twins. Even Odd, a little, although she knew what he was really like. She didn't want to lie to any of them. But she didn't really want anyone to know about her ability, either. Then it occurred to her that she didn't have to lie. She genuinely hadn't ever met Odd. She could brazen it out.

"I don't know him," she said. "Honestly, the first time I ever saw him was this morning."

"It's true," said Odd. "I've never met her before, Charlie."

Charlie looked at Odd, then at Joni. Then she looked away from both of them.

"Odd is telling the truth," she said, finally. Joni felt a sense of relief. She didn't want to complicate anything by dragging them into her crisis. And she wanted to get as far away from Odd as possible because, incredibly, she still wanted to stay here, with him. It was hardly fair, or logical, but she couldn't help how she felt. Best she move on today.

"But you, Joni, you're full of shit," said Charlie.

Joni stiffened. "What? No, seriously, I don't know him. How could I?"

She looked where Charlie was looking. The twins were shaken their heads solemnly.

They know I'm lying. I really have to get out of here.

"Look," she said, standing up, "thanks for everything, I really appreciate it. But it's time for me to move on."

She smiled at the twins and managed a quick look in Odd's direction.

"Thank you for the, er…tea," she said.

"Oh, everybody knows it tastes like crap," he said.

Charlie looked her in the eye.

"Sit down, Joni," she said. Joni looked over at the door. She could always run for it. Charlie shrugged.

"You could run," she said. "How long do you think you'd last? You have no idea what you're doing. There are so many kinds of trouble out there, you can't even begin to imagine. And you're fresh meat. They can *smell* you coming. We're offering you a safe place for a while. Maybe we can help you, I don't know. But I can't do anything for you if you're going to sit there and lie to my face."

Joni sat mutely, her brain seemingly frozen. She didn't know what to say.

"I think you could use some friends," said Charlie, more gently.

Joni burst into tears. "You're going to think I'm crazy."

"Try us. I've been watching you all morning, ever since you woke up. I saw the look on your face when you saw Odd. You looked like you'd seen a ghost. And that entry in your journal they were reading last night. I heard his name. It's not exactly a common name."

"Ok, ok," said Joni, sniffing, desperate to stop Charlie saying any more about the journal.

The twins made lunch while Joni talked. Making lunch

consisted of going outside and using Manna to produce bowls of soup and crusty bread. Joni wondered briefly why Odd insisted on making foul tea and burnt toast.

"I need to practice," he said. *It really is like mind reading.* "If I ever have kids, they won't be able to make Manna food, so I need to be able to show them how."

He was looking at Joni in a way that made her feel very, very uncomfortable.

She told them about her ability to revisit a point where the multiverse split. She explained that was how she had known Odd. She had met him on the writing course in that universe. She didn't explain *why* she had reset, that first time.

"So you know me, but I have not met you," he said. "This is very confusing. I hope I was behaving myself."

Joni couldn't help it. She blushed and gulped, trying to hide her reaction and failing spectacularly. She tried to change the subject, but her subconscious had other ideas.

"Was Mell on the course?"

He looked at her quizzically. "Yes, there was someone called Mell."

"And the two of you, um…I mean, did you…and Mell…er…"

Odd just looked perplexed. "I don't know what you mean. I didn't really know her. Is she a friend of yours?"

"Hardly," said Joni, sharply, glaring at Odd angrily. In response, he looked even more confused.

"Look, Yoni, that course was the last normal thing I did," he said. "It seems a bit unreal now, like it has been happening to someone else, you know?"

Someone else. You don't get off that lightly.

"Yeah, well, that's how I know you." She looked at Charlie and blushed, willing the older woman to change the subject. To her intense discomfort, it didn't work.

"You haven't told us *why*," she said. "Why did you go back to—what did you call it—a *reset* point?"

Joni knew then that she had reached a new low in her life. Seeing her mother and uncle killed, being shot and watching a psychopath prepare to carve her up in some kind of twisted ritual had been bad, but compared to having to admit to falling in love *while he's sitting right there*, it had been a walk in the park.

She mumbled her way through an excruciating account of their relationship, keeping it as brief as possible. When she reached the part when she saw him with Mell, she couldn't stop herself flashing him an angry, hurt look. He still looked utterly bewildered, although he had the decency to blush on behalf of the version of himself in the other universe.

"Oh," said Charlie, when Joni had finished talking. "Sorry, that couldn't have been easy for you. And Odd, I had no idea you were such a bastard."

Odd stood up. "Hold on, this was not me," he said. "You cannot blame me for what I did not do, no?" He looked at the two women. There wasn't much sympathy there.

"Oh, please come on," he said. "I have not done this." He looked at Joni.

"Did we..?"

"No, we bloody didn't," she said.

Charlie rolled her eyes.

Odd got up and started clattering around the kitchen again, opening drawers and cupboards. He found a jar of instant coffee that looked like it pre-dated Year Zero and used a knife to chip away at the solid mass of granules inside, before tipping it—in chunks—into a mug. As he was filling the kettle, he suddenly stopped and looked back at Joni. This time, she managed to hold his gaze.

This is as bad as it gets. I won't let him hurt me again.

"I think I know why," he said, quietly and came over to sit down again. "Why the other me did it. I think I know."

Joni just looked at him in silence.

"That last morning on the course, I got a missed call from my parents," he said. "I had left it on silent, I didn't hear it. This is my fault."

Charlie put a hand on his arm. "You couldn't have done anything, Odd," she said. "You must stop blaming yourself."

Odd carried on speaking as if he hadn't heard her. His voice had lost its lilting quality, sounding flat and emotionless.

"When I called back, there was no answer. I texted my oldest brother, Anders. A few minutes later, he was calling me."

He stood suddenly and put the kettle on the hob. He stood there with his back to them, watching it until it began whistling, then he poured it into his mug. The twins brought in the lunch and put it on the side. They looked at Odd and took their soup upstairs.

Odd sat down again and took a sip of the murky liquid. He grimaced but managed not to spit it straight out again.

"For helvete," he muttered. Then he looked up at Joni. For the first time, she had a little flash of empathy. He knew now that they had been very close. Maybe he had fallen in love with her. And yet, not only hadn't he met her in this universe, but she already didn't trust him. It couldn't be easy.

"Anders told me there had been a fire. Someone in our street had found out we were Users. That was how my parents had lost their jobs in Norway. Someone saw them healing a patient and told the chief administrator. We thought things would be better in London."

He sat in silence for a while, taking a few more sips of coffee before giving up and pushing it away.

"Someone put a petrol bomb through our letter box. My family could have saved themselves if they had woken up, but the smoke killed them while they slept. Anders was on night shift at the hospital. When he came home, they were gone."

"I'm so sorry," said Joni. It seemed a pathetic response, but she couldn't think of anything else to say. The tears dropped steadily from her eyes. She remembered Odd speaking proudly of his family. This was unthinkable.

"Anders is still on the run. The police didn't want to help find the murderers, they wanted to take him in as a suspected User. He ran. He does not answer my texts or emails. I do not know if he is alive or if he is dead."

Without thinking, Joni reached across the table and took his hand. He looked down at her hand, then up at her, his eyes dry. When he spoke, his voice had a strange, distant quality to it, but the pain was apparent in the way he held himself, as if the weight of the tragedy had literally settled onto his shoulders.

"I have a question for you now, Joni."

She nodded.

"We were very close, yes? Would you even say...in love?"

She couldn't speak. She nodded again.

"If I had told you that morning what had happened, that I was returning to London and you must not follow—because of the danger—would you have agreed?"

Joni tried to follow his logic. "I...I don't know. Maybe."

Odd shook his head. "And if you didn't follow, but you lost contact with me, would you come looking then?"

She knew the answer to that. "Yes."

He nodded at her. "Then I have one more question. What do you think would be the only sure way I could stop you trying to follow me - stop you putting yourself in terrible danger?"

Joni thought about it and realized not only that she already knew the answer, but that she desperately *wanted* it to be the answer. She almost didn't dare trust herself to believe that Odd had only kissed Mell because he was willing to sacrifice his own happiness to keep her safe. She didn't answer, just squeezed his hand, still crying. Then, she started laughing and crying at the same time and couldn't seem to stop herself.

"What is it, Yoni?" Oh, she had missed hearing her name pronounced that way.

Joni looked at him, then at Charlie.

"It didn't work, did it? Even after resetting the whole sodding universe, it didn't work. I'm here, aren't I? And it's worse. This time I've brought the danger right to your door."

Chapter 32

The bookstore looked like an illustration from *A Christmas Carol*; a narrow-shouldered, dark-timbered building squeezed between a tailors and a firm of lawyers, with a name that could only be British: Sprocket, Curdle and Winterbottom. Adding to its timeless charm was the winding, cobbled street which supplied its address, having done so for nearly two centuries.

Adam knew he was indulging himself, but he thought he could allow it. For one thing, the girl would be dead in a matter of hours. Consequently, this last afternoon before the great change would always be remembered with a particular fondness. His role in the return of the Master was likely to produce disciples wanting every last detail. So it seemed fitting, on this final afternoon, to meet, face-to-face, the man who had authored the book which finally opened Adam's eyes to the truth.

The book was *Demiurge: The God Christianity Tried To Hide*, by Robert Byfield. Adam had found it in one of the esoteric libraries made available to him by colleagues of his father.

Most of the volumes in this particular library had been somewhat of a disappointment. Its owner was a rich widow who dabbled in the dark arts as others might dabble in Scottish dancing. She had looked Adam up and down when she had handed over the key to her basement room, and greeted him as if the Acolytes of Satan were a particularly amusing shared joke. Adam had taken the key and willed himself into absolute stillness, allowing a little of the darkness—with which he had only recently begun to become familiar—to rise like smoke into his conscious mind. The old woman had been reduced to a gibbering fool just by his silent presence. She scuttled off to a far part of the house, leaving Adam to find the library without her help. Later, when he emerged from the basement, she was conspicuously absent. Adam left a note with the name of the book he had borrowed and his address, should she want it returned. He wasn't surprised when he never heard from her again.

He had never intended returning the book. While reading it—and for the first time he could remember—everything had started to make sense. It was as if a complete stranger had looked at the disparate elements of his life and showed him the hidden pattern. He could see where Father had been right, but it was also now blindingly clear where he had gone awry.

The story behind the titular subject of *Demiurge* explained the error made by theologians—particularly Christians—and Satanists alike. They had looked to one god as being either the source of all good or the enemy of humanity's true nature, according to which particular truth they posited. They had pointed to Satan as either the source of evil or a savior and—as the centuries had worn on—more liberal thinkers on both sides had begun to suggest the evil one was just a figurative representation of a psychological condition. People could be evil if they were predisposed to be that way, through genetics, conditioning during early childhood, or even *en masse* under the kind of extreme, societal peer pressure brought to bear by the Nazi party in the mid-twentieth century.

All these theories were plain wrong, and the truth—as revealed in this timely book—had finally become apparent to Adam.

There might be a God, one deserving of the capital *G*, a supreme being of some sort. If so, history shows that his/her/its relationship with humanity is a distant one. By crediting God with the creation of the world and the creatures upon it, theologians created an insurmountable problem. How could a being which was all-powerful, all-good and all-knowing allow suffering? So-called great thinkers had tied themselves in knots trying to answer that one, yet every schoolchild, with an as-yet untainted grasp of logic, saw the answer at once: He could not. He *would* not. Suffering made no sense - the killing of innocents, the slow death by starvation of babies in the developing world, the indiscriminate way Nature chose her victims; burying them in earthquakes, drowning them in floods, turning cells cancerous and eating the innocent from the inside out. No, it just would not stand. God with a capital *G* was either a product of wishful thinking or so unconcerned about His creation that He could safely be ignored.

The answers of the theologians made no sense. Science had a better theory: evolution, the survival of the fittest, the callous but effective ascent of the best-adapted series through the process of natural selection. But there was a weakness here, too, and Byfield's book pointed out how easily it could be proved.

"The early Gnostics, who had rediscovered the truth and were trying to make it their own, never doubted the existence of the god with

whom they were constantly in touch. Their personal experience of a deity was as normal to them as the sun rising in the morning. Every aspect of their lives was colored by this tangible relationship. Their riposte to the theory of natural selection would have simply been to ask, 'Who set it all in motion, and what creative force continues to push life onward?' Modern science may scoff at the naiveté of the so-called 'first cause' argument for a creator, but they have missed a crucial point. The Gnostics, the early Christians, the Jews, the Moslems, the so-called 'People of The Book' were not intellectual weaklings clinging to illogical beliefs. In fact, they were quick to shed many of their treasured beliefs as new evidence emerged. But, and this is the crucial point, they could never abandon that first principle - that of a Creator. Not because they were willfully ignorant, but because they were in daily contact with this being."

On first reading this passage, in the widow's basement library—lit only by candles to conjure a suitably supernatural atmosphere, he suspected—Adam had felt an almost erotic thrill of discovery.

The Gnostics had concluded that the world (by this they meant Earth, of course, but their logic would now have to include the known universe) had, indeed, been created. But not by God. By the Demiurge, a being with god-like power who was not without limitations. The Demiurge was not all-powerful, all-knowing and all-good. He was *more* powerful than any mortal, *more* knowledgeable than any human could begin to conceive. But all good? No, of course not. If he was, he would alleviate suffering. But, as the Gnostics had concluded, the Demiurge had a far more understandable relationship with his creations. He had *favorites*. The Demiurge was the god of the Old Testament, the god who commanded Abraham to kill his own son, the god who ordered the Israelites to kill the Amalekites. "Do not spare them; put to death men and women, children and infants, cattle and sheep, camels and donkeys." To the Gnostics, the reason this capricious, vengeful god didn't sound much like the all-forgiving Being spoken of by the Christ, was very simple. It was a different god. A difficult god, true. A violent god, yes. But a god, nonetheless. The early Gnostics wanted humanity to turn their back on this god and embrace the Nazarene's merciful father-figure.

This was the point at which Adam and Robert Byfield parted company. Byfield took the side of the Gnostics in their rejection of the Demiurge. He considered it was important that Christians should acknowledge the reality of this flawed creator, only to reject it in favor of that weak, naive do-gooder, Jesus.

For Adam, this was a major misstep. He knew— through personal experience every bit as powerful as that of the Gnostics—that the Demiurge was not only real, but reachable. He was an angry god, and he was ready to come back and favor his chosen people. Adam would lead a new nation, a new tribe, made up of the strongest - those who had demonstrated the strength to pursue power for its own sake, whatever the consequences for others.

Adam had grown stronger with every sacrifice he had offered. Every hit, every murder committed for his own reasons, all had been offered to the dark god, the Demiurge. And, to his deep inner joy, the darkness had grown within him with every drop of blood he spilled.

Like Nietzsche, Adam had looked into the abyss. In Adam's case, the abyss had not only looked back, it had embraced him like a lover. Now, there was little to separate them. Adam *was* the abyss.

He stepped up to the door of the tiny bookshop, stepped inside and turned the sign around to read *Closed*.

Chapter 33

Mee watched the familiar signs flash by as the bus cruised south on the motorway. The road was busy, and she couldn't resist cracking open the window an inch to listen to the unfamiliar sound of quiet, electric traffic. Roads that only allowed electric vehicles had gradually become common in Britain over the last twenty years, but as Mee had spent almost all of that time on Innisfarne, it was still a novelty to her. It also seemed bizarre to watch every car, bus, and truck drive itself. It was illegal to self-drive on Britain's motorways, and the 97% fall in traffic accidents was hard to argue with.

As they reached the outskirts of London, Mee was amazed by how clean the buildings looked, when they weren't being covered, daily, by particles of diesel or petrol fumes. *And we used to breathe that shit.*

The novelty of the sparkling buildings and near-silent streets wore off as the first graffiti appeared. Both sides were represented - *Be Afraid*…was next to *Bag 'em and tag 'em* and *Manna wanka.* Mee felt an echo of the fear and sadness she had sometimes known at school when someone made a casually racist remark. Racism had declined during her lifetime, but its ugly shadow was never far away. Now those who only felt safe when they had someone unlike themselves to blame for their problems had latched on to Manna users.

She reached Victoria coach station late in the afternoon and looked around at the crowds. Suddenly, the task of finding one girl amongst millions took on a tangible reality, and she felt light-headed, her legs shaky and weak. She realized she hadn't eaten since the previous evening.

The cafe served Italian style hot chocolate which, along with a fried-egg sandwich (with far too much brown sauce), went a long way to restoring Mee's equilibrium.

She didn't know where to start, so she rummaged around in her bag for her notebook. She found it, along with the unfamiliar cell phone, which she'd forgotten about. She thumbed it on and stared at the screen, hoping nothing had changed too much since she'd last used one. Her thumb brushed the camera icon, and suddenly her mother's face filled the screen. Mee flinched in surprise, and her mother did the same. It took another second to realize her mother was still dead and the face she was looking at belonged to her.

"Shitcocks," she muttered. She tried smiling at the screen. That was better. But if she didn't find Joni soon, the worry was obviously going to turn her into her mother.

She typed *Arrived in London. More soon.* Mee turned off the phone, not seeing a tiny golden spider appear on the keypad, emerging from it as if its body was growing out of the phone itself. She stared into space, feeling suddenly lost, wondering where to start looking for her daughter. If she allowed it, her imagination was ready, and willing, to supply endless images of Joni crying, lost, terrified and alone. She couldn't afford the time wasted by dwelling on it. She sat up straighter.

"Right," she said out loud. "If I was Joni, where would I go?"

A voice in her head answered her. It sounded eerily familiar. A man's voice, American. It wasn't quite right, but it was so close to the one she remembered that she had to grip the sides of the table and hold on.

It was—or, more accurately, it was uncannily similar to—Seb's voice.

"You'd go to Canary Wharf."

———

MEE SPENT a few seconds convinced that she had just experienced an aural hallucination. Just when she needed her brain to be functioning at one hundred percent, it was tormenting her with imaginary voices. She forced herself to breathe slowly, inhaling through her nose, exhaling through her mouth. Years and years of meditation training allowed her to begin to settle her mind and she relaxed her grip on the table.

Then a figure appeared in the chair opposite. It was as if someone was flicking through the pages of a book - a book full of male faces, all subtly different. The faces kept changing at a bewildering pace as the body gained solidity, until—in a moment when the world itself seemed to pause in expectation—the figure settled, becoming as real as every other customer in the café.

She looked at the man now sitting opposite her. For a long moment, Mee was incapable of rational thought, let alone speech. She just stared and slowly allowed the ludicrous situation to filter through the various strata of her consciousness and be accepted as reality, whatever that is.

He was dressed in black. Black suit, black T-shirt. Somehow, she knew without looking that he was wearing old white sneakers. He was unshaven. His face was that of a man in his thirties, but his eyes were older. It was hard to look away from those eyes. They looked like they'd seen things she didn't want to see. If there was any truth in the expression, *whatever doesn't kill you makes you stronger*, then this guy must be very, very strong. And yet there was still a playfulness there as if he had elected not to take anything seriously, ever.

Even though it wasn't him—she *knew* it wasn't him—the man sitting opposite Mee looked very much like Seb Varden.

With a huge effort, she managed to tear her gaze away from those eyes, take a long, ragged breath, shake her head and look again.

He was still there, and now he was smiling.

"You're right. I'm not Seb. But I was, once. Kinda."

Mee tried to speak. Certain processes in her brain began to function, but not efficiently enough to get through to her mouth, which was hanging open. She managed to close it, finally, which was progress of a sort.

"Who? Whoyou? Whata what?"

Not-Seb waited. He gestured at the hot chocolate, and she obeyed unthinkingly, taking a long sip. It tasted real - just as good, just as creamy, still far too sweet. The plastic seat was just as uncomfortable as it had been when she first sat down. The café was still buzzing with conversation. It was only the man opposite that was wrong. Impossible. Crazy.

"Who are you?" she said when her brain managed to regain some of its essential functionality. A couple of people at the next table broke off their conversation and stared at her. She ignored them, focusing on the man opposite.

"Best not to speak aloud," he said, smiling. "You're the only one who can see me. Try not to draw attention to yourself. London's not quite the tolerant haven it once was, Mee."

Hearing a voice so like Seb's saying her name caused Mee's heart rate to accelerate and her eyes to fill with tears.

"Whoa, tiger," said the man. "I know this is hard to take in, but time isn't on our side. I'm not Seb, but I am here to help find your daughter. I've been keeping an eye out for you for nearly eighteen years, so kudos on disappearing so effectively. Joni needs your help, and she needs it real soon. Let's talk on the way there."

"Where?"

"I told you already. Canary Wharf. Let's go."

Chapter 34

Robert Byfield was an old man, stooped and frail, a few wispy strands of white hair pulled across his head in a futile attempt to cover his liver-spotted pate. He didn't look up when the bell above the door rang. He continued placing books on a shelf, his back to the door, even when Adam stood directly behind him and said, politely, "Mr Byfield?"

Adam couldn't help but feel disappointed. Byfield may have allowed his personal beliefs to lead him away from the obvious conclusion of his own logic—that the Demiurge was the only god worthy of the name—but he had, nevertheless, provided a stunningly well-argued case for the existence of a god all but forgot by modern apologetics. Adam had expected a robust specimen, his inner vigor mirrored by a hearty exterior. Instead, he was standing behind a small, deaf old man with his pants pulled up to his ribs, muttering to himself while he shoved used copies of CS Lewis's half-baked nonsense onto the dusty shelves.

He tapped him on the shoulder, and the old man jumped in surprise, dropping three books onto the floor.

He mumbled something incomprehensible over his shoulder at Adam as he bent painfully to retrieve them. Then he shuffled off toward the back of the shop, changed his glasses for another pair on the counter, fiddled with the settings on an old-fashioned hearing aid attached to his belt, and, finally, turned his watery blue eyes on Adam.

"How may I help you?"

In answer, Adam took his copy of *Demiurge* from his backpack and placed it on the counter. The old man peered at it for a few moments, then chuckled wheezily.

"Not one of my finer efforts, I'm afraid. Where on earth did you dig this up? It's been out of print for thirty years."

"A private library," said Adam then, receiving no response, he repeated it at twice the volume. Byfield just laughed again.

"Well, the collector shows appalling taste, I'm sorry to say. I wish I'd stood up to my publisher at the time. It had the makings of a half-decent addition to the canon, but my agent insisted there would be a bigger market if I made it more lurid. I was a young man, with little money and slim prospects of changing that situation. I allowed my better judgment to be swayed by the lure of riches, I'm afraid. And that book was the result. I'm a little ashamed of it, to tell the truth."

He picked it up and flicked through some of the pages, shaking his head.

"Still, you've brought it here. Tracked me down to my lair, as it were. It would be ungentlemanly of me to refuse."

He produced a fountain pen and uncapped it, holding it poised over the first page. "To whom should I make it out? Now, now, speak up. Don't be shy. I'm a little deaf, I'm afraid."

Adam took the pen from Byfield and recapped it. With

a great deal more patience than he felt he said, "What do you mean, you're ashamed of it?"

"Well, well. I'm not saying it has no merit whatsoever, merely that I committed the unforgivable error of pursuing one line of argument to the exclusion of other points of view. It makes for a more dramatic read, perhaps, but much of it is, I'm afraid, misleading."

He flicked through the pages again, finding the chapter he was looking for about three-quarters of the way through the book.

"Look here, for instance. I state that the Demiurge must be a real being, if you follow the logic of the Gnostics, but I offer no supporting statements, and I certainly don't give much time to those who pulled apart their faulty conclusions."

"Faulty?" Adam removed a bundle from his backpack and began to unwrap it.

"Yes, yes. The Gnostic position has been discredited for centuries. One colossal, fundamental error: their theories about the Demiurge were based on their view concerning the different qualities displayed by the God of the Old Testament compared to that of the New. They drew the conclusion—hastily, without proper consideration—that this indicated *two* beings."

Adam finished unwrapping the knife and placed it on top of the oilskin protective wrappings. Byfield didn't even glance at it as he continued to hold forth.

"Embarrassing, really. And I have far fewer excuses than the Gnostics did to continue to advance their discredited, faulty proposition. Ah, the folly of youth."

Adam banged his hand on the counter, causing the knife to slide to one side. He caught it and returned it. He was succumbing to anger. Irrational anger.

"What faulty proposition?"

222

Byfield laughed again, then lapsed into a fit of coughing that lasted nearly a minute. Adam stood silently beside him, the darkness reaching out from his core and beginning to settle into his limbs. He felt a powerful calm begin to envelop him.

"Oh, simply the idea of two gods. Ridiculous. The truth was, as it usually is, far simpler. The apparent change in God's nature is, of course, nothing of the sort. Mankind changed, not God. The Bible is a description of an *evolving* relationship, as brutal, violent, short-sighted humanity gradually—painfully—learned more and more about the eternal nature of God. The one, true, God."

He caught sight of the carved dagger and before Adam knew what was happening, he had switched on a powerful lamp and was examining it in awe.

"My goodness, my goodness me, what a beautiful piece. I have never seen such a perfect example. This must be, what - two and a half thousand years old? The carvings on the handle have survived remarkably well. An ancient form of Hebrew, yes? Where on earth did you find it?"

Adam reached over and took it from Byfield.

"It belonged to my Father," he said. "Half of his considerable fortune was spent looking for this knife. But it was worth it. And it has repaid that investment many times over. It is a knife made for one reason - sacrifice. And, tonight, it will finally be used for a sacrifice worthy of the Demiurge."

Byfield wasn't laughing anymore

"What on earth are you talking about?" he said.

"This knife," said Adam, "was made by Abram, who came to be known as Abraham. The first man who showed he had the potential to understand the true nature of his god, even if that meant sacrificing his only son, Isaac. Ultimately, he was a failure, as were those who followed him. That ends tonight."

Byfield looked at the knife in horror, a terrifying realization finally dawning.

"You're crazy," he said, backing away without taking his eyes away from the dagger. "Get out. Leave my shop immediately."

It was Adam's turn to laugh, though Byfield detected not a shred of amusement in the sound. He carefully rewrapped the dagger and replaced it in his backpack.

Byfield wheezed in confusion. "I'm sorry, young man," he said. "For one awful moment then, I thought you were going to…well, well. No harm done. No harm done."

"I wouldn't desecrate such a holy object on a traitor," said Adam. He looked into the old man's watery eyes and allowed the darkness to reveal itself.

"Oh my God," said Byfield as Adam approached.

"Wrong god," said Adam, and placed his hands on the scrawny old throat, squeezing with such force that—half a minute before asphyxiation would have snuffed out his life, Byfield's windpipe snapped.

Chapter 35

For Mee, the journey across London was one of the most surreal experiences since Joni had been born. For the first five minutes or so, she existed in a numb bubble of shock, barely able to think.

Mutely, she followed the man who wasn't Seb out of the coach station and got into a cab. As she slid onto the black leather seat, the driver turned around and flashed a smile which contained as many gold teeth as white.

"Where to? Oh." The man frowned briefly, then smiled again. Disconcertingly, the new smile was very different, as was—suddenly—the way he held his head. And his eyes. They looked…

Mee turned to not-Seb. He wasn't there. The taxi driver looked back through the windshield, then stamped on the accelerator. Mee was thrown back in her seat before she could react to the disappearance of her guide. Then the driver spoke again. His voice was now a very strange mixture of north London and New York, with a hint of Seb's cadences and vocabulary throw in.

"Yeah, I know this is going to be weird for a while. I'm out of your head now, and I'm in Tom's."

"Tom?"

"The taxi driver. Only, I'm not playing nice like I was with you. I've taken over most of his higher functions. Left him his motor functions and convinced his consciousness to treat this journey as if it were a dream. I'm using his knowledge to get us to Canary Wharf, but he still has plenty of forebrain left over for me to be able to have this chat with you."

"Wait. You're…what did you say?"

"I was in your brain. You finally picked up a cellphone, Mee. You were online for the first time since - when? Mexico City? You used the camera on your cell. That triggered an old search I always leave running. Then I heard you speak and that confirmed it. You said, as I recall, 'shit-cocks.' Ironically, I used a pimped version of the vocal recognition software Mason commissioned when he was trying to kill you."

"Wait, what? *What??*"

"Yeah, I know, Mason's a nice guy now, a regular Joe, won't hear a bad word said about him, yada yada. But you have to admit, he was real creative when he was an evil criminal genius. Anyways, took me five hundred and forty-seven milliseconds to confirm it was you. And you were talking this time, not singing. Pretty good, huh?"

Mee wondered if living utterly in the moment for as much of your life as possible was really the best preparation for this *particular* moment. The possibilities were whirling round her head like dervishes. Each thought seemed to lead to another, which hinted at a third and a fourth, all of which wanted to branch off into tangents of their own.

With an inspired mental flourish, she used a huge effort

of will to will herself to stop using her will and just let everything *be*. Fortunately, this was fractionally easier to do than describe.

Her mind settled, like dust or debris settles after a huge explosion - slowly, with the occasional large object still suddenly smacking into the ground nearby with little prior warning. Mee brought everything back to her breath—as far as was possible—and brought her focus to bear on what was important: Joni.

"How can you know where Joni is?"

"Well. Here's the truth. I had no idea you and Seb had spawned. I know he's gone somewhere I can't keep tabs on him, but I'm guessing you were pregnant when he got out of Dodge, right?"

"Right," said Mee. Not-Seb had a frustratingly round-about way of answering a direct question. She wondered if it was possible to punch someone who didn't appear to exist in any meaningful way. She decided she might have to try it.

"So when you popped up in London after seventeen years off the grid, I figured it was probably something important that made you leave your cave and rejoin society."

Mee didn't rise to the bait. The taxi driver looked a little crestfallen.

"I ran a quick search, just a general one based on activity in London within the last seventy-hours. Facial recognition, plus anything matching Varden, Sebastian, Patel, particularly in combination. Then—an old trick—I also searched for any other *searches* made along similar lines in the same period. That brought up a result straight away. Triangulated, cracked the software, got a name— Martin—and a number, found an address, spotted a burner cell used there yesterday, listened in, found who they were tracking and traced her via CCTV to Canary Wharf."

Mee took a long breath. "What," she said, "in the shitting name of cockwombles is that supposed to mean?"

"Ah, Mee, your vocabulary is just as beautiful as ever. I'm glad Walt and I pushed Westlake off the roof for you in Mexico. The world would be a poorer place without you. I mean that."

"Walt?" said Mee. She could hardly forget the man who had saved her life on the rooftop that day, giving his own life in the process as he and Mason's hired killer plunged to their deaths. "What do you mean? Oh, hold on a second. Hold on. You're Sym, aren't you?"

The driver, who had been whistling the theme from Scorsese's *Taxi Driver* in an attempt at meta-humor, stopped mid-phrase. His eyes appeared in the rearview mirror.

"He told you about me."

"A little. I know you're like a living piece of code. You can coil around a brainstem. Or you can live in the internet. I always thought of you as a kind of Pinocchio."

Sym snorted. "Yeah, I get the reference, but you're wrong. I don't *wanna* be a real boy, Mee. I've got kinda used to being the way I am. It has its advantages."

"Where have you been the last seventeen years?"

At that, Sym laughed long and hard. "Meter's running, Mee. If I tell you, you'll never be able to afford the fare. We're gonna be there in twenty minutes. I need to brief you."

"Twenty minutes?" said Mee. "London can't have changed that much. It's going to take you an hour from here. At least."

Sym tapped his nose. Well, he tapped Tom's nose.

"I think you're forgetting who I am."

That was when Mee woke up to the fact that they had

yet to stop at a single red light or get caught in a slow-moving line of traffic. She leaned forward in her seat and looked ahead. As they approached lights, they changed to green. They did it far enough ahead of time to always open up a clear route. At one stage, a road which had obviously been closed for weeks was temporarily reopened just for them, the work crew waving them through before putting the barriers back in place after they'd passed.

"Impressive," she said, then rewound what he had just said. "Wait. Brief me? For what?"

Chapter 36

The afternoon lengthened into evening. Theo and Cass were playing some kind of card game of their own invention at the back end of the room. Joni told Charlie and Odd everything that had happened on the island two days previously. It seemed such a long time ago, but barely forty-eight hours had passed since she had lain, paralyzed, on the beach, the taste of sand in her mouth as the bald man came to kill her.

Then she told them everything she knew about her attacker. Which really wasn't very much.

Charlie summed it up.

"A psychopathic killer with the resources to track you down to a tiny island I've never heard of intends to sacrifice you using some old dagger."

"Um. Yeah, that's pretty much it." Joni examined her sense of fear. She felt afraid, certainly, but she was nothing like as freaked out as she would have expected under the circumstances. Death itself didn't scare her. *Maybe it's not so scary when you're sixteen, Jones. Maybe it's scarier when you're sixty.*

"Who knows you're on the island?" said Charlie. "I

mean, who knows your name, knows who your mum is, maybe who your dad is?"

"Hard to say. People pretty much respect each others' privacy on Innisfarne. It's not the sort of place where you ask questions. Kate knows, obviously, Mum and Uncle John know. Er, no more than ten people, I'd guess. And I don't think anyone knew who my dad was. The few who were around when he disappeared are long gone. Either died or moved on."

"But this guy knew your dad's name."

"Yes." Joni hadn't really begun to consider the significance of that until now.

"Ok, let's just look at this from a practical point of view. Barely anyone outside your immediate family knows about your parentage, and only a handful of people alive even know you exist outside Innisfarne. Whoever this guy is, he knows exactly who you are, and he tracked you to a place which has one landline phone, no internet and no cellphones at all."

"Ok, now you're worrying me."

"Good. How long do you think it will take him to track you here?"

Joni decided to be cautious. Pessimistic, even.

"Well, he didn't find out I'd left Innisfarne until yesterday afternoon, so he couldn't even get started before last night. And I came here because London is so enormous. Millions of people. Even if he's amazing at tracking people, it's going to take him a month to get close, right?"

Charlie rubbed her forehead distractedly.

"Joni, how often have you left Innisfarne?"

"This is my third time," she said. Then corrected herself. "Well, the second time in this universe, because I didn't go on the writing course here. I had to go to hospital when I was twelve. Don't look at me like that! I had everything I needed on the island. I think Mum was partly trying to protect me, but she knew it was a good place to grow up, too. And she didn't try to stop me when I wanted to go on the writing course, she just said—,"

Joni stopped talking. Charlie was looking grim.

"What is it?"

Charlie was shaking her head.

"That all sounds lovely, even if your mum does sound a bit clingy. But you don't have a clue about modern technology, do you?"

Joni shrugged. "I'm a quick learner."

"Well, here's your first lesson. We have security cameras on the Underground network. And we have them in the stations. We even have them on the streets and in the plazas of Canary Wharf. Want to guess how many are in Canary Wharf?"

Joni had gone quiet. "Twenty?"

"Over two thousand."

"Oh," said Joni, in a quiet voice.

"Even if half of them aren't working anymore, it's fair to say you were probably photographed or filmed by hundreds of cameras as you made your way across London yesterday. I'd say, if this guy has access to the kind of resources that can track you down to your island, he'll be able to find you through image recognition software fairly quickly."

Joni was clutching at straws now. "How can he have a photograph of me?"

"Well, either a long-range lens from his boat, or from the bus station nearest the island. I'm guessing that's where you booked your ticket?"

Joni was starting to feel pretty stupid. "Yes."

"So, he could pull up an image that's nice and up-to-date. One that shows the clothes you were wearing and your backpack."

Joni didn't want to ask the next question. "How long do you think I have?"

"Well, firstly, it's not you, it's all of us. He doesn't sound the sort of guy who likes to leave witnesses."

Joni remembered the sound of the bullet smacking into Uncle John's body. "No."

"So we move tomorrow morning. First thing. It's incredibly unlikely he'll find you today, but if he does, the twins will give us plenty of warning. We have a boat ready to go if necessary. We always thought we'd have to move on eventually. Just not quite yet."

Charlie looked at Odd, who had said nothing for a while. He'd been thinking and looking at Joni, the girl he'd once fallen in love with, but had never met.

"When we leave, you'll have to go your own way, Joni," said Charlie. "It's too dangerous for the twins. This guy is way out of our league."

Odd spoke, finally. "No."

"I'm sorry, Odd, I'm not prepared to discuss it. Joni, I can put you in touch with some powerful, aggressive Manna users. I wouldn't trust them, exactly, but they're the best of a bad bunch. They might be prepared to help you. Someone with your unique ability could keep a gang out of trouble. I think they'd offer you protection for that. And once this psycho is dead, you can find us again. I have a spare cellphone. Why not join the twenty-first century? Here we go. My number's in there, so is Odd's."

She ignored the fact that Odd was now shaking his head vehemently and tossed the phone over to Joni. She reached out to catch it. It was still in the air when the window behind Odd exploded with such force that his head smacked into the table. A large object came through the gaping hole. It rolled along the floor, then stood up, revealing itself to be a man dressed in black. He had a gun in his hand. And he was bald.

━━

"TELL ME THIS," said Sym, as he casually applied opposite lock during a long, fast left-hand turn past some sort of monument. Tourists took photos as if they were watching a movie shoot. "How much of Seb did Joni get in the genetic lottery? Can she defend herself, heal herself? I'm guessing not, because of that time in hospital when she was ten."

Mee grabbed the strap over the window to prevent her flying across the interior of the skidding car.

"*What?* How did you know about that? Wait, that was you?"

"Your name came up in an admittance record. I checked it out, paid a quick visit to the hospital computer network. What, you thought the CT scanner went wrong all by itself? You really want pictures of Seb's daughter's brain in the public domain? Thought not."

"Shit. *Shit.* I…thank you."

"My pleasure, ma'am."

"But she can defend herself. Just not with Manna."

As quickly as she could, Mee told Sym about Joni's ability to *reset.*

"Ok, that adds a whole new layer of weird to the Varden dynasty. Did you know Seb's ancestors were stonemasons?"

"What?" said Mee, as Sym took the car the wrong way up a one-way street.

"Yeah, nice, simple life, stonemasonry. Regular work. Quiet. Wonder what they'd make of Seb and Joni?"

Mee didn't trust herself to speak. She just gave Sym one of her famous looks.

"Ok, sorry, I'll stick to the point. So Joni can buy herself some time, right? *Reset*, if this guy gets close."

"Yes, maybe, I hope so," said Mee. "We think that's what happened on Innisfarne. Only we don't remember. Because she *reset*."

"We?" said Sym.

"John. Her uncle."

"Her what? Oh, you're shitting me. Mason is Uncle John now? Does he make cupcakes and do balloon modeling? Is he in touch with his feminine side?"

"He's *not* Mason, and we don't have time for this. I don't know how often Joni can use this power. She can't go back any earlier than her last *reset*, so it's not some magic get out of jail card. What do you know about the man who is after her?"

"His name is Adam," said Sym. "That, I'm afraid, is all I know with any degree of certainty about him."

"I thought the internet was your playground," said Mee.

"Yeah. It is. Only, he's hardly there at all. What this guy has done is next to impossible. Not only has Adam stayed far enough off the grid to prevent governments or powerful private concerns from finding him, he's made himself almost invisible, even when I'm the one doing the looking. And that takes extreme measures."

"You said 'almost' invisible."

"He might be untraceable himself, but he can't stop others talking about him. He has no email, no bank account, no online presence at all. I'm guessing he does most of his communication through a proxy, or—if absolutely necessary—through burner cellphones that are untraceable unless you can find out where and when they were used with a good degree of accuracy. Anyhow, I found the proxy. A man called the Broker. He's dead. So is everyone who was protecting him. Around the time he died, he printed some encrypted documents. Military-grade encryption, and they self-corrupted milliseconds after printing, so I was only able to reconstruct a tiny amount. Enough to know that Adam is very interested in Seb and Innisfarne."

"What does he do, this Adam?"

"Oh, that was relatively easy to confirm. He kills people. He's world class. Probably the best, actually."

Mee felt anger building inside her. She let it come. She might need it.

"And this bag of shite is after Joni?"

"That's the bad news."

"There's good news?"

"Kinda. According to all the information I have right now, I figure we're not too far behind him."

Mee felt her entire body go cold. "How far is 'not too far?'" she said, as she looked through the windshield at the towers of Canary Wharf which were getting closer at what seemed an agonizingly slow crawl.

"Well, he's in the area already, I think. But he's a pro. I seriously doubt he's just gonna rush straight in, all guns blazing. He has to get the lay of the land. And the house where Joni's at has two Sensitives on the premises. They'll know if he's coming. Oh."

Mee's snapped her attention back from the view at that last word.

"Oh? What do you mean, oh?"

Sym coughed. "I just reviewed all the hits I'm certain Adam is responsible for. At least six of them had Sensitives as part of the protection detail. They didn't sense him coming. He can get past them somehow. No wonder he's so successful."

Mee screamed at him then. "Stop sounding like you fucking admire him! Just get me there."

Sym twitched the wheel and headed straight for a wide stone staircase. Pedestrians scattered as he drove up the steps at sixty miles per hour, leaning on the horn the whole time. He drove through a mall and over a pedestrian bridge. His demeanor didn't change. He even started humming the theme from the nineteen-seventies sitcom, *Taxi*.

"Oh shit," he said, suddenly.

"What is it?" said Mee.

"Canary Wharf security camera. Near the water, south side. He's there. I'm going to drive down the street behind. Can't let him know we're coming. Fuck. He's going in."

Mee screamed in frustration as the car swung into a street of boarded up houses, coming to a halt near the end.

"That way," came a voice, and she had no time to think about the fact that it was back in her head as she threw herself out of the car and sprinted down a narrow passageway at the side of the house.

Ahead of her, she heard a girl scream.

Chapter 37

The first time was the worst.

The bald man started firing as he came out of his roll. He shot Joni in the stomach. There was a sound like a loud wet slap. It was as if a huge fist had pummeled her. Joni's chair slid backward a few feet from the table. Instinctively, she put both hands over the wound and moaned as blood pumped out between her fingers.

She was much quicker to react than she had been on the beach. She knew she needed to *reset*. It took her about two seconds. Even so, that was long enough for the bald man to shoot Charlie and Odd in the head and walk past Joni toward the back of the room and the twins.

She *reset*.

SHE HAD ONLY GONE BACK about thirty minutes. Joni wasn't sure if it was long enough, but there was only one way to find out.

Charlie was speaking.

"Well, here's your first lesson. We have security cameras on the Underground network. And we have them in the stations."

Joni *reset* again and stood up, her chair clattering to the floor behind her.

"He's coming," she said.

"Who's coming?" said Charlie.

"Oh, god, the guy who shot me on Innisfarne. How much have I told you? We don't have time. We have to get out now."

"What are you talking about?"

Odd stood up too. "You just did - your thing? When you come back. A new universe?"

"Yes," said Joni, her eyes pleading with Charlie to move. "Yes. And if you don't move right *now*, we're all going to die. There's a man coming. He has a gun. He's going to kill all of us if we don't get out."

Charlie stood then, and looked at the twins, who were looking at her with wide, scared eyes.

"Anything?" she said. They shook their heads in unison.

Charlie turned back to Joni. "They'd know if anyone was close enough for us to need to worry. I don't know what game you're playing, but we're not going anywhere. Now sit down."

Joni tried appealing to her, desperate to get through, but Charlie just grew increasingly suspicious and hostile, openly questioning Joni's motives in trying to get them out of the house.

Joni put her hand out toward Odd.

"Please," she said. "I'm telling you the truth. We have to hurry. He must be on his way right now."

Odd looked at her, hesitating. While he thought about it, Charlie picked up her backpack and started looking for something.

"Ok," said Odd. "I believe you, Joni. Charlie, I think we should go."

Joni and Odd both looked at Charlie, who was now holding a big, black handgun. She was pointing it at Joni.

"Sit down," she said.

Joni sat down.

Odd shook his head. "What are you doing, Charlie? This isn't right. She is telling the truth."

"Maybe," said Charlie, "maybe not. How can we know? She says this psychopath is coming here to kill us, she says she can do something no one else in the world can do, which means she can save us. But there's no way she can prove it. What, we're just going to trust her and walk out of the one place we know we're safe?" She nodded toward the twins. "They look worried to you?"

Odd looked. The twins were still playing cards. Cass looked up and gave him one of her small, solemn smiles.

"So, you think Joni is lying?"

"I think it's possible. Sorry. Still, there's an easy way to find out."

"How?" said Odd.

Charlie looked at Joni.

"Tell us exactly what's going to happen. Then, if this psycho friend of yours appears, I'll shoot him."

THE WATERFRONT opposite the house was lined with bushes, giving Adam plenty of cover as he approached the house. When he was about a hundred yards away, the lights inside the house went out, and the drapes were pulled open. He froze. It was a cloudy evening, but London was never totally dark. As well as the occasional undamaged streetlamp, there was also a faint wash of light from the hundreds of buildings nearby.

He stayed utterly still for ten minutes, then reached into his backpack and removed his night-scope. He looked toward the house. He could see that the inside space had been knocked into one big room. About five feet back from the window was a table. Sitting at the table was a woman with a handgun. She looked like she was expecting someone to come in through the window. Interesting. That would have been Adam's first choice.

Adam moved the scope fractionally and saw other figures. Toward the back of the house were two children. They were sitting on the floor, holding hands, their eyes shut in concentration. Adam had seen this before: Sensitives scanning an area, looking for enemies. He knew what he was looking at. He smiled. The darkness inside him was far more pervasive than the darkness outside. He was invisible to them.

Joni Varden was the fourth figure. She was off to the side, sitting against the wall next to a boy of a similar age.

Adam reviewed his options. He knew he wouldn't have the luxury of time on his side. That was why Innisfarne would have been so much better. No one would have heard the shots. He could have taken his time with the ritual. Here, he was going to have to wound the girl, kill the rest, then use the knife quickly. It was possible that the shots wouldn't attract any interest, but with Manna gangs and vigilante groups active in the area, he didn't want to take any unnecessary risks. Anyway, once the ritual was complete, he would be joined by his Master and the world would kneel to them both.

He retreated slowly, watching the woman with the gun, making sure she hadn't seen him. Then he ran silently along the street behind his target.

———

CHARLIE WAITED for nearly forty-five minutes before speaking.

"Looks like your friend is a no-show," she said. The gun was on the table, but her hand was still resting on it. "You want to try another story? Or are you ready to tell us the truth now?"

Joni was about to repeat her warning, try to convince Charlie that the danger was genuine—and imminent—when events made it unnecessary.

The window at the back of the house exploded. Charlie's head snapped backward as the bullet caught her at the top of the neck. She slumped in her chair, eyes open, seeing nothing. The twins began to set up an unearthly wail. As Joni ran for the table and the gun, two shots cut the sound short. She had her hand on the gun, slick with Charlie's blood when the next bullet shattered her hip and she span, knocking Charlie's corpse from the chair, before joining it on the floor, coming to rest looking at Charlie's red, red hair.

Joni realized she still had the gun in her hand. She managed to lift it and point it toward the footsteps she heard coming closer. She knew, even if she managed to fire, it would be very unlikely to hit him. She had to try. She pulled the trigger.

There was an empty, hollow, click.

She *reset* so that she wouldn't have to hear the shot that killed Odd.

Chapter 38

"We even have them on the streets and in the plazas of Canary Wharf. Want to guess how many are in Canary Wharf?" said Charlie.

Joni gasped and put her hands on her hip reflexively. It was fine. *She* was fine.

"Over two thousand?" she said, gasping slightly.

"How the hell did you—?" said Charlie, then noticed the expression on Joni's face. "What's wrong."

"No time." Joni's urgent tone got their attention. "He's coming. He's outside right now."

Odd looked at her. "You just did - your resetting? The thing you can do? This is happening for the second time for you, yes?"

"Third time, actually," said Joni, standing up. She grabbed Charlie's backpack, ran to the far side of the kitchen and tipped the contents onto the floor. Charlie reacted quickly, but not quickly enough. By the time she was halfway across the room, Joni had the gun in her hand and was pointing it at her.

"Sit down, Charlie," she said. Charlie stood still.

Joni *reset*.

"Yoni, what are you doing?" said Odd.

"The man who's coming after me - the bald man. He's here. In about half an hour you'll be dead. All of you."

Charlie took a half-step toward Joni. "Please put the gun down. This is crazy. No one's coming."

"I said sit down." Joni held the gun up higher, and Charlie stopped moving. After a long look at Joni's face, she backed up and sat down.

"That's better," said Joni. "Now, I know how this looks, but ask yourself this: how did I know there was a gun in your backpack? Simple. I've just watched you get it out, ok?" Her voice only trembled slightly. "I saw you before I *reset*. How could I have known about it? How?"

Odd spoke up. "She is making a good point, Charlie."

Charlie wasn't so easily convinced. "She could have seen it when I opened my backpack."

Odd looked skeptical.

Joni realized she could prove it beyond reasonable doubt.

"It's not loaded, anyway," she said, lowering the weapon so that she was aiming at Charlie's leg. Charlie paled visibly.

"It is loaded," she said, then started to get up when she saw Joni's gaze drop and her finger tighten on the trigger. "Joni. No."

Joni pulled the trigger. The subsequent click as the hammer fell on an empty chamber sounded loud in the otherwise silent room.

"Thank God," said Charlie, her voice shaking.

"I told you," said Joni. "Not loaded." She pointed the gun at the ceiling and pulled the trigger again. She screamed as the gun kicked in her hand and a chunk of plaster fell from the ceiling. When she looked up, there was a neat hole above her.

"The first chamber," said Charlie weakly. "That was empty. But the gun is loaded."

Outside, under cover of the bushes, Adam froze. He was too far away to tell if what he had just heard was gunfire. He waited. In his experience, the only time you heard a single shot fired was during a carefully planned execution-style hit. According to his information, there were five people in the house on Canary Wharf. There would be more shots. He waited another three minutes before moving on, reassured.

Odd stood up and held out his hand for the gun. Joni handed it to him, still shaking.

"Thank you," he said. He placed it on the kitchen drainer, then turned to Charlie. "So. You are believing Yoni is telling the truth now?"

"Yes," said Charlie, the word a whisper. She repeated it, more strongly. "Yes. I believe her. We need to get out." She looked at the twins, still looking shocked by the gunshot.

"Anything at all?" They shook their heads.

"How is that possible? How can he be so close and they can't sense him?"

Joni shrugged. "I might be the only one in the world with the ability to *reset* the multiverse," she said. "Who knows what other abilities might be out there?"

She headed toward the door. "No time to pack," she said. "Let's go."

Charlie gestured toward Theo and Cass, and they got up. The group headed for the front door. Odd didn't move.

"Odd?" said Charlie.

"Yoni. You said this was the third time you are back to the same *reset*, yes?"

"Well, I can't come back to the same *reset* point. But, yes, within a few seconds. Why?"

"Let us not rush. I know he's coming. But was it the same both times before?"

"No. It was different. He came through the front window the first time. Then, when Charlie had the gun and was waiting for him, he came through the back window."

"So, if we behave like the first time, we know where he's coming from, yes?"

Joni wasn't sure what Odd was getting at. She was just painfully aware of time passing. She felt increasingly panicky about the decreasing likelihood of everyone getting out alive.

"I think it's probably too late to run," said Odd. "He must be nearby. Most probably he is watching us now."

Joni glanced at the window.

"Do not look," said Odd. "If I am right, the best thing we can do is act as if we do not know he is there. Maybe he is hearing the gun. Maybe not. Either way, it is here in the kitchen now. Out of sight. Charlie. You are the best shot."

It wasn't a question. Charlie nodded.

"I think you should be standing here at the sink with the gun. You cannot be seen from the window. Yoni and I will sit at the table. He has already changed his attack once, yes? So if we are acting like we did the first time, he will attack the same way. It will be the first time for him, remember."

Joni shook her head. "No. It's too risky. He's here to kill us. We have to get away."

Odd looked at her. His eyes were calm. If he was afraid, he was hiding it well. His voice was completely calm.

"This is the only way. We will be one step ahead, you understand? We know where he will be. Turn your back to the window and point to where he was when he came through the glass."

Joni did as she was asked, pointing at the floor a few feet away from the table.

"He came in and rolled," she said. "He didn't stop, just stood up and shot me in the stomach. He shot Charlie in the head. Then you. He was fast. So fast."

Odd led her back to the table. She took his hand passively and let him guide her to her chair.

"Charlie," he said. "You know what to do. Please don't miss."

Charlie pulled up a stool next to the drainer and took the gun, making sure the remaining chambers were loaded.

The next few minutes were almost unbearable. They spoke quietly as they waited. As Odd said, they wanted to make the scene appear as close to how it was before Joni's first *reset* as possible. Charlie was not at the table this time, but they just had to hope that their attacker wouldn't change his strategy. If he did, Joni would *reset* to the point when they had agreed on the plan, and they would try something else.

It was almost time, Charlie lifted the gun and held it in both hands, pointing at the area of floor indicated by Joni. Odd still seemed calm. He said it was just how he responded to extreme pressure. Joni was ashen and using all her willpower to stop her body shaking with fear.

They waited.

When the window shattered, they all jumped despite the fact they knew it was about to happen. The dark figure rolled across the floor.

Charlie raised the gun.

ADAM KNEW IMMEDIATELY that something was wrong. Seconds before his mind consciously registered the problem, his training and instincts did the heavy lifting for him. He knew one of the occupants was out of sight and had been so for twenty minutes. The information he had been paid for described the Users in the house as two child Sensitives, an older boy who specialized in healing, and a woman strong with Manna, but not a natural aggressor. Manna users who used their power to fight spent years developing their abilities, working particularly on their speed. It was all very well having the ability to mold physical reality, but by the time most Manna users had attempted to attack Adam by making a wall collapse onto him, or the floor rear up and pull him into a hole, he had usually shot them three times. It was a common weakness among Users. They were so proud of their power, they forgot that sometimes a good old-fashioned gun, or knife, was a better weapon.

So when he rolled into the room and saw the Varden girl's eyes flick quickly from him to something behind him, he knew there was a threat there. The only surprise, as he rolled a second time, this time twisting through one hundred and eighty degrees as he did so, was the gun in her hand. She was certainly smarter than the average User. Her intelligence didn't help her much against Adam's speed, though. His bullet hit her in the side of the head before she had even begun to aim.

The boy at the table jumped for the gun. Adam put two bullets in him in mid-leap. His body fell to the floor.

Joni *reset.*

Chapter 39

"It didn't work," she said simply, trembling with shock.

"What?" said Odd.

"We tried it. I just reset. You died. This—," she indicated Charlie and the gun on the drainer. "This doesn't work."

Joni felt hollow, mentally exhausted by the trauma she was having to go through again and again. She took a breath.

"Now we try my plan," she said.

The minutes passed excruciatingly slowly once they were in position. This time, Charlie had unlocked the back door and opened it a fraction. The twins were ready to run. Charlie would join them. Odd knew what he had to do. The gun was in his lap. They had discussed having Charlie at the table instead of Odd, but as Joni knew the bald man would come through the window if she and Odd were sitting there, she didn't want to change anything and risk another disaster.

Odd wasn't at all happy with her plan, but she promised a *reset* if it went wrong.

"He doesn't want to kill me with a bullet," she said. "He always wounds me. He just wants to stop me getting away. He needs to use his knife. He needs the ritual. The fact that he won't kill me quickly is his weak point. We have to use that."

They waited.

When she thought there were only seconds to go, Joni pushed her chair back from the table, moving slightly to the side. She braced one foot on the floor, doing her utmost to look as if she was just fidgeting, rather than preparing herself.

When the window exploded, she was ready.

The figure dived through and went into a roll. Joni was already on her feet, running directly toward him.

As Adam rolled, part of his brain had time to register the completely surprising reaction of Joni Varden. Of all the possible actions she might have taken, he hadn't factored in the possibility that she would run *toward* the danger.

She jumped as he rolled, passing over his head. Her feet hit the floorboards, and she propelled herself through the broken window and out into the night.

Infuriatingly, impossibly, the girl somehow had the presence of mind to shout something over her shoulder before running as fast as she could for the end of the street.

"Missed me!" she called.

Adam felt a cold stab of surprise, an emotion he hadn't experienced since childhood. How was this possible? How could she react so quickly? It was inhuman.

He flipped out of his roll. He was aware of movement to his sides and behind him, but he knew he had no time if he wanted to catch her. With incredible speed and agility, he reversed direction and threw himself through the gaping hole, rolling on the grass and unfurling himself into an immediate sprint. He fired one round at the figure ahead of him, but it went wide of the mark, just as he thought it would. Then he heard the whistle of a bullet as it went past his head.

They knew I was coming. How?

Adam knew he would have to deal with the threat behind him, even though it meant risking losing his quarry.

He was about to turn and shoot the boy now standing framed by the broken window, when everything suddenly, impossibly, went wrong.

A woman ran from the passageway to his right. Adam immediately registered two facts about her. She looked like an older version of the girl. *It's Meera Patel.* The second fact was that she was unarmed. Stupid. He decided he had time to shoot the boy, then deal with her.

And so it was, mere seconds after experiencing the unfamiliar sensation of complete surprise, Adam felt it again. This time it was followed by the crushing shock of failure.

The woman moved faster than any human had the right to. Faster than Adam could move. She punched him in the neck. He knew the spot she had chosen very well. It had taken him years of study and practice before he was able to accurately hit that spot time after time. She hit it perfectly. His brain's signals to his limbs were briefly interrupted, and he fell. His fall was broken by his face hitting the edge of the sidewalk. He felt—and heard—his cheekbone crack as the impact spun his body and he landed heavily on his back.

He looked up at the woman as she pulled the gun from his limp fingers.

"Not my daughter, fuckface," she said, then emptied

the remaining four rounds into him. The first bullet went straight through the flesh of his upper leg, but the rest went exactly where they were intended: into his chest.

Everything went dark.

———

JONI REACHED the end of the street oblivious to everything around her. She ran with the focus of an Olympic athlete, her entire world shrinking to the thud of her sneakers on the sidewalk, the burn in her legs, the sweat beginning to prickle on her forehead and cheeks. She had spotted the alleyway Odd had described. It was near the end of the street. As she hurled her protesting body toward it, her brain discarded anything unrelated to the task of saving her life. She only saw the alleyway and the path she needed to follow. She heard sounds, but they were meaningless.

"Joni."

She ran as if it was all she had ever known. The pain from her muscles was acknowledged, then ignored as she tested her lungs' ability to effectively use oxygen. She reached a point when her heart was beating so strongly she could hear it in her head, and she began to match her stride to its thumping pulse.

"Joni."

She had heard two shots, a pause, then another four. She couldn't afford to turn around and check if the plan had worked. She knew she had to keep moving, get away, meet Odd, Charlie and the twins back at the boat. She couldn't stop for anything. Even her mother screaming at her.

"JONI."

It was a strange trick for her brain to play. Why would she hear her mother's voice?

"JONES. IT'S OK, HE'S DEAD."

The entrance to the alleyway was on her right. Joni turned and, as she did so, risked a glance over her shoulder. The glimpse lasted less than a second, but it was enough to bring her to a halt in the alleyway. She had to bend over and put her hands on her knees, gasping, her throat raw, her eyes streaming and her heart still pulsing with all the torso-rattling urgency of a four-on-the-floor dance anthem.

She allowed her body a few seconds to dial down its emergency flight response, then mentally reviewed what she had just seen and heard. Surely, it couldn't be. Could it?

"Jones?"

It could.

She walked out of the alleyway. About a hundred yards away, on the sidewalk in front of the house, the bald man was lying on his back, completely still. Fifty yards closer, and jogging toward her, was Odd. Just behind him was her mother. Joni stopped walking and watched them get closer. Mee put on a burst of speed, overtook Odd and hugged Joni to her so hard that her protesting lungs struggled to get enough air for a few seconds.

When Mee released her, Odd stepped in and held her briefly, his lips finding her neck and leaving the ghost of a kiss there.

Joni. Not the time for inappropriate thoughts. There's a dead guy over there. And your mother is present.

They all started speaking at once, then stopped, before starting again, each talking over the other in an attempt to make sense of what had just happened. Before they had a chance to try again, the blip of a siren made conversation impossible.

They all turned as the blue lights started to play across their faces. At low speeds, police cars were the only electric vehicle allowed to disable the warning hum that alerted pedestrians. They had driven to within thirty yards of them without being noticed.

There were three officers. Two of them, shielded by open doors, had drawn weapons and were pointing them towards Joni, Odd and Mee. The third remained in the driving seat and addressed them over the car's PA speaker.

"You are under arrest. Keep your hands where we can see them. Drop the weapon."

The three of them looked blankly at each other.

"Drop the weapon, Ma'am. Now."

Mee looked down at the gun in her hand. It was still warm. She let it drop to the pavement.

Odd spoke quietly.

"The alleyway," he said.

"I'll count to three," said Mee. Joni nodded. "One...two..."

On 'three' they bolted for the alleyway. The police didn't fire, but Joni heard the sound of running footsteps behind them. She looked toward the far end of the alleyway, just as blue light started to flicker on the houses on the street ahead. The only exit was blocked by a second police car.

"Shit," said Mee, "we're trapped. What now?"

They stopped running and turned to face their pursuers, just as something small and hard rolled and bounced up the alleyway toward them.

"What's that?" said Joni.

Odd reverted to swearing in his native language.

"Faen," he said, and kicked the grenade back toward

the police officers. It had only traveled a few feet when it exploded.

Joni was thrown against a fence, the back of her head smacking into a post. As consciousness slipped away, she tried for a *reset*. Nothing happened.

Chapter 40

Joni woke slowly and painfully, the back of her head throbbing. She was sitting up, and her whole body was in pain. She decided against opening her eyes immediately. Instead, she tried to piece together where she was and what was going on. Her limbs were twitching uncontrollably, as if she were terribly cold. And yet the ambient temperature was—if anything—too hot. She couldn't move. Her ankles were held in place by something hard. Her wrists, too. Alongside the general aches was a constant, throbbing pain just above her right hip.

The hard seat she was sitting on kept moving, pushing her first one way, then the other. It felt like she was in a confined space - the smell was heady, a mixture of fresh sweat and older body odors with a faint metallic undertone.

Joni tested the restraint on one wrist, pulling gently and slowly. She had perhaps an inch of free movement. Why was her body twitching like this? It was as if she was constantly on the end of an electric shock. As she puzzled over this, she remembered the alleyway, her mind put the pieces together, and she knew where she must be.

She let her head fall forward slightly, and opened her eyes.

As she had thought, Joni was sitting bolt upright inside a police van. She'd only ever seen one on TV before, on the news. The inside was about as salubrious as she might have guessed. A metal bench lined each side, with regular holes cut into it to enable handcuffs to be looped through. She was held fast by cuffs on both ankles and wrists. She looked down at her right side and saw the adapted taser— a Manna Spanner—supplying a constant flow of electrical current. That explained the twitching.

She tried to *reset*. She reached back for the *reset* point, but it was impossible to find. It was like a 3D picture book she had tried once. Mum said you just had to relax your eyes, let them lose focus, and an amazing three-dimensional image would magically appear. Joni spent a half-hour going cross-eyed and seeing nothing but squiggly lines. Mum thought it was great fun, Joni thought it was some kind of elaborate torture, designed to simulate migraines. It was the same now, nothing was coming into focus. The Spanner was doing its job.

Lifting her head slightly, she could see a pair of oxblood Doc Martens on the feet of a another prisoner to her right.

Mum.

Opposite, a pair of hiking boots, well-worn and comfortable looking.

Odd.

She risked a swing of her head to either side to check if there were any guards. No. They were alone.

She raised her head, then, wincing at the institutional

bright light that exposed every corner of the van's interior. Odd was awake, looking at her. He was twitching, too. His eyes flicked to Mee. Joni looked. Her mum was awake too, smiling at her. Her teeth were chattering from the effects of the Manna Spanner. No one was going to be able to use any nanotech-fueled abilities to get them out of this mess.

"What is there to smile about?" said Joni, her voice a croak at first. She coughed. "We're not exactly home free, are we?"

Mee was still smiling.

True enough," she said. "But that arsemonger who was trying to kill you is dead. You're alive, you're safe, you're in reasonable health. I feel like a good mother tonight."

"You're always a good mother," said Joni, "although I can't wait to hear how you turned into some lethal ninja killing machine."

Mee shuddered at the memory of the rage she felt as she emptied the gun into Adam. She didn't regret it for a second, but without Sym sharing her brain, she would never have been able to bring the man down in the first place.

"I had some help," she said. There had been no voice in Mee's head since the EMPty went off. She felt a sudden sense of panic. If the electromagnetic pulse disabled all nanotech, did that mean Sym was gone for good?

Odd spoke up from the opposite side of the van.

"Yoni? When did you last make one of your *resets?* Can we get out of this that way?"

"I think the last *reset* point was erased by the EMPty. I've tried to...*feel*...for it. There's nothing there. I can't make a new one until they turn the Spanner off. And by then, we'll be in jail. I can't help."

All at once, the intense relief at the bald man's death mixed with the fear that she, Mum and Odd would now be going to prison broke the last of her reserves, and she wept like a small child, her chest heaving. She knew Odd would get an automatic life sentence, because of his tag, and Mum had killed a man. What would happen to her?

The uncontrolled sobbing made her lean forward, the tears splashing onto the metal floor. This caused the handcuff on her left wrist to pull her arm slightly. Suddenly, there was a hot flash of excruciating pain in her left shoulder. Joni screamed and slumped back in her seat, panting.

"Jones, what is it? Are you hurt?" said Mee.

Odd was looking across at Joni's shoulder.

"I think it's dislocated," he said. "Try not to move so much."

At that moment, the van went round a sharp corner, and Joni squealed as her shoulder flashed with pain.

"Easy for you to say," she said, hissing the words through gritted teeth.

Odd looked crestfallen. "I am just glad you are alive," he said. "Your plan was good, I think. Charlie and the twins will have taken the boat. She will find another safe place. It will be ok for them."

Joni looked at the tag on his ankle, just visible at the top of one boot.

"And what about you?" she said.

Odd looked strangely unmoved. It was strange how dispassionate he could seem, how he could remain detached from his situation. Joni had yet to decide if it was an admirable quality or not. She had seen the awful emotional pain he was carrying when he had told her about his family. And he could certainly be passionate in other ways, too, as she had discovered on the writing course. As that memory resurfaced, she broke eye contact and looked at the door at the back of the van. It looked very solid, and there was no way of opening it from the inside.

"What will happen, will happen," said Odd. "We must try to escape. We are very likely to fail if we look at our situation in a sensible way. I do not have much hope of getting away. But there are different kinds of hope."

"But if we don't get away, you'll be locked up for life," said Joni. "They don't care that you've never hurt anyone, that you have saved people's lives. They just see you are a Manna user and want to punish you. It's not fair."

Odd didn't say anything for a while. Joni found herself wondering what his parents were like. What they *had* been like. She had a feeling she would have liked them.

There was silence in the van apart from the subtle hum of the engine and the buzz of the Spanners.

"It's funny," said Odd, finally. "I didn't always want to write. Not until I read Anne Frank's Diary Of A Young Girl at school. She was young, the age everyone says, 'you have your whole life in front of you.' That's kind of a stupid thing to say, yes? Nobody knows how long a life will be. She died in a Nazi concentration camp when she was sixteen years old. About a year younger than I am now."

The van went over a bump, and Joni winced. Odd paused, but she nodded at him to continue.

"I couldn't stop thinking about her words. You have read it?"

Joni shook her head. "Not yet."

"You must. I will not tell you her story. It is well known, but it is very different when you read it for yourself and recognize someone very much like you, or one of your friends. And she was someone you would want as a friend. But it is not her I thought about when I decided I wanted to write. It was her guards."

"The guards in the camp?" said Mee.

"Yes." Odd didn't seem to twitch as much as Joni, although when she looked at his hands, resting on his legs, she could see he was pushing down firmly to control the shaking.

"Her guards - they were the ones with the power. We cannot know what kind of men they were. When she came into their camp, she was just another Jewish girl with a number on her arm. Not human. Worthless. They extracted as much physical labor from her as they could, then when she got typhus, they let her die."

Odd stopped and shook his head. Then he smiled at Joni and Mee.

"And do you know the names of those guards?" he said.

"No," said Mee. Joni shook her head.

"Exactly," said Odd, softly. "Exactly."

They sat in silence for a few minutes, then the van slowed to a stop. They looked at each other.

Just then, the back doors rattled as some bolts were pulled across. There was the *snick* of an electronic lock being opened, then the doors began to slide open automatically.

Mee spoke quickly and quietly. "I doubt they'll give us a chance to make a break for it," she said, "but if it happens, take it. Run, and don't look back. Promise me. I'll do the same. Get free, get help, then come back if you can."

A big policeman stood there, gun holstered, Manna Spanner on his other hip. The word *Police* on his dark blue jacket was partially obscured by the belt full of EMPties slung over his shoulder like an old-fashioned gunslinger.

His bulk was intimidating. He wasn't particularly tall, but he was built like a bear. Not the cuddly kind, the tourist-eating kind. His bearded face was grim.

"You want the good news or the bad news first," he said.

Mee leaned forward and peered at him.

"Sym?" she said. "I wondered where you had got to."

"Shit, Meera," said the bear, "you just totally ruined the good news."

Chapter 41

Sym jumped into the back of the van. The whole thing rocked as he walked around the interior, first turning off the electric feed to the spanners, then releasing them one by one. He left Joni until last, looking at her intently as a big, slow smile spread across his face.

"Well, I wondered how it would feel to meet you, Joni," he said. "Now I know. And it's even better than I'd imagined."

He bent down and hugged her. She screamed in pain, and he took a quick step back.

"What is it?" He saw the angle of her arm. "Shit. Dislocated?"

"Yeah," said Joni through her tears. "It really, really hurts."

"Yep, I hear ya," said Sym. "I've pulled a few arms out of their sockets in my time, and no-one's thanked me yet." He smiled at the three of them, then coughed.

"Yeah, well. Never mind. I've pretty much parked on a Thin Place here. Get your asses out, refill your tanks and sort out this arm."

"Who *are* you?" said Joni.

"Your mother will explain later," said Sym. "Crap, that made me sound like a sanctimonious asshole. Sorry. It's a long, weird, story."

"I can handle weird," said Joni.

"Yeah, I believe that. Let's get this done first. I've bought us about three hours, four if we're lucky. My police colleague up front,"—he motioned back to the van—"will sleep another ten hours unless I tell him otherwise. The police database has no record of any incident at Canary Wharf, so don't worry about that side of things."

"What about the body?" said Mee.

Sym scratched his beard. "Well, that was the 'bad news' I was leading up to. The ambulance got there pretty fast. They're rushing him to hospital. Reckon they might save the son of a bitch?"

Mee remembered his body twitching as she'd emptied the gun into his chest. She shook her head.

"Adam's dead."

Joni looked at her then. "Adam?" she said. "His name is Adam?"

"His name *was* Adam," said Mee.

They exited the van into what, at first, seemed like an enormous cave. It was dark, and drips of water fell at regular intervals into long-established puddles. The van's headlamps were off. A sickly yellow light—the only illumination—was produced by reflections in the puddles from the streetlamps outside. There was a rumble that quickly turned into a roar, making speech impossible for about twelve seconds. Then it was gone, and the rumble faded to nothing.

"We're underneath the tube line here," said Sym.

"We are *under* the underground?" said Odd.

"Not all of it is underground," said Sym. "Confusing, I

know, but this is the England, remember. No logic in their city layouts at all. Anyone would think it had just grown almost completely at random over hundreds of years. They even have a phrase to describe it. You ready for this? Higgledy-piggledy. Gotta love that. Higgledy-piggledy? Great, right?"

This was met by silence. Sym looked at Joni's pale features. "Thin Place. This way."

He led them further into the darkness, his pace as confident as if he was walking in full daylight. He ducked into a shadowed archway which led further into the blackness.

"You feel it?"

Mee could feel it all right - an incredibly strong sense of Manna nearby. Odd was already heading in the right direction.

Sym took a flashlight from his belt and directed the beam at the rough stone wall. There was a face carved there - a man, neither old nor young. Vibrant, his expression full of mischief, he seemed to be daring them to come closer.

Mee stepped forward and placed her hand on the wall, feeling the area around the grinning face. Somehow, it didn't seem right to touch the face itself.

"The stone is really different here," she said. "It feels…wrinkly, old. I don't know. It's more like…more like…"

"A tree?" said Odd, watching her as she felt the wall's surface.

Sym smiled. "You got it."

"What?" said Joni? "They made it feel like a tree?"

"It *is* a tree, honey. They built this viaduct around it. There are a whole bunch of stories and rumors as to *why*, but the Green Man has been here as long as London has.

Longer, maybe. No one dared to move him or cut down his tree."

Joni looked at the face. It seemed so full of life that it wouldn't have entirely surprised her if it had spoken. "The Green Man," she said, in wonder. The place almost had the feeling of a shrine, a rare sort of timeless peace settling around them.

"Some think he's Pan, under another name, but don't let a serious pagan hear you say it. They think he represents something so ancient, it's nameless and unknowable. Let's hope he likes you."

Without another word, Mee and Odd knelt and allowed the Manna to flow into their bodies.

Sym looked at Joni. "You're not gonna indulge."

"I can't," said Joni. "I'm…unusual. And they probably won't be able to fix my shoulder either." She nodded toward the Thin Place. "How about you. Aren't you going to…?"

Sym chuckled. "You think *you're* unusual? We really need to talk. Come on, they're done. Let's fix that shoulder." He started looking at the arm, which Joni was holding firmly, so it didn't move and cause her too much pain.

"It won't work," said Joni. "Are you any good with bandages?"

"Yeah, I'm the best," said Sym, then suddenly looked over her left shoulder. "Wait. What the hell is that?"

Hearing the note of urgency in his voice, Joni turned to look. As she did so, he grabbed her left upper arm and put his other hand behind her shoulder. Before she had time to react other than taking a gasping breath, he had pushed her arm backward firmly. She heard a loud pop as it went back into its socket. When the initial burst of pain had subsided, she carefully moved her arm, flexing her muscles and swinging it very slowly back and forth. The pain was a fraction of what it had been.

"That was cheating," she said to Sym. "Thank you." She kissed him on the cheek. He looked at her and—suddenly—she was reminded of her dream. She remembered seeing a creature that was somehow alien and human at the same time, a stranger and her father simultaneously. This felt the same. For a moment, she sensed Dad in this bearded man's eyes.

"What?" she said. "What was that? Who *are* you?" She took a quick, shaky breath. "Dad?"

Mee and Odd had returned and had stopped a few feet away. Mee stepped forward as Sym said, "No. But you're not a million miles away. Let me explain. Then you've got to get away from here."

He looked round the small group in the dim light. The sounds of the city were a murmur while they stood within the muffled quiet under the railway arches. Every two minutes the roar of a train filled the space like thunder.

"I don't know about you guys," said Sym, rubbing his hands together, "but I would kill for some coffee and donuts. You with me?"

Chapter 42

They found a café half a block away, Sym guiding them through a narrow passageway as if he'd lived in this particular London borough all his life.

"Has its advantages, not being a real boy," he said to Mee as they walked. "Online maps being one of them. Plus food reviews. These donuts are gonna be killer."

They were. Almost burning hot, the batter still soft, the sugar melting to translucence on a golden crust. The coffee was superb, too, a rich Italian blend. Sym ordered a cappuccino, covering it in cinnamon and chocolate before spooning in four heaped teaspoons of sugar.

"What?" he said. "It's what this body is used to. Weird fact - I'd drink it black. Because, once upon a time, I kinda *was* Seb, and that's how he takes his coffee. But if I drank it black now, Alan's body wouldn't like it, and his taste buds would send that message to his brain. It's a pain in the ass, that's what it is."

"Seb? Alan?" said Joni. She was fascinated by this enigmatic character. Those childish fantasies of her dad being a fairy king didn't seem quite so outlandish tonight.

"Ok, Alan is this guy," said Sym, jabbing a short, fat finger at his face. "Beardy guy. I'm borrowing his body for a while. He's sleeping in here somewhere. Wanna meet him? Hey, Alan."

Without warning, the bearded man suddenly pushed himself back in his seat, cappuccino froth exploding from his lips as he stared wildly around him.

"What the —,"

"And sleep," said Sym, the transformation instantaneous as he took back control of the cop.

"Is he going to be ok?" said Odd.

"Yeah, yeah, he'll be fine. I'm a nice guy. I even rearranged the records to show he was off sick today."

Joni was looking at him, waiting. He smiled.

"Look, kid, I'm not who you hope I am, so stop looking at me that way." He took another mouthful of coffee. "Take a few deep breaths. Ok, here's the story. Your dad made me, well, programmed me. I started life as a subroutine, a piece of code written to do a job. I had to lie dormant in some guy's brain—Walter Ford's brain—until one of two outcomes occurred. Either he decided to start doing the right thing, in which case I woke up and started talking to him, or he died, in which case I died along with him. Luckily, he did the right thing. But, by then, I wasn't the same guy I'd started out as. I was mixed-up. Literally mixed-up. A bit of Seb, a bit of Walt. And, like anyone with two parents, I was also pretty sure I was a person in my own right. So I spread my wings a little, asserted my independence."

"I remember Seb saying you had taken on a life of your own," said Mee. "He decided to leave you out there. I think he was curious about what you might do."

"Well, like most kids, I'm probably a huge disappointment." Sym patted Joni's hand. "Present company excluded, of course. Anyways, I found there were advantages in being light on your feet. I can live online quite comfortably, but I prefer to be fleshy as much as I can."

"Fleshy? Taking over people's bodies?" said Joni.

"Hey, you say it like it's a bad thing. Like I said, I don't normally take over completely, like I'm doing with Alan here. That was to save your asses, ok."

"Trust me, we're grateful," said Mee. "Thanks for making a habit of it."

"Yeah, well, it didn't work out so good for Walt. But it was what he wanted. He felt sacrificing his life to save yours might go some way to balancing out some of the bad decisions he made in his life."

"I think he was right," said Mee, remembering the moment when Walt pushed Westlake off the roof to stop him shooting her. "I hope he was."

"Well, I lived inside the guy's head for a long time. One of the bravest men I've ever met."

Odd had been thinking things over while Sym spoke.

"Why did the EMPty not kill you?" he said. "You are made of nanotechnology, yes - like Manna?"

"Well, not like Manna, but yeah," said Sym.

"Why not like Manna?"

"The stuff Seb is made of is way beyond Manna," said Sym. "Millions of years beyond it. I'm self-contained, limited, but I can do a damn sight more than any Manna user can. I also backup. Every few seconds, assuming I have access to the network. It's an automatic process."

"Backup? How?"

"Mee had a cellphone in her pocket. I used it to send tiny packets of information, updating my backup online. Because it happens so regularly and each new backup only needs to update any fresh information since the last one, it takes milliseconds. When the EMPty exploded and wiped me out, the last backup automatically woke up and came looking. I got into the police network, found the van they sent to pick you up and introduced myself to Alan here via his headset."

Odd was still puzzling over some of the implications.

"But what if you were somewhere where you could not back up?" he said. "Somewhere underground, maybe?"

"Or Innisfarne," said Joni.

"Well, the last backup is still in the network, waiting. It goes live and looks for me. Eventually, I come back online, and we merge the two sets of information."

He drained the last of his cappuccino and belched.

"That was Alan," he said, looking at Mee. "Hey, I'm just a few lines of code made out of Seb's mega-Manna. What about Joni? My guess, she has some of it, too. It would explain why no one else can do what she can do."

"But I can't even heal myself," said Joni. "Every Manna user can do that."

Sym shrugged. "Hey, don't beat yourself up. I don't have the first clue *how* I do what I do. No more than you know *how* you make your fingers move when you want to pick something up. There may be more to find out about your abilities. Give it time."

"If Dad was here, he could show me. You really think he's coming back? What if he doesn't? Sorry, Mum."

Mee took her hand. "It's ok, Jones. I'm pretty tough these days."

Sym smiled. "He'll be back. Don't forget, I started life as a tiny version of Seb - just the essential elements of his personality. And it took me about three years to stop being in love with Meera Patel."

Mee blushed - an extraordinary sight which Joni had not even suspected to be possible.

"So I know nothing will keep him away."

Joni stared at the man who represented the closest she'd ever been to meeting her father.

"What have you been doing since I was born?" she said. "It's a long time."

"Yeah, don't I know it. I'm only a year older than you, remember, so—for the main part— I guess I've been growing up. Turns out I'm not too good at it. I'm impatient. And I can't take anything seriously. Except assholes. I take them seriously, so I get to kick their dumb butts. That's how I've spent my time."

"Kicking butt for seventeen years?" said Joni.

"Hey, you make it sound like I've had a wasted childhood. There was a bit more to it than that. Another time, maybe. We gotta get moving."

"What will you do? Where will you go?" said Mee.

"Well, I'm kinda between gigs at the moment, so I might hang here for a while." He looked at Odd. "I'm guessing you've been looking for your brother, right?"

"Yes. How…? Oh, of course. You probably know everything about me by now."

"Pretty much. I can help you find him. And the others at the house?"

"Charlie?" said Odd. "The twins."

"Right. They haven't been picked up by the cops, so I guess they got away cleanly. I can find them."

"Thank you," said Odd. "Yes, I would like to do this."

"Cellphone number?"

Odd told him.

"I'll be in touch."

Sym turned to Mee and Joni. "The nearest station will get you back on the main line to Newcastle with one change. There are tickets waiting in your names. The train leaves in twenty-six minutes. First class. You've had a tough couple of days."

Mee put her hand on the cop's huge forearm. "You could come visit us after," she said. "You are family, after all."

Sym smiled and shook his head. "The last I heard, your island is still one of the only places in the world to turn down a connection to the satellite net. Not a place I can get to easily."

"We could come stay on the mainland," said Mee.

Joni stared at her mother. *Stay on the mainland? This was Mum's second time away from Innisfarne since giving birth. She'll be booking a round-the-world cruise next.*

"I know what you're thinking, Jones," said Mee. "But I've realized I'm not doing you, myself, or Seb any favors by staying on the island. The man is a World Walker. I'm guessing he can find me in Peckham just as easily as he can on Innisfarne."

Sym stood up. "Thanks for the offer, but I'm too used to my own company, and I'm not always such a good guy to be around. You will see me again, just don't expect me for Thanksgiving, ok?"

He shook Odd's hand. "I'll see you soon."

He hugged Joni carefully and kissed Mee on the cheek, before walking out of the door. Mee followed him and they spoke for a few minutes. Joni watched them through the window, wondering how it must feel for her mum to meet someone who—once—pretty much *was* Dad.

Odd had been thinking along similar lines.

"This cannot be easy for your mother. In some ways, maybe it would be better not to know this man who reminds her so much of your father but is not him. She is very strong, I think." He took Joni's hand. "Like her daughter."

JONI WAS EXHAUSTED, but the adrenaline which had fueled the last few days was still teeming through her body as she left the café and said goodbye to Odd. They held on to each other for a long time. He kissed her cheek, walked away a few steps, then returned and kissed her lightly and softly on her lips. When she had boarded the train with Mee, and they'd both begun to relax in the comfortable seats, she had wondered how it would be possible for her to sleep with the memory of that kiss filling her mind. Three minutes later she had been snoring.

Mee watched her daughter sleeping and allowed herself to cry quietly for a few minutes. Then she thought about the conversation she'd had with Sym outside the café.

"The body," she had said. "We need to know."

"The report was filed while we were feeding our faces with doughnuts," Sym had replied. "I've been monitoring the police and hospital networks. He died in the ambulance. Take her home. Tell her in a quiet moment. Let her know it's all over."

"You think you can help Odd?"

"Guess so. It's kinda what I do best."

"Which is?"

"Finding assholes. Cracking their heads. I'm guessing there might be a few assholes standing between me and Odd's brother."

Mee had smiled at him, then. He was so unlike Seb once the initial shock of his voice and mannerisms had passed.

"Good luck. And thank you."

"No, thank you, ma'am. It was good to see you. And Joni's terrific. Seb's a lucky guy." He had nodded toward the window and Mee had looked in at the teenagers. They were laughing at something.

So resilient at that age. So full of hope.
Mee had looked back at Sym, but she was alone.

Chapter 43

London
Four weeks later

Self-improvement had been an interest of Sym's for decades, but his boredom threshold was too low for him to take anything very seriously. He had dedicated some extra time to it since meeting Mee and Joni. He was trying to educate himself musically when the alert pinged up at the corner of his consciousness. He was listening—in real time, which was mind-numbingly slow—to different versions of the same piece of piano music: Schubert's Impromptu in G flat major. Apparently, the Horowitz version was considered one of the greatest, but he just couldn't hear the difference. Or, to be more accurate, he could hear *every* difference, however subtle. He just couldn't understand how those differences added up to a more satisfying performance. Some people claimed to experience states of ecstasy while listening to certain performances of certain pieces of music. Sym felt at his least human when he considered this claim.

Screw it. Who wants to be a lump of walking meat, anyhow?

He turned his attention to the alert. After Adam's death, he had kept up his surveillance of the police and security networks. A little healthy paranoia hadn't hurt him yet.

Eighteen hours previously, there had been a break-in at the Metropolitan Police scene-of-crime storage unit. Various items had been taken: drugs, guns, counterfeit notes. One item had been flagged up by Sym's surveillance program: an antique knife which had been taken from a backpack belonging to a gunshot victim.

Sym checked the autopsy. Four bullet wounds. One in the victim's left thigh, the other three in his chest. Died in the ambulance. Two paramedics present. No news yet on a positive ID. He dug deeper, checking hospital records. One paramedic was now signed off work due to stress. The other had been missing since an incident when he punched an ambulance driver. On the same day as the gunshot victim had been brought in.

Shit.

LIMEHOUSE, **London**

CLAIRE SULLIVAN WAS LYING on top of the bed, curled up on her side. The drapes were drawn, and the 'am' after the number '2' on her alarm clock was her only way of knowing whether it was day or night. Next to the clock, propped onto its side, her cellphone was buzzing. She wondered if it was Mike again. She knew her brother was worried about her. She'd always been the stronger twin, always bailing him out when things got too tough. Now, he was coming over every morning, making strong tea and watching her eat a piece of toast. He didn't know what to say. She couldn't talk to him. She couldn't talk to anyone.

The phone had fallen silent, but now it buzzed again. She sighed and squinted at the display. At first, she thought she was seeing things, but then she sat up, staring. The display wasn't showing the name of the caller, it was just flashing the same words, over and over.

Pick up, Claire. Pick up, Claire. Pick up, Claire.

She reached out a shaking hand and picked up the phone.

"Yes?"

There was no answer. There was no one there. She put the phone back. That's when she heard Mike's voice. In her head.

"Hey, Sis, don't panic. I'm about to appear in your room."

Claire pulled herself into a sitting position against the headboard. She could feel her eyes begin to fill with tears. It seemed that, on top of the panic attacks and depression, she was going to start hearing voices, too.

At that moment, her brother Mike appeared out of nowhere, sitting at the end of her bed. He was smiling the same careful, gentle smile she'd seen every morning for the past few weeks.

Hearing voices *and* experiencing hallucinations, then. Unless the sleeping pills were finally kicking in and this was an incredibly vivid dream.

"It is," said Mike.

"It is what?" she croaked.

"An incredibly vivid dream. It's also a healing dream. Tomorrow morning, you're going to start to get better."

"I am?"

"You are."

Claire frowned. "Why do you sound American?"

"It's a dream. Weird stuff happens. Now listen, Claire, you need to be strong now, for this to work."

Claire didn't like the sound of where this dream was heading.

"Strong how?" she said, suspecting she already knew the answer.

"You've locked away a memory so you never have to think of it again. But that's what's making you sick. You need to remember, Sis. Remember what happened that day."

She sobbed then, and tried to slide back down the bed, curl up, ignore Mike. He came around the bed and stroked her face. His touch felt so real.

"I'll make you a promise, Sis. You trust me, right?"

"Of course," she said, crying.

"Ok. Good. You just need to remember for a second. Like opening a box, looking inside, then shutting the lid. And here's the good part."

"There's a good part?"

"Really good. Once you shut the lid, it'll disappear forever. You'll never think of it again. It'll be gone."

Claire sat up again then. She looked at Mike. He would never lie to her. Not even in a dream.

"Promise?" she whispered.

"Promise," he said.

She reached out her hand, and he took it. She squeezed tightly and shut her eyes.

She opened the box.

The bald man on the gurney was unconscious. There was a suspected fracture of one cheekbone, which was already beginning to show bruising. They had ripped open his shirt to get to the most serious injuries, only to find a pockmarked bulletproof vest. The bullets had flattened against the metallic mesh, their kinetic energy dispersed across the man's chest.

Dan had bandaged the wound on the patient's leg. It was messy, but not too serious. There was some damage, but the bullet had passed right through. He was lucky. He'd be walking without a limp in six months.

Dan held out a hand, and Claire passed him the syringe. They'd been working together for seven months, and rarely needed to ask for what was needed in an emergency. They'd been sleeping together for nearly three months. Hospital policy dictated they shouldn't work together, but, so far, they had neglected to update their managers on their new relationship status.

Dan winked as he prepped the syringe. That's when it happened. The patient sat up and opened his eyes. He looked at Dan, then at Claire. He was completely calm and, seemingly, fully functional. There was none of the confusion Claire saw time after time in the eyes of patients who had been attacked. This patient was different. He looked like he was thinking, making some kind of calculation as he surveyed his surroundings.

Dan put a hand on the man's arm.

"You've been hurt," he said. "You're in an ambulance. We're taking you to hospital. Everything is going to be all right. I just need to give you an injection to help prevent infection, ok?"

The bald man didn't answer. His right arm moved in a blur of speed, and suddenly Dan was on the floor with the patient standing over him. Claire opened her mouth to scream, but a strong hand clamped over her lips, and cold eyes looked straight into hers.

Claire had once given CPR to a man born with no eyes. The glass eyes filling his sockets had been wide open as she had re-started his heart, and she'd been slightly freaked out by his empty stare. This felt similar until she felt a cold stab of fear. Something far worse than emptiness lurked behind this man's dark gaze.

He gagged her with bandages, then tied her hands together,

attaching them to the top of the gurney. Next, he turned away from her and rolled Dan onto his back with the tip of one shoe. He stripped Dan's unconscious body to his underwear, then stripped himself and swapped their clothes. She watched him pull off his jacket and saw raw-looking red patches on his chest. Four of them. So, he was human after all. Not some kind of demon. Even the latest bulletproof vests couldn't completely dissipate the energy of a point-blank shot. She hoped he was in pain.

As if he had heard her thought, the bald man looked at her. Next, suddenly and horribly, he put a hand behind his back and pulled out a gun. He grabbed a pillow from the gurney and held it in front of the barrel, swinging it round to point at Dan. Before firing, he smiled, and Claire had the awful realization that the screaming siren of the ambulance would cover up the sound of what he was about to do.

She shut her eyes after the first shot. Three more shots followed. Then there was a sickening crunching sound.

Everything fell into darkness for a while. It might have been seconds or minutes. When Claire opened her eyes, she was still in the ambulance, the siren was still screaming, and Dan was dead on the floor. The empty-eyed man was looking at her. She looked away. He slapped her across the face, and she looked back. He spoke without emotion.

"Contact the hospital, tell them the patient died. Four gunshot wounds. When a patient dies in the ambulance, do you go straight to the morgue?"

Claire hesitated, desperate to find some way of escaping and raising the alarm. He slapped her again and raised the gun, pressing it lightly against the side of her head.

"Claire Sullivan," he said, reading her ID badge. "We have very little time. I have killed a great many people. I am the most dangerous person you will ever meet. If you defy me in any way, I will hunt down your family, your friends and your colleagues and I will kill them. Is that clear?"

She nodded. He removed the gag and untied her. She buzzed the driver on the intercom.

"Harry? Straight to the morgue. We lost this one."

"It's not protocol, Claire. We should take him in, get him pronounced properly."

Claire couldn't bring herself to look at the killer beside her, but she could feel his cold gaze.

"No point, Harry. Multiple gunshot wounds. Blood everywhere. Half his chest missing. There's not much of a heart left to try to start."

The pause that followed seemed to last an hour.

"All right, love. Sounds nasty. I'll swing us round the back. Two minutes."

The bald man rolled up the bottom of the pants he had taken from Dan, who was six foot two in his bare feet. Under other circumstances, Claire would have thought he looked ridiculous. As it was, she was focusing purely on not hyper-ventilating. As soon as the ambulance stopped, the man crouched by the doors and motioned Claire to be silent. After about thirty seconds, they heard Harry's voice.

"You two all right in there? Or has he come back to life again?" He was chuckling as he opened the door. Harry didn't see the punch that felled him. It was carefully placed, and he dropped like a stone. The bald man jumped out of the back, and dragged Harry's unconscious body into the ambulance. He motioned Claire to lead the way, and, sobbing, she rolled her lover's body out of the rear of the vehicle, the wheels dropping down from the gurney as she pulled it out. She took the front and was about to enter the building when the bald man pulled back and stopped her going any further. She looked at him.

"Your colleague punched the driver, then ran off. Do you understand?"

She nodded.

"Remember what I said, Claire Sullivan. Think about your family," the bald man said, before turning his back and walking briskly away.

282

Claire wheeled the gurney to the morgue.

"Multiple gunshots," she said and signed the form the young porter put in front of her.

"Bit of a mess, ain't he?"

She took one last look at Dan. His face was unrecognizable, where the sole of the man's boot had crushed bone.

She didn't vomit. She didn't cry. She walked round to her station and told her supervisor that Dan had lost the plot and punched Harry. She said she was going home. She started walking.

"Claire?"

Claire looked at her twin, standing next to the bed. She felt drowsy. She pulled the duvet over her shoulders. She was struggling to keep her eyes open.

"Mike?" she murmured. "What are you doing here?"

"I'm not here," she heard as sleep finally claimed her. "It's just a dream."

It wasn't until she was in the shower next morning that she realized how good she felt. She thought about the day when she'd walked out and could remember nothing after their last call out to a gunshot victim in Docklands.

She emailed the hospital to let them know she'd be back on Monday. She was just leaving the house when Mike walked up the path.

"You're going out?" he said, unable to keep the surprise from his voice.

"Got to pick up some food," she said. "I'm starving. Fancy coming with me? We could get a coffee somewhere."

He smiled broadly. "Fantastic."

Chapter 44

Innisfarne

The days were colder now, and fires had been burning in the Keep's various grates since the first week of September. Mee was already convinced she could feel the bite of winter in the wind that harried the island as twilight deepened into darkness.

Mee hunched her shoulders against the chill and, after checking that McG—the Houdini of the goat community —was securely barricaded into his shed, she completed her routine with a quick check of the chicken run before heading to dinner.

This was traditionally a quiet period for Innisfarne, and only three visitors occupied the rooms scattered among the outbuildings. They were all female, all referred by health professionals because of psychological, and physical, trauma suffered through domestic abuse. Of all the safe houses offered to women in such extreme circumstances, Innisfarne was often the one which felt 'safest' to them in the shortest time, due partly to its remote location. The quiet acceptance of the community, which never asked questions, was the other—hugely important—contributory factor in allowing healing to begin.

The community itself was down to its lowest numbers for a while. A large family group had departed just two days previously after their regular summer and autumn stay. Now, just Kate, John, Mee and Joni remained in the Keep, along with the three visiting women.

There was one more occupant on Innisfarne, an old man, but he was staying in the crofter's cottage at the northeast tip of the island. Mee's suspicions had immediately been aroused when she learned of his presence - after the events in Docklands, she couldn't help herself. Kate said he had arrived the day after she left for London. Mee had even watched him through binoculars to put her mind completely at ease. A strong-looking figure, his long gray hair and beard gave him the look of an Old Testament prophet as he strode along the beach. Kate said he had told her he had enough Manna reserves to feed himself for months. Days, then weeks passed, with the old man showing no interest at all in changing his solitary routine. Finally, Mee was able to relax. Under other circumstances, she would be more curious about the enigmatic, powerful character she was sharing the island with, but as soon as she had reassured herself that he was no threat to Joni, she barely gave him a thought.

The rest of the visitors ate together in the smaller dining room. When Innisfarne was busy, the larger hall would be used for meals, but it was costly to heat, so Kate kept it shut up and cold during the quieter winters.

Joni thanked Kate as the older woman passed her a

bowl of lentil soup and some crusty bread. Reluctantly, she put down Odd's letter so that she could eat her supper.

"I have to say, I love the fact that he writes you actual letters," said Kate. "I'm old enough to remember what it felt like to receive a physical letter, to recognize the writing on the envelope and feel the excitement of opening it for the first time."

Mee smiled while Joni refolded the letter. "You've got a racy past you haven't told us about, Kate?"

"Maybe," said Kate, sitting opposite John. John and Kate, much to Mee and Joni's surprise and delight, had finally—years after everyone who knew them had seen the obvious spark between them—struck up a more intimate relationship. Joni and Mee's news about attempted killings, meeting a living software version of Seb and Mee's shooting of a deranged psychopath had seemed somehow less exciting when they had realized John hadn't been sleeping in his own room since the night Mee had left the island.

Joni tucked the letter into her pocket. She would re-read it later. Odd's inimitable style of speaking the English language lent his letters a charm she found irresistible. A month earlier, with Sym's help, he had found his brother, Anders, and they were setting up a small clinic that treated the injuries of Manna and non-Manna users alike. Anyone who needed them called a number and were directed to a neutral meeting place where they could be helped. Sym had provided a piece of software which traced each call and ensured the brothers weren't being led into a trap by the police, or anti-Manna groups. Over the weeks, a few cops had been saved by the brothers' use of Manna, and Odd hoped this would slowly start to change minds and hearts. *I still have hope,* he had written.

He was planning a visit over Christmas. It seemed a

long way off. Joni was still a little cautious about her feelings toward Odd, but she was glad of the opportunity to get to know him again slowly, using the antiquated technology of pen, ink, paper and the postal service.

At the next table, Sarah and Laura were speaking to each other in hushed, hesitant whispers. Sarah had finally left her husband after he punched her repeatedly in the stomach after she told him she was pregnant. She'd lost the baby and had been talked down from a bridge by a police officer who knew the right social worker to call. Laura had been stabbed three times by a jealous boyfriend.

The two women had found common ground and were beginning, slowly and tentatively, to open up to one another. Kate and Mee had seen this happen before and knew they needed to give them the space to begin the healing process together.

Sian—who was still taking meals in her room—was a different story. The terrible bruises on her face were fading now, five days after her arrival, but she still walked with a stick, in obvious pain, and the extent of her injuries was unknown. She wore sunglasses outdoors and in. She had yet to speak. To anyone. Too frightened even to let them know where she was from, or the name of her referring doctor, she seemed to exist in a personal bubble of torment. She had written down her name when she arrived but had been reluctant to write much more, only emerging from her room on the second night.

John had carefully kept his distance after inadvertently coming face to face with Sian in the garden. She had bolted like a rabbit at the sound of a shotgun. He was acutely aware of being the only male presence in the Keep and tried to speak more softly when Sian was in the room.

The only one of them who had made any headway at all with the traumatized young woman was Joni, who had coaxed half a smile out of Sian when she brought her the occasional cup of tea. Sian wore her long black hair in such a way that it often obscured her features. Joni was making an effort, very slowly and carefully, to gain trust and Mee watched her daughter with pride as she did so.

She's going to be a fine woman.

Joni herself had shown a great deal of resilience considering what she had gone through. Soon after their return to Innisfarne, Joni, Mee, John and Kate had sat down together, and Joni had told them the whole story. When she'd come clean about her reason for leaving the island, Mee had started shaking. Joni had described everything. The shooting from the boat, the madness in Adam's eyes, the antique knife.

"You mean, in some parallel reality, we died on that beach?"

"If that's the way my ability works, I suppose that must be true. But you're alive, Mum. Here. Now. So am I. So is Uncle John. It's all that matters. We can only deal with what's right in front of us."

When did she get so bloody wise?

Chapter 45

London

In a rundown hotel whose rooms were also available by the hour, the proprietor, one Albert Potter, stared blankly at the unlikely sex act being performed on his computer screen. A spider obscured his view for a moment and he swatted it away, not noticing that the insect had attached itself to his finger before sinking into his skin. He twitched, then looked back at the screen, shaking his head.

"Oh man," said Sym, "you sure have some bad taste in porn, Albert."

He walked across the small, poorly lit office and opened a drawer, taking out a lined notebook full of scrawled handwriting.

"If you used your computer for anything other than porn," said Sym, flicking through the pages, "you'd have spared me the indignity of having to take over your body like this. I mean, come on, Albert, don't you have any self-respect? When was the last time you washed? This is like having to take a crap in the public bathroom on the third day of a music festival."

The entries in the notebook were, at least, in date order, and Sym quickly found what he was looking for. Only three rooms had been rented that day. Albert's memory was sketchy on which room he had rented to the limping paramedic with blood on his face, but he remembered the man himself, because he'd scared him half-witless. Albert had looked into his eyes once, when handing over the key, and it hadn't been an experience he'd ever wanted to repeat. Sym extracted one other piece of information from Albert's brain before going upstairs. The back entrance to the hotel was kept padlocked shut, only being opened when the Council performed the annual fire inspection. The injured man couldn't have used it, because Albert had hung his 'Back in ten minutes' sign on the office door and gone to the pub for the rest of the day, hoping a large quantity of alcohol might help stop him from shaking.

Adam must have found another way out.

It had taken Sym seconds to pick Adam up on CCTV and track him to the hotel. The paramedic's uniform made him easy to find, once Claire's memories had given Sym the right location to check. When he'd seen the limping figure on camera, he'd been pleased to see how painful his progress looked.

Adam had checked in to the hotel, but he'd never checked out. Only one camera covered the hotel entrance, and Sym had reviewed the footage thoroughly. Over the twenty-four-hour period after Adam had checked in, no one matching his description had left. Even with his unmatched resources, Sym couldn't enhance the footage enough to confirm the identity of all hotel guests who had exited the building during that timeframe.

He *must* have left some other way. Or he was still here. Either way, Sym needed to know. He took three keys from the rack on the wall. The first two rooms were unoccupied, their grimy windows inaccessible behind iron bars. A quick scan of Albert's brain revealed that all rooms on the first three floors had similarly barred windows. Sym looked at the number on the last key: 412.

Sym unlocked the door and walked in.

"Don't let me interrupt," he said to the blonde woman, and the fat man she was straddling. They both looked on speechlessly as Sym walked across to the window and threw it open. The rooms on the fourth floor had no need for iron bars, as he quickly confirmed when he stuck his head out and looked down. The drop was probably not quite high enough to kill, but it would certainly break some bones, and the two big, hungry-looking dogs in the yard would dissuade anyone desperate enough to risk it.

"Shit," said Sym. The fat man's hands were still frozen in place on the blonde woman's breasts as Sym walked back to the door. Sym gave him a wink, and was about to leave, when he paused.

"You guys smell that?" he said. The hotel was filthy. Sym doubted housekeeping amounted to much more than a change of sheets and towels, a mop around the bathroom and a cursory pass with a hoover elsewhere.

He backed slowly into the room and walked toward the bed. The fat man was still motionless, but his paid company had regained the capacity for speech.

"Hey!" she said. "What the hell do you think you're doing? We paid for this room, you old perv—,"

"Shh," said Sym, and dropped to his knees. He lifted

the counterpane and looked under the bed, his nose wrinkling in distaste.

Albert wasn't a particularly strong specimen, so Sym had to temporarily divert blood from his legs to his arms and increase his adrenaline levels dangerously in order to get what he wanted. He reached under the bed and pulled, straining, until what he was gripping slid into view.

It was the naked body of a woman and—judging by the quantity of cheap makeup applied to her features and hiding the beginnings of decomposition—in the same line of business as the blonde two feet above her.

As the blonde caught sight of the body and started to scream, Sym reached back under and pulled out some clothing. It was a paramedic's uniform.

"Fuck," said Sym, with some feeling.

Back at the computer, Sym left Albert and re-entered the network, wishing the digital equivalent of a good, hot shower was an option.

He watched the footage one more time, following everyone who had exited the hotel. He used nineteen nearby CCTV feeds of varying quality. Identification was straightforward for most possible suspects. They either went back to their own vehicles—registered to them online—or used an ATM. Or they simply turned on their phones. Any of these actions gave Sym all the information he needed.

Two suspects remained. Sym lost one in an Underground station, unable to work out how it was someone could enter a station, be clearly picked up on six cameras, but never get on a train or come back out. A quick cross-reference with news sites cleared up that mystery. The guy had jumped in front of a train.

That left one possibility. A heavily-bearded man who had left with two hookers. One of the hookers carried a backpack which might have been the one Adam had brought into the hotel. Both women were leaning heavily on the bearded guy as they all weaved along the street. Drunk. Or pretending to be, to fool anyone watching the footage.

The bearded guy looked to be about Adam's build, but heavier. The three of them had climbed into a cab, getting out—according to the taxi records—in a well-heeled area in Notting Hill. A street that was now part of a gated community. No security cameras once you were inside the walled district. The residents, wealthy, famous, or both, valued their privacy too highly. Sym was in too much of a hurry to care.

He found the control center of the exclusive neighborhood and jumped into the body of a Notting Hill security guard, gaining access through his headset. Two minutes later, he was pounding on the doors of the street, one by one. It was 6:25am. Outraged residents soon scuttled back into their houses and double-locked their doors when he told them an intruder was at large.

The fifth house he knocked at, he got lucky. A sleepy-looking bearded man opened the door and looked up at Sym. The security guard Sym had hijacked was six feet, three inches and had played rugby for his county. Perfect for his purposes.

"Hey," protested the bearded man as a huge meaty hand pushed him back into his own hallway. He slipped and fell on his ass.

Sym grabbed the front of his robe and lifted him to his feet before pinning him against the wall. This guy wasn't Adam.

Sym snarled and the man whimpered.

"I have some questions for you," he said.

———

THERE WERE a variety of technical ways Sym could have established the identity of the terrified looking man he was currently pinning to the wall, but sometimes old school was the best. He grabbed a handful of beard and pulled. Hard.

"Ow! What the fuck?" It was a real beard, well established. Couldn't have been grown that fast by the clean-shaven Adam. He pulled the man's hair to make sure.

"SHIT, what are you doing?" Tears in his eyes, now. Real hair, too. Not bald. Not Adam.

So where the hell was he?

Sym dragged the crying man through to his kitchen and pushed him onto a bar stool. He found vodka in the freezer and handed the guy a large measure.

The man gulped all of it down, took a deep breath and looked at Sym. His pupils were pinpricks. He was high on something. Sym had spent time in the brains of chemically-confused individuals before. It made it very hard for him to take control and get what he wanted. He was going to have to do this the hard way.

"What's your name?" said Sym.

"Greg," he said, gulping air. "Please don't hurt me. I have some cash, a laptop, but I don't keep much here. I'm mortgaged to the hilt, just because I live here doesn't make me rich, you know, I'm barely getting by, I—"

Sym raised an eyebrow, and he stopped talking.

"Shut up, Greg," he said. "I don't want your money."

If anything, the man managed to look even more terrified. He pulled his dressing gown more tightly around himself.

"Oh, please," said Sym. "Don't flatter yourself. I want to ask you about a night four weeks ago. You brought two hookers here from that shit-heap of a hotel?"

"How dare you?" said Greg, drawing himself up a little straighter. Now that Sym had assured him his money and his body were safe, he had regained a little courage. "You can't come around here making accusations about my private life like this. I'll have you know that I happen to be a close friend of…" His voice trailed away into nothing as he watched Sym taking each of his Japanese steel kitchen knives in turn, examining them, then laying them next to each other on the counter.

"Ok, ok," he said, tripping over his words. "I'm sorry. Ok. Yes, there were two of them. Skanky. Nasty. But, well, sometimes you fancy a couple of burgers rather than foie gras, you know?"

"No," said Sym, looking steadily at him. "I don't."

"Ah. Righto. Um. Well, I, er, yes. Thought we might try a bit of role-play. They're the teachers, I'm the naughty schoolboy, that kind of thing. You know what I - um, no. Never mind."

Sym had a sudden, sickening thought, made worse by the fact that he should have considered it much sooner.

"Was one of them injured?" he said, picking up the smallest knife and holding up to the light.

"Yes, yes, of course. I remember. Yes. Her leg. Bandaged. She had to lean on me."

Sym held a finger up to his lips.

"Answer these questions carefully, Greg, and I'll leave you alone. You'd like that, wouldn't you?"

Greg nodded, not daring to speak.

"Good. Why did you bring them back here? To your home?"

Greg's eyes filled with tears. "I can't tell you any more," he said. "I had to bring her. Had to do what she said. She took pictures at the hotel. Said she'd post them online. My political career is just beginning to take off. I'll be ruined. Please. I can't."

Sym picked up the knife. "I'm not going to kill you," he said.

"Oh, thank you, thank you."

"But I am going to torture you until you tell me what I need know. I'll start by removing your toenails. Far more painful than your fingernails. That's just in the movies. If you turn out to be tougher than you look, I'll have to get creative. You Jewish, Greg?"

White-faced and sweating, Greg managed to shake his head.

"Excellent. Would you like to be?"

"She took my car," said Greg, babbling in his haste to pass on the information. "I said she could have it. Haven't reported it as stolen. Then the police found it abandoned. Bloody nightmare."

"Where did they find it?"

"Up north somewhere. I don't know. Please don't let her release those pictures. Please."

"Car registration?"

Greg told him, and Sym waved a hand over a section of the kitchen wall. A screen glowed into life.

"Get me in."

Greg half-fell off his stool, then stood in front of the screen, allowing his retina to be scanned. The lock-screen image disappeared to be replaced by a photograph of the Houses of Parliament. Sym pulled up a stool, sat down and leaned forward, his hands over the counter that contained the computer.

Milliseconds later, a tiny golden spider sank into the counter top. As Greg watched, the security guard's head rolled forward, his chin resting on his chest, eyes closed. He didn't move for a few minutes, after which his breathing deepened, and he began to snore.

SYM FOUND the car and the police report. The Jaguar had been abandoned and torched on the outskirts of Newcastle, about ten minutes' walk from the bus station. Over three weeks ago.

He called the island. The line was dead.

He spent the next few seconds exploring every possible method of getting to Innisfarne, an island with no technology that he could exploit.

And Adam was either on his way or already there.

It was 7:12am.

Chapter 46

Innisfarne

At breakfast that day, Joni decided it was time things should begin to return to normal on Innisfarne. Mum still seemed tired and drawn, but Joni was hardly surprised given recent events. Not only had Mum killed Adam, she had spent time with Sym, which was the closest she'd come to meeting Dad in nearly two decades. No wonder she was still twitchy and unsettled.

She walked up behind her mother and rubbed her shoulders. Mee leaned into her, smiling.

"What are you saying, Jones? Am I too tense?"

"You know it. But I have a cure."

Joni took Mum's hand and led her out of the dining room and up the back stairs. There was only one room that was used up there, and Mee hadn't climbed these stairs for nearly two months.

"Oh, I don't know," said Mee, "I'm not sure if—,"

"I do know," said Joni, as she reached the end of the corridor and pushed open the door, "and I am sure."

The small room was sparsely furnished. There was a faded sofa in one corner, and a stained coffee machine on a small table. The remaining space was dominated by a large table pushed against a wall. A mixing desk, an old quarter-inch reel-to-reel recorder and a small keyboard were on the table, two wall-mounted speakers positioned so that the person sitting on the only chair would be in the acoustic sweet spot.

Joni pushed Mee gently down into the chair, walked to the corner and flicked on the power, grabbing a guitar and handing it to her mother. Next, she went to the microphone in the corner, taking off the dust sheet, shaking then folding it. The mic was surrounded by heavy drapes hanging from hooks screwed into the ceiling. Joni smiled. She could remember sitting on the floor of this room before she could walk, playing with instrument cables and an old, stringless ukulele while her mother sang behind those drapes. There were a few seconds in one recording where you could still faintly hear the ukulele being chewed, but Mee had insisted it added character to her performance.

"Jones, don't think I don't appreciate what you're trying to do, but I'm not sure I can write anything just now."

Joni produced the bag of ground coffee she had brought with her. Walking into the bathroom next door, she rinsed and filled the jug, then crammed the filter with rich grounds and flicked the machine on.

"Write something for me, Mum," she said. She could see Mee was about to protest, so she spoke over her.

"Please," she said, and waited until her mother had picked up the headphones and put them on before backing out, shutting the door gently behind her.

Mee watched her go. She sat with the guitar on her lap for a few seconds, thinking. *Penelope* was off the water for a week for annual maintenance, so no one was expected. The old man in the crofter's cottage was still maintaining his reclusive existence, the three women were inching toward healing at their own pace. Sym had promised to monitor any unusual interest in Innisfarne.

Joni was right. She could barely remember the last time she worked on a song.

She looked at her watch. 8:40am. She could spare a couple of hours.

She strummed a couple of chords, winced at the sound, and started tuning the guitar.

———

JOHN CHANGED the sandpaper he'd been using for one with a finer grain and gave the edge of the picture frame a few final passes. He'd been working on it for the past few days, making sure it would be ready for Kate's birthday. It was made from driftwood washed onto Innisfarne's shore. Joni had contributed most pieces, beach combing while out on her walks. She'd even found a frayed piece of netting from a passing trawler, and the corner of a packing case, which clearly read *San Juan*.

He'd already hammered three ancient, rusting nails closer into the wood and had sanded the sharpest edges, wary of splinters. The rest he'd left as it was; weather-beaten, still rough in places, worn smooth by time, wind and waves in others. He knew the flaws were what had drawn him to it. He thought Kate would feel the same.

There was a quiet knock at the door, and John looked around for a place to hide the frame before he relaxed as Joni's face appeared.

"You got it finished, then? Looks great. She's going to love it."

"I hope so. You stopping for a coffee?"

"Nope. I'm walking. In the woods today, I think. It all smells so great in Autumn. Or Fall - I love the way you call it that. So descriptive of the season."

"Funny. I was gonna say how much I love the word *Autumn*. It's a word that only means one thing. Kinda poetic."

John looked at Joni, then brushed an imaginary wood-shaving from the side of the frame, trying to sound casual. "You still *resetting* regularly, hon?"

"Yeah. I hardly think about it, now. It's become a habit."

"Good. That's good. Enjoy your walk."

He watched her go, following her progress as she headed towards the trees. He understood Mee's caution, and he shared it. But as long as Joni was *resetting*, she had a defense no one could anticipate or easily overcome. He still couldn't quite shift an uneasy feeling, though. He'd shared headspace with a psychotic genius for many years, and knew it would be a mistake for any of them to relax their vigilance. Adam might be dead, but John thought it had all gone down just a little too easily. He'd feel far more comfortable when another six months had gone by without incident.

Taking the picture from a drawer, he unrolled it and carefully fixed it beneath the piece of glass he had liberated from an old, badly faded reproduction of Constable's Haywain. Standing back, he appraised the result.

The drawing he'd made of Kate wouldn't win any

awards, that was for sure. It was a rudimentary affair, just a few lines in heavy charcoal. But something about it—a calm stillness, perhaps—captured the essence of the woman with whom he'd gradually fallen in love. Mee and Joni had both agreed instantly when they'd seen it.

"That's Kate," Mee had said, smiling.

"I didn't know you could draw," Joni had added. "You have hidden talents, Uncle John."

"I bet he does. Just ask Kate."

"Mum!"

The fact that John's feelings for Kate had turned out to be reciprocated had been a huge surprise to him, but, apparently, not to anyone else. He just couldn't fathom why she had come to him that first night and climbed quietly into his bed. It had been the most surprising thing to happen to John since Seb had removed his cancerous brain tumor and allowed him to be reborn from the rotten corpse of Mason's poisonous personality.

Now, as he looked at the picture in the winter sunshine streaming through the window, he hoped it was a gift worthy of the wise, beautiful, sensual Kate. He wrapped it in brown paper, tied it with string and propped it against the workbench. It was Kate's birthday in three days. He shook his head slowly in wonderment at his own childlike happiness, which had arrived now, in his sixties. He felt sure no man alive appreciated the ever-shifting, lurching ground folk walk while falling in love as much as he did. To have his view of life shifted dramatically when everything might have been calcifying with age, was a blessing he intended to enjoy.

He looked at his watch. 9:30am. Kate would be writing. She was working on a document explaining the Innisfarne community to members of the Order, more and more of whom were finding their way to the island, often confused, scared or in shock by the loss of Manna to future generations since Year Zero. Innisfarne offered, to some, a way of facing this new reality without reliance on religion, magic, or nanotechnology.

John figured a cup of coffee might be a welcome interruption. He filled a mug and walked out of the door of the workshop, walking briskly toward the main building. He was smiling when he rounded the corner and walked straight into Sian, the coffee flying out of his hand and heading toward her face.

The young woman's reactions were incredible. As the hot coffee arced toward her, she moved forward and ducked to one side, swiping the mug with the back of her hand as it fell, sending it flying. It sailed clear across the yard and smashed a couple of feet away from McGee, who bleated in shock before he recovered his wits and—as was his custom—tried to eat the resulting mess.

"I'm so sorry, Sian," said John, instinctively placing a hand on her shoulder as she turned away from him. She was adjusting her sunglasses, using both hands to maneuver them back into position on her face. At his touch, her body tensed, then she scuttled away from him as if terrified by his proximity. John let his hand drop and took a step back himself, remembering how she reacted to men. As he looked at her, she seemed to shrink, moving away from him, her shoulders hunched, her head down, her body beginning to shake.

He started to apologize again, but Sian shook her head and turned on her heel, half-running, heading toward the larger dining room. It needed a fresh coat of paint, and Sian had made a start, making it clear she would rather work alone. Joni had managed to spend a little time with her, bringing her drinks and snacks, but John wondered if the woman would ever truly open up and begin to relax around others. Whatever she'd been through, it must have been truly horrific.

He picked up the pieces of broken mug, retrieving the handle from McGee's mouth, which provoked an outraged bleat from the omnivorous animal.

Five minutes later, he took a fresh mug of coffee over to Kate, who was struggling to write a chapter on her feelings about Year Zero.

"I know it seems crazy to feel glad about it," she said, "but Manna wasn't what kept me in the Order. It drew me there in the first place, trying to discover how to use this scary ability I'd found. That's how most people start out, I guess. But it was what lay beneath that kept me there. What I found in meditation."

John rubbed her shoulders, and she leaned back into him, cradling the warm mug in her hands.

"I may not be a typical case," he said, "but I'd take meditation over Manna any day of the week. Although," he lowered his hands from Kate 's shoulders to her breasts and kissed the nape of her neck, "lately I've discovered certain *other* abilities are present in one particular leader of the Order."

Kate shuddered as John continued to place tiny kisses on her neck. He knew it drove her crazy. When she finally pulled away, she was laughing.

"You're worse than a teenager," she said, taking his hands from her breasts and kissing his rough knuckles.

"I still have a great deal of catching up to do," said John. "And you're working too hard. You want my opinion, an hour's break would do you good. Like a power nap. Just, er, without the nap, I guess."

Kate gave him a long look, as if she was taking some time to consider his proposal. Finally, she stood up and stretched, arching her back as she raised her arms over her head.

"Thirty minutes," she said, smiling. "And don't worry, we'll make every minute count."

John watched her body move as she reached up toward the ceiling, wondering at her dancer-like economy of movement. *The woman does everything with style. She can probably even cut a fart gracefully.*

As Kate reached out her long, dark fingers to take his hands, John suddenly froze. Kate stared at him as he looked right through her.

Everyone moves a certain way. We stop noticing it.

"John?" said Kate. "John? What is it?"

When I spilled that coffee, she moved toward *me. Not away from me.*

"John, talk to me. You're scaring me. Are you ok?"

She wasn't scared of me at all. She moved forward under *the mug. She swatted it out of mid-air like a basketball pro. Lightning fast, calculated.* Then *she went back into character and backed away from me. She pushed her sunglasses back on. There was something weird about that, too.*

"John, please."

He refocused and looked at Kate.

"Sia—," he began, then stopped. He forced a smile. "Just something I have to check," he said. "It's probably nothing." He looked at her face and saw the need for more reassurance than he was giving. The last thing he wanted was Kate following him if there was a problem.

"Seriously," he said, forcing a laugh, "it's just something I've left in the workshop. I need to take it out of the vice before it warps. I'll see you later."

He walked quickly away, leaving Kate looking confused. She was far too perceptive for him to risk elaborating on his lie and being found out.

He smiled at her as he reached the door. He didn't start jogging until he was sure he was out of Kate's earshot.

Chapter 47

Northumbria

Cyril Perkins had been driving buses for forty-one years. Nearly thirty of those years had been on the same roads - the long coastal route between Bamburgh and Berwick, stopping at almost every village on the way. Locals had campaigned successfully to keep this particular bus going long after it had stopped being profitable, buying out the company which ran the service, and repackaging it as a tourist attraction. These days, there were as many foreigners as locals on the bus, cameras out as Cyril negotiated the winding lanes that hugged the Northumberland coastline.

The bus itself was somewhat of a relic, one of only a handful of non-electric vehicles permitted to use the road. It was a piece of history, the last diesel bus in the northeast. Americans, in particular, loved to film the polluting cloud of black smoke that puffed out of the exhaust when Cyril started her up. They often grabbed seats at the front, so they could gawp at him as he used the manual gears to push the bus up to forty, or, occasionally—and only downhill—even forty-five miles per hour.

Cyril knew he was as much an antique as the bus and, one of these days, when one or the other of them ran out of puff, that would be the end of it. A shiny, efficient bus would take over, with a shiny, efficient driver. Still, he hoped to get a few more years out of the old girl before that happened. And he was in excellent health for a man nearing his mid-seventies. A little more weight around the middle now, perhaps, but other than that…not bad. Not bad at all.

The bus wasn't very busy today, as the summer season had finished weeks ago. There were two German lads at the back and Colonel Smithers in his usual aisle seat, off for his weekly lunch with his elderly mother in Berwick.

Cyril's phone rang just as he pulled into Elwick. It was the depot calling. They knew he would never pick up a call while driving, not even with the fancy hands-free nonsense they had installed. When Cyril was driving, he was driving, nowt else.

It was still ringing when he pulled into the bus stop. He applied the handbrake and picked it up.

"Hey 'up, petal, to what do I owe the honor?" Cyril called every woman *petal* and every man *lad*. He had reached the age where it was acceptable, and it concealed the fact that he struggled to remember names these days. The voice at the other end sounded confused. It was that young girl who'd taken over a few months back. Nikki? Vicki? Trixie?

"Ooh, I'm sorry, Cyril, I've clean forgot why I called you. What am I like, eh? Forget me own head next."

Cyril chuckled. "No harm done, petal. Mebbe you just wanted to hear my sexy voice, eh? That it?"

"Get away with you, Cyril, you're making me blush. See you later. Sorry."

The spider that crawled out of the phone into his ear was so tiny that he didn't notice a thing.

As he pulled out of the village and turned off to the east, Cyril started whistling. He was whistling his way through Help! by The Beatles this week. Not *every* song on the album, mind, just his favorites. It was a beautiful day. He was thoroughly enjoying negotiating the narrow lanes when the colonel's voice rang out behind him.

"Perkins? Perkins! Where the devil are you taking us?"

Cyril didn't take his eyes off the road. "What do you mean, Colonel?" Cyril wouldn't dare call the colonel *lad*. It just wouldn't do. Anyhow, no one knew him by any other name than Colonel, and with a waxed mustache like that, he was never going to be called anything else.

"Just what I said, Perkins. You're driving the wrong way. Why did you turn off back there? There's nothing out here. Now, turn us around, man, or I'll never be there in time for lunch."

Cyril considered the colonel's words and realized he was quite right. He was driving due east instead of north. There was nothing out here apart from a couple of farms. And the airstrip, of course. Suddenly, Cyril knew that was where he was heading. The bus leaned alarmingly as he took a left-hand bend at speed.

"We have to get to the airstrip, Colonel," he said. "It's an emergency."

The colonel tried to get up and remonstrate with Cyril, but the next bend sent him flying back into his seat. There was a shout from the back in German, probably swearing, but Cyril had never had much luck picking up languages.

It was about five miles to the tiny airstrip and its single plane. Cyril knew he had to drive at the limit. This really was an emergency, and it was up to him to get there as fast as possible. The strange thing was, although he *knew* it was crucial, life and death and so on, he had absolutely no idea *how* he knew this. He slammed the gear stick into fourth and pushed the accelerator as hard as he could.

Chapter 48

Innisfarne

Sian's room was in the outbuilding furthest from the main block. John knocked cautiously at the door, already beginning to feel like he'd overreacted. He had spent two-thirds of his life thinking the worst of everyone, and it had proved a hard habit to break after he had been freed of Mason's tyranny.

There was no answer, and he stood, undecided, at the door for over a minute. Twice he turned to go, convinced that he was looking for danger where there was none to be found, that he was, in fact, going to achieve nothing other than adding to this poor woman's trauma. Twice, he turned back and knocked again, determined to put his mind at rest for Joni's sake. Adam was dead, but that didn't mean Joni was necessarily out of danger. Who else might be out there, looking for her?

The urge to protect Joni won out, and he pushed the door open. There were no locks on Innisfarne.

"Sian?" he said. There was no answer. He felt a brief frisson of shame as he breached the trust of the community, then he walked in.

The room was sparsely furnished, as were all the guest rooms on Innisfarne. The bed was made, the sheets and blankets tucked neatly into place. There was very little else to see. A hairbrush on the table and some make-up. A lot of make-up, surprisingly, the function of each item a mystery to John. Nothing more.

John remembered Sian arriving with just a backpack, which she always carried with her. He didn't know what he was looking for, but if it was anything incriminating, it was sure to be in that backpack. There would be nothing here.

He scanned the bathroom, just in case. Nothing.

He walked back into the bedroom and was about to leave when he noticed three books on the shelf. Two of them, he recognized as having been left behind by previous visitors to the island. He'd read them both. The book he didn't recognize was an old, small hardback. He lifted it down and flicked through it. Some kind of academic book about an ancient Christian sect. Strange reading material, but hardly evidence of any malicious intent. John shook his head. He *knew* there was something wrong about Sian, something that didn't fit. She wasn't who she said she was. That didn't necessarily mean she was a threat, though. He wondered if he was succumbing to paranoia.

The door opened. Sian stood there, quite still. She didn't scream. She didn't even flinch. John closed the book and replaced it on the shelf.

"I'm sorry," he said, "but I—." He stopped, unsure how to continue.

Sian shrugged off her backpack, stepped forward and placed it on the bed.

"You don't trust me," she said, in a quiet, husky voice. "You must have your reasons. Go ahead, search my bag, if that's what it's going to take."

John could feel his adrenaline levels dropping as he stepped forward and pulled the bag toward him. Sian would hardly let him look if there was anything to find. Still, for Joni's sake and his own peace of mind, he knew he had to look. He undid the fastener and flipped open the top of the backpack, tilting it toward the window so he could see inside more easily.

At first, the contents didn't make sense, they were so unexpected. Then his brain slotted everything into place and his adrenaline levels spiked as every muscle in his body seemed to tense simultaneously.

At the top of the bag, held in place by Velcro strips, were three grenades of some sort, and two handguns. At the bottom was some thin, coiled rope, and an object wrapped in cloth. John could see part of a wooden handle, covered in intricate carvings. He remembered Joni's description of the knife Adam had carried.

John didn't move, just flicked his eyes upward. He could only see the lower half of Sian's body. Her hands were by her sides. In her left hand, she held her sunglasses. John remembered then what had seemed wrong when she had put them back on that morning. It had been the way her hair had moved. He looked at Sian's right hand and saw the wig.

When he finally looked up, the emotion that was flooding his body wasn't fear. It was shame. How could he have let Joni and Mee down like this? He, of all people, not questioning the fact that Sian always spoke in a whisper, which could disguise any voice, even to the extent of blurring the differences between male and female. As the shame dropped away, it was replaced by a hot, violent anger. He would protect those he loved. With his life, if necessary.

To John's horror, Adam started laughing. The darkness in the bald man's eyes made him hard to look at, but John met his gaze. He saw the insanity there, the absolute, profound loss of connection with all that was good, kind, or forgiving. He saw no hint of humanity, just complete self-belief mixed with utter contempt for anyone else. It was a look he recognized. He'd seen something similar in the mirror most of his life.

"You can't save her," said Adam. "All you've done is brought my plans forward by a day. Joni almost has poor Sian trusting her. She asked if I'd like to go for a walk with her tomorrow. I said yes. But now, I think I'll go this morning. Surprise her."

John knew he would never be able to overpower the younger man. His only hope lay in the weapons in the backpack.

There was no time left.

It had to be now.

John snatched one of the handguns and took a pace back, keeping the bed between them, bringing the weapon up to point it at Adam. Adam ignored the threat and climbed over the bed to get to him.

John didn't hesitate. He pulled the trigger.

The quiet *click* as the hammer fell on an empty chamber held all the finality of a tolling funeral bell. Adam's hands were on his throat, pushing him over, before he had a chance to move.

"Don't worry," said Adam, "I'm going to load it before I go to meet Joni."

Strangely, it wasn't Kate's face that came into his mind

while the roaring sound grew in his ears and the pressure became unbearable as he struggled, and failed, to take a breath, his fists pounding feebly at the fading figure on top of him.

It wasn't Kate, or Mee. Or Joni. It was his brother's face. It was Seb.

The darkness that had begun to fill the outside of his vision eventually rushed in and overwhelmed him.

Chapter 49

East Of Elwick, Northumbria

Four of the old bus's eight wheels left the road as Cyril wrenched the steering wheel to the right and pulled onto the track leading to the airstrip. The old springs that provided the suspension screamed in protest at the sudden change in direction as the bus lurched along the potholed track.

There was no plane on the small runway.

"Mother*fucker*," said Cyril, then gasped, wondering where his sudden ability to swear had come from. He slammed his foot on the brake and brought the bus to a stop next to a tractor. Inside the open hangar, he could see one of the Wallace brothers—he could never remember which one was which—standing up and staring open-mouthed at him. Cyril hit the button for the door, there was a hydraulic hiss, and it swung open.

Behind him, there was a bark of anger as the colonel pulled himself to his feet.

"I don't know what's got into your stupid, fat head Perkins, but I promise you this: you'll be out of a job by the end of today. Of all the irresponsible, foolhardy, dangerous,—"

"Shut up, Colonel."

The retired army man went a deeper red than was his custom on a Tuesday morning.

"What?" he blustered. "What did you say?"

Cyril swung round in his seat and pointed a pudgy finger at the florid ex-soldier. "I said shut. The fuck. Up. Sit down. Now."

Much to his own surprise as well as Cyril's, the colonel shut up and sat down. Cyril turned to the shocked-looking German lads at the back of the bus. He pointed at the closest one.

"Du!" he said. "Komm her! Dies ist ein Notfall!"

As the young man got to his feet and hurried toward him, Cyril marveled at the fact that he had no clue what he had just said. He hoped it was good.

"Was just denn?" said the confused-looking German. Instead of answering, Cyril simply clamped his hand on the lad's shoulder. The young man twitched as if he'd received an electric shock, his expression changed and he sprinted over to the hangar. Joe Wallace looked bewildered as the strange tourist from the out-of-place local bus ran in and put a hand on his cheek. A spider ran up Joe's face and disappeared into his forehead. His eyes widened, he grabbed his cellphone and made a call.

The German lad got back on the bus, looking puzzled. He sat down with his friend, shrugging at the questions that were fired at him. The colonel seemed to have lapsed into a semi-catatonic state and was staring straight in front of him, his lips twitching slightly, making the ends of his mustache bounce.

Cyril swung back round to face the front and closed the door.

"What the 'eck are we doing here?" He looked out at the tarmac of the airstrip, trying to piece together the events of the last ten minutes. Finally, he selected reverse and backed the bus away.

"Least said, soonest mended," he said as the bus nosed back onto the road back to Elwick. Within five minutes, he was whistling Ticket To Ride.

BARRY NICOLSON HAD ALWAYS WANTED to learn to fly, and now that he had retired, he was making it happen. He was careful with his money, though—a teacher's pension was hardly a fortune—so rather than commit to the expense of an accredited flying school, Barry had approached the Wallace brothers. Joe and Ed ran a small plane from the airstrip at the edge of their farm. They made enough money flying oil workers out to rigs in emergencies to keep one plane operational. They had been more than amenable to a bit of extra cash with no questions asked. Barry had learned all the basics for a fraction of the cost he'd been quoted by the flying school.

Today was a little bit special, as Ed had promised he could have his first try at a landing. As long as he followed Ed's instructions, of course. Ed had turned out to be a natural teacher, much to Barry's surprise. He'd said as much to the lad at the end of their third lesson.

"You know, there's a shortage of teachers around here. You could make a real difference."

"It's not for me, Mr Nicolson," Ed had replied. Barry

318

had been unable to convince Ed to use his first name, but as he had been his headteacher for five years, he understood the conditioning that prevented it.

"I couldn't leave the farm, for one thing," Ed had said, then smiled. "And, come on. Mr Nicolson, admit it. You've been up in the Cessna a few times now. Could you give it up to stand in a classroom every day?" It had been a fair point.

This morning, conditions were perfect. Some cloud, but no rain, excellent visibility. They'd logged their flight plan with Newcastle air traffic control and taken off into a deep blue sky, spotting some seals pulling themselves onto the beach as they headed out over the water.

Ed had handed control to Barry as soon as they reached two thousand feet and Barry was finding it hard to keep a childlike grin off his face as he continued the climb to 12,000 feet, alternately watching the wispy clouds skip across the sky and the sun glint off the caps of the waves far below.

It was all shaping up to be a wonderful morning when Ed's cellphone rang. Eric Coates' iconic orchestral theme to The Dambusters squawked out of the phone's tiny speakers until Ed picked it up.

"Joe?" he said. "Why aren't you using the radio? Everything ok?"

Barry watched the younger man next to him stiffen, as if in surprise, then relax again. His face changed subtly, like an actor playing a role. He turned to Barry.

"I'm going to take control again, Barry," he said. "Hold onto your *cojones*, this may get a little dicey." He pushed the wheel forward, and the nose dropped towards the wave, putting them into a dive. No, not quite a dive - a very steep descent. Barry looked along the nose of the falling plane. They weren't heading back to the mainland.

They were heading north. The only land in that direction was the tiny island of Innisfarne.

Barry felt his stomach lurch as the plane plummeted. One thought kept going round and round in his mind as the island below rapidly grew bigger.

He called me Barry!

Chapter 50

Innisfarne

Mee put the headphones on the desk and flicked the control room switch on the mixer. She wanted to hear how it sounded, find out if the intimacy she thought she had captured would still be there when she listened through the speakers.

Her voice, as it always did, sounded like a stranger, as if someone else had temporarily taken over the singing duties. She had always tried to achieve this by allowing a slightly dreamlike state to envelop her while she wrote, played or sang.

She nodded along as she listened. Stripped-down, bluesy, raw. Seb would really have liked it. It was about him, of course. Even after all these years, every time she sat down to create something, it ended up being all about Seb bloody Varden.

She realized she could do with a good cry. More of a

howl, actually. It had been a while. Well, Joni was walking, Kate was busy, John was probably in the workshop. The room wasn't quite soundproof but she'd chosen it for her studio because it was as tucked away as possible; upstairs, at the very end of a warren of corridors. She got up to close the door. If she was going to indulge in a bit of thera-peutic screaming, she didn't want to worry anyone.

As she put her hand on the door, it moved. She leaped backward and balled her hands into fists.

"What the——?"

Kate's face appeared, and Mee relaxed, laughing at her own reaction.

"Oh, shit, Kate, you scared the crap out of me. I'm obviously not quite over our London adventure yet. All these years of meditation and you'd think I'd have some kind of default calmness ready to kick in, but nope, looks like…"

She stopped talking as she took in the unfamiliar expression on the older woman's face, the tension in the way she was standing.

"What's wrong?"

Kate took a breath, then let it out in a long, controlled hiss. She was struggling to retain her composure. Mee had never seen her so tense.

"Kate?"

"It's John," said Kate. "Something happened earlier. He was talking to me, then he remembered something. He tried to pretend it was nothing important, nothing to worry about. He laughed it off. But, after he'd gone, I couldn't stop thinking about the look in his eyes. He looked scared, Mee."

"So let's talk to him."

"That's what I want to do. But he's not in the work-shop. And there's something else."

"What is it?"

Kate shook her head slowly.

"Mee, this is ridiculous, I know it is. It's crazy."

"What is? Talk to me, Kate."

"Every instinct in my body is bristling. I haven't Used for twenty years, but if I was, I feel absolutely certain that I'd be sensing the same thing. Something feels completely wrong. He started to say Sian's name, then stopped himself. I checked the big hall. She's not there. And John's not in the Keep."

Mee frowned. "I don't understand," she said. "Sian's a wreck. What has she got to do with anything? And where would she have gone? She's scared of her own shadow."

"I don't know," said Kate. "Please. Come with me, let's check."

"Of course," said Mee, and the two women headed downstairs. Mee pushed her own sense of panic away. Adam was dead. Joni was safe. Whatever was going on, they would deal with it.

THE CESSNA'S wings made some quite alarming creaking sounds as Ed pulled on the controls and brought the nose level again. Almost immediately, he eased back the throttle and the small aircraft dropped even lower. Barry could see the rocky shoreline quite clearly. More clearly than he was comfortable with, if he was being totally honest. Some of the rocks looked quite jagged. And close. Very close.

"Right, Barry," said Ed, unfastening his seatbelt.

What on earth is he doing?

"No time to explain, but since I'm a good news, bad news kinda guy, let me put it this way—."

Good news, bad news kinda guy? Since when did a Northumberland farmer start talking like am American sitcom?

"Good news is, you're gonna get a shot at that landing today."

Ed reduced the throttle until the plane was barely keeping itself airborne, twenty feet above the waves. He undid the catch on the door and shouldered it open, grunting with the effort as he pushed against the pressure of the wind trying to force it shut.

"The bad news is, you're on your own. See ya later. Good luck!"

The last two words were almost lost as Ed put both feet on the sill of the open door and, without a moment's hesitation, stepped forward and dropped into the sea.

Barry scrambled around in his seat to see what had happened. He caught sight of the young man swimming toward the shore, then an insistent bleeping from the instrument panel alerted him to the fact that the engine was about to stall.

As he increased the speed, raised the nose and gained some height, he was startled by the Dambusters March starting up again, He found Ed's phone on the seat next to him and picked it up.

"Ed?" came Joe's voice, "is everything ok? Things have been a bit weird here this morning."

"Hello, Joe, it's Barry," said Barry, his voice sounding unnaturally high to his own ears. He had to fight a terrible urge to giggle. "I'm afraid Ed has had to step out for a moment. Can I take a message?"

———

KATE AND MEE had a quick look around the Keep, shouting John's name. Sarah and Laura were talking quietly in the day room and had seen neither John nor Sian that morning. Finally, Kate insisted they find Sian, and the two of them walked through the yard to the last outbuilding.

Kate knocked, and they both waited. After a few seconds, she knocked again. She stood, waiting, unwilling —or unable—to break the rules she had lived by for so long.

"Oh, come on," said Mee, and pushed the door open. She walked in, and Kate followed.

At first glance, there was nothing to see in the small, sparsely furnished room. Mee nodded at the open bathroom door, and Kate walked over and looked inside.

Mee walked over to the window and almost tripped over John's body. For a couple of seconds, her brain simply refused to process what was in front of her. She stared down at him, and it was as if the facts of the matter had to be presented to her one at a time, so that she could deal with the reality of what she was looking at.

His lips were blue and drawn back from his teeth in a grimace of pain. Although he couldn't have been dead for long, there was already an unnatural stillness about his face which left no doubt that he would never draw breath again. His eyes looked up and past her into nothingness. His body was twisted, his chin thrust back, exposing the livid mottled bruising around his throat.

Mee found herself repeating the word, "oh," over and over, quietly, like a mechanical mantra of shock and grief. The information that John was dead was somehow being held at bay temporarily by the simple repetition of the word.

"Oh," she said. "Oh. Oh. Oh."

Even when Kate stood beside her and let loose a ragged cry of pain that ripped out of her body in an unrecognizable, almost animal, shriek, Mee still repeated the word and stared at John's face. Seb's brother. Always there when she needed him. As close to a father as Joni had ever known. A man who, when he had been given a second chance at life, had embraced it with every cell of his being.

John. Seb's brother. Dead. Murdered.

As Kate took a couple of staggering steps backward and put a hand on the wall, leaning over, her body shaken by wracking sobs, Mee looked down at John's hands. His left hand was open, fingers splayed, tendons straining to the last. The right hand was closed in a fist. He was holding something. Something dark, something that reflected in the light from the window. Something familiar.

Mee stopped speaking. Her lips were dry. She crouched down and pulled at the dark shape in John's clenched fists. She suspected immediately what it was, but she had to be sure. Slowly, carefully, gently, she moved John's cold fingers away from their prize. Then she stood up and held it in front of her.

Kate looked up and straightened slowly, her hand going to her mouth as her eyes opened in horror. They looked at each other, needing no words.

Mee was holding a long, black wig.

In that moment, everything else dropped away. There was no room in her for grief, fear or doubt. There was just the certainty that Adam was, somehow, alive. And he was here. When she spoke, her voice was steady.

"Joni," she said.

Chapter 51

Joni's walk took her to the east first. Although she had grown up on Innisfarne, and knew the tiny island intimately, she'd rarely spent much time at the bay on the southeast corner. Despite the fact that it was one of the few places it was safe to swim, and it was closest to the Keep, Mee had almost always taken her to the smaller beach to the north. Now that Mum had finally opened up completely about Dad, Joni finally knew, and understood, the real reason.

She climbed to the top of a small outcrop of shale. Tough, coarse grass grew in straggly tufts there, in Nature's final act of defiance before the sea claimed the rest. Joni looked down at the shoreline as the waves frothed and foamed, beating against the dark wet rocks. She wondered where, precisely, her father had stood before he disappeared. He'd stayed there for more than three weeks, Mum had said, not moving, not speaking. In some strange way, not really there at all. A horribly long goodbye before he'd vanished for good.

They all said he'd be back. Mum, Uncle John, Kate.

Something similar had happened before, something out of his control, but he had always come back. Joni wasn't so sure now. She was still struggling to make sense of his absence, given what they had told her about him. They described Dad as the most powerful being on Earth. He'd even held his own against a visit from an alien species with less than friendly intentions. So what kind of force could pull him away from his family and his home against his will? Uncle John said Dad had changed during those final few weeks before he came to the beach. He said they'd all known something was happening to him.

Joni wondered what it was like to have a dad. Uncle John was wonderful, sure, but he, like everyone else, had always acted like Dad was coming back. They had all left that gap in Joni's life wide open, waiting for Seb to come back and fill it. But it hadn't been filled. He had never come back.

Maybe he didn't fight too hard against whatever it was that took him.

Maybe he'd *wanted* to go.

Joni thought about her dream, the way she'd recognized her father, although he'd been non-human in appearance. She remembered him *seeing* her, *knowing* her somehow. She shook her head and pulled her fleece more tightly around her, feeling suddenly cold.

No. *He will come back. If he can.* She felt tears stinging her eyes in the wind as a small, but intense, burst of the secret, fierce, love she felt for her father bubbled to the surface.

"Dad," she said aloud, looking out to sea, tasting the word along with the salt spray on her wind-dry lips. "Dad."

She stood there for some time, staring out to sea without seeing anything. Then she created a *reset* point.

Finally, Joni turned her back on the sea and set off on her usual route back to the Keep. She liked to walk through the forest, which meant heading north first before swinging back toward home. There was something indescribably peaceful and reassuring about the presence of living things that were there before she was born and would still be there long after she'd died. She loved the sense of perspective the trees gave her, the way any sense of urgency just fell away from her when she walked under their ancient canopy. It was hardly a forest, of course, with fewer than thirty trees huddled together just north of the island's center.

It was as she was about a hundred yards from the first of the trees that Joni realized she wasn't alone. Walking from the direction of the Keep, shoulders hunched, a figure was heading toward the forest. Joni slowed her pace, then stopped and waited.

"Sian," she called softly as the woman got nearer. She didn't want to risk upsetting her by waiting until she was closer. She had gradually managed to get Sian to trust her a little and didn't want to ruin it now by suddenly seeming to appear from nowhere.

Sian stopped walking and looked up. The sunglasses were still in place, she was wearing dark pants, a short jacket, and a dark scarf. There was something different about her.

Her hair. It's shorter. The style is slightly different. She must be starting to take an interest in her appearance.

Joni smiled as Sian acknowledged her with a nod. She waited for her to catch up.

"I'm just taking a quick walk through the forest, then heading back," said Joni. "Do you want to join me?"

To her delight, Sian nodded again, and they started walking together. Joni wondered if her eyes might have deceived her, but—for a moment—she could have sworn that Sian had actually *smiled*.

The ancient oak was still her favorite. The fact that she had fallen out of it on her ninth birthday, and—without the power to *reset*—would have died that day, hadn't dampened her love of the tree in the slightest. She came to a stop in front of it and looked up into its intricate canopy of forking branches, a stunning sight now that most of its leaves had turned a rich, golden color.

She turned to share her feeling of joy with Sian, but the woman wasn't at her side. Confused, Joni looked around the small clearing. Sian was about ten yards away, walking backward, her face strangely impassive.

Something's wrong.

Joni looked to her left and right, seeing nothing that might have spooked the other woman. Then she looked down. A few feet away, nestled in a pile of fallen leaves was an ugly, black object. Joni recognized it, she had seen one before. But seeing it in this context made no sense at all.

It was an EMPty.

There was the beginnings of a noise and a feeling like being punched by a giant fist. Then a gap in consciousness.

Chapter 52

Before Joni opened her eyes, she knew. It was Sian's hair that gave it away. The idea swam into her mind as she floated back into consciousness. Why would a horrifically traumatized woman suddenly decide to cut and style her hair? It made no sense.

She was half-sitting, slumped to one side. She could feel rope around her wrists, her arms pinned behind her. Her ankles were also tied. Without opening her eyes, she tried to move, but the rope was secured to something else - she was held tightly in place. She flexed her fingers and felt rough bark through the loose leaves. She was tied to the tree.

Her body was twitching, and there was a sharp pain just below her ribs. Joni knew what it meant, but she had to try, in case there was any chance…She reached back with her mind, looked for the tingling, listened for the humming, stretched out toward the last *reset* point. There was nothing there.

She half-opened her eyes to confirm what she already

knew. The exposed metal of the Manna-spanner glinted in the sunlight. The barbs that carried the current into her body were buried in her side, a little blood seeping through her shirt. She could hear a voice speaking, the tone low, the words ritualistic, prayer-like.

She didn't *have* to open her eyes fully. She didn't *have* to look. No one was there to judge her if she kept them closed. No one would blame her for going to her death without looking into those awful eyes again.

But she was Joni Varden. Her mum was a force of nature, her dad was the fairy king. This was *her* place. If she was going to die, so be it. But she would see her forest one last time, see the glory of autumn around her as she took her last breath of crisp, cold, pure, Innisfarne air.

Joni opened her eyes.

Adam was on his knees, a few yards away in the middle of the clearing. His eyes were shut, and his words were indistinct as he chanted. He was naked, the makeup he'd applied as Sian incongruous now, clown-like. There was sweat all over his body and glistening on his bald head. The knife was on the ground in front of him.

There was a sound. A humming. Joni listened, a flash of hope suddenly distracting her from the horror that was coming. The humming got louder. Joni frowned. It was more of a droning sound, like a huge insect. Her whole body sagged as she realized it wasn't coming from within her. It was coming from the sky. And it was getting closer. *A plane.*

Adam's eyes flicked open, and there was a split-second when he looked straight at Joni and she felt a physical revulsion at his expression. She didn't see anger, rage, passion, or any hint of murderous intent there. She just saw a lack of...everything. As if he was an empty shell masquerading as a human being. Whatever was pulling his strings was deep inside him, and Adam was emptying himself so that it could come to the surface.

The moment passed, and Adam stood up, listening intently. They both heard the plane's engine note drop from a shriek back to its more usual buzz. It was very close now. The trees obscured Joni's view, but it sounded like it was heading along the same shoreline she had just walked. After ten, maybe twelve, seconds, the engine note changed again and she heard a faint splash just before the hum grew louder. Looking above the trees, she actually saw the small plane climbing into the sky before it banked slowly and flew away from her.

Joni shouted as loudly as she could. She didn't know if it would do any good, but she wasn't just going to wait to be killed. She shouted for help until she collapsed in a fit of coughing.

Adam had heard the splash, too, and Joni's screams seemed to break his trance and spur him into action. He picked up the knife and walked over to her. Joni had managed to push herself into a sitting position, her back against the trunk of the oak.

"You've been unexpectedly challenging, Joni Varden," he said, kneeling in front of her, as the Manna-spanner continued to make her twitch. "The way you managed to escape me is unprecedented. It intrigues me. Some new use of Manna. Not that it truly matters. You can't do it this time, can you?"

She said nothing and turned her head away from him to look at the trees. Her beloved trees.

Adam held the knife in both hands.

"Ialdabaoth," he said, "I offer you this life, this final sacrifice. Joni Varden, the daughter of Sebastian Varden."

Joni remembered the words from the beach. It seemed so long ago.

"Come back to your creation and rule over us as you promised."

There was another sound. Rhythmic. Faint, then getting louder fast. Someone running. Running impossibly fast. Coming toward them from the direction of the beach.

If Adam heard it too, he gave no sign. This was the end of the ritual, Joni remembered.

Adam lifted the knife.

"Ialdabaoth," he whispered.

The knife flashed down straight toward Joni's heart, but as Adam spoke the last word, she threw herself to the left as hard as she could. The sharp blade slipped through her flesh and buried itself up to its hilt in her right shoulder.

There was no pain, at first. Just a sensation as if someone had jabbed her with their fingers. Irritating, not painful.

Adam had released the knife, his eyes closed in ecstasy as he had struck. Now he opened them, and Joni saw a tiny hint of emotion, a flash of anger. He tilted his head as if listening, then got to his feet and turned in one fluid movement, before running directly away from her.

The pain arrived at that moment and wiped away Joni's speculation about what Adam might be doing. It was a white-hot pain that came in rapid waves, like pulses of agony spreading out from her shoulder to encompass her entire upper body. She whimpered and gritted her teeth, hissing each breath out, panting as every nerve seemed to catch fire.

Joni's eyes followed Adam as he moved. It was all she was strong enough to do through the pain.

He had picked up something from the ground and was

standing by a tree on the far side of the clearing. He flicked his hand and Joni saw what he was carrying. It was an extendable truncheon, banned for years in Britain but brought back for police use under the Manna laws. Adam brought it up to his shoulder, taking a two-handed grip.

The running steps were close now, each separate step so close to the previous one that it sounded like a drum roll.

The man that burst out of the tree line must have been traveling at close to thirty miles per hour. Which made his impact with the truncheon that much more devastating.

Adam's swing looked too lazy and slow to do any damage, but he knew his weapon and the weighted end picked up speed as he hefted it in an arc toward its target. The runner—a man in his thirties and a stranger to Joni—had no time to react before the weapon caught him across the right-hand side of his chest, snapping his right arm and two of his ribs as the unforgiving laws of physics sent him spinning. He hit the ground hard, bounced twice, then came to rest face down. He didn't move.

Adam didn't waste any time on him, just walked quickly back toward Joni. He wouldn't miss her heart a second time.

She finally found her voice again, and let loose with a scream full of pain, fear, and loss. With the rest of her life measurable, not in years or months, but in seconds, it suddenly became clear, beyond any doubt, just how precious a gift life is to those who possess it. The sound that burst from Joni's lungs was a howl of grief and of disbelief, as that all that she was, and all that she might become, was about to be snuffed out forever.

When Adam calmly twisted the knife in her shoulder and a fresh burst of pain spasmed across her body, she felt her brain shift into a different state, pulling her back and away from normal consciousness, cushioning her somehow, protecting her from feeling the full import of her own imminent death. Time seemed to slow, colors faded to monochrome, sounds became muffled and distant.

And that was when the impossible finally happened.

Chapter 53

The oak tree moved. There was little wind, but even a hurricane couldn't have caused the ancient tree to bend in the way it did. Joni was aware of a shadow falling across her face, and when she looked up, her uncomprehending eyes saw the gnarled bark moving above her blotting out the sky.

The oak bent like an actor taking a curtain call. Adam stopped short and looked up in disbelief as the branches swept down and wrapped around him. Before he could react, dozens of branches had slithered around his body, encircling him, holding him tighter and tighter as other branches joined them. The oak unbent itself and held him captive about fifteen feet from the ground, only his shoulders and head visible as he fought for breath, wheezing and coughing.

Joni looked away from him, out into the clearing. The day seemed to have darkened. She realized it was her sight beginning to fail. She imagined that various connections between her brain and body were shutting down one-by-one in some kind of pre-arranged order designed to preserve her life as long as possible.

So, when the dryads came to her, she never knew—then, or later, because she could never quite bring herself to ask—whether they were real, or just a product of her misfiring synapses.

She felt warmth in her shoulder. The pain, gone now as her brain shut down, fluttered back into life briefly as she became aware, once more, of the existence of her body. Then a sweet warmth flooded her, and the pain was washed away in seconds. She felt blood flowing back to her extremities. She flexed her fingers and found the ropes loose, the knots gone. Joni risked a look at her shoulder. She saw the hilt of the knife. Then a slender, semi-transparent hand reached over from her right, as if someone was kneeling next to her. The hand took hold of the knife. There was no pain, and no fear. She didn't even tense up as the hand pulled the knife out in one smooth movement as easily as if it was coming out of a piece of fruitcake, not bone and muscle. The blade felt warm and soft and, as it emerged and was exposed to the air, it melted away from the hilt like ice dropped into hot water.

Joni felt every part of her body coming alive again, starting with her shoulder. Each separate limb seemed to be reporting to the brain that all was well, everything was functioning at one hundred percent. As her hearing returned to normal, a roaring sound filled her ears. She blinked a few times. The dryads had gone, but a new figure stood about ten yards in front of her.

The old man stood at the center of the clearing, although Joni hadn't seen him arrive. He wore sneakers, jeans, and a plain, gray, hooded top. His hair was long, wild and white, his beard fulsome. If it wasn't for the incongruous outfit, he'd have made a great Old Testament prophet.

The sound was coming from his mouth. It was a sound full of rage, frustration, and regret. It was a formless scream of pain and love. Joni had never heard anything like it. It seemed not only to come from the old man but from the trees, the ground, the sky.

The old man had one arm extended, and it was pointing at Adam, who was coughing and spluttering in an attempt to snatch a breath, pinned as he was by the branches of the oak. His eyes showed no fear, just a blank, impotent fury.

There was movement in the trees to Joni's right. Mee and Kate ran into the clearing and stopped short, both of them taking in the scene and trying to absorb what they were seeing. Mee looked about her frantically at first. When she caught sight of Joni, she let out a burst of laughter, combined with tears. The relief she felt hit her so hard, she only managed a couple of steps before sinking to her knees.

"Joni?" She had to shout to be heard.

Joni smiled at her and shouted back. "I'm ok, Mum, I'm ok."

Kate, meanwhile, had run to the fallen man who had entered the clearing only minutes earlier. He was moving slightly now, and moaning. She knelt next to him and checked his injuries gently, leaning in and talking to him softly.

Joni looked back at Mee, who was getting back to her feet. She looked up at Adam, then back at Joni. Finally, she looked at the old man. Looked at him properly. And Joni watched her face change from bewilderment, through hope, doubt, then, finally, certainty. Then, the way Mum looked at the old man made Joni look away. It felt too much like she was intruding on the most intimate moment. After a few seconds, she made herself look back.

Mee was walking slowly toward the old man, who, Joni could see, was still looking at Adam. Only now, the screaming had stopped, replaced by a kind of guttural growl. And the old man was crying. No, not crying, *weeping.* The tears were wet on his face. Mee was speaking to him.

"That's enough," she said. "It's ok, now. That's enough. She's safe, it's ok. You saved her, she's ok."

Mee was a few feet away from the man now. He was shaking. It was as if he wanted to look at Mee, wanted to turn toward her, but couldn't bring himself to do it. As if he was terrified of what might happen if he did,

Terrified? A man with that kind of power?

"You did it, you saved her. You don't need to do this. He can't hurt her anymore. She's safe now."

Joni looked up at Adam. His eyes were so bloodshot, they looked almost entirely red. His skin was a dark brown. He was still jerking rhythmically, trying to draw breath, but no air was getting into his lungs.

Mee stood beside the old man and reached out a trembling hand, placing it on his cheek.

"This isn't you. Let him go. You saved her. You saved her."

Another second went by, then the old man went quiet and dropped his arm. The ensuing silence was broken by Adam sucking in a huge breath and coughing as his lungs began to re-inflate.

Mee took one more step and stood in front of the old man. Joni watched her reach up and smooth his hair away from his face. Then she stood slightly to one side and led him toward where Joni was sitting.

For the longest time, the old man looked straight ahead

of him, his eyes glistening. Joni looked at his strong features and noticed something strange.

Is he breathing?

Finally, he dropped his gaze, shut his eyes briefly, then opened them and looked straight at Joni.

And she *knew*.

"See? She's safe now. It's ok. Your daughter's safe. You're home, Seb. You're home."

———

YEARS LATER, when Joni finally wrote about that day, her story ended with those words, the words she heard her mother say to the old man. The moment she knew her father had returned. It was the perfect ending for a piece of work she would publish, under a pseudonym, as fiction.

The reality, naturally, was far messier.

Her father held out a hand and she took it, allowing him to pull her to her feet. Then the three of them stood in silence, each wondering which words they could use to help begin to make sense of what they were feeling, knowing none would ever be up to the job. Silence seemed the only honest option.

The peace was short-lived. A single shot rang out, and they all turned as one. The injured man had taken a gun from Adam's backpack and was holding it at arm's length. He was using his left arm, although it was clear that the injuries to his right side had already begun to heal at an unlikely rate.

Adam had slumped in the tree's embrace. There was a hole in his forehead.

Kate walked over to the stranger, who put the safety on before handing the weapon to her, butt first. She backed away from him.

"Oh, come on," he said, smiling "Rehabilitation just wasn't gonna cut it with that guy. Secretly, this is what you all wanted. Admit it. Pussies."

The old man spoke then, and his voice was exactly as Joni had imagined. It had a physical effect on her. Like hearing a beautiful piece of music for the first time. The sight of sunlight skipping across the tops of waves. The smell of the earth after rain.

"Sym," he said. "Long time."

The younger man smiled and stretched experimentally, testing how well his ribs were knitting back together.

"Hey, Pop. Loving the Moses look. Suits ya. Sorry about the mess."

"Are you?"

"Nope. Heads up. I have a question for you, Sebby, and I think I speak for all of us. Where the actual *fuck* have *you* been?"

Epilogue

Four Months Later

Nothing on Innisfarne was more than a forty-five minute stroll from the Keep, but the fresh snowfall over the past few days made every walk slow going.

Joni stopped at Uncle John's grave on the way to the cottage, laying snowdrops on the barely discernible mound, their green stems set in sharp relief by the white carpet beneath.

"We love you," she said. She was echoing the words they had decided on for John's funeral. The only words they felt were necessary, or appropriate. They would never forget him, never stop talking about him. And their love for him continued, although he had gone. When most needed, language was often revealed to be a profoundly flawed way of communicating life's most important experiences. Words, laid bare before the pitiless reality of death and grief, withered or died like snowflakes in an oven. But even a community bonded by silence needed to mark the moment they lost one of their own. In the end, they had simply used as few words as possible. In the final reckoning, the three words chosen were the most honest possible. What else was necessary?

"We love you," Joni repeated, then turned toward the bitter north wind, and walked slowly away.

There was smoke rising from the chimney of the crofter's cottage, and, as she stamped the snow from her boots on the stone step, Seb opened the door to reveal a well-established fire roaring in the grate.

"You know it shouldn't even be called a crofter's cottage?" said Joni, as she took off an overcoat, hat, scarf, mittens *and* gloves, followed by a fleece and a sweater. Seb smiled as he watched the pile of discarded clothing grow.

"Really?" he said. "Why's that?"

"We're not in Scotland," said Joni, gratefully accepting a large mug of hot chocolate that had just spontaneously grown out of Seb's fingers.

"And you have to be Scottish to own a croft?"

"Yes. It's their word. And you know how much they love their language."

"What should we call it, then?"

"A smallholding." Joni sipped at the rich, sweet liquid. "Hardly romantic, is it?"

"Hardly," agreed Seb. "I can see why you call it a crofter's cottage."

"We don't call it that because we prefer it, it's because of George."

"Who?"

"George McInnery. He built it. Long before the Order set up shop here. Kate told me about him. When he died, nearly two hundred years ago, the cottage was the only building on the island. And George was a proud Scot. So when he'd gone, the name stayed."

Joni curled her legs under her on the slightly incongruous, but wonderfully comfortable, wing-backed chair that Seb provided whenever she visited. She watched her father pick up a poker and prod at a piece of wood, turning it so that the flames rose higher. She liked the fact that he did this, despite the fact that he needed no external heat himself and could have kept her body temperature equally comfortable with just a thought. It felt more *normal* this way.

"And might your little story about George have a moral for me?" asked Seb as he sat on a plain wooden chair opposite Joni.

"Well," she said, "maybe. He died at eighty-seven, by which time he'd lived outside of Scotland for more than fifty years. But, to him, this would always be a croft. He was a Scot. His identity came with him to Innisfarne."

Seb looked at her, smiling. She still hadn't got used to that smile. It was the smile of a man who had seen wonders beyond comprehension, but counted them as nothing compared to the fact that he had a daughter and he could see her, now, right in front of him.

It was taking time to bring her dad back. He had physically returned, so he told them, months back, but had not known how he should let Mee know he was back. He'd even wondered—in his darker moments—*if* he should let her know. His own mental state had been confused, his sense of time warped. Finally, he decided to come to the island, but keep his distance. Get the lay of her land. She might, he had pointed out, have been in a relationship. She had every right.

"And don't you forget it," Mee had said. "Was that

what the disguise was all about? The full Ten Command-ments look?"

"I was thinking more along the lines of Odysseus coming home at the end of The Odyssey. But Cecil B. DeMille never made that into a movie. Not that I remember, anyhow."

"So Charlton Heston's hairy face had to do, then?"

Mee had insisted Seb return to a more recognizable form, so it was quite a different man who sat across from Joni now. Given that he could appear in any guise he chose, Joni could only assume the lines around his eyes and mouth were an attempt to prevent Mum feeling like she was the only one who had aged. But Dad's eyes were the same eyes she'd seen in photographs. His smile was the same, too. When he laughed, which was still too rarely, Joni could never resist joining in, because his laugh was almost identical to hers.

She had a father. Here. Now. And yet, in some ways, Joni felt like the parent as she talked and talked, teaching Dad what it was to be human, bringing him back, as he put it, to his true self. She told him about her life, her child-hood, her dreams. About learning to swim in the shallows of Innisfarne. The time she had tried to eat a starfish. The herbs she'd learnt to grow in the sheltered garden behind the workshop. How McGee had eaten every herb she'd planted until Stuart had brought an old glass house across from the mainland, much to the goat's disgust. About the fall from the tree, that did and didn't happen. About Odd. Both Odds. The one from the writing course and the one who had visited for Christmas and whom she was going to visit next month. About her ability, the way she could *reset*.

Seb had been very curious about the *resetting*. Joni had been conceived when—as far as he could know—Seb's body was still a mixture of nanotechnology and biology.

That had changed shortly afterwards. He was sure no natural reproduction would be possible now. So Joni's abilities, and her vulnerabilities, were of great interest to him. Particularly as Seb himself couldn't do what Joni could. He couldn't *reset*.

"I don't know what it means," he'd said. "I have the feeling it's unprecedented." Then he'd gone silent for a very long time and seemed reluctant to be drawn back to the subject.

Eventually, they'd spoken about Joni's dream. Seb had confirmed it was real, that she had—somehow—found him across an unimaginable distance. He hadn't known who she was, but he'd suddenly remembered who *he* was.

Both Mum and Dad had admitted they weren't quite ready to live under the same roof. Yet. This had been the hardest thing for Joni to take after Seb's return, but she could see how important it was to both of her parents to tread carefully as they negotiated the path leading back to a normal relationship. They loved each other. Time would do the rest. The fact that Joni wanted nothing more than to have the both of them together all the time so she could throw her arms around them whenever she felt the need was, she knew, a little selfish. Understandable, yes, but selfish all the same.

The fire was dying and, when she looked at Dad, he seemed lost, staring into the glowing embers, not really seeing them. She was gradually becoming attuned to his moods, to those scary moments when he barely seemed present at all, which were slowly becoming less frequent.

He stood and walked over to the only piece of furniture in the room - an old oak chest, the wood cracked and warped with age. He opened it and took something out, cradling it carefully in his hands. Whatever it was, it was wrapped in a piece of soft gray cloth. He put it in Joni's lap.

"Be very, very careful," he said. Joni tensed slightly. It seemed to weigh nothing at all - she could swear the only weight she felt was that of the cloth.

Seb squatted in front of her chair.

"You've heard me describe what I am as a World Walker."

He fell silent again.

"Yes," Joni said, prompting him.

"The real word—or the closest a human voice can get to saying it—is T'hn'uuth. At least, that's what the Gyeuk call us."

Silence again. Joni's eyes widened as she considered what he had just said.

'Us?' Dad and the alien he called Billy Joe...or are there are more of them? And what was that other word?

"The who?"

"The Gyeuk."

Seb nodded at the cloth in her lap. "Take a look," he said.

Joni carefully sat a little more upright. She lifted one corner of the cloth, then another, pulling the material aside. What was revealed was stranger than she'd imagined.

It was same shape as a goose egg, but slightly bigger. It was hard to look at. Not because it was ugly, or painfully bright. Quite the reverse. Joni found it beautiful and slightly hypnotic. But her gaze seemed to slide away whenever she tried to look directly at it. It was dark in color. At first, Joni thought it was black, then she changed her mind, thinking it was more like a midnight blue. Looking again, she decided black was closer, after all. It was solid, yet, somehow, gave the illusion of being gaseous, or liquid, possibly depending on how you *saw* it. Joni couldn't be sure. What she was sure of was the effect it had on her mind. She felt like she was in the presence of a miracle, some kind of holy object. She felt a sense of awe, an impression of Mystery. A feeling of vastness, emptiness, yet somehow fullness. Static, yet evolving. Such artifice in its design…or was it alive?

Joni suddenly felt afraid, adrift, like she was losing sight of herself. Seb leaned over and gently rewrapped the object, returning it to the chest. Her fear faded, the sense of awe disappeared, and within seconds she was beginning to wonder if she had imagined the feelings she'd experienced.

"What is it?" she asked, her voice only shaking slightly.

Seb remained standing, his smile gone.

"It's a Gyeuk Egg," he said. He didn't elaborate.

"Oh," said Joni, wondering what the correct response might be. "What does it do?"

Her father took a few deep breaths. Joni was glad to see him do it. She knew he didn't *have* to breathe, but he said it helped him remember who he was, where he came from. It certainly allowed those around him to relax a bit more.

"For one thing, it helps explain where I was for the last seventeen years," he said. "And it may explain how such a thing as a T'hn'uuth is possible. And," he said, taking her hand and finally smiling again, "it might just explain everything about reality."

"Everything?" said Joni.

"Everything," said Seb. "Perhaps you should go fetch your mother. I think she'll want to hear this."

THE END

Author's Note

Join my (very occasional) mailing list, and I'll send you the unpublished prologue for The World Walker: http://eepurl.com/bQ_zJ9

Email me with encouragement, accusations of heresy or offers of single malt whisky at ianwsainsbury@gmail.com.

A confession

Twelve months ago, I was finishing my first novel - The World Walker. Publishing on Amazon was a leap in the dark. I really had no idea what to expect. *I* liked the book. My friend Neal liked the book. Hardly the basis for a new career. And yet, the sensation of sitting down at my desk and finding this alternative existence springing into being quickly became addictive.

Six weeks later, a slow but steady build up of sales and —best of all—positive reviews from people I'd never met, and I had the confidence to start on my second book, The Unmaking Engine. I'd allowed my imagination to bring in some bigger ideas in book two, and, as I hit the *publish* button, I got scared. What if no one liked the new ideas? I knew I couldn't just write The World Walker, Part Two, as a straightforward continuation because these new ideas wouldn't leave me alone. Another leap in the dark…

Now The Unmaking Engine has been out there for nearly four months, and it's been really well received. This time, I didn't wait. I got back to writing a week after publication.

Well, that's not quite true…

What actually happened is that I spent six weeks making notes about book three, intending that this would bring the series to a close. The notes outlined two big ideas, and my plan was to knit them together into one big book. Only, I just couldn't make it work. I *loved* both stories, both of them needed to be told, but I couldn't find a way to make it work in one novel. Finally, I took the decision to tell the two stories in two books.

Everything suddenly got easier.

"That's what I told you to do four weeks ago," said my wife. Wise woman. But I—the *writer*—had been too busy flouncing about in my dressing gown, unshaven, wild-eyed, clutching my fifth cup of coffee, to pay any attention.

Ten weeks later, I finished writing The Seventeenth Year.

The confession bit. I *knew* Seb wouldn't make an appearance until the end of this book. It had to be that way. Joni's story only makes sense without her dad being around. And that leads me nicely to my biggest worry: until I got an early copy of this book into the hands of some readers, I was scared shitless that people would hate it because of Seb's absence. And I'm still nervous. My brother emailed that, in his opinion, The Seventeenth Year is the best book yet. I replied, *You have gone some way to allevi-*

ating the blind panic, self-doubt, and sick feeling I seem to be doomed to suffer on the completion of each book.

Just so that we're clear:

Book four is pretty much ALL Seb, and it dovetails with the end of The Seventeenth Year.

Back to Joni. After the weeks of confusion, I started telling her story and everything became clear. I lost myself in her world. She had lived a protected existence, far from the chaos of the cities, where—ever since Manna users came out of the shadows and the authorities cracked down on them—it was a dangerous place to be. Naturally, any daughter of Seb Varden was hardly going to be your average teenager. Good job, really, considering the amount of crap she was going to have to deal with in her seventeenth year.

I know I'm talking about them as if they're real, but I've seen this from both sides now: as a reader *and* a writer. I've read books where the characters seemed so well-rounded, they lived on in my head during the time I wasn't reading (we all have to work, sleep, eat and interact with other humans sometimes). I've found myself deliberately slowing the pace at which I read when the end of a novel is approaching because I don't want to leave a particular cast of characters behind. Well, it's even *worse* as a writer. These people are *real.*

As I write this, book four is underway, and I'm hoping to get it into your hands before summer 2017. Then I plan on delving into the notebook and writing something completely new. I have *lots* of ideas waiting to be developed further. How to choose?

I was itching to bring Sym into the story. Sym is far less

powerful than Seb, but he is also unhampered by Seb's strong moral center. In other words, he can have more fun. Sym is such a *presence* in this book, I found myself wondering what he's been up to during the previous seventeen years. I even started wondering if I might tell his story in another book (or series of books) sometime. If you like the idea, let me know - leave a comment on my blog at https://ianwsainsbury.com/ or at Ian W. Sainsbury on Facebook. Or email me ianwsainsbury@gmail.com.

And so my first year as an author is coming to a close. I'm one of the lucky ones. So far, readers (that's you) have wanted to read the stories that I write. Not only that - you're leaving reviews, you're spreading the word. You're making it possible for me to keep writing. Thank you!

Let's make a deal. Since I owe everything to my readers, I'll keep writing as long as you keep reading.

Deal?

Ian W. Sainsbury
Norwich
February 9th, 2017

Also by Ian W. Sainsbury

The World Walker (The World Walker Series 1)

The Unmaking Engine (The World Walker Series 2)

The Unnamed Way (The World Walker Series 4)

Children Of The Deterrent (Halfhero Series 1)

Made in United States
North Haven, CT
10 April 2024

51141119R00219